Rare Objects

Rare Objects

A Novel

Kathleen Tessaro

HarperCollins*PublishersLtd*

Rare Objects
Copyright © 2016 by Kathleen Tessaro.
All rights reserved.

Published by HarperCollins Publishers Ltd

First Canadian edition

HarperCollins books may be purchased for educational, business,
or sales promotional use through our Special Markets Department.

HarperCollins Publishers Ltd
2 Bloor Street East, 20th Floor
Toronto, Ontario, Canada
M4W 1A8

www.harpercollins.ca

Library and Archives Canada Cataloguing in Publication
information is available upon request.

ISBN 978-1-44344-311-1

Printed and bound in the United States
RRD 9 8 7 6 5 4 3 2 1

A man's character is his fate.

HERACLITUS, *Fragments*

This book is dedicated to my dear friend ROBERT TROTTA, whose remarkable character has forever shaped the fate of my son for the better and given me proof time and time again of true heroism in this world. I am beholden to you, sir.

Rare Objects

L ooking back is a dangerous thing. I've spent much of my time studying other ages, searching out the treasures of ancient worlds, but I've always found it best to move forward, eyes front, in one's own life. Hindsight casts a harsh, unforgiving light, and histories too tender and raw are stripped bare of the thousand shadowy self-deceptions that few of us can afford to see ourselves without.

But even the most conscientious of us can forget. The past dangles before us, as innocently as a loose thread from a sleeve. For me it began with a few lines in the local newspaper.

"Renovation works scheduled to begin at the Museum of Fine Arts, Boston."

It had been years since I'd been there. I'd thought of going, many times, and even gotten so far as to be standing on the front steps before something stopped me. I suppose the place held too many memories, maybe even a few ghosts. Is there anything more haunting than the ambitions of youth?

But one of the great myths of age is that it brings us wisdom. It had been too long, I decided, folding the paper. This time I will knot the thread, tie the untidy end of my past or cut myself free of it.

And so, like Orpheus in the underworld, I talked myself into turning back and looking one last time at what I shouldn't see.

I made the mistake of going on a rainy Saturday afternoon in March. The museum was full of families with small children careering from one room to another. They're encouraged to touch everything these days—sticky handprints on all the glass cases.

I managed to avoid being tackled by toddlers and found my way to the Art of the Ancient World wing. The room I was looking for was sealed off with a red velvet rope and a sign that read "Closed to the Public." I stepped round the rope, behind the sign, and into the abandoned gallery.

It was cool inside, and wonderfully quiet. There were tins of unopened paint and folded dust sheets, a few cigarette butts floating in some empty Coca-Cola bottles, but no work had actually begun. They hadn't moved any of the displays yet or stored away the artifacts. Above the marble arch of the entrance it read "The Treasures of the Golden Age" in gilded lettering. I could see from where they'd constructed the scaffolding that they were probably planning to rub it out.

The mural was still there, though faded and cartoonish—Greek temples and dancing nymphs, satyrs playing flutes. I was surprised to feel a nostalgic twinge of sentimental affection for it, even though I hadn't liked it at the time. Aging does that; it makes you amenable to far more ambiguous feelings and opinions than the inflexible black-and-white thinking of youth.

I walked past the statues of the mythical brothers Kleobis and Biton, frozen in rigid perfection, and paused by the vase and plate by the Harrow Painter, the archaic red-figure master. I even read the plaque beneath them, although I already knew what it said.

I remembered the first time I'd seen them, and the thrilling, slightly terrifying anticipation came flooding back, like déjà vu. Among the finest aesthetic accomplishments of their age, they'd been entrusted to my care one strange, ill-fated evening.

How young I'd been! How desperate and frightened and arrogant, all at the same time!

I continued, moving from case to case.

And then there it was, in one of the cabinets along the far wall: the black agate ring. I wasn't sure it would be there; I just had a feeling.

Even after all these years the sight of it made my skin go cold.

"Excuse me, madam?"

The voice startled me. I turned.

A young guard was hovering tentatively by the entrance as if he didn't dare disobey the sign.

"Yes?"

"I'm sorry, madam, but this gallery is closed."

I feigned surprise. "Really?"

He nodded. "Can I help you? Are you lost?"

I didn't answer right away. Instead I looked round one last time. The thread of my past unspooled before me—memories, dreams, and regrets.

"Do you need some help?" he repeated, louder this time.

I shook my head. "No, thank you." And lifting my chin, I pulled myself up to my full height, tucked my handbag under my arm, and marched past him. It's a trick I learned from my mother—when in doubt, act like you know what you're doing, and you'll be treated like you do.

And of course, if you can convince others, there's a chance that someday you might just be able to convince yourself.

Part One

I opened my eyes.

It was still dark out, maybe a little after six in the morning. Lying on my back in bed, I stared at the ceiling. I could just make out the wet patch in the corner where the roof leaked last spring and the wallpaper had begun to peel away—pale-green wallpaper with pink cabbage roses my mother had put up when we first moved in, over twenty years ago. At the time, it seemed the epitome of feminine sophistication. Outside, the rumble of garbage trucks drew closer as they made their way slowly down the street, and I could hear the faint cooing of the pigeons Mr. Marrelli kept on the roof next door; all familiar sounds of the city coming to life. They should've been reassuring. After all, here I was, back in my own room; home again in Boston. But all I felt was a dull, gnawing dread in the pit of my stomach.

I couldn't sleep last night. Not even Dickens's *Great Expectations* could still my racing mind. When I did finally drift off, my dreams were disjointed and draining—full of panic and chaos, running down endless alleys from some black and terrible thing, never fully seen but always felt.

I hauled myself out of bed and put on my old woolen robe and slippers, navigating the narrow gap between the end of the bed and the stacks of books—I collected secondhand editions with broken spines bought from street stalls or selectively "borrowed" from the library: Jane Austen, the Brontë sisters, Dickens, Thackeray, Collins. Great heavy editions of Shakespeare and Milton,

Yeats, Shelley, Keats. "You've read them already, why do you need to keep them? All they do is take up space!" my mother complained. She was right—there was no room for anything, not even a chair. But where Ma saw only old books gathering dust and smelling of mildew, I found comfort and possibility. Other worlds were within my grasp—better worlds full of rewarded ambition, refinement, and eloquence. I clung to them as a pilgrim whose faith is proportional to the extremity of their need clings to a relic or a prayer.

Shuffling into the bathroom, I paused to press my hand against the radiator in the hallway. Stone cold as usual. I don't know why I kept checking. The triumph of optimism over experience. Or good old-fashioned stubbornness, as my mother would say.

Turning on the bathroom light, I blinked at my reflection. It was still a shock. I used to have long hair—thick, copper red, and uncontrollable, a dubious gift from my Irish heritage. Now it was cropped short, growing back at least two shades darker in deep auburn waves. It made my skin look even paler than usual. I put my finger on the small cleft in my chin, as if covering it up would make it disappear entirely. It always struck me as a bit mannish. But I couldn't hold my finger there forever. Bluish-gray shadows ringed my eyes, the same color as the irises. My eyes looked huge—too large, too round. Like a madwoman's, I thought.

I splashed my face with cold water and headed into the kitchen.

My mother was already up, sitting at the kitchen table reading the paper and smoking her morning cigarette. Even in her curlers and dressing gown, she sat upright, straight back, head held high, at full attention. Regal. That was the best word for it. Apparently even as a young girl she was known as Her Majesty in the Irish seaside town she grew up in. It was a nickname that fit her in more ways than one.

The rich aroma of fresh coffee filled the air. It was a tiny room, mostly taken up by the black cast-iron stove recessed into the mantelpiece. On one side there was a built-in dresser and just enough room for a small wooden table and a couple of chairs. Two narrow windows looked out over the street below and a clothes airer was suspended from the ceiling, to be lowered with a pulley. The rest of the neighborhood used the public lines hanging between buildings, but not us. It was common, according to my mother, and that was the last thing we Fanning women wanted to be.

Ma frowned when I walked in—anything out of the ordinary was cause for suspicion. "What are you doing up this early?"

"I couldn't sleep." I checked the gas meter above the sink. It was off. "It's cold," I said, knowing that I was asking for trouble.

She shot a long stream of smoke at the ceiling, a combination of exhaling and a world-weary sigh. "When you get a job you can stuff the meter full of quarters. Now eat. You need something in your stomach, especially today."

"I'm not hungry." I poured myself a cup of strong black coffee and sat down.

The heat, or lack thereof, was always a sticking point between us. But since I came back it had become the central refrain of almost every encounter. It's funny how some arguments are easier, more comforting, than real conversation.

I looked round the room. Nothing had changed except for the Roosevelt campaign leaflet pinned on the wall with the slogan "Happy Days Are Here Again." Otherwise it was all just as I remembered it. Above the stove were three books—*Mrs. Rorer's New Cook Book: A Manual of Housekeeping*, a copy of *Modes and Manners: Decorum in Polite Society*, and a small leather-bound Bible—our entire domestic library. Next to that, displayed on the dresser shelves, were my mother's most precious possessions: a photograph of Pope Pius XI, a picture of Charles Stewart Parnell of the Irish Nationalist Party, and in the center of this unlikely partnership, a small wooden crucifix. Below, my framed diploma from the Katherine Gibbs Secretarial School took up the entire shelf. And on the bottom a genuine blue-and-white Staffordshire willow-pattern teapot with four matching cups and saucers sat waiting for just the right occasion, a wedding gift brought all the way from Ireland.

"So"—Ma decided to get straight down to business—"what are you going to wear today?"

"My blue dress. Maybe with the red scarf."

"Really." She sounded distinctly underwhelmed. "That dress isn't serious enough."

"Serious enough for what? It's only an employment agency."

She ignored my tone, folding the newspaper neatly. It would be saved and used again—to line the shelves of the icebox or wash windows, maybe even to cut out patterns for clothing. I used to wonder what it felt like to waste something; as a child I couldn't imagine anything more delicious or sinful than the extravagance of throwing things away. I've wasted a few things since then; it's not as liberating as I imagined.

Ma made me an offer. "I'll tell you what, Maeve. You can borrow my gray wool suit. I pressed it last night, just in case."

She said it as if she were handing me the keys to the city.

And in her mind, she was.

Ma worked in a high-end department store called R. H. Stearns in downtown Boston. She'd been there years in the alterations department, working as a seamstress. But her real ambition was to be a saleswoman. More than anything she fancied herself a fashion adviser to wealthy women—the kind of society mavens with enough money to buy designer gowns and a different fur for every outfit. To this end she wasted precious quarters on copies of *Vogue* and *McCall's* every month, poring over them, memorizing each page. She'd bought the gray suit years ago when she first began applying for a sales position, but they passed over her year after year. Perhaps it was because she was so skilled a seamstress, or perhaps because they thought she was too old, at forty-three, or maybe too Irish. But in any case the gray suit, the proud uniform of her future self, still hung in her wardrobe, outdated now.

"The blue dress fits better," I told her.

"This is a job interview, not a date." She was hurt. I could hear the wounded pride in her voice, as if she'd just proposed, been turned down, and now had to get up off her knees from the floor. "Also I fixed that hat of yours, the one with the torn net. I steamed it back into shape but in the end I had to take the net off." She got up, went to the sink. "Where'd you get a hat like that anyway, Maeve? It's a Lilly Daché! They cost a fortune!"

Trust her to notice the label.

"It was a gift," I fibbed.

"Well, you certainly didn't take care of it. And a 'Thank you' wouldn't go amiss."

"Cheers, Ma."

She started to wash up.

I stared out the window, pressing my palms tightly against the coffee cup for warmth. Sitting here in the kitchen just before the day truly began, looking out into the darkness, calmed my nerves. The city was shadowy, lit only by streetlamps. But still the North End was already awake and opening for business.

The fruit seller across the street, Mr. Contadino, was setting up his stall, squinting as he cranked open his green-striped awning in the icy wind, the air swirling with snowflakes. He had on a flat cap and a heavy woolen vest under his clean apron, and a pair of knitted fingerless gloves protected his stubby hands. Soon he would light the chestnut stove—a large iron barrel near the shop doorway with a coal fire in the base and fresh chestnuts roasting in the top. He sold them tender and hot in little brown paper bags for a penny. Contadino's chestnuts were a glowing beacon of civilization in the North End. The smell of the buttery flesh roasting and the delicious combination of cold air and the crackling fragrant heat radiating from the belly of the stove made it all but impossible not to stop as you passed by. Men collected there, speaking in Italian, smoking, laughing, warming their hands. In the morning they held tiny steaming cups of espresso, and in the evening cigar smoke, sweet and luxuriant, billowed around them in clouds.

As Ma was fond of pointing out, Contadino knew what he was doing. That chestnut stove brought him twice as much trade as any other fruit seller in the neighborhood had. "See, the Italians are smart. And they don't drink. We made the right choice; we're better off here."

Here was the North End of Boston. Waves of immigrants had made the North End their home over the years. It had been a Jewish ghetto before the Irish took over, but most had since moved south; it was firmly Italian now. We had second cousins living in the South End, but Ma always considered herself a North Ender, valuing privacy over familiarity. "We don't have to live in everyone's back pocket," she used to say.

"A suit looks more professional." Ma hated to lose an argument. "Just because you're not working doesn't mean you can't look respectable."

Respectable was one of Ma's favorite words, along with *ladylike* and *tasteful*. Quaint, old-fashioned words. To me they sounded as relevant as *bustle* and *parasol*; faded echoes from another era when good looks, pleasing manners, and modesty were all that were required in the female arsenal. Nowadays, they just made you seem backward.

"I'll think about the suit," I told her, watching as Mrs. Contadino, wrapped in a shawl, came out into the cold with her husband's coat. He waved her away, but she won in the end; he had to put it on before she would go back inside.

Then I remembered what day it was.

"It's the eighth today, isn't it?"

I saw her smile. Maybe it pleased her that she didn't have to remind me. "That's right. It's a sign. Mark my words: it'll bring you luck!"

Underneath Ma's worldly exterior a superstitious child of Ireland still lingered, clinging to all the impossible magic of the supernatural.

"Do you think?" I swallowed some more coffee.

"Absolutely! You were born at night, Maeve. That means you have a connection to the world of the dead. If you ask for their help, they're sure to come." She topped up my cup. "I'll be going to mass later if you want to join me. I'm sure he'd like it if you came too."

It had been a long time since I'd been to mass. Too long.

I looked out at the pale gray dawn, bleeding red-orange into the sky. "Go on, Ma, tell me about him," I said, changing the subject. It was also a tradition, something we did every year on the anniversary of my father's death. And who knew, maybe today it would make a difference; maybe against all reason, my dead father would lure good fortune to me.

"Oh, Maeve!" She shook her head indulgently. "You know everything there is to tell!"

Every year she protested—not too hard.

"Go on!"

And every year, I insisted, for old times' sake.

She paused, teasing the moment out like an actress about to play a big speech. "He was a remarkable man," she began. "A graduate of Trinity College in Dublin. A true gentleman and an intellectual. Do you know what I mean when I say that?" She took a long drag. "I mean he had a hunger for knowledge; a deep longing for it, the way that some people yearn for food or wealth." She smiled softly, exhaling, and her voice took on a tender, dreamy tone. "It made him glow; like he was on fire from the inside out. His eyes used to burn brighter, his whole being changed when he was speaking on something that interested him, like literature or philosophy. He was good-looking, yes," she allowed, "but if you only could've heard him *talk*. . . . Oh, Maeve! His voice was a *country*—a rich green land populated with mountains and rivers . . ."

She had the gift, as the Irish would say, an ear for language. Her talents were wasted as a seamstress.

"He drew you into other places. Other worlds. He made the obscure real and the unfathomable possible. He would've been a great man had he lived. There was no doubt. His brain was like a whip." She flicked a bit of ash into the sink, pointed her cigarette at me. "You have that. You have a sharp mind." Her words were an accusation rather than a compliment. "And his eyes. You have his eyes."

There was just one photograph of Michael Fanning. It sat on the mantelpiece in the front room, a rather startling portrait of a handsome young man staring directly into the camera. His broad, intelligent forehead was framed by waves of dark locks, and his features were fine and even. But it was the fearless intensity of his gaze and the luminous pinpoints of light reflected in his black pupils that drew you in. It was impossible not to imagine that he was looking straight at you, perhaps even leaning in closer, as if he'd just asked a question and was particularly interested to hear your answer. It was an honest face, without artifice or pretension, and as far as I was concerned, the most beautiful face in the world.

I'd never known him. Ma was a widow and had been all my life. But his absence was the defining force in our lives, a vacuum of loss that held us fast to our ambitions and to each other. He'd always been Michael Fanning, never father or Da. And he wasn't just a man but an era; the golden age in Ma's life, illuminated by optimism and possibility, gone before I was born. I'd grown up praying to him, begging for his guidance and mercy, imagining him always there, watching over me with those inquisitive, unblinking eyes. God the Father, the Son, the Holy Ghost, and Michael Fanning. In my mind, the four of them sat around heaven, drinking tea, smoking cigarettes, taking turns choosing the forecast for the day.

"What time are you going to mass?"

"Six o'clock. I want to go to confession before."

Confession.

Now there was the rub. I certainly wasn't going to confession.

"Well," I said vaguely, "I'll see what I can do, Ma."

My parents met in Bray, a small seaside town in county Wicklow, Ireland. Fresh from university, Michael Fanning turned his back on his family's considerable resources to teach at the local comprehensive, where Ma was a student in her final year. After a brief and clandestine courtship they married, against both their parents' wishes, when she was just seventeen. They planned to immigrate to New York, where Michael's cousin was already established. But he contracted influenza, and within three days was dead. No one from either family came to the funeral.

With what little money remained after burial costs, seventeen-year-old Nora set sail for America rather than turn to her family for help. The only ticket she could afford landed her in Boston, and so I was born six months later, in a tiny one-room apartment above a butcher's shop in the North End, with no heat, hot water, or bathroom. I was delivered by the butcher's wife, Mrs. Marcosa, who didn't speak English and had seven children of her own, most of them kneeling round the bed praying as their mother, sleeves rolled high on her thick arms, shouted at my terrified mother in Italian. When I finally appeared, they all danced, applauded, and cheered.

"It was one of the most wonderful and yet humiliating days of my life," Ma used to say. "The Marcosa children all loved to hold you because of your red hair. They found it fascinating. The whole neighborhood did. I couldn't go half a block without someone stopping me."

She took in seamstress work during the day, piecing together cotton blouses for Levin's garment factory nearby, and in the evenings she traveled across town to clean offices, taking me with her in a wicker laundry basket, wrapped in blankets. Setting me on the desks, she made her way through the offices, dusting, polishing, and scrubbing, singing in her low soft voice from eight until midnight before heading back across the sleeping city.

But she always hungered for more. And even when she joined the alterations department at Stearns, she'd already had her sights set on moving from the workroom to the sales floor. She enrolled in Sunday-afternoon speech classes from an impoverished spinster in Beacon Hill, taking me with her so that I could learn to enunciate without the telltale lilt of her brogue or, worse, the flat vowels of the Boston streets. I suppose that's something we have in common—the unshakable conviction we're destined for better things.

Year after year she continued to apply for a sales position, ignoring the rejections and snubs, refusing to try elsewhere. "It's the finest department store in the city," she maintained. "I'd rather mop floors there than anywhere else." She could endure anything but failure.

Stubbornness is another trait we share.

She still wore the plain, slim gold band her husband had given her on her wedding ring finger, not just as a reminder but also as a safeguard against unwanted male attention.

"Your father would've been proud of you, Maeve, getting your secretarial degree." She took a final drag from her cigarette, stubbed the end out in the sink.

I looked down. "Oh, I don't know about that."

"Well, I do."

All my life, she'd been a medium between this world and the next, advising on what my father would've wanted, believed in, admired.

"He had everything it took to really be someone in this world—intelligence, breeding, a good education. Everything, that is, except luck. I just hope yours is better than his." She sighed.

"What do you mean?"

"Nothing. You're a clever girl. A capable girl." Leaning in, she scrubbed the coffee stains out of the sink. "It's just a shame you lost that job in New York."

A knot of guilt and apprehension tightened in my stomach. This was the last thing I wanted to talk about. "Let's not go into that."

But Ma was never one to let a subject die an easy death if she could kick it around the room a few more times.

"It just doesn't make sense," she went on, ignoring me. "Why did Mr. Halliday let you go after all that time?"

"I told you, he's traveling."

"Yes, but why didn't he just take you with him, like he did before? Remember that? You gave me the fright of my life! I didn't get a letter from you for almost six weeks!"

It was if she knew the truth and was torturing me, the way a cat swats around a half-dead mouse. I glared at her. "Jeez, Ma! How would I know?"

"It just doesn't make sense. You've been his private secretary for almost a year, and then, out of the blue, you're suddenly out of work and back in Boston!"

"Well, at least I'm home. Aren't you glad about that?"

She gave a halfhearted shrug. "I'd rather have you make something of yourself. You were on your way in New York. Now you'll have to start all over again." Scooping some porridge into a bowl, she set it down in front of me. "I'll hang the gray suit in your room."

I gnawed at my thumbnail. I didn't want porridge or the suit. The only thing I wanted now was to crawl back into bed and disappear.

She gave my hand a smack. "What are you doing? You'll ruin your nails! Don't worry so much. With your training and experience, you're practically a shoo-in."

I prodded the porridge with my spoon.

My experience.

If only my experience in New York was what she thought it was.

SOMEWHERE IN BROOKLYN, NOVEMBER 1931

I was falling, too fast, with nothing to stop me . . . down, down, gathering speed . . .

I came to with a jolt. I was sitting on the side of a bed wearing only my slip and stockings—a wrought-iron bed in a cold, dark bedroom. Only it wasn't my bed or my room.

Suddenly the floor veered beneath me, the walls spinning, faded yellow flowers on the wallpaper melting together. *Please, God, don't let me be sick!* I pressed my eyes closed and held on to the bed frame tight.

I had to think. Where was I, and how exactly had I gotten here?

It had been a long, dull night at the Orpheum dance palace on Broadway where I worked. The joint was full of nothing but out-of-towners and hayseeds—guys with little money and lots of expectations. By the time we'd closed and I'd cashed in my ticket stubs, I was ready for some fun. Another girl, Lois, had made a "date" with a customer, and he had a friend . . . Was I game?

Why not? After all, it wasn't like I had anything to lose.

I remembered two big men, grinning like excited schoolboys, in New York for a convention and laughing the way tourists do— too easily and too hard, willing themselves to have the best night of their lives. One was reasonable-looking, and the other—well, let's just say no one was going to mistake him for Errol Flynn or Douglas Fairbanks. But there's that old adage about beggars and choosers, and tonight I felt like a beggar for sure. The last thing I wanted was to be alone and sober at the same time. So we all piled into a cab. Hip flasks were passed round; I remembered Lois sitting on someone's lap, singing "Diggity Diggity Do."

We drove to Harlem, to a place called Hot Feet. There was a band from New Orleans and a chorus line of smooth-skinned Negro girls dressed up with grass skirts and bone necklaces, shaking and shimmying for all they were worth. The moonshine had kicked in by then, and I was feeling a bit less rough round the edges. Lois was sure she saw Oweny Madden and the boxer Primo Carnera at the next table, and one of the guys, the ugly one, forked out for a bottle of real gin.

God, my mouth was as dry as the Sahara! What time was it now? What had happened to Lois?

I tried to stand. My head pounded, my stomach swooned. Easy does it. Not too fast.

Someone shifted in the bed next to me.

Shit. Please don't let it be the ugly one.

I tried not to look. A face you never saw was a face you never remembered. I'd learned that much in New York.

I eased myself up. My knees were sore, and there were holes in my stockings. I guess I must've fallen. Going over to the window, I pushed aside the curtain. The street was residential, narrow row houses with uneven terraces crammed together, lamps glowing eerily over abandoned lots between. I searched for something familiar on the skyline, a bridge or a building, but couldn't see anything. One thing was certain: I was definitely on the wrong side of the river.

I seemed to remember talk of going to a hotel to carry on the party—someplace like the Waldorf or the Warwick. So why was I stranded in some cheap boarding house in Queens or Yonkers with no idea where I was or how I was going to get home?

The man rolled over on to his side and began to snore. I had to get out of here, before he woke.

Where were my clothes?

I nearly stumbled over something and picked it up. But this dress wasn't mine.

Then a memory came of the day before. I'd borrowed a dress from Nancy Rae, the girl down the hall at the Nightingale boarding house, where I rented a room. It was Nancy's good-luck dress, a hunter-green serge she'd been wearing when she landed her job at Gimbles; all the girls wanted to borrow it for interviews. I'd given her a dollar for the privilege and even gotten up early to steam the box pleats of the skirt through a towel to make them crisp and sharp without going shiny. When I finished, they fluttered open like a fan round my legs.

See that's the thing about luck—it has to be courted. You have to seduce it; reel it in slowly without arousing suspicion. It's so precious that every tiny thing matters—what you wear, which side of the road you walk on, the tune you whistle, or how many birds you see out the window. Nancy Rae's hunter-green dress had stood in fate's presence and felt its light touch. And when fate favors anything, you'd best pay attention.

I'd been working as a taxi dancer at the Orpheum for months, waltzing with strangers night after night for a dime a dance. But when I saw the advertisement in the back of the *Herald* for "a young woman of exceptional executive secretarial skills," I knew that my luck was about to change.

So I gave Nancy the dollar, ironed the dress, and set out first thing in the morning with my notebook and résumé in hand.

But when I arrived at the address, a full hour ahead of time, there were already fifty girls ahead of me, lined up around the corner of the office building, all clutching notebooks and reference letters, all looking hungry and determined and ferociously confident. I lasted three hours waiting in the cold before the girl ahead of me, a short brunette with a frizzy permanent wave and a big run in her stocking, turned round and announced, "You know they're not going to see all of us, don't you? I've been standing in lines for months, just trying to get my foot in the door. I tell you, we're waiting here for nothing, like a bunch of saps!"

No one answered her. You can be six inches from someone's face in New York City and they can still stare straight through you, like you're not even there. But when I looked around, I could see from the other girls' faces that what she said was true.

Then she leaned in closer. "I know a guy who runs the door on a joint off Lexington. If you sit at the bar and are friendly to the customers, they don't mind serving you for free, especially if you're good-looking."

I didn't know why she was telling me. Did I look like the kind of girl who was at home on a barstool? I lifted my chin a little so I was looking down at her and sneered, "What of it?"

She wasn't put off. "Besides"—she jerked her head at the others, shivering ahead of us—"today's not our day, sister."

There *were* an awful lot of us. The line stretched right up the block and disappeared round the corner. And it would be so nice to sit down and get warm. I didn't have any money for breakfast that morning, so my stomach was playing a selection of squeaky, off-key tunes all on its own.

Still, if they could only see my qualifications, give me a chance.

The poodle-haired brunette wasn't waiting any longer. "Fine!" She rolled her eyes, the voice of reason in a world full of idiots. "I was trying to do you a favor, but if you want to catch frostbite just to be told thanks but no thanks, that's up to you!"

"Is it heated?" I'm on the thin side, being warm is something of an Achilles heel for me.

She shot me a look like I was from the backwoods of West Virginia. "Sure it's heated! And they got free peanuts at every table, as much as you can eat."

As soon as I stepped out of line, the girl behind me shoved forward like I was all that was standing between her and destiny. I tossed a sad smile her way just to show her I knew better. I was off to be fed and watered for free. I'd graduated from waiting around.

The poodle brunette had a name like Ivy or Ida or Elsa, and

once inside the club on Lexington, she told me right where to sit and how to play it. She got us both a basket of peanuts and we ate as much as we could stand before she brushed the shells off the table and swung into action. Hers was an entirely democratic brand of lazy hospitality—everyone was included in its warm glow, but no one was singled out; every guy figured he had a chance. Maybe because of this she was a past master at getting men to buy more rounds. It wasn't long before the morning slipped into the afternoon and the afternoon into the evening. I probably ate a pound of peanuts that day. Soon it was time to head over to Broadway to begin another shift at the dance palace.

Now here I was, eighteen hours later, tripping over Nancy Rae's lucky green dress, crumpled in a heap on a stranger's floor.

My life was full of cracks, ever-widening gaps between the person I wanted to be and the person I was. When I first came to this city, they used to be small enough to laugh off or ignore. But over the past year they'd grown wider, deeper. I'd fallen in one again last night.

This was the last time, I promised myself.

The very last time.

I found my coat in the corner, thrown over a chair. My new hat, the one I'd splurged on when I got my first job, had been stepped on, squashed into a flat felt circle, the black net that had framed my face so charmingly torn and dangling miserably from a few threads.

I got dressed. Unfortunately I'm good at this—navigating creaky floorboards and sleeping men, finding clothes in the dark. It's a loathsome talent.

All I needed now was my handbag.

I searched the floor, the bedside table, then on the dresser. A watery blue beam of moonlight streamed in from the crack in the curtains. An old-fashioned gold pocket watch and a pair of cufflinks sat on top of it. Next to them was a photograph of a dark-haired woman holding a toddler. Both were smiling—big, wide, foolish grins. "To Daddy, with all our love" was written in a woman's rounded hand across the bottom right-hand corner.

I wanted to throw up.

The guy in the bed snorted, coughed. I spotted my bag, jammed between the bedposts, and eased it out.

The room was quiet except for the snoring and a gentle ticking sound; a steady march of time.

I picked up the watch. Solid, smooth, and heavy, it had a pleasant, reassuring weight. My fingers closed round it; it fit neatly into the palm of my hand.

Three twenty-three a.m.

Plenty of time to get back to the boarding house and sleep it off before work tonight. Plenty of time to re-iron Nancy Rae's dress before returning it. Maybe I'd buy a paper on my way home, get a head start on finding another job. That's what I told myself. But more likely I'd just stay in my room, too ashamed to let the other girls see me coming in at dawn, lock the door, and lie in bed all afternoon, listening to the music of the landlady's radio seeping through the floorboards. And I'd imagine how maybe soon things would be different; a man would come into the dance hall who was decent and kind or I'd stumble across a real job or maybe finally I'd just give up altogether, go home . . .

Tomorrow my luck would change. Tomorrow I'd try again.

Only I had to get through tonight first.

I don't know why I took the watch. Maybe it was just an accident. Or maybe because of the stupid hopeful grin on the woman's face in the picture, or because of the way the man in the bed smelled like mothballs and sour sweat. Maybe just because it gave me something to hold on to.

I don't know why. But I did.

And I really wish I hadn't.

Because after that, things got a lot worse.

New York City was the knife's edge of opportunity—modern and progressive. A place where a girl could leave her past behind and get a job and a life that really mattered. Every day smart young women with bobbed hair and cherry-red lips poured out of the subway stations at eight in the morning to take over the world, and no one batted an eye. No one cared either when they ended the day sipping cocktails in underground clubs next to their male colleagues.

I told everyone that I went to New York City because I didn't want to end up just another pair of hands in a typing pool. Sharp, efficient, able to anticipate every need before it arose, I saw myself rising through the ranks and becoming indispensable to a high-powered corporate executive. I wanted freedom and excitement; that's what I said. And that was partly true, but it wasn't the whole story.

I had just enough ability to make my hubris seem like healthy ambition. Even after the Crash hit, I'd always landed on my feet in Boston; even been able to take my pick of jobs. I thought I could make it. And for a short time, I suppose I did. I got a job at a brokerage firm working for the CEO and bought myself a fancy new hat to celebrate. But after six months the business went bankrupt and they found him underneath his desk, burning pages from his address book. After that I received an extended lesson in humility.

Turns out I wasn't as uniquely talented as I thought, that the city was crammed to the gills with girls with the same credentials, and the landlady at the Nightingale wasn't very patient when it came to rent. I ended up working as a taxi dancer at the place on Broadway, the Orpheum. They were short on redheads and prided themselves on catering to all tastes. So I got a job dancing with strangers.

I went from top of my typing class to bottom of the pecking order in the girls' locker room. I rented a secondhand gown from one of the other dancers and borrowed a pair of slippers until I got paid. The other girls weren't particularly nice or mean, just jaded and tired. And luckily for me, there wasn't that much competition in the redhead section. You have to sit in groups round the edge of the dance floor, blondes with blondes, brunettes with brunettes, and the guys stroll around eyeing you up the way a woman looks at an apple at a fruit stall—trying to find one that's not too bruised, not too soft. Some girls winked and flirted, others carried on chatting among themselves as if ignoring the customers sharpened their appetite. I used to close my eyes and try to drift inside the music—I didn't like to see the look on the guys' faces if they passed me by.

You think you're lucky when you're chosen, but of course now you've got a whole other world of difficulty ahead of you—keeping their hands where they belonged was a full-time job, and one that had to be done with a smile on your face. And it's not easy to make small talk with a guy who doesn't speak any English, or who's trying to hustle you for a free date. But every misfit in the city is your sweetheart for the next three minutes—the gropers and the bullies, the small-town Casanovas; the shy boys, the physically deformed, foreigners fresh off the boat; older men, looking for company. You have to charm them while letting them know you're not for sale. Only you are, really.

Of course I didn't tell Ma where I'd landed. I made up a story about being a private secretary to an eccentric millionaire—Mr.

Halliday. I gave him odd habits and a demanding personality. That explained away the late nights and why I was never at the boarding house when she called. And also why I never came home.

After all, it was only meant to be temporary. But it turns out there's a lot of money to be made as a taxi dancer—almost forty dollars a week sometimes. And I pretty much had the redhead market cornered after about a month. I found that if I had a few shots while I was getting ready and then kept myself topped up through the night, it was just about bearable. I wasn't the only girl with a bottle in her locker—most of us had something. And it wasn't like we went out of our way to hide it either. The management knew the score and never bothered anyone unless a girl was stupid about it and got sloppy or sick.

Pretty soon a few of us started going out after the dance hall closed, just to finish up the night. That's when the clubs got really interesting. Sometimes I'd make it back to the boarding house and sometimes I wouldn't. It wasn't something I was proud of. Sleeping all day, working all night, in a city like New York gets lonely.

But then I took the watch.

Turns out that guy was really fond of that watch; his father had given it to him, and his father before that. Turns out too that he remembered where I worked and showed up the next night hellbent on getting it back.

By that time, I didn't even remember I'd taken it. But he found it in my coat pocket, so there was no way I could talk my way out of it. He started making a scene, right there in the middle of the dance floor, shouting that I was a thief and a liar, and then the management had no choice but to let me go.

Only that wasn't enough for him. He figured I still owed him something. And when I came out of the back entrance of the building after cleaning out my locker, he was waiting there to get it.

You have to give it to New Yorkers—they're pragmatic people. They don't get involved unless they have to. They can turn a blind eye, ear, or anything else you want to name. When he was done, he left me lying in the alleyway. Somehow I managed to get up, button my coat over my torn dress, and walk twenty-three blocks back to the Nightingale.

Then I ran a bath, poured another drink, and took a razor blade with me into the bathroom.

That's how I ended up at the Binghamton State Hospital, otherwise known as the loony bin.

🌸 BOSTON, FEBRUARY 1932

In the end, Ma won; I found myself standing in the empty outer office of the Belmont Placement Agency in Dewey Square, wearing the gray suit. I'd lost weight; the jacket sagged around my bust like a deflated tweed balloon. I tried to cover it up with my scarf, but it was hopeless.

I wondered where everyone was. I'd known the woman who ran the agency, Maude Williams, since I began secretarial school. As a star student, I was singled out as early recruitment material, and she gave me the pick of any position I wanted. It wasn't long ago I'd been sitting across from her, turning down extra pay because I couldn't wait to get out of Boston. But things had changed. There was a time when Maude had a receptionist of her own; when these dingy little rooms were crammed with girls, ready to go anywhere Maude sent them. Now I was the only one there.

On the way the trolley had passed by Boylston Street, near the

Common. Crowds of homeless sat huddled around campfires in a makeshift shantytown. There'd been outrage and shock over their invasion before I left, but now there were twice as many. They had become invisible in their poverty, sleeping on cardboard boxes in doorways, selling apples on street corners. It wasn't quite as bad as New York and the sprawling Hooverville that had taken over Central Park, but still it sent a chill up my spine.

In the North End, too, there were things I hadn't seen before—big signs hung from the front gates of the shoe factory and the railroad yard: "Jobless Men Keep Walking—We Can't Feed Our Own." And on Hanover Street this morning, the corner was crowded with men, maybe fifty or sixty. They were all waiting for the construction trucks to drive past on their way to the building sites in the city, looking for day workers. When they stopped, all hell broke loose—swarms of bodies engulfed them, shouting, shoving, clambering aboard. The foreman had to push them down like animals, banging on the side of the truck to start moving again.

Please God that didn't happen to me.

I jammed my hands into my pockets.

"Ouch!" Something sharp stabbed my palm, and I pulled out a bent safety pin. Another one of Ma's superstitions: "A crooked pin in the pocket brings good luck."

A minute later I was sitting across from Maude—short and solid, somewhere in her late fifties, a hard smear of red lipstick highlighting her thin lips and thick black glasses framing her eyes. Straight-talking and unflappable, Maude was the first and often only port of call for anyone looking for a truly professional secretary. Or at least that's the way it used to be.

"Jesus, kid!" She took a hard drag on her cigarette and leaned back in her desk chair. "I never thought I'd see you again! What are you doing back?"

"Guess I'm not cut out for the big city after all," I said.

She nodded sagely. "Not many people are. Though I have to say, you look a bit, well, underfed. And I can't say I like that hairstyle on you."

"I'll never go to that hair dresser again!" I laughed, automatically running my hand through the short curls. "It'll grow back," I reassured her. "Faster than you think."

"Have you been sick or something?"

"No, no, I'm fine. Maybe I was a little homesick."

"Perhaps you should take it easy. Rest up. Why not come see me in another week?"

It wasn't like her to worry about anyone's health.

"I'm right as rain. So"—I sat forward, gave her a smile full of history and complicity—"what have you got for me?"

Maude flicked a bit of ash into a mug, where it fizzled in the remains of her cold coffee. "Nothing."

"I'm sorry?"

"I haven't got anything for anyone, kid. Don't you read the papers? The whole country's out of work."

This wasn't the reception I'd been expecting. Maude always had some lead tucked up her sleeve.

"But, Maude"—I tried to laugh, but it came out forced, like a broken machine gun—"there has to be *something*!"

She picked up a single sheet in her in-tray. "See this? This is it— I've got one job. And about two hundred girls waiting for my phone call. And I'm sorry to say, kid, but you're not what they're looking for."

"What is it?"

She squinted as she read the heading. "A temporary clerk/salesgirl."

"But I can do that!" This time my laugh sounded real—full of relief. "I don't care if it's not secretarial. I'm not going to be picky!" I added graciously.

"Yes, but not just any clerk. It says"—she referred to the paper again—"'The girl in question should be a young woman of quality, well-spoken and professional, able to create a favorable impression with affluent clientele.'" She peered at me over her glasses. "Allow me to translate: that's 'No Irish redheads, thanks.' They want a blueblood. Or at least someone who passes for one. It's one of those fancy shops on Charles Hill."

"Look, I can't go home with nothing, Maude. You don't understand. I've got bills, debts to pay."

"No, you're right," she said flatly. "I've never had a bill in my life."

"What about the telephone company? They always need girls, don't they?"

"Not anymore. They let fifty go last month." She stubbed her cigarette out in the mug. "I'm sorry, really. I am."

"What's the address of this shop?"

"Oh, no!" She shook her head. "No, I'm not taking any chances! I need this commission!"

"I know how to speak properly and which fork to use at dinner!" I had an idea. "You know what? I'll just dye my hair blond!"

"Are you kidding me? And end up looking like every two-bit secretary I already have on the books, all of them trying to be Joan Blondell or Jean Harlow? These people want a young woman of quality, not a chorus girl!"

"Please, Maude!" I was starting to sound desperate. "Just give me one chance. That's all I'm asking."

She winced; the conversation was painful for both of us. "I've known you a long time, Maeve. And you're a smart girl with a lot of potential. But my God, if you haven't got lousy timing!" A buzzer sounded in the room next door. "Things are tough here. Real tough. Maybe you should've stayed in New York."

She got up and went into the waiting room to unlock the door.

I grabbed the paper from her in-tray. A card was attached to the bottom. I tore it off and shoved it into my pocket.

It wasn't until I got outside in the street that I took it out again and looked at it.

WINSHAW AND KESSLER
Antiquities, Rare Objects, and Fine Art

Under the address were the following lines:

EXTRAORDINARY ITEMS BOUGHT, SOLD, AND OBTAINED UPON REQUEST
Absolute discretion guaranteed

———

R. H. Stearns had long been established as the most exclusive department store in Boston. Located in a tall, narrow building overlooking the Common, its hallmark green awnings promised only the finest, most fashionable merchandise inside. Already the windows were dressed with pretty pastel displays of spring fashions in stark contrast to the customers, still bundled in thick winter coats and furs, browsing through the long aisles.

I didn't go in through the polished brass doors, though, but went round to the back of the building. Normally visitors were prohibited from using the staff entrance, but I managed to walk in behind a couple of cleaning girls unnoticed. There was only one person who could help me now, and unfortunately, she wasn't going to like it.

The alterations workshop was a large windowless room in the

basement between the stock rooms and the loading bay, filled with long rows of sewing machines, ironing boards, and clothing rails. The constant clattering of the machines echoing off the cement floor and ceiling made it sound like a factory. Twenty or so women worked side by side, wearing white cotton calico smocks over their street clothes. The department was presided over by Mr. Vye, a very particular, exacting man in his mid-fifties who sat at a desk near the door. He assigned each garment, liaised with the customers, and oversaw the final result. Everything had to go through him, including me.

Ma had a sewing machine at the front of the room in a prime position. It was widely acknowledged that her abilities with difficult materials like silk, taffeta, organza, and brocade were extraordinary, and as a result she was the first choice for eveningwear alterations. Behind her on a dress form was a fitted gown of black velvet with rhinestone straps. When I arrived she was kneeling on the floor, pins in her mouth, taking up the hem.

Mr. Vye scowled at me, an intruder in his domain. "May I help you, young lady?"

"Oh, that's my daughter!" Ma got up, brushed the stray threads from her knees. "You remember my daughter, Maeve, don't you? She's just come back from New York!"

"I'm sorry to disturb you," I apologized. "Only I wondered if I could have a quick word with my mum."

He nodded begrudgingly, and we went into the hall.

"I need a favor, Ma."

"Tell me what happened at the interview. Did they have anything for you?"

"There's not a lot out there, but there is one job. Only I need your help." I lowered my voice. "Ma, I have to dye my hair."

"Dye your *hair*?" She recoiled as if I'd just slapped her across the face. "Certainly not! You have beautiful hair! It was bad enough when you cut it. Only fast girls do that sort of thing!"

"But it's for a job, Ma!"

"What kind of job? A cigarette girl?" She folded her arms across her chest. "Absolutely not!"

I would've happily taken a job as a cigarette girl, but I didn't tell her that.

"Look, I don't want to look fast, or cheap," I explained. "Which is why I came to you. It's for a job in Charles Town. An antiques shop. They want a woman of quality."

"Really?" Now she was indignant. "And what are you, may I ask?"

I lost my patience. "What do I look like, Mum? Do you think anyone's going to figure me for Irish? Why don't I just go in clutching a harp and dancing a jig?"

"There's no need to be vulgar!" But she frowned and bit her lower lip. We both knew she'd spent years erasing all traces of her Irish brogue for exactly the same reason. But dying one's hair was vulgar and brazen as far as she was concerned. She tried to sidestep the question. "Well, I can't help you tonight. I'm going to mass."

"We can go to mass any night! And we haven't got time—the interview is first thing tomorrow morning!"

But she dug in her heels. "I'm afraid I have a prior arrangement, Maeve."

"If you help me, it will turn out all right, I know it will. I won't look cheap or fast. But I can't manage it on my own. *Please!*"

I could feel her wavering between what she thought was respectable and what she knew was necessary.

"Who knows when I'll have another chance?" I begged.

"Maybe. *If* you come to church." She drove a hard bargain, leveraging my eternal soul against the certain depravity of becoming a blonde. "But I'm warning you, Maeve, this is a terrible, *terrible* mistake!"

Nonetheless, she took me up to the ladies' hair salon on the top floor and introduced me to M. Antoine. M. Antoine was French to his wealthy clients and considerably less Gallic in front of staff like Ma. Originally from Liverpool, he'd apparently acquired the accent along with most of his hairdressing skills on the boat on the way over.

He gave me the once-over from behind an entirely useless gold pince-nez. "It's a shame, really." He poked a finger through my red curls. "I have clients that would *kill* for this color!"

I avoided my mother's eye. "Yes, but you can see how it limits me, can't you?"

"It's true," he conceded, "especially in this town. Some people have no imagination."

M. Antoine sent us home was a little bottle of peroxide wrapped in a brown paper bag, which Ma quickly jammed into her handbag as if it were bootleg gin. "No more than twenty minutes," he instructed, firmly. "The difference between a beautiful blonde and a circus poodle is all in the timing. And remember to rinse, ladies, rinse! Rinse as if your very lives depended on it!"

The sign above the door read "Winshaw and Kessler Antiquities, Rare Objects, and Fine Art" in faded gold lettering. It swung back and forth in the wind, creaking on its chains like an old rocking chair.

I stood huddled in the doorway, waiting.

Maude's voice rang in my head: "The girl in question should be a young woman of quality, well-spoken and professional, able to create a favorable impression with affluent clientele."

A blueblood.

I'd looked the word up the night before. The term came from the Spanish, literally translated *sangre azul*, describing the visible veins of the fair-skinned aristocrats. But of course here in Boston we had our own special name for these social and cultural elite, Brahmins—old East Coast families who'd stumbled off the *Mayflower* to teach the English a lesson. There was an even more telling lineage behind that word; it referred to the highest of the four major castes in traditional Indian society. The Boston Brahmins were a club you couldn't join unless you married into it, and they didn't like to mix with anyone who'd floated in on one of the newer ships, landing on Ellis Island rather than Plymouth Rock.

Adjusting my hat in the shop-window reflection, I wondered if it would work. The effect was more dramatic than I'd expected. I looked not just different but like a whole other person; my eyes seemed wider, deeper in color, and my skin went from being white and translucent to a pale ivory beneath my soft golden-blond waves. But would it be enough?

To my mother's credit, she'd been thorough, covering every inch of my scalp in bleach at least three times to make certain there were no telltale signs. And when it was rinsed clean, she wound it into pin curls to be tied tight under a hairnet all night. When I woke, she was already up, sitting by the stove in her dressing gown sewing a Stearn's label into the inside lapel of my coat. "It's one of the only labels people ever notice," she said. "And a coat from Stearn's is a coat to be proud of."

"Even though it's not from Stearn's?" I asked.

"They won't know that. They'll look at the name, not the cut."

For someone who didn't approve of what I was doing, she was dedicated nonetheless.

Now here I was, on a street I'd never even been down before, in my counterfeit coat and curls.

It was almost nine in the morning, and no one was around. In the North End everything was open by seven; there were people to greet, gossip to share, deals to be struck. The streets hummed and buzzed morning till late into the night. But here was the stillness and order of money, of a life that wasn't driven by hustle, sacrifice, and industry. Time was the luxury of another class.

So I practiced smiling instead—not too eager, not too wide, but a discreet, dignified smile, the kind of gentle, unhurried expression that I imagined was natural to women in this part of town, an almost imperceptible softening of the lips, just enough to indicate the pleasant expectation of having every desire fulfilled.

Eventually an older man arrived, head bent down against the wind. He was perhaps five foot five, almost as wide as he was tall, with round wire-rimmed glasses. He glanced up as he fished a set of keys from his coat pocket. "You're the new girl? From the agency?"

"Yes. I'm Miss Fanning."

"You're tall." It was an accusation.

"Yes," I agreed, uncertainly.

"Hmm." He unlocked the door. "I ask for a clerk, and they send me an Amazon."

He switched on the lights, and I followed him inside. Though narrow, the shop went back a long way and was much larger than it looked from the outside.

"Stay here," he said. "I'm going to turn on the heat."

He headed into the back.

I'd never been in an antiques store before—the dream of everyone

I knew was to own something new. And I knew all too well the used furniture stalls in the South End where things were piled on top of one another in a haphazard jumble, smelling of dust and mildew. But this couldn't have been more different.

Crystal chandeliers hung from the ceiling, the floors were covered with oriental carpets, and paintings of every description and time period were crowded on top of one another, dado rail to ceiling, like in a Victorian drawing room. There were ornate gilded mirrors, fine porcelain, gleaming silver. I picked up what I thought was a large pink seashell, only to discover that an elaborate cameo of the Three Graces had been painstakingly etched into one side. It was the most incredible, unnecessary thing I'd ever seen. And there was a table covered with maybe thirty tiny snuffboxes or more, all decorated with intricate mosaic designs of famous monuments, like the Leaning Tower of Pisa and the Great Pyramid at Giza, none of them bigger than a silver dollar. It was more like a museum than a shop.

Little cards with neatly printed descriptions were everywhere.

Here was a "17th-century French oak buffet," a "gilded German Rococo writing desk," a pair of stiff-backed "Tudor English chairs" in mahogany so old they were almost black. Tall freestanding cases housed porcelain vases, pottery urns, a trio of Italian Renaissance bronzes. A row of bizarre African wooden figures squatted on the floor, staring through round cartoon eyes, comical and yet shockingly sexual at the same time. And the prices! I had to keep myself from laughing out loud. Five hundred dollars for a dresser? You could buy a brand-new automobile for less! Near the back of the shop in glass display cases trinkets, watches, and fine estate jewelry were arranged against waves of dark green velvet. The ticking of half a dozen clocks hanging from the wall, ornamented with inlaid wood and gold, sounded gently.

The place even had a smell all its own, a rich musty scent of aging wood, old textiles, and silver polish. This was the perfume of centuries and continents, of time.

Now I knew why they'd wanted a "young woman of quality." People didn't come here to replace a table or sofa; they were collecting, searching out the rare and unique. They wanted a girl who knew what it was like to acquire things out of amusement rather than need. Who sympathized with those whose lives were so pleasantly arranged that they hungered for beauty and meaning rather than food.

The old man returned, took off his hat. His thinning hair was weightless and fine, circling the widening bald spot on the top of his head like a white wreath. "It'll warm up soon. I'm Karl Kessler." He gave a tug at his suit vest, which was struggling to cover his stomach. "What was your name again?"

"May. With a *y*, of course," I added. (I didn't want to use the Irish name Maeve.) "I was named after the month of my birth," I lied.

"And do you know anything about antiques, May with a *y*?"

"Oh, I know a little." I tried to seem casual. "My family had a few good pieces. I was wondering, that buffet over there . . . is that oak, by any chance?"

"Why, yes. It is."

"I thought so." I flashed my well-practiced smile. "I'm so fond of oak, aren't you?"

He fixed me with a sharp black eye. "Where is your family from?"

"New York. Albany, actually. But I'm here staying with my aunt." I ran my fingers lightly along the smooth finish of a Flemish bookcase, as if I were remembering something similar back home. "You see, I had a particularly troublesome beau, Mr. Kessler. We all thought it best that I get away for a while."

"And you can type?"

"Oh, yes! I used to type all Papa's letters. But to be honest, I've never considered a sales job before." I frowned a little, as if pondering the details for the first time. "I suppose it means working every day?"

"Yes. Yes, it does." He nodded slowly. "But I thought the woman from the agency was sending me a girl with secretarial skills?"

"Dear old Maude!" I gave what I hoped passed as an affectionate chuckle. "You see, she's a family friend. I told her I'd try to help her out. Though, as it happens," I added, "I did attend the Katherine Gibbs Secretarial School. Of course, it was more of a diversion than a necessity. But if I do something, Mr. Kessler, I like to be able to do it properly. I was taught that excellence and hard work are virtues, no matter what your situation."

"I see."

"And the wages?" I didn't want to seem overeager. "I suppose they're . . . reasonable?"

"Twenty-five a week. Does that seem reasonable to you?"

"I'm sure it will do very nicely."

"So"—he leaned back against the counter—"do you have other interests?"

"Oh, yes! I like to travel and read, English literature mostly. Also I do a little painting and drawing. . . ." I tried to remember what the heroines in Jane Austen novels did. "I'm terribly fond of long walks and embroidery."

He nodded again. "You read a great deal?"

"Absolutely. I love books."

"So you know how to tell a story?"

"I certainly hope so, Mr. Kessler."

"Well, selling isn't so different from telling a story. Everything here has a history. Where it comes from, how it's made. Why it's important. Once you understand that, the rest is easy. For example, take this piece." He walked over to a small writing desk. "This is an eighteenth-century German Rococo *Toilletentisch*. This little table had many uses in its day. Primarily it would have been a dressing table, which is why it has a mirror in the center. Inside, below the mirror, the wash utensils would be stored." He opened up the small drawers. "And to the sides, jars, combs, and jewelry. But that's not all. There's space for writing and working, playing card games. These tables are light enough to be easily carried from room to room. Mechanical fittings enable them to change use, for example from tea table to games table. It's a fine example from the workshop of Abraham and David Roentgen, specialists in constructing such furniture."

"Why, it's ingenious!"

"Isn't it?" he agreed. "But that's not why someone would buy it. Someone would choose this little table over all the other little tables on this street for one reason alone: because it belonged to Maria Anna Mozart, Wolfgang Amadeus Mozart's older sister. Because this little table, with all its uses, sat in the same room, day after day, with the world's greatest composer as he learned his scales as a boy." His hand rested tenderly on the delicate inlaid wood top. "She wrote in her diary here, the same diary that her brother would later steal and fill with false entries about himself, all in the third person."

"Really?" Suddenly I pictured it in a room with a harpsichord and a violin, overlooking the cobblestone streets of Salzburg, snowflakes dancing in the icy winter air. "How do you know all that?"

Mr. Kessler gave a little shrug. "You doubt me? I believe it because that's what I'm told. Just as I believe you're from Albany and used to type all your father's letters."

My heart skipped a beat, and I felt the heat rising in my cheeks. "Why . . . I'm not sure what you mean . . ."

He raised a hand to stop me. "A good counterfeit is as much a work of art as the real thing. Perhaps even better, May with a *y*. You see, I spoke to the lady at the agency yesterday afternoon. She rang to say she had a nice, reliable girl for me named Roberta, but she needed my address again because someone had stolen my card."

I opened my mouth but nothing came out. I'd pushed it too far.

"And that, Miss Fanning, is how you sell an antique table. With a story and a smile and a healthy dose of truth and lies." He cocked his head to one side. "The woman from the agency also told me to be on the lookout for a very determined redhead. I'm beginning to wonder, is your hair really blond?"

"Well, it is now!" I headed to the door.

"Where are you going?" he called.

I whipped round. "I beg your pardon?"

"You're angry!" Mr. Kessler chuckled. "Well, that beats all!"

"You think I'm *funny*?" Embarrassment vanished; now I was furious. "There's nothing funny about it, Mr. Kessler! I'm flat broke, and I need a job!"

"And I still need a clerk. In fact"—he ran his fingers through his beard—"a blonde from Albany would suit me very well."

"Ha, bloody, ha!" I flung open the door.

"Hold on a moment! I need a girl who can make sales and keep the books, and who fits in with my customers."

"What about Roberta?"

He gave a distinctly Eastern European shrug, a kind of slow roll of the shoulders that came from centuries of inherited resignation. "I doubt Roberta has your dramatic intuition. Now calm down and close the door. Let's see your dress."

"Why?"

"Come now!" He made a soft tutting noise, as if he was luring a stray cat with a saucer of milk. "No one's going to hurt you."

I closed the door and took off my coat, careful to hold it so the label showed. I was wearing the navy blue knit. It was the nicest outfit I owned, and even at that, I'd spent the night before darning moth holes beneath the arms.

Mr. Kessler opened up the jewelry cabinet and took out a long string of pearls and a pair of pearl clip-on earrings. "Here," he said, handing them over. "You can wear what you like from the display, as long as it goes back at the end of the day. If a man comes in, he likes to see the jewelry on a pretty girl. It's the easiest way to sell it."

I wasn't sure I understood. "Are you *hiring* me?"

"If you can keep the fiction for the customers, you might be rather useful. I'm looking for someone adaptable, with a pragmatic disposition. And I have to admit, your stories have flair." He winked, tapping the side of his nose. "The bit about the persistent beau was clever. You'll be good at selling."

"But . . . but aren't you afraid I'm going to steal something?"

He gave me a rather surprised look. "Are you?"

"Well, no."

"You're an actress, May with a *y*. Not a thief," he informed me. "A real thief doesn't warn you of their intentions."

I followed him back behind the glass counters to a room

divided into two offices. He hung his coat up in one and pointed to the other. "You can use that desk. It's Mr. Winshaw's."

"Won't Mr. Winshaw need it?"

"Mr. Winshaw isn't here. Do you drink tea or coffee?"

"Coffee, please."

"So do I." He gestured to the back storage room. "There's a sink in the bathroom and a kettle on the hot plate."

Then he went inside his office and closed the door.

I stood there, unsure of what exactly had just happened.

Then I slipped the pearls over my head. There was no mistaking the real thing. They were heavy with a creamy golden-pink luster. The echo of some long-lost perfume clung to them; sensual, sharp, and sophisticated, it could be muted by time but not silenced.

Instantly they transformed that old blue knit; when your jewels are real, your dress doesn't matter.

But no sooner had I put them on than an eerie feeling came over me, at once familiar yet anxious and uncertain.

The pearls reminded me of someone—the girl on the far ward.

❀ BINGHAMTON STATE HOSPITAL, NEW YORK, 1931

She was wearing pearls. That was the first thing I noticed about her. Large and even, perfectly matched, falling just below her collarbone over the thin blue cotton hospital gown. She strolled into the day room of the Binghamton State Hospital with its bare, institutional green walls and floor stinking of strong bleach like she was wandering into the dining room of the Ritz. Willowy and fine boned, she had blue eyes fringed by long, very black lashes and deep brown hair cut in a straight bob, pushed back from her face. A navy cardigan was draped casually over her shoulders, as if she were on her way to a summer luncheon and had turned back at the last minute to grab it, just in case the weather turned.

The rest of us were in the middle of what the nurses referred to as "occupational therapy," or making ugly hook rugs. The girl with the pearls moved slowly from table to table like visiting royalty, surveying everyone's work with a benign, interested expression.

"Oh, how interesting!" she'd murmur, or "What an unusual color choice!"

Then she stopped beside me. Up went a perfectly plucked eyebrow, like a question mark. "Well, now! Surely that's the most deeply disturbing thing I've ever seen in my life!"

"Well, no one's asking you, are they?" I was tired of crazy people. And this place was bursting with them in all shapes and sizes.

"There's no need to take it that way. It's a very powerful piece."

I glared at her. "It's not a piece. It's a rug."

"A very angry rug, if you ask me." She sat down, picked up a hook. "Go on then—show me how you do it."

I wasn't in the mood for a demonstration. I was only here because the staff made me come, hauling me out of my usual spot in the rocking chair by the window. "Ask the nurse if you're so interested."

She laughed. It was a drawing-room laugh—the practiced jocularity of a hostess, high and false. "Don't be so serious—I'm only teasing you!" She nodded to the other women in the room. "You're the best of the lot, you know. An artist!"

It wasn't much of a compliment. There were maybe a dozen of us rounded up for the afternoon session, all dressed in shapeless blue smocks, heads bowed over our work. There'd been a lice outbreak, and we'd all been clipped. But this girl still had a good head of hair. She must be new. The two of us were the youngest in the room by maybe ten years, although it was hard to tell for sure.

"So you're a connoisseur, is that it?" I pointed to a thin, wiry woman in her mid-fifties with no teeth, furiously hooking across the room. "Mary's pretty good. Why don't you go bother her? She doesn't speak. Ever. But she can make a rug in an afternoon."

The girl twirled the hook between her fingers. "But you have talent—a real feeling for the medium, possibly even a great future in hooked rugs. Provided of course that people don't want to actually use them in their homes. So"—she leaned forward—"tell me, how long have you been here?"

I yanked another yarn through. I'd been here long enough to wonder if I'd ever be allowed out again. Mine was an open-ended sentence: I needed the doctor's consent before I'd see the outside world again. But I wasn't about to let her see that I'd never been so alone and terrified in my life. I gave a shrug. "Maybe a month, I don't know," as if I hadn't been counting every hour of every day. "What about you?"

"I'm just stopping in for a short while," she said vaguely.

"'Stopping in'?" I snorted. "On your way where, exactly?"

She ignored my sarcasm. "Why are you here? In for anything interesting?"

"This isn't a resort, you know," I reminded her.

"Are you here voluntarily or as a ward of the county?"

I gave her a look.

"You never know"—she held up her hands apologetically—"some people come in on their own."

"Did you?"

For someone who liked asking questions, she was less keen on giving answers. Crossing her legs, she jogged her ankle up and down impatiently. "They say it's an illness. Do you believe that? That we can all be magically cured?"

"How would I know? Where did you get those pearls?"

"My father gave them to me." She ran her fingers over them in an automatic gesture, as if reassuring herself over and over again that they were still there. "I never take them off."

"Neither would I."

"I like them better than diamonds, don't you? Diamonds lack subtlety. They're so . . . common."

She was definitely crazy. "Not in my neighborhood!" I laughed.

"Well . . ." Her fingers ran over the necklace again and again. "He's dead now."

"Who?"

"My dear devoted father."

I considered saying something sympathetic, but social niceties weren't expected or appreciated much here. Besides, I didn't want her to feel like she could confide in me.

The girl watched Mute Mary across the room, working away. "What are you really in for?"

"What's it to you?"

"Come on! Your secret's safe—who am I going to tell?"

I don't know why I told her, maybe just so she'd shut up and go away, or maybe in some sick way I was trying to impress her. "I cut myself with a razor blade."

She didn't miss a beat. "Deliberate or accidental?"

"Deliberate." It was the first time I'd ever admitted it aloud.

But if I expected a reaction, I was disappointed; she didn't bat an eye.

"So no voices in your head or anything?"

"No. What about you?" I looked across at her. "Do you hear voices?"

"Only my own. Mind you, that's bad enough. I'm not entirely sure I'm on my side."

Actually, that made me smile—for the first time in weeks.

"So at least you're not *really* insane," the girl with the pearls cheerfully pointed out.

"What about you? Why are you here?"

"Oh, they've given me all kinds of diagnoses. Hysterical, suicidal, depressive, delusional . . . Big Latin words for 'a bad egg.' This place is all right, actually. Not like some of the other ones I've been to before." And she smiled again, as if to prove her point.

"So why haven't I seen you on the ward? And why isn't your hair cut?"

She picked up a ball of red yarn. "I don't know. Are they meant to? I'd prefer they didn't. I've just managed to grow it out from the most frightful French bob." She stifled a yawn. "God, I'm tired! The woman in the room next to me moans all night."

I stopped. "You have your own room?"

The nurse walked in and clapped her hands. "Work tools down, ladies! Stack your rugs on the table and follow me. It's time for exercise."

I got up and stood in line with the others. Then Mrs. Verdent, the head nurse, appeared in the doorway, casting a dark shadow across the floor. Instantly everyone went quiet.

Mrs. Verdent's mouth was twisted into an expression of permanent disapproval and her white linen uniform was tightly fitted, covering her formidable curves so completely that she gave the impression of being upholstered rather than dressed. She scanned the room before advancing ominously toward the girl.

"I'm not sure you're meant to be here," she said pointedly.

"I quite agree." The girl stood up, brushed off her hospital gown. "Have them bring the car round while I get my things."

The joke did not go over well.

We all held our breath in dreadful anticipation of what would come next.

Mrs. Verdent's eyes narrowed and her voice took on a subzero iciness. But she remained remarkably calm, far more civil than she ever was with any of us. "You're not meant to mix with others. You know that. It's time you went back to your room." And taking the girl firmly by the elbow, she escorted her out.

"Good-bye, ladies!" the girl called out as she was trundled down the hall. "It's been a real pleasure! Truly! Keep up the good work!"

As luck would have it, one of the other girls at the Nightingale Boarding House worked an early shift at a diner and found the bathroom locked from the inside at five in the morning. When no one answered, the landlady got the police to knock down the door, and there I was, passed out, job half done.

Had I known what would happen next, though, I would've paid more attention to what I was doing. I was committed to the Binghamton State Hospital in upstate New York, declared temporarily insane, induced by extreme intoxication.

The building itself might have been nice if it were used for any other purpose. Formerly the Binghamton Inebriate Asylum, it was a rambling Gothic Revival structure with ornately carved wooden staircases and high vaulted ceilings. The main entrance featured stained-glass windows depicting scenes of Jesus healing the sick, helping the lame to their feet in rich jewel tones that cast rainbows on the parquet floor. All the other windows were covered in metal mesh. Wide, gracious corridors led from one terrifying therapy room to another, and though the hospital was set on acres of rolling green landscaped lawns, the grounds were deserted; no one but the gardeners were allowed outside.

The first week I was there, they gave me the famous belladonna cure, known among the patients as "puke and purge." Regular doses of belladonna, herbs, and castor oil were meant to "clean out the system." But all I remember is being doubled over with stomach cramps, vomiting, and diarrhea, drifting in and out of hallucinations. Two large nurses dragged me to and from the toilet to the bed, occasionally hosing me down with cold water in between. The doses came every hour on the hour for three days straight. And then the hydrotherapy and chemical shock treatments began. Only after another week of those was I finally deemed lucid enough to meet with Dr. Joseph, the psychiatrist.

With his closely trimmed beard, spectacles, and shiny bald head, Dr. Joseph looked like a modern-day Santa Claus. But looks were deceiving. Beneath his benevolent exterior, he held our fate in his hands. Without his signature on the release papers, none of us was going anywhere. Every question he asked was a test, each answer proof of either recovery or illness, and all the while he took endless notes with a shiny silver pen. It must've had a broken nib because it made a soft scratching noise on the paper like a thorn scraping against skin. I couldn't work out if more notes meant a right answer or a wrong one.

He wanted to know everything—why I went to New York in the first place, about my job, why I'd tried to do myself in.

I gave him the edited version—told him about the customer

who accused me of stealing, described the scene he made on the dance floor. I could still feel the shame; the humiliation of being escorted to my locker by the manager, the other girls standing around, watching, more indifferent than sad . . . Lois hadn't even bothered to look me in the eye.

"I felt so exposed."

"Exposed?" More scratching, pen against paper. "What do you mean by that exactly?"

How could I explain it? A feeling that all my life I'd been heading down an endless hallway lined with mirrors, running as fast as I could, doing anything to distract myself and avoid seeing my own reflection.

"Miss Fanning," he prompted, "you were saying?"

I realized my mistake at using such an open-ended word. "I don't know. That was a stupid thing to say. I don't know why I said it."

"And that's what precipitated the incident? Losing your job?"

"Yes."

He seemed unconvinced. "Are you sure nothing else happened? Before?"

I didn't understand.

"You may have been aware," he continued, "that we performed a complete physical examination on you when you were admitted. I have the results of that examination here." He paused, resting his hand on a folder in front of him. "Are you certain there isn't anything you want to tell me, Miss Fanning? Something you would like to confide?"

I looked down at my hands folded in my lap.

"The report says you've had an operation within the past six months. An abortion. You were pregnant when you came to New York, isn't that right?"

My head felt weightless and my mouth dry.

"And the father? Who was the father?"

"No one . . . I mean, someone I knew in Boston," I managed.

"That was the real reason you left, wasn't it? You were running away."

I couldn't answer.

Sighing heavily, he leaned back in his chair. He already had low expectations, and still I'd managed to disappoint him. "Most women see children as a blessing." He waited for me to explain myself but I had no excuses. We both shared the same poor opinion of me. "Can you see that your problems are of your own making?" he asked after a while. "That in trying to escape life you've only made yours worse?"

"I guess I'm not like other women," I mumbled.

"No, you certainly are not. There's a line between normal and abnormal behavior. You've already crossed that line. Now you must work very hard to get back on the right side of it again. Make no mistake: it will require all your efforts. You're in a very dangerous position." He held out his hands. "Look at where you are, Miss Fanning. You're a burden on society. Sexually promiscuous, morally bereft; if you don't change, then this is most likely where your descendants will end up too. I've seen it time and time again. The apple doesn't fall far from the tree."

The mirrored hallway came to an abrupt end; the reflection I'd been avoiding stared back at me, ugly and void of hope.

"Do you want to spend your life locked up in institutions?"

"No, Dr. Joseph."

"Then stay away from dance halls, strange men, and speak-easies. And avoid drink all together. No one likes a fast young woman, and a drunkard is repulsive in the extreme." He stared at me hard. "It's a matter of discipline and character. Of willpower. I'll be frank: you have a long road ahead of you."

His words frightened me. "But I will be able to leave? I mean if I try very hard to change, will you let me go?"

"If you cooperate and do what's required, you'll be released in due course," he allowed. "But it's up to you to continue to reform your ways out in the real world. Otherwise you'll end up right back inside."

He made a final note to my file and then looked up.

"When a person becomes dependent upon the habit of escaping their difficulties, they lose touch with reality and deteriorate rapidly. But there is hope. Remove the habit and sanity returns. It will take effort, but if you change your ways and monitor yourself carefully, you can recover and be like everyone else. You can live a normal life."

He let me go after that, back to the dayroom with the rows of rocking chairs and wire-mesh-covered windows.

I sat down and stared out at the gray winter sky.

A normal life.

Who in the world wanted anything so small?

I only saw the girl with the pearls one more time after that, two weeks later.

It was a Tuesday morning, just before they let me out. Tuesdays and Thursdays were treatment days. Extra orderlies were called in, banging on the doorframes of the wards with wooden clubs to round the patients up. "Time for treatment! Get in line! Treatment time!"

Treatment was a form of shock therapy that took place in a room at the end of the ward. Outside was a long row of wooden chairs that went all the way down the hall, overseen by nurses and orderlies standing with their backs to the windows, keeping the line moving.

It was early morning and the sky was clear and bright. Outside, a thin coating of snow was melting on the sunny side of the sloping lawn.

One by one, we all went into the room, and the line moved down. I wanted to be last; to feel that after I was finished, there would be only peace and stillness.

But I didn't get my wish. Instead a nurse appeared at the other end of the hallway with another patient from a different wing. It was the girl. Even from a distance, I knew it was her from the way she moved, as if she'd spent her entire life walking from one cocktail party to another balancing books on her head. The nurse was talking quietly to her, hand on her elbow, pulling her gently along. Her eyes were wide with fear, footsteps slow. For all her bravado and sophisticated talk before, she was clearly frightened now.

The nurse put her in the chair next to mine.

"You'll see." The nurse gave her a terse smile. "It will be over before you know it."

Instinctively, the girl reached for the pearls but they were gone now; confiscated by the staff. She wrapped her arms around herself and curled inward.

I hadn't liked her much before, or rather I'd resented the way she'd swanned in, pretending to know everything. But now I felt for her, bent double with apprehension, cradling her dread like a mother with an infant.

We sat for a few minutes before she said, quite softly, "Tell me about a time when you were happy."

Normally I would've ignored her. But today I was getting out, about to be free again and in the unique position to give her what she was asking for—hope.

I thought a moment. "There was the time at my second cousin Sinead's wedding, after the ceremony, when we were in the church hall, having a ceilidh."

"A what?"

"A ceilidh. It's an Irish word. It means a dance, but with traditional music, proper reels. There's always lots to drink, plenty of food, people fighting . . ."

"At a *wedding?*"

"Wouldn't be an Irish wedding without it." I leaned forward, elbows on my knees. "You see, the first thing you need to understand is that I was tall for my age. I've always been too tall. And skinny as a broom—no figure to speak of. So I was never much to look at as a kid, and I always felt pretty awkward. But that night I had one important advantage. My mother, she's a very good dancer, and she taught me. A step dancer, they call it. There's quite a lot of fancy footwork involved, and it takes real skill. For some reason I was good at it too, which was a miracle because I was all arms and legs. But when I got going and felt the music pulsing through me, I could really dance. And that night, for the first time in my life, I was nothing short of magnificent, dancing with everyone, showing off." I smiled a little. "People stood round and watched me, clapping and cheering!"

The door at the end of the hall opened again, closed.

The girl's face drained of color. "Go on," she said. "Then what happened?"

"Some of the men took to teasing me. I suppose I looked ridiculous bouncing up and down with my red hair. They were calling me Matchstick because I was so thin, and my hair, well, I guess it looked like a flame. I wanted to get even with them, show them. So when the band took a break, they offered me a whiskey. I think they were trying to make a fool of me. I'd never had one before, but I lied, I told them I had. And then I drank it down in one. I don't know how I did it, but I managed not to cough or choke. Well, that shocked them."

"I'll bet it did!"

"They thought it was funny. 'She holds her whiskey like a man!'" I could still remember the way the liquor felt, burning down the back of my throat like fire. How it hit me like a punch to the stomach. It was like I'd never been born until then. Everything inside me suddenly felt warm and right and comfortable. "So they gave me another and I drank that too. Same thing, right back. And now I was their mascot, see. And when the band came back, I danced even harder."

"So you were the belle of the ball." She wanted to believe in fairy tales today, happy endings.

"Well, not quite."

"Maybe you'll do that again someday. When you get out." Her eyes scanned my face, searching for something to cling to. "Don't you think?"

"Sure. Maybe."

I didn't tell her that at some point my legs gave out, and the next thing I knew I was being sick, out in the alleyway behind the church. One of the men took me out, tried to hide me from my mother. I was dreadfully ill the next morning. Ma made an awful fuss with my cousin, and we never went to another ceilidh again.

"Your turn," I said. "Tell me about a time you were happy."

She looked out of the window covered in metal mesh that separated us from the sharp winter air, from the blue skies, snow, and sunshine. "I don't have any memories. That's why I'm here. To get rid of them all."

❧ BOSTON, FEBRUARY 1932

On the way home from my new job, I stopped by Panificio Russo on Prince Street. Open for business from six every morning till late at night, it was more than a bakery, it was a local institution. Just before dawn you could smell the bread baking, perfuming the cold morning air. Rich butter biscuits, dozens of different cannoli and biscotti, delicately layered *sfogliatelle* and *zeppole*, little Italian doughnuts, were made fresh each day. Traditional southern Italian cakes like *cassata siciliana* vied for space with airy ciabatta and hearty *stromboli* stuffed with cheese and meats, and fragrant *panmarino* made with raisins and scented with rosemary, all stacked in neat rows. Three small wooden tables sat by the front window, in the sun, where the *anziani*, the elderly men of the community, sipped espresso and advised on all manner of local business.

Well known throughout Boston, Russo's delivered baked goods to many restaurants and hotels in the city. But they were first and foremost a family-run business and a proud cornerstone of North End life. It was widely known that once Russo's ovens were hot and their own bread under way, poorer families from the tenements were welcome to bring their own dough, proofed and ready, to the kitchen door to be baked. Children waited in the back alleyway, playing tag and kick-the-can until the loaf was pulled out and wrapped in newspaper so they could hurry home with it, still hot. When a family finally graduated in fortunes from the alleyway to buying their bread from the front of the shop, Umberto Russo proudly served the woman himself, and his son Alfonso would make a treat of a few choice pastries.

I'd grown up with the Russo children and could remember when the bakery was little more than a single room with an oven. They were famous for their tangy sweet *zaletti*, dense breakfast rolls flavored with orange rind, vanilla, and raisins, and covered in powdered sugar. There was a time when I'd come in every morning to get one on my way to work. It had been a while since I'd been able to afford such treats, but now things were looking up.

The front of the shop was run by the three Russo women, sisters Pina and Angela and the formidable Maddalena Russo, their mother. They were all small and voluptuous, their figures accented by the white aprons pulled tight round their waists. I watched for my chance to catch Angela's eye as she bustled from one end of the counter to the other, slipping between her mother and sister in an unending, seamless dance as they ducked down, reached over, slid around, or stretched high to grab the string hanging from the dispenser to tie the boxes tight. Above them, a picture of the Virgin Mary smiled calmly, radiating feminine modesty.

With her broad round face and large brown doe eyes, Angela looked just like the portrait of the Holy Mother that watched over them. Her hair curled gently, spilling out of her black crocheted hairnet to cascade softly on her cheeks. And she had a natural grace and gentleness that belied her often surprisingly sharp sense of humor.

I tried to remember the first time I'd met Angela and the Russo family but couldn't. They'd simply always been there. For a while we'd all lived in the same tenement building, the one I still lived in now. The Russo children, especially the older boys, had "owned" the front stoop by virtue of being in the building the longest, but were gracious about sharing it with us younger ones. Angela and I were inseparable growing up: playing jacks and skipping rope, making little woolen dolls from old socks with button eyes that we pushed up and down the block in a broken-down old baby buggy that was used for everything from grocery shopping to junk collection. I was on my own a lot during the day while Ma worked piecing blouses together. But Mrs. Russo always made an extra place for me at her table, even though she already had five mouths to feed.

Angela and I made plans to run away from home and become professional dancers at eight; fell in love with the same boy, Aldo Freni, with his unusually long dark lashes, at ten; and were caught stealing lip rouge from the drugstore at thirteen, and received the same number of lashes as a result. She was the closest thing I had to a sister. And yet it was months since we'd spoken. My shame at my circumstances in New York had prevented me from writing, and she'd gotten married while I was in the hospital, a wedding I was meant to take part in as the maid of honor. Pina had to step in instead. Ma made excuses for me, told them the same tales I told her of eccentric millionaire bosses and unexpected trips abroad. But now that I was here, I felt a sudden attack of nerves and regret. The Russos knew me, could see past all my fictions.

It was Pina who spotted me first. When I left for New York, Pina was a newlywed. Now she was heavily pregnant. But though she may have enjoyed the rosy-cheeked sensuousness of a Rubens nude, there was nothing soft in her manner. "Oh, my, my!" She thrust her chin at me. "Look what the cat's dragged in! Jean Harlow!"

Angela turned, and her face lit up. *"Ciao, bella!"* She made it sound light and natural, as if she'd only seen me the other day. "I didn't recognize you! What have you done to your hair?"

The tension in my chest eased. Still, I couldn't help noticing the wedding band that flashed, catching the morning sun as Angela expertly whipped the string around a cake box and tied it in a knot.

"Mamma mia!" Angela's mother gasped, holding her palms to the heavens. "Maeve! What have you done to your beautiful red hair?"

All eyes turned.

"I cut it and . . . well . . ." I was turning red. "It's for a job, actually."

Pina snorted. "What, are you a Ziegfeld girl now?"

"Not exactly. A salesclerk. But no Irish."

There was a time when the city was full of signs declaring "No Irish Need Apply." We were considered little more than vermin. Then the Italians came, and suddenly we moved up a little in the world, only not quite far enough.

"Yeah, well, I'm surprised to see you here at all." Pina folded her arms across her chest. "I thought this town wasn't good enough for you. That only New York City would do."

"Stop it!" Angela glared at her sister. "Just because you've never left Boston!"

"I don't need to leave Boston. And evidently neither do you!"

Pina laughed, nodding at me. "I hope you left a trail of bread crumbs so you could find your way home." Pina always had a tongue like a stiletto blade. Even as a kid, she had a preternatural talent for verbal vivisection.

"*Basta!*" Her mother shot Pina a look. "We've missed you. Your mother told us you had important business in New York and couldn't come to the wedding," she continued evenly, resting her hands on her hips. "We're sorry you couldn't get away."

Guilt stung beneath my smile.

"I'm sorry too. I mean . . ." I looked across at Angela; I was speaking to her more than anyone else. "I was working as a private secretary for a very wealthy man. Quite a difficult character, very demanding. . . . I wanted to come, really I did."

We all knew I wasn't being honest. My story didn't explain why I hadn't written or called.

"Well, I'm just glad you're here now," Angela said, in that way she had of simply closing the door on anything difficult or unpleasant. "It's good to have you back." Then, popping a fresh loaf of bread into a paper bag and handing it across the counter to Mr. Ventadino, she flashed me a naughty smile. "*La mia bella dai capelli biondi!*"

"*Ah, bella!*" Mr. Ventadino laughed, eyeing me up and down. "*Molto bella!*"

The old men at the tables by the window laughed too, and Mrs. Russo rolled her eyes. "Girls! *Comportatevi bene!*"

Comportatevi bene—Italian for "behave yourself"—was the constant refrain of our childhood. When we were together, five minutes didn't go by without Mrs. Russo saying it, usually with a rolled-up newspaper in her hand, ready to whack one or both of us on the back of the head.

Mrs. Russo turned to me, her face serious. She had a way of looking straight into your eyes, as if she could see right down into your soul. *"Come stai davvero?"*

"Bene. Meglio, grazie. E tu?" I answered.

When Mrs. Russo spoke in Italian, I knew all was forgiven.

"Bene, bene." As she counted change and handed it to Mr. Ventadino, she shook her finger at us. "You girls need to grow up. And you!" She gave Mr. Ventadino a dark look too. *"Dovreste vergognarvi di voi stesso!* And how is your mother, Mae? I hope she's well."

Mrs. Russo had the knack of switching between conversations; she could reprimand Mr. Ventadino and still set an example for her daughter of civilized manners without missing a beat.

I stepped aside so Mr. Ventadino could slink past. "She's fine, thank you."

Mrs. Russo always asked after my mother, even though she didn't entirely approve of her. After all the years they'd known each other, theirs was nonetheless a formal acquaintance, maintained by courtesy rather than affection. I suspected it had something to do with the fact that Ma had never married again, a fundamental feeling Mrs. Russo had about the wrongness of a young widow raising a child on her own when she could have easily taken another husband and had more children. In her world, independence was an extravagance, a kind of selfishness.

In truth, I'd always been torn between Ma and the formidable Maddalena Russo. I'd spent so much time in the Russos' household growing up that she was a second mother to me—only of the more traditional variety.

Small and strong, fiercely disciplined, and certain of everything, Maddalena Russo never doubted, never questioned. She *knew.* The Russo home was strict, loud, vivid, and real. Nothing else existed nor needed to exist beyond the North End. It was an entirely self-sufficient universe. When I was younger, I used to pretend that I'd been left on the Russos' doorstep one night as a baby, and they'd adopted me as their own. It was a betrayal I couldn't resist, and my affection was transparent to everyone—including my mother.

"Is that a new hat?" Mrs. Russo nodded approvingly. *"Very* handsome!"

"It used to have a net, but it was torn . . . my mother fixed it for me." I was babbling. "Anyway, I stopped in for a *zaletti.* I'm celebrating, you see. I got a job today."

"Congratulations!" Angela beamed.

Pina passed a tray of fresh biscotti to her mother. "What you need is a husband!"

"Maybe I'm not the marrying type."

Mrs. Russo clucked reprovingly. "Why do you say that? Any man would be happy to have you!"

"I don't know."

"Of course you know!" Pina and her mother looked at each other and laughed. "Don't talk crazy!"

Reaching over, Angela handed a *zaletti* wrapped in waxed paper across to me. "I'll stop by later."

"I'd like that."

I tried to give her a nickel for the *zaletti,* but she wouldn't take it. "Go on, now. Tell your mother the good news."

I lowered my voice. "I really am sorry, Ange. About missing your wedding." I knew I'd hurt her, and I knew too that she had too much pride to let me see how much. "How was it?"

"It was lovely."

"You should've been there." Pina wouldn't leave us alone for a minute. "Oh, that's right! You were too busy taking notation for millionaires. One of these days, Jean Harlow, you're going to have to wake up and realize you're just like the rest of us."

When I got home, Ma was scraping carrots in the kitchen. "Is that you, Maeve?" she called when she heard me come in.

"Who else would it be, Ma?"

"There's no need to be sarcastic. Where have you been?"

I paused in the doorway. Potatoes, onion, celery . . . she was making a stew again. There was only ever the smallest bit of beef, a cheap cut softened with the hours of slow braising. She made it last through the week, adding extra potatoes to cheat it out.

"I got the job, actually," I told her, setting the *zaletti* down on the table with a flourish.

She stared at it; I think she'd half hoped I wouldn't get the position and then would dye my hair back. But of course work was always better than no work. "Good," she said finally. "So, what's it like?"

"Fancy. Very posh." I hung up my coat on the hook in the hallway, pulled off my gloves. "You know, they have a silver service there that costs as much as a house! I showed it to a woman this afternoon."

"Did she buy it?"

"No. But only because apparently it was missing lobster tongs. Have you ever even heard of lobster tongs?"

She frowned, began paring the potatoes into quarters. "Do you get commission?"

I checked the coffeepot on the stove. "I only just got the job, Ma!"

"You should ask for commission."

"It's just me and the old man." I poured a cup. It had been too long brewing and was bitter and strong. I drank it anyway.

"What difference does that make?" She tossed the potatoes in the cooking pot. "A sale is a sale!"

"Yeah, well, I haven't made a sale yet."

"And they're not going to fall into your lap!" she warned, pointing the paring knife at me. "You need to be friendly. Outgoing."

"I *am* friendly!"

"But you're not outgoing, Maeve!" She scraped the carrots so hard one snapped in two. "You're an introvert. Even as a baby you were quiet. All that time spent in your room reading!" She shook her head. "Too much time daydreaming—that's always been your trouble! You have to make a concerted effort. You need to act like you're the hostess at a party!"

What had gotten into her today? "Didn't you hear me? I got the job!"

She stopped, wiped her hands on her apron. "Mrs. Shaw's retiring next week."

"Does that mean . . ."

"It means they've hired a new saleswoman in Ladies Wear. And it isn't me," she added bitterly.

Here was the crux of the matter. Unfortunately we'd been here before, and I'd exhausted my repertoire of conciliatory clichés.

"I'm sorry, Ma. You're too good at your job, that's the problem." It was a stupid thing to say, but I had nothing left.

She stirred the stew on the stove, staring fixedly into the pot. "You're lucky. You don't realize it, but you are. You can really make something of yourself. It's too late for me. But you can be somebody."

I didn't know what to say.

"You mustn't waste your opportunities. Do you understand?" She turned. "You can be anything you want, anything you set your mind to, Maeve. You're so clever, so much more capable than I ever was."

"That's not true."

But she was serious. "You mustn't fail yourself. Do you understand, Maeve? You mustn't settle."

There was a knock at the door.

"Who's that?"

"Angela said she would stop by."

"Angela?" Suddenly she seemed small and forlorn, caught off guard. "Tonight?"

I got up. "I'll tell her I'll see her another time."

"No." Yanking the strings of her apron, she pulled it off, handed it to me. "Keep an eye on dinner. I'm going to lie down."

I poured some fresh coffee into one of my mother's Staffordshire willow-pattern teacups and passed it to Angela. "Sugar?"

"Yes, please. These are nice." She held up her cup, admiring the delicate blue-and-white oriental design. "I've never seen these before. Where did they come from?"

"They're my mother's. A wedding gift." I smiled. "But we only use them on special occasions." I wanted to make things up to her.

"I'm honored!"

I sat down across from her at the kitchen table. "I'm sorry we don't have any cream."

(In truth we never had it.)

We divided the *zaletti* in half on a plate.

"Here's to you and your new job!" Angela raised her cup.

"Here's to you and your new husband!" We took a drink, and then I asked, "So, what's it like, being married? I want to hear everything!"

"Oh, Mae!" She blushed, gave me a slightly embarrassed grin. "I don't know! It's different. I mean, from what I thought it would be like."

"How?"

Cupping her cheek in her hand, she pretended to concentrate on stirring the sugar into her coffee. "Faster!" she whispered back with a giggle. "Seems no sooner do we close the bedroom door than . . . you know, he's on top of me!"

"Well, men are like that. You have to slow them down."

"Mae!" She gave me a stab in the ribs. "You shouldn't know these things! And it hurt." Her face flushed pink again. "He kept apologizing!"

"What about the rest of it? You know, the bits that happen *outside* the bedroom."

She rolled her eyes. "I hate living at his mother's house. It's like being a bug in a glass jar; everyone knows everything you're doing all the time. But we haven't the money to move yet."

I lit two cigarettes on the stove and passed one to her. "No one's got any money. At least he has a job."

"Oh, he'll have more than that when he graduates from pharmacy school—he'll have his own business. We've got our eye on that corner shop on Salem Street. It would make a perfect drugstore." She tilted her head, looking at me sideways. "What about you? How was New York?"

"Fine. Good to be home."

Her eyes met mine. "Really?"

She could always see right through me.

I felt an awkward flush of shame, took a long drag. "Well, maybe it didn't go quite the way I planned."

"You never answered my letters."

"No . . . I'm really sorry about that."

"Are you upset at me?"

The hurt in her voice pricked my conscience. "No, Angie. Not at all. I wanted to write, really I did."

"So why didn't you?"

"I didn't want you to worry, that's all. It was hard." I shrugged, tried to smile. "I had troubles."

"What kind of troubles?" Her voice became stern, maternal. "What happened, Maeve?"

I wanted to tell her; I wanted to *be able* to tell her. But it was all so far away from anything she was used to, and it had been so long since we'd really spoken. Instead I grabbed at a half-truth, hoping that any confession might draw us closer again.

I inhaled. "I got in the habit of going out after work, hanging out in clubs. I guess I started to drink too much, Ange."

"Oh, Mae!" The shock and disappointment in her face surprised me. "You mean bootleg gin?"

I knew Angela didn't approve of drinking. In fact, I'd always hidden how much I'd drunk from her, knowing she thought of it as something only men did and distinctly unladylike. Wine was the exception, but like most Italians we knew, she didn't count wine as alcohol. The homemade version her father and brothers made in the summer and kept stored in wooden barrels in the basement of the shop was sweet, fruity, and mild. Not even the police bothered to confiscate it. But still, I'd expected her to be more worldly and understanding.

"I wasn't the only one! Everyone drinks in New York," I said, "men, women, young, old, Park Avenue right down to a bench in Central Park! But it sort of sneaks up on you. And it does make everything messier . . ."

"Then just don't drink."

Nothing was complicated for Angela. It was one of the things about her that I loved but also resented. Everything that was black and white for her was gray for me.

"Well, I didn't want to, not really," I tried to explain.

"Then just don't! Honestly, Mae!" She'd run out of patience. "They put anything in that stuff! You should hear the stories Carlo tells me!" Brushing some loose crumbs off the table into her hand, she shook her head. "You really need to settle down. You're too old for that sort of foolishness."

That was always the answer, no matter the question. If only I would settle down, behave myself. When we were younger, it was a reprimand leveled at both of us. But Angela had since become the model daughter, sister, and now wife. I was alone in my delinquency.

Tears welled up in my eyes. She was right, of course, and I suppose exhaustion and the stress of the day had gotten to me.

I started to cry, something I hadn't done in almost a year. "I'm so sorry about the wedding! About everything! I'm really sorry I let you down."

I hate crying; I'd rather be caught naked than with tears on my face.

Angela put her hand over mine. "I just think if you stopped running around and got married you'd be better off," she said gently.

I wanted to laugh, but couldn't muster it. "Believe me, no one wants to marry me now!"

"Mickey did. Remember? Probably still does," she added hopefully.

A year ago, no one thought my old boyfriend Mickey Finn was good enough. Now he was an opportunity.

She lowered her voice. "He doesn't know what you got up to in New York, does he? So don't tell him. Any man is better than no man, Mae."

I stared at her. We were so different now. Tapping my ash into the ashtray, I brushed the tears away with my fingertips. "It doesn't matter. I'm sorry I'm weepy. So"—I changed the subject—"how's the rest of your family?"

Frowning, Angela ran her finger along the milky-white porcelain edge of the willow-pattern teacup. It was so delicate, so fragile you could almost see the light through it.

"That's not everything that happened, is it? You're not going to tell me, are you?"

She knew me well enough to know I was deliberately shutting her out. I stared down at the uneaten *zaletti*.

She took a deep breath. "You're better now, though? Right?"

"Yeah." I nodded. "It's all in the past." Outside the window, the evening sky softened, and the men standing round the chestnut stove below were reduced to shadowy outlines, the ends of their cigars glowing and bobbing in the air as they spoke. "It's good to be back."

Winshaw and Kessler was quiet. Not just quiet but holding its breath, waiting. After the constant jostling and hustle in New York City, it was strange to walk down an almost empty street each morning, unlock the door, and step into a world dominated not by people but by things. There was a sense of solemnity and guardianship, like being in a library or a church. And like a church, the shop had a muted, remote quality, as if it were somehow both part of and yet simultaneously removed from the present day. The essence of aged wood, silver polish, furniture oil, and the infinitesimal dust of other lives and other countries hung in the air. I could feel its weight around me, and its flavor lingered on my tongue. Time tasted musty, metallic, and faintly exotic.

Almost everywhere else, time was an enemy; the thief that rendered food rotten, dulled the bloom of youth, made fashions passé. But here it was the precious ingredient that transformed an ordinary object into a valuable artifact—from paintings to thimbles.

I'd never been around such extraordinary things. I was content to sit and hold the carved cameo shell for half an hour at a time, running my finger over its variegated, translucent surface, wondering at the imagination that brought the Three Graces to life. The regular clientele, however, were not so easily mesmerized. Most, in fact, were disconcertingly focused.

"Do you by any chance sell eighteenth-century naval maps?"

"You haven't any Murano glass, have you? Nothing common, mind you. No red earth tones. I want something *special*. Do you have anything blue? Perhaps influenced by Chinese porcelain?"

They weren't casually browsing, but on an unending quest for very specific prizes. And they would accept no substitutions.

"I can't even get them to *look* at anything else!" I complained to Mr. Kessler one afternoon.

He took off his glasses, rubbed them clean with his pocket hankie. "Perhaps it's better if you don't even try."

He didn't make sense. "But how am I meant to sell anything?"

Instead of answering he asked, "Are you by any chance a collector, Miss Fanning?"

"*Me?*" I laughed. "I haven't got that kind of money!"

He gave me a reproachful look. "It's not about money. You know that. Tell me, did you ever save anything when you were a little girl?"

"Well"—I paused a moment—"I had a cigar box that I kept under the bed."

"And what was inside?"

"Just junk. Kid's stuff. Maybe a clothes-peg doll or some buttons strung together on thread. Ticket stubs my mother saved from the pictures or the foil wrapper from a bar of chocolate that still smelled sweet if you pressed your nose into it. Nothing special."

"And yet you kept it. See!" He smiled knowingly. "You *are* a collector! You collected for nostalgia, the most natural, instinctive thing in the world."

"Nostalgia?"

"Sentimentality. You sought out little pieces of the world you wanted to live in—a world of chocolate and pretty buttons and picture shows—and you created that world as best you could."

I thought about the old wooden box, the earthy, sweet smell of tobacco that remained from the cheap cigars. Mr. Russo had given it to me, much to Angela's indignation, after a meeting of the San Rocco Society one evening when we were five. He was a very quiet man. It was unusual for him to say anything or show any affection. But I could remember how he'd swayed a little that night, unsteady on his feet from too much red wine as he bent down to hand it to me. "Here you go. Something for your secrets," he said in his thick accent.

For a while I shared it with Angela, but she campaigned relentlessly until she got one of her own. Together we used to scour the streets for old chocolate wrappers—gold and silver foil peeking between the grates of gutters or sparkling in the dirt of empty lots. We pressed them flat with our fingers and stacked them in neat little piles, taking almost as much pleasure in smelling them as if we'd eaten the chocolate ourselves.

As I got older I kept other things in the box too, things I didn't show to anyone else, not even Angela—a man's black bow tie I'd stolen off a washing line when I was eight; a used train ticket I'd seen a stranger toss into a rubbish bin, stamped from Boston to New York. I'd pretended the bow tie belonged to Michael Fanning and that the ticket was his too—that he wasn't really dead, he was only traveling and someday he'd be back. That's when I began to hide the box under my bed, where no one could find it.

"Can you remember why you did it?" Mr. Kessler asked.

"I suppose it gave me comfort—the sense of having something only I knew about."

"Anything else?" He pressed.

"Not that I can think of . . ."

"It gave you two things," he elaborated, "purpose and hope. Think of the hours you spent looking for treasures—were they pleasant?"

"Yes," I admitted. "They were."

Patrolling the streets for discarded candy wrappers and ticket stubs had kept Angela and me happily occupied for most of a summer. And it had also given us, as Mr. Kessler pointed out, a tangible link to the movie-going, chocolate-eating world we longed to someday inhabit. They weren't just wrappers—they were talismans, gathered in the faith that each one drew us nearer toward the fruition of our dreams.

"Of course not everyone collects out of sentimentality. Some only appreciate usefulness and market value; they want items with excellent craftsmanship and aesthetics—porcelain, glass, furniture, and clocks fall very much into this category. A brilliantly functioning timepiece is a triumph of engineering, as is an exquisitely turned Adam chair. These things consistently maintain their value and often prove to be wise investments. These customers are easy to please—quality and tradition are what they want. You have only to convince them of a piece's merits and they're sold. Then there are the true connoisseurs, in search of the distinctive, obscure, and unknown."

"In what way obscure?"

"See these?" He pointed to three tiny silver containers in the jewelry case, each in the shape of a heart with a latched lid. "These are Danish *hovedvandsaeg*—extremely rare, made somewhere between 1780 and 1850. They hold sweet smelling spices and were popular as betrothal gifts. You can see their charm, can't you?" He regarded them with affection. "I have a customer who collects them exclusively, but he won't touch these because he believes them to be too pedestrian. I blame myself." He seemed dismayed by his own lack of foresight. "It's the heart design—too common for his taste. He wants something more unusual now. And yet only about three other people in the whole of Boston even know what a *hovedvandsaeg* is."

Each container was over a hundred dollars. It wasn't difficult to understand why someone would invest in something practical like a chair or a clock, but these? "How can anyone afford to spend so much on a tiny little trinket?"

"Well, we don't sell as many as we did," he allowed, "but for many serious clients, collecting isn't a luxury but a necessity—like an addiction. I know people who will go without food or new shoes to buy just one more piece."

"They would do that to their families?"

"Few of them have families; most are unmarried men, often professionals who have money to spare and no one to tell them how to spend it. In fact"—he peered at me over the tops of his glasses—"just the sort of people who might be swayed by a pretty blonde."

"Yes, but I don't seem to have much influence," I reminded him. "If I haven't got what the customers want, they're out of the door before I can stop them."

"That's my point, though. These aren't just customers, they're pilgrims, searching for a holy grail. So ask them about the journey. Get them to tell you about the other pieces they have. *Listen*. And before you know it, you'll be able to show them almost anything you like. But they like to feel they've discovered things for themselves. There's something furtive about a real collector; it has to do with the thrill of the hunt. And then, of course," he added, "there are the eccentrics."

I had to laugh. "It gets *more* eccentric than eighteenth-century Dutch spice boxes?"

"Oh, yes! I have one man who only wants to buy rare porcelain that's been repaired in some unusual way, long before the days of glue. Exquisite teapots with ugly twisted silver spoons for handles, platters held together by metal staples and twine, broken glassware with shattered bases replaced by hand-carved wooden animals. Actually, I have to admit, as an anthropologist, he's one of my favorites." He leaned against the counter. "You see, a well-curated collection always tells a story. His tells a tale of resourcefulness and industry; of people who had the foresight to salvage something even though it will never be pristine again. I like to think of it as the moment when aspiration meets reality."

"You were an anthropologist?" It never occurred to me that he had been anything other than a shopkeeper.

"That's right. I taught at the University of Pennsylvania." He seemed to grow several inches as he said it. "But this is absorbing too, in its own way." He cast an eye round the shop like a ruler surveying his kingdom. "It's anthropology of another sort. You see, in its purest form, collecting is designing—selecting objects to create sense, order, and beauty. To us, we're simply selling a serving dish or an ivory comb. But for the buyer, he's fitting another intricate piece into a carefully curated world of his own construction. At its root is an ancient belief, a hope, in the magic of objects. No matter how sophisticated we think we are, we still search for alchemy."

I thought of the cigar box, of the black bow tie and train ticket.

And then suddenly I remembered the gold pocket watch in New York; the thick chain and the solid, satisfying feel of it in my hand. The hairs on the back of my neck stood up; I knew why I'd taken it.

Some distant part of me knew it belonged in the box under my bed, too.

Even with Mr. Kessler's expert sales advice, business at Winshaw and Kessler continued to be slow. Every day Mr. Kessler put three bills into the cash register in the morning and took them out again, often unsupplemented, in the evening. It didn't bode well. But he remained unfazed. "We're hunting for bears, Miss Fanning," he told me. "You don't need to catch one every day, just a few a season."

The last thing I wanted was to be out of work again. I liked having heat in the mornings and the luxury of being able to afford new stockings rather than darning and redarning the same pair until they were more cotton thread than silk.

So I made work for myself. Each morning I went in determined to prove myself indispensable by rearranging displays, cataloguing inventory, polishing, and cleaning. And I enjoyed it. After the bleak emptiness of the hospital, the shop was a feast for not only the senses but the imagination too. While dusting the furniture, I found myself pretending this was my drawing room filled with fine antiques. Or as I polished silver, I mulled over which pieces might give the most favorable impression of excellent taste. (The plain English serving dishes were elegant without being ostentatious.) Sometimes when Mr. Kessler was out, I took all the jewelry from the cases and tried it on in different combinations, mixing Victorian opals with strings of red coral beads and Art Nouveau cloisonné bangles. I was playing dress-up, like a child— pretending to be a woman of means and charmingly eclectic sensibility.

Mr. Kessler seemed more bemused by my industry than anything else. I asked a thousand questions, wanting to know when and how and even why things were made, their worth, how long they'd been there. He was used to being alone, and while he enjoyed teaching me things, he perhaps wasn't quite prepared for the way I set about rehanging all the paintings by "mood" rather than period or displaying the glassware in rows of color instead of style. Some of my methods were more successful than others. It turns out china collectors, for example, are extremely particular about mixing patterns and makers and they wasted no time setting me straight.

But gradually, in spite of my overzealousness, a precarious order began to prevail. There was only one place that remained impervious to all my improving efforts.

Even though he'd been away a long time, nothing had been touched in Mr. Winshaw's office; the drawers were bulging with letters and receipts; books and piles of old newspapers and journals were stacked high, all just as he'd left it. A fat tabby called Persia slept curled up on the old red velvet seat cushion of his chair. Stubbornly territorial, he guarded the place like a sentinel. I was allowed to use the office for paperwork and to take my lunch sitting at Mr. Winshaw's massive Victorian desk, amid this spectacular monument to disarray. At first it was maddening; I had to physically restrain myself from throwing things out. But there was also something intriguing about being privy to the intimate belongings of a complete stranger. Scientific journals, volumes of world mythologies, old playbills, and overdue library books formed unstable, teetering towers around me as I unwrapped my daily meal of two hard-boiled eggs from waxed paper and peeled them. Atlases from different corners of the globe and translation dictionaries for half a dozen languages bore cracked spines from excessive use. Correspondence from countries like Australia, Cuba, and India remained tantalizingly unopened, crammed into cubbies.

But this wasn't just messiness or neglect. It was knowledge, rich, chaotic, and diverse.

And everywhere there was evidence of Mr. Winshaw's constant intellectual curiosity; notes jotted down on the backs of envelopes, dog-eared pages in books, underlined passages, and articles torn from newspapers. Like an excavation site, different eras of obsession were layered one on top of another. Here was an entire collection of books on African art, and on top of that a thick stack of newspaper articles explaining German Surrealist cinema. Then came an examination of eastern American Indian rites and rituals. What his interests lacked in cohesion, they more than made up for in variety. Sometimes I'd open one of Mr. Winshaw's books and find myself unexpectedly lost in another of his fascinations—like the making of medieval tiles. But the most compelling thing was the map of the ancient world that hung on the wall above his desk, with pins marking destinations. At lunchtime I stared at it, wondering at the places he'd been, the things he'd seen, and where he was now.

"Where exactly is Mr. Winshaw?" I asked Mr. Kessler one day.

He looked up from a pile of invoices he was going through, peering at me over the top of his wire-rimmed glasses in a certain way he had, like a mole poking its nose aboveground to sniff the air before venturing out. "Well, I haven't heard from him in some time."

"When will he be back?"

"I'm not sure." He put the papers down, taking off his glasses and rubbing his eyes with his fists. "You see, Winshaw's an archaeologist—a *serious* archaeologist, not just an academic. A year ago, an opportunity came up that was too good for him to miss; he joined a dig with an old friend of his, Leonard Woolley, in Iraq. What used to be Mesopotamia, the ancient city of Ur."

I'd studied the map long enough to remember where that was. "In Arabia?"

"Yes. But the truth is, I'm not exactly certain where he is now. Winshaw's something of a loose cannon. It's a bit worrying," he conceded. "There's been violence in that area. Bombs, air attacks on local tribes. But I'm fairly certain he'll turn up sooner or later."

"*Fairly* certain?" He appeared disconcertingly calm. "But what about his family? Haven't they heard from him?"

"Oh, he hasn't got a family."

"Couldn't we write to Mr. Woolley?"

Mr. Kessler took a handkerchief from his breast pocket and cleaned his glasses. "There's no need to jump to conclusions. Winshaw occasionally wanders off course. But he always turns up again, usually with something extraordinary. If it will make you feel better though, here's an address, a postal box in Baghdad." He took a note card from his desk drawer. "Actually, you can send his mail on for me. Could be important. Now, are you any good with numbers, Miss Fanning?"

"Yes, sir."

"Have a look at these." He handed me a thick ledger bulging with loose receipts. "Don't lose anything. That's the only copy I have."

I went back to Mr. Winshaw's office, put the ledger down.

Leaning in closer, I studied the map again. Tattered and frayed, it was worn at the edges as if it had been hung and rehung on many walls over the years. It was drawn in a delicate, florid style, painted in rich, sun-bleached colors that were the fashion at the turn of the century. Here was ancient Egypt with the pyramids, and the golden walls of Troy; another pin marked the island of Crete, home of the mythical Minotaur. It reminded me not of a worldly man but of a small boy planning future expeditions, eager to discover the world of his heroes—to walk in the footsteps of Virgil and Homer, and see with his own eyes the Hanging Gardens of Babylon, the Great Colossus, and the Sphinx. The very fact that it existed, pins and all, betrayed a child's ambition and enthusiasm, as well as lasting awe.

A shiny silver pin marked the ancient city of Ur in Mesopotamia.

Was this where the story ended?

I sat down in the wooden swivel chair. Its arms bore the initials of several previous owners, the kind of boyish vandalism of students. I had an almost irresistible urge to open all the drawers, go through every book and paper. But Mr. Kessler was just across the narrow hallway, door open.

Reaching for a pen, I brushed against a stack of books. A thin old volume toppled to the floor, a book of Alfred Lord Tennyson's poems. It had naturally fallen open on a dog-eared page of "Ulysses" on which certain lines had been underlined in pencil.

How dull it is to pause, to make an end,
To rust unburnished, not to shine in use!
As tho' to breathe were life! . . .
. . . that which we are, we are:
One equal temper of heroic hearts,
Made weak by time and fate, but strong in will
To strive, to seek, to find, and not to yield.

Something quickened in my chest as I read it, an indefinable excitement and longing.

. . . that which we are, we are . . . to shine in use . . .

Someone, presumably Mr. Winshaw, had scrawled "Yes!" in the margin.

I'd read *The Odyssey* in high school and admired the mythic realm of skies tinted rose and gold by dawn's light fingertips and a wine-dark sea; of a life defined by bold actions, loyal companions, and true hearts. But I'd never read this poem before.

To strive, to seek, to find, and not to yield.

My eyes were drawn to the emphatic "Yes!"

Yes!

The word moved me, though I wasn't sure why. Perhaps because it had been such a long time since I'd felt pure, unrestrained enthusiasm for anything.

Mr. Winshaw was still alive; I felt sure of it.

A man who believed in "Yes!" couldn't simply disappear from life without ripples extending to every shore.

———

Dear Mr. Winshaw,

My name is May Fanning. I'm Mr. Kessler's new assistant at the shop, and he's asked me to forward your post on to you. I realize we haven't met, but there is a great deal of concern here as to your current whereabouts and welfare. We are both, Mr. Kessler and I, eager to know that you are safe. If you would be so kind as to drop us a line or, indeed, any form of correspondence, it would be greatly appreciated. Likewise, if there is anything we can do on your behalf, please don't hesitate to let us know.

I paused.

I was alone in the shop. The ticking of the clocks and Persia's deep purr were the only sounds.

"Occasionally," I continued,

I have used your desk for brief periods in order to complete paperwork and I have come to admire the great map on your wall. I am curious as to whether you have been to all those places and what they were like.

Again, I stopped. He might, quite rightly, find the idea of me sitting in his office intrusive. Then again, I reasoned, this letter would most likely rot in the postal box in Baghdad, along with the rest of his mail.

I envy you your freedom, Mr. Winshaw. I wish I too could leave Boston behind. I would like nothing better than to be somewhere new, where people weren't so bound by convention and narrow-minded ideas of right and wrong, good and evil. I think there's

nothing duller than trying to be good nor any task more thankless.
If I were you, I would stay missing as long as I could.

> *Sincerely,*
> *May Fanning*

Well, that was childish.

I tore the sheet off the writing pad and began again.

When I had finished the second letter—a brief, polite inquiry—I looked for envelopes in the drawers of his desk. Failing to find any, I took one from Mr. Kessler and then packaged up the rest of Mr. Winshaw's mail into a small parcel covered in brown paper and twine and took it to the post office. It took three clerks twenty minutes to figure out the postage to Baghdad. They were naturally curious about who I was corresponding with, what was in the package . . . I exaggerated a little, explaining it was my husband, the famous explorer, who was abroad and that I needed some urgent signatures on very important business documents.

By the time I left, they were looking at me differently—as if I was fascinating, handling difficult situations on my own, braving the absence of my beloved with dignity and poise. The fantasy lent the afternoon a certain tender hue of melancholy, an imaginary sadness and courage that made everything just a little more interesting.

So I pretended that, in my own way, I'd somehow said "Yes!" to life too.

I was walking past a barbershop in Prince Street when I spotted it, hanging in the window. "Boxing," the poster advertised in bold red letters across the top, "Five Bouts, Thirty-Six Rounds at Boston Garden."

I don't know why I stopped; maybe out of habit, maybe just because things had been going well and I had to test them, poking and prodding at my own happiness the way a child picks at a newly formed scab.

I read through the list of names, searching, looking for the one I wanted to find. And sure enough, there it was, down near the bottom: Mickey Finn.

A sudden wave of loneliness hit me hard. I had my freedom back, a new job, money in my pocket, but still my chest ached the way an empty stomach gnaws and clutches for food that isn't there.

Michael Thomas Finlay.

For years he'd been as much a part of my life as my right hand.

We'd grown up together, been in the same class for a while in grammar school. But as soon as he'd grown tall enough, in sixth grade, Mick had been pulled out to work on the docks, loading and unloading with his father, brothers, and uncles. Still, I saw him every Sunday at church, sat next to him in confirmation class. When I learned how to waltz, he was my first and only partner.

I must have been staring—there was a rap on the window, and when I looked up the guys in the barbershop were laughing and blowing kisses at me.

I ignored them, walked on. But the emptiness in my chest grew and spread.

I could still remember the first time Mickey kissed me, in the alleyway behind the cinema; the soft, warm pressure of his lips on mine and, most of all, the way he held me—gently, as if I were made of delicate glass he was afraid of breaking. No one before or since had ever thought I was that precious. It was a pure, uncomplicated affection, almost like siblings, based on unquestioning loyalty.

Of course Ma didn't like him. He was black Irish, she said, with his thick dark hair and brown gypsy eyes. He'd been taken out of school and would never amount to anything.

But I didn't want anyone Ma approved of.

Then Mickey's brother started boxing, and Mick took to hanging out at the Casino Club. As luck would have it, he turned out to be even better than his brother; just the right combination of height, muscle, and speed. And there was money to be made, a lot of money, for just one night's work.

Everyone knew all the best boxers were Irish. Kids from nowhere could rise to the top of the boxing world in no time—going from brawling in basements and back lots to Madison Square Garden in a matter of months. We watched their breakneck rise to stardom on the newsreels every week—Tommy Loughran, Mike McTigue, Gene Tunney, and Jack Dempsey. Punching their way out of tenements straight into movie careers and Park Avenue addresses.

The first time I went to a fight, I was terrified. But Mickey won that night, and my fear became excitement. Soon I looked forward to the sweaty, raw nerves that snapped like electricity moments before the bell sounded; to the fighters, dancing in their corners, skin glistening, muscles tense. All the chaos, the smells, the din of the crowd, the rickety wooden chairs, the hot roasted peanuts and calls of the ticket touts; gangsters smelling of French cologne sitting cheek by jowl with old-money millionaires; the blood, the fear, the speed, the unholy fury of it all, I came to relish every bit. And Mickey, at the center, fighting, conquering the world.

Overnight he had a manager and a nickname—the Boston

Brawler. His face appeared on fight posters, and his name climbed up to the top of the listings. And afterward, in the pubs and clubs, we drank and danced and felt the glorious relief of those who'd outwitted fate. With our pockets crammed full of bills from Mickey's winnings, the future was ours for the taking.

Mick was my champion, punching his way out of this drab, relentless grind into a new life of unfettered possibility.

Only it turned out Mick was a good boxer, not a great one. Someone else came along, an Italian; they called him the Boston Basher, and Mick couldn't seem to get out from under his shadow.

And then I got pregnant. Suddenly our limitless future shrank to the size of a one-bedroom walk-up in the South End and a dockworker's pay packet.

He would've married me, had I told him. But I never did. I didn't tell anyone.

I went to New York instead. There was more work there, I said; better opportunities and a chance to really make something of myself.

We talked about what we would do, how we would live when I got back. But we both knew that wasn't going to happen.

And Mick was such a stand-up guy, he even loaned me the money to leave him.

The Casino Athletic Club on Tremont Street was located up a steep flight of stairs on the second floor of an old grain warehouse. It smelled of generations of young men, training nonstop, in all seasons; of sweat, fear, and ambition. As soon as I stepped inside, a thick sticky wall of perspiration engulfed me. There were four rings, one in each corner, weights, punchbags; the sound of fists slamming against flesh and canvas beat out a constant dull tattoo.

It was a familiar sound; I'd spent hours here, smoking and watching Mick train. Pausing in the doorway, I scanned the hall. Then I spotted him.

Mickey was in the far left-hand ring, sparring with a tall Negro man. His trainer, Sam Louis, was hunched over the ropes, shouting, "Look out, Mick! Come on! Look lively!"

And seated on a folding chair and wearing a molting chinchilla wrap over a cheap red dress was Hildy.

Of course.

Poor old Hildy was a permanent fixture at the Casino Club and something of a running joke. When she was younger, she'd worked in the office. With her blond German hair and blue eyes, she broke her fair share of hearts. But as the years passed, her sharp tongue and ruthless gold digging earned her the nickname Sour Kraut. Now she moved from man to man, shamelessly latching on to anyone she could. I looked around and wondered which of these saps she'd been bleeding dry lately. It had to be someone new, someone who didn't know her game.

I watched as the other boxer, a big man, landed a heavy right to Mickey's jaw. Sam blew the whistle and they stopped, heading back to their corners for water. Mickey spat out a mouthful of blood into a bucket and Sam mopped him down.

Now was my chance. As I moved through the gym, men stopped and a few catcalls and whistles followed. I knew better than to take it personally—it was just because I was a woman in a place women didn't go—but I flattered myself into thinking that I was still worth whistling at.

Across the room, Hildy looked up, irritated that someone else was getting attention. And when she saw me, her eyes narrowed and her mouth twisted tight. Tossing the magazine down, she flounced over, barring my way. "What are you doing here?"

"Hi, Hildy." I looked past her to where Mickey was doubled over, hands on knees, catching his breath. He hadn't seen me yet. "I need to talk to Mickey."

"What for?" She had a honking Boston twang and far too many facial expressions. Right now she was glaring, gaping, and smirking, all at the same time.

"What's it to you, anyway?"

Across the room, Sam gestured at us, and Mick looked up. Surprise spread across his face. I gave a little wave.

He said something to his partner, who nodded, and climbed out of the ring.

"I'll tell you what it is to me: you owe us money!" Hildy spat the words out.

Now she had my attention. *"Us?"*

"Yeah, *us!*" Her upper lip curled in triumph. "What Michael earns is my business now too!"

I felt like I'd taken one of Mick's left hooks straight to the kidney.

He was behind her now, staring at me like I was the Ghost of Christmas Past.

No longer the golden boy, Mickey wore his history on his face; resignation weighted his brow, and his nose was flattened out from being broken too many times. But if anything, it only added interest to his dark eyes, black hair, and well-muscled physique. Although handsome, Mickey was and always had been slightly unsure of himself, self-deprecating and shy. It was the most attractive thing about him. But now his battered features bestowed a gravitas that had been lacking before.

With one look, I'd always been able to win him back. I searched his eyes. *"Us?* Really, Mick?"

He laid a hand on Hildy's shoulder. "I'll deal with this," he said in his soft, lilting brogue.

My heart disappeared through the bottom of my stomach. I hadn't been sure what I was doing here, why I'd come. But now I knew I'd been kidding myself, imagining that after all we'd been through, he might still want me.

Hildy flashed him a warning look.

"Let me deal with it," he said again.

"I know you—you'll end up giving her more!" she hissed.

It was charming the way they both talked about me as if I weren't standing right in front of them. "Actually"—I pulled my chin up—"I just stopped by to pay you back, Mickey."

"See?" He gave Hildy a gentle push, back toward the chair. "I'll handle this."

"Well, you better!" She marched into the office instead and slammed the door. It echoed dramatically through the hall.

Mickey ran his hand across his eyes wearily, like a man forced to mediate between his mother and his wife. "Jesus, Maeve!"

"Jesus yourself!" I shot back. "What are you doing, Mick?"

He pointed a finger at me. "I don't have to answer to you! You left! Remember?" Still, the color rose in his cheeks, and I knew he was embarrassed.

"Sure." I shrugged. "You don't have to answer to anyone. Least of all me."

"Damn right I don't!"

"I guess I'm like a bad penny: you just can't get rid of me."

He sighed, shook his head, but his eyes softened. At six foot three, he was one of the few men who could ever look down on me. "Aw, now, you know I didn't want to be rid of you, Maeve. I never wanted that."

I nodded to the office door. "You do now."

A shadow of guilt flickered in his eyes. "What did you expect me to do? Wait?"

"Well, no . . . I don't know . . ." I frowned down at my shoes as if the answer was written across my toes. "I just thought I'd . . . I mean . . . well, I didn't know you'd . . . moved on."

We both stared at the floor awhile.

"So, you came back," he said, changing the subject. "I guess it didn't work out, huh?"

"It's a big city. Too big for me."

"That's what they say." His face twisted into a soft smile. "Jesus, Dante! What'd you go and do to your hair?"

"You don't like it?" He'd christened me Dante when I was in high school, reading *The Inferno*. "You're hair's an inferno," he used to say, laughing. He was the only person I let call me that.

"I dunno know." He reached out, touched one of the blond curls. "You look fine. But I guess you'll always be a redhead to me."

"I had to dye it, for a job. They didn't want an Irish girl, you know?"

He nodded. "It's good you got a job. There's not a lot about."

"Speaking of which . . ." I pulled some bills from my coat pocket. I'd never given him money before. No matter how poor he'd been, Mick was a gentleman: he'd always paid.

"What's this?" He glared at it.

"I meant to pay you back sooner, a bit at a time. But things were hard, really hard." Suddenly it was difficult to look him in the eye; I focused instead on the doorway at the top of the stairs, the dark, filmy world of entrances and exits. "I just wanted to say I'm sorry. It was stupid of me running off like that, staying away so long. I acted like an ass. But I wanted you to have this."

He pushed it back. "Put it away."

"It's what I owe you. It's yours."

"I don't care. I don't care about the money, Maeve. I never did."

"Come on, take it! Please!" I took a step closer. "We've been through a lot, you and me. I just want to settle my debt. So it can be okay between us. That's all."

In his eyes, an entire landscape of disbelief and betrayal unfolded before me. "And you think *money* will do it?" He took a step back, as if he didn't want to breathe the same air. I'd never seen him look at me like that before. "Is that really what you think?"

This wasn't just pride talking, but something deeper, still raw to the touch.

"But it's what I owe you!" I tried again, struggling to make him understand. "Don't you see? It's the least I can do!"

He folded his arms across his bare chest. "I got your letter."

"Letter?"

Then I remembered. A rambling, drunken fiction I'd sent from New York, right after I'd started at the Orpheum—full of stories of my wonderful new job and fascinating friends. I'd handed him the same line I'd given everyone else.

"You finally found the right crowd, huh?" he added bitterly.

"You have no idea what you're talking about," I told him. "That isn't how it was at all!"

"You know, I would've done anything for you," he continued. "You could've had anything you wanted from me, Maeve. *Anything!* As much as I had to give and more! Only"—he flung his arms wide in a gesture of hopeless resignation and confusion—"you didn't want it! Nothing I gave was enough for you!"

"That's not true!"

"Your mother always used to look at me like I was dirt on your shoe. And now I can see it—you feel the same way. Swanning round New York with millionaires and showgirls! Going to fancy clubs and meeting famous people. I was just holding you back, wasn't I?"

"Please, Mick, listen to me, I never thought that! *Never!*"

"Really?" His eyes narrowed. "All right, then, answer me one simple question: why did you run off to New York in the first place?"

My brain seized. "I . . ."

"I want the truth!" he warned.

"I . . . I just needed to get away . . . to be on my own for a while." I pulled the words painfully from the air around me. "I didn't mean to hurt you. It had nothing to do with you, I swear!"

"Jesus, Maeve!" He pounded his fist on the wall in frustration. "Can't you ever be honest? Just *once?*" He grabbed my arm and pulled me in, his face inches from mine. "You knew I was going nowhere, and you thought you could make it on your own—without me!"

My heart was beating so hard and fast I could hear it pounding in my ears.

He was right. I did want my own life; I had betrayed him.

"Why are you shaking?" He let go, backed away. "I wasn't going to hit you. I'd never hurt you."

"I have to go. I'm sorry. Really, I am." To my shame, tears blurred my vision as I hurried back across the hall.

"Maeve!"

I stumbled down the stairs and out into the street.

It was dusk now; shadowy velvet crept through the alleyways, pressing up against the anemic halos of light from streetlamps. Every sound seemed sinister, every movement menacing. My hands fumbled as I struggled to light a cigarette.

"Hey! Hey! Wait!"

Hildy came running out, bouncing on the balls of her feet in her high heels like a performing poodle. She tossed the rotting chinchilla around her shoulders and thrust out her hand.

I stared at it. "What?"

"Do you think I'm an idiot?" She snapped her fingers impatiently. "I've got my eye on you all the time! I'll take that money, thank you very much." She stood waiting, her lips pursed into a little red sphincter.

I didn't bother to argue; I didn't care anymore. I took out the bills and gave them to her.

She counted them before dropping them inside her handbag. "Michael doesn't have any sense when it comes to money. He'd lend a hobo his last dime. Or a two-bit floozy," she added, folding her arms across her chest. "And just in case you didn't get the message, he doesn't want to see you again. He may have been soft on you a long time ago, but he's over that now. He loves me. Consider your debt paid." She turned on her heel, calling back over her shoulder, "You don't need to call again!"

It was a cold, moonless night. Leaning up against the side of the building, I took another drag to steady my nerves.

Poor Mick.

He hadn't been the champion we'd both counted on. And I hadn't been the girl he'd imagined either.

And yet we'd both carried on, a little compromised, a little worse for wear, a lot more cynical.

The wind whipped off the water, cutting right through my thin coat. Pulling up the collar, I pressed on into the darkness.

Maybe that's what I liked about boxing.

It wasn't that the best man won or the even most powerful or that the fights weren't brutal or unfair. It was that the fighters continued, round after round, landing and taking punches long after they were willing or even able.

One morning a few weeks later Mr. Kessler had dramatic news when I came into work. "There's a shipment due in today from Liverpool! Something big. I need to go down to the docks to pay the customs charges. You must look after the shop on your own," he informed me, pulling on his coat.

"A shipment? A shipment of what?" There were no records of an impending delivery, and more importantly, no money to pay for one. Having spent hours every week trying to balance the accounts, I was only too aware of the limits of our budget.

"I have the documents right here." He pressed a stack of official-looking papers into my hands. "They arrived by courier this morning."

"By courier?" I opened them up. "Decorative ceramic vase and plate shipped from the port of Istanbul, Turkey," I read aloud, staring up at him in astonishment. "You bought something from *Istanbul?*"

"Me? No! Of course not!" He tossed a scarf round his neck with a particularly flamboyant flick of the wrist. "That's Winshaw's work!" He chuckled.

"Mr. Winshaw? But what would he be doing in Turkey?"

Up went the bushy white eyebrows. "What indeed?"

He was so animated and excited that for a moment I wondered if he'd been drinking.

"But . . . but how will we pay for this?" I was still struggling to catch up. "Look!" I pointed at the last line of the forms. "The customs fees alone are a fortune, Mr. Kessler!"

He put on his hat, cocking it just so. "I'm pleased you're taking an interest in your work, Miss Fanning. But it would be more expensive to send it back than to keep it. Besides, we can't leave it on the docks; they'll impound it." He smiled, patting my hand as if I were an idiot or an invalid. "Don't worry. You worry too much. I told you, Winshaw has a way of landing on his feet. And an eye, Miss Fanning! He's got a *very* good eye."

"It's not his eye I'm worried about—it's our bank account!"

"Chances are, he heard about something in Turkey, an opportunity that couldn't be missed." He tapped the side of his nose with his finger. "And now we're going to reap the benefit! This business is built on private acquisitions—specialist commissions. And Winshaw's got the talent of obtaining just the right object at just the right time. Trust me"—he opened the door—"this could be just the thing we need right now."

I watched as he scurried away, disappearing into the thick morning fog.

Unbuttoning my coat, I went back into Mr. Winshaw's office and stared at the old map on the wall.

Then I took a pin out of the drawer and stuck it into Istanbul.

Mr. Winshaw was on the move.

It was midafternoon by the time Mr. Kessler returned with the shipment. He had Charlie in tow to do the heavy lifting. Charlie was a skinny young man who'd been laid off from the docks recently. With his long face and large hangdog eyes, he looked like a bloodhound begging for scraps. His duties included picking up and delivering items, storage and packing, and hanging and displaying new pieces in the shop. He also took it upon himself to perform minor repairs. Clearly he was trying to make more work for himself, but Mr. Kessler either didn't notice or didn't mind.

Now Mr. Kessler and I watched anxiously as Charlie prised open the wooden crate with a crowbar.

The lid eased off, and together Mr. Kessler and Charlie pulled out handfuls of soft wood shavings. Then Mr. Kessler lifted out a cheap woman's vanity case in a dubious shade of coral pink.

"What's that?" I frowned.

"Be patient," he told me.

Wedged tightly inside the case was something wound in layers of fine linen, like a swaddled infant. With great care Mr. Kessler unwrapped it.

"My goodness!" I was taken aback by its beauty.

"Yes, my goodness indeed!" he agreed.

It was a Greek vase standing just over a foot tall, largely black apart from the figures and ornamentation, which were in rich terra-cotta red.

Removing a magnifying glass from his inside jacket pocket, Mr. Kessler leaned in closer. "What we have here," he began, "is a red-figure amphora, or vase, approximately 480 to 470 BC. And if I'm not mistaken, it looks like the work of the Greek pot specialist known as the Harrow Painter. Which makes it rare"—he looked up—"*very* rare. As you can see," he said, pointing to the main figurative motif, "we have a young man wrapped in his cloak or himation, holding a lyre. There is a red apicate fillet in his hair, the mark of an athlete, and the bearded man standing in front of him, leaning on his staff, is his teacher, patron, perhaps even lover. And here"—he indicated the figure on the other side of the vase—"we have the young man alone. It's known as 'The Music Lesson.' "

Mr. Kessler straightened, adding with a triumphant smile, "And I'm pleased to say it's in excellent condition."

"How do you know it's called 'The Music Lesson'?" I asked.

"Because this is a very valuable piece, quite well known, though it's been many years since it's been on the market."

I dared to run my finger lightly along the side, over the smooth clay that had seen empires rise and fall. "Why do they call the artist the Harrow Painter?"

"After another famous vase of his displayed at the Harrow School in England. It features a young boy playing with a hoop. He produced maybe ninety different vases that have survived today. He has quite an elegant, recognizable style."

How could something this old look so contemporary? "The painting is so precise—like it was all done in a single stroke!"

He nodded. "It's a remarkable level of mastery."

Charlie dug out a second small woman's traveling case from the crate, this one a rather insipid powder blue. He handed it to Mr. Kessler. Inside was another swaddled object, a plate. Again, the design was relatively simple, mostly black, with a red figure of a youth astride the back of a giant rooster, his toes braced against the framing line of the design motif. The boy was smiling, the rooster swollen-chested, with full, elaborate plumage. It was a striking, surprising piece, refined and yet bold.

"The vase is worth at least fifteen thousand, maybe twenty. And the plate"—Mr. Kessler frowned, stroked his beard—"sixteen thousand, easily."

"Are you serious?" I stared at him in amazement. "As much as that?"

He grinned. "I told you Winshaw knew what he was doing!"

His excitement was contagious. "Well, where's a good place

to put them, then?" I looked around. "In the window, don't you think? Maybe with a sign?"

"Oh no! No. These won't go on display." Mr. Kessler folded up the customs forms and put them in his inside pocket. "Believe me"—he smiled—"these pieces already have a home."

It wasn't until later that evening, when Mr. Kessler had gone and I was left behind, trying to figure out how we were to cover the import charges, that Charlie came to the office door, hovering just outside. "Miss Fanning?"

I started. "Jeez! Don't sneak up on me!"

"I didn't mean to frighten you." He smiled slowly.

"What are you doing here this late?" I asked.

His shirtsleeves were rolled up, brow damp from sweat. Mr. Kessler had asked him to pack the pieces in something more suitable than old vanity cases. Never one to miss an opportunity, Charlie had somehow conjured up a whole day's work, making a bespoke crate. But now he was holding something. "I found this. In the side pocket of one of them cases."

It was a dirty silk handkerchief, dusty and yellowed, tied into a little bundle.

But it had weight; there was something inside.

"We'll have to show this to Mr. Kessler in the morning," I told him. "It's late. You ought to get off home now."

"Yeah, I suppose." He yawned, stretching his arms high, but still lingered by the door. "Or I could wait for you, if you like. Walk you to your stop."

"No need to worry about me. I'll be fine." It came off sharp and prissy, like a schoolteacher correcting a student.

He didn't seem to notice.

"Okay, then." He shrugged. "Guess I'll see you in the funny papers, huh?"

Once he'd gone, I unknotted the bundle.

It was a ring: heavy gold and fitted with an intricately carved black stone, engraved with an image of a winged woman. She looked like an angel at a spinning wheel, long, fragile threads between her fingers. At her feet stood a pudgy cupid, and around her head floated a tiny butterfly.

This was an antiquity, I was sure of it. Either Greek or Roman. And the scene must be mythical, though I didn't know which one.

I ran my finger over the inky stone, tracing the outline of the woman, draped in her flowing garments, her fine profile accentuated by her hairstyle, wound back from her face in plaits.

Who was she?

I went into Mr. Winshaw's office and dug out his copy of *Cowper's Classical Mythology*. In the glossary I searched under the words *goddess* and *spinning wheel*.

CLOTHO

Clotho is one of the Moirai—one of the three Fates in the ancient world. They control the thread of life and the destiny of each human from birth until death. They are daughters of Annake, the goddess of necessity. Clotho spins the thread of life on her distaff; Lachesis, the allotter, measures out how much each person will have with her measuring rod; and Antropos, the most dreaded sister, finally cuts the thread with her shears.

The Fates.

It was a ring of destiny.

I shooed Persia out of the way and sat down in Mr. Winshaw's chair. This was a great deal more sophisticated than a crooked pin in a pocket.

The burnished gold began to warm from the heat of my hand. I slipped it on my index finger. It was more than just beautiful; it had a darkly compelling, otherworldly quality—as if it obeyed different physical laws from the rest of the universe and was beholden to no one, not even gravity.

No one else knew it existed; not even Charlie had seen it.

I should've put the ring in Mr. Kessler's office.

But I didn't. I hid it in the top drawer of Mr. Winshaw's desk instead.

I knew I couldn't take it; I didn't want to lose my job. And eventually I would show it to Mr. Kessler.

But for one night, I wanted to be the only person who knew exactly where it was.

It wasn't long before "the special client" paid us a visit. Mr. Kessler's instructions were simple but firm. "Tomorrow we have an important visitor arriving quite early. I will need you here by eight a.m. Please look your best, and under no circumstances should you speak unless spoken to."

I gave him a look. "Unless I'm *spoken* to?"

But he was perfectly serious.

So I did what I was told and came in at eight, in my blue knit. Mr. Kessler was already there, rearranging things on the shop floor—moving them from one spot to another and then back again, like a nervous housewife before a party. I made coffee, which he insisted I put into a Limoges coffeepot that was part of a very expensive French tea service. Then he told me very solemnly that I was "in charge of refreshments." The vase and plate were already in pride of place at the center of the English oak table.

At eight thirty precisely a Duesenberg pulled up outside and a uniformed driver got out and opened the door. A gentleman wearing an expensive camel-hair overcoat with a white carnation in his buttonhole climbed out. He moved precisely, with the automated efficiency of a piece of industrial machinery designed to find the shortest distance between two points. Mr. Kessler greeted him at the door, but the gentleman barely acknowledged him, offering just a curt bob of the head before going straight to the table. Reaching into his inside coat pocket, he took out a small gold magnifying glass of his own and leaned in close to examine each piece.

He did this in complete silence. Mr. Kessler, in turn, offered no pleasantries to distract him. I stood behind the counter, wondering if the coffee would go cold.

After about five minutes the man looked up. "Yes," he said, nodding as if in response to some unspoken question. "Yes, indeed."

Mr. Kessler gave me a signal. Or at least I thought it was a signal.

"Sir, may I pour you some coffee?" I offered.

The man spun round, staring at me as if he'd only just noticed that I existed. "No." He managed to sound shocked and slightly offended at the same time. "That won't be necessary."

Then he nodded again to Mr. Kessler and left.

The whole episode had taken maybe ten minutes.

"Well, that went better than I could have hoped!" Mr. Kessler seemed genuinely delighted. "We have just sold two extremely rare and valuable Greek artifacts!" Then he proceeded to pack the pieces away again while I threw away the cold coffee.

By that afternoon, further arrangements had been confirmed.

"You are to deliver them this evening," Mr. Kessler informed me.

"*Me?*" I looked up in surprise from the copy of *Vanity Fair* I had hidden behind the counter.

"A driver will collect you at six. You will be given a check upon arrival, which you must be very careful to keep safe."

"But why me? Surely you should deliver them."

"I don't do business after sunset. It's the beginning of the Sabbath."

"But can't the driver come earlier?"

He frowned, uncharacteristically annoyed. "It's just better if you do it."

These were the most expensive, important pieces we'd ever had. I certainly didn't want to be in charge of them. "But you're the expert, Mr. Kessler. What if they have questions? You know so much more than I do."

"Miss Fanning! *Please!* It's better this way, don't you understand?" He sighed, suddenly on the verge of losing patience. "Mrs. Van der Laar doesn't like Jews!"

I was mortified that I'd pushed him to say such a thing out loud, and that there was anyone who would knowingly treat him with such disrespect. "Mrs. Van der Laar? Who's she?"

"She is our client, a very wealthy and important collector. It doesn't matter what she thinks of me. I'm trusting you with a great deal. Can you do this for me?"

"Yes, of course. I'm sorry."

His confession made him seem suddenly fragile. Jewishness was a mark you couldn't remove as easily as red hair.

"Mr. Winshaw used to deal with this sort of thing. But he isn't here," Mr. Kessler explained wearily. "So this time, Miss Fanning, it will have to be you."

The car was different from the one that had come that morning. Just after six a long black Packard pulled up outside the shop and sat there, waiting, motor purring thick and low like a contented cat. The driver didn't bother to get out or honk the horn; I was expected to be watching and ready. As I put on my hat and coat, a nagging uneasiness gnawed at me. Already my palms were beginning to sweat. I was about to turn out the lights and lock up when suddenly I went back into Mr. Winshaw's office and took the black agate ring from the top drawer. Maybe I was foolish and superstitious, just like my mother, but I needed luck tonight, something to hold on to. So I put the ring in my coat pocket.

When I finally came out of the shop, the driver collected the crate, and I sat beside it in the back, with a blanket over my knees for warmth. He drove south, out of town for some time, following the water. He was so far away, in the front, that I couldn't ask him where we were going without shouting. So I sat quietly, trying to enjoy the unfamiliar experience of being driven. Out of the window, the landscape altered dramatically, and eventually we reached the rural, rocky seafront town of Cohasset. The car came to a stop in front of a high wrought-iron gate. A man hurried out of a gatehouse to open it, and the car carried on, up a private winding road that threaded its way along a curved outcrop of land, jutting out into the water. Perched there, overlooking the ocean, an enormous stone mansion stood guard, lights blazing in the softening dusk. I counted six other cars parked in the drive.

Without a word the driver opened the door and offered me a gloved hand. I stepped out onto the gravel drive and the sea air whipped round me, bracing, briny, and electric. We were so far away from the ashen factory smoke, oily coal dust, and damp fog that rolled in from the harbor to engulf Boston. Beyond the house was a pilgrim's view of unspoiled coastline; black water dissolved into the vast expanse of gray-pink horizon. Sea gulls circled above, their shrill cries echoing forlornly against the distant roar of the waves thundering against the rocky cliffs below. The place seemed to have its own clearer, rarified atmosphere.

The house had a wide terrace, and the grounds a particular, barren, windswept beauty, the rolling lawns populated by giant chestnut trees, their massive branches raised like ancient arms toward the heavens, twisted by time and the elements.

The front door opened. A gentleman waited on the threshold; behind him the white marble entrance was lit by a dazzling crystal chandelier. I followed the driver up the front steps. He handed the crate to the man, and I stepped aside.

"Miss Fanning?"

"Yes."

"I'm Mr. Abbott, Mrs. Van der Laar's secretary. Will you kindly follow me, please?"

He led me into a room that was easily the size of the entire ground floor of the public library. Flames flickered in two great marble fireplaces, and settees, ottomans, and armchairs were clustered on four massive oriental carpets.

Mr. Abbott put the crate down on one of the low ottomans. "If you would like to make yourself comfortable, Mr. Kimberly will be with you in a moment."

"Mr. Kimberly?" I didn't want to stay; I just wanted to get the check and leave.

"He oversees all of the acquisitions in Mrs. Van der Laar's collection. Now, if you'll excuse me . . ."

Mr. Abbott left, and I sat gingerly at the edge of one of the armchairs, my handbag on my lap. The room was sweetly scented; a vase of pink hothouse lilies, each as big as a man's hand, were arranged on a table at its center. Somewhere a door opened; I heard music and laughter. It closed again, and the noise died.

I'd wondered who Mr. Kessler's clients were. Who was wealthy enough to spend $100 on a silver trinket or $500 on a desk? Now here I was, sitting in a room that held more fine pieces than the whole of Mr. Kessler's shop put together. And it was only one room of many.

Then a terrifying thought occurred to me. What if these people thought I was an expert, too? What if someone asked me a question or expected me to value something?

I looked around in a panic, racking my brain to remember all of Mr. Kessler's lessons. Those chairs were French, weren't they? But what were they called? *Fauteuils* or *bergères*? And the table in the center of the room—was that cherry or mahogany? My hand felt for the ring in my pocket, twisting it nervously between my fingers.

Suddenly a strange face blinked back at me, and my heart stopped. Then I realized, with a pathetic sense of relief, that the blonde in the overmantel was me.

As I stared back at myself in the reflected grandeur of the room, I remembered what Mr. Kessler had told me: a good counterfeit is as much a work of art as the real thing.

"Good evening."

I turned. It was the same gentleman who'd visited the shop, but now he was followed by a second man dressed in a dinner jacket and tie, clearly in the middle of entertaining.

"I'm Philip Kimberly," the first man said, closing the door.

"May Fanning, sir. From Winshaw and Kessler."

The man behind Mr. Kimberly stepped forward, hands in his pockets. His hair was dark and wavy, his features strong and uneven, and he had unusually clear, seemingly transparent blue eyes. He had an easy, gracious manner that could only come from ownership and there was an audacity in his gaze, a confidence and directness that was both intriguing and unnerving.

"James Van der Laar," he introduced himself, with a slightly apologetic grin, as if just saying his name was a trump card played too early in the game. "I believe you have something for me."

"It's just here." I walked over to the crate, and the two men followed.

"Allow me." Mr. Kimberly lifted the lid, took out the vase, and handed it to Mr. Van der Laar.

The glossy black surface of the vase reflected the darting flames in the fireplace, and for a fleeting moment the old adage about Nero fiddling as Rome burned came to mind.

The flames were also captured in the black orbits of Mr. Van der Laar's eyes. He stared at it for a while, almost as if he were memorizing each detail, before putting it down on the wide marble mantelpiece.

"You say that's the finest one you can find?" He didn't sound convinced.

"Oh, yes!" Mr. Kimberly assured him. "The finest example we'll see available on the market again for another four generations."

Then Mr. Kimberly took out the plate.

"Yes, see!" He smiled, handing it to Mr. Van der Laar. "Now, this is without equal!"

Mr. Van der Laar held it up, frowning a little like someone trying to work out a puzzle. "It's plainer than I thought it would be."

"Simplicity is the hallmark of the Harrow Painter. It's what makes these pieces so elegant. The integrity of the line is exquisite."

"I'm not concerned with elegance. It has to be superior."

"Oh, but this is! These are first-rate. Here is proof, if proof were needed, of the golden age!"

Mr. Van der Laar gave a disparaging laugh. "You and your golden age! The only age I care about is the one I'm in now."

Mr. Kimberly clearly wasn't a man who took kindly to being dismissed. The skin on the back of his neck flushed red, and his ears turned pink. He caught my eye, and I quickly looked away. But now I'd suddenly appeared on the horizon of his notice, if only as a suitable outlet for his irritation. He turned on me. "Do you even have any idea what we're talking about, Miss Fanning?"

I looked up, startled. "I'm sorry?"

"The golden age." His voice was icy with condescension. "Have you even heard of it?"

In my pocket, I felt for the ring. "I believe the golden age refers to a time long gone when mankind lived without difficulty or strife. Almost like gods. Or at least, that's the legend in Greek mythology," I managed.

He blinked, pursed his lips together.

"*Et in Arcadia ego*," he said, tilting his chin down to see my reaction. My insolence had earned me another challenge.

I'd never studied languages. "Pardon me?"

"*Et in Arcadia ego*," he repeated, savoring my ignorance.

I could feel Mr. Van der Laar watching me too.

Firelight flickered across the plate in his hands. The image of the boy on the rooster seemed to be laughing at me.

Luckily years of listening to mass in Latin had taught me at least a little. "Even in Arcadia, there I am," I translated roughly.

"Yes." Mr. Kimberly awarded me a terse smile. "Death triumphs over everything."

He turned his attention back to Mr. Van der Laar, but Mr. Van der Laar was still looking at me, an expectant expression on his face, almost as if he were silently goading me on.

"But does it?" I asked.

Kimberly hadn't expected me to challenge him; the smile faded.

I pointed at the plate. "Death hasn't conquered this. Here we are, centuries later, wondering at the aesthetic perfection of a lost age. Who of us doesn't long for such immortality?"

Mr. Van der Laar chuckled. "She's right, Kimberly. Isn't that why we collect beautiful things—to cheat death?"

Suddenly the door opened; a swell of music and laughter filled the room. "There you are! I've been looking everywhere! We're all waiting for you!"

I knew that voice. I turned.

A striking young woman was leaning against the doorframe in an emerald-green silk gown, a low V neckline exposing the smooth white skin of her long neck. Her dark hair was tousled, her cheeks flushed, as if she'd been laughing, chased or teased into a state of breathless exhaustion; in her hand she held an empty champagne glass, and around her neck was a string of faultless pearls.

I couldn't take my eyes off her.

It was the girl from the far ward.

My confidence vanished. I had to get out of here, quickly, or risk being unmasked.

But before I could do anything, an older woman came up behind the girl. Thousands of jet beads sparkled on her evening gown as she swept past her into the room. "So are they worth all the fuss?" Her hair was iron gray, worn back from her face, and she had the same unusual blue eyes that both Mr. Van der Laar and the girl shared. Her voice was accented, but it wasn't an accent that I recognized. It was like German, but softer, less guttural.

"They're perfect," Mr. Kimberly assured her, crossing to her side. "In fact, they're without question the finest I've ever seen."

"I should hope so, at that price. Show me," she demanded.

The girl spotted the crate. "What's going on? What are those?"

Mr. Kimberly held up the vase.

"Is that it?" The woman was disappointed. "It's not very big!"

"It's not the size, it's the condition." Mr. Van der Laar put the vase down on the table.

"But I have hats bigger than those!"

"I'm sorry, Mother, but unfortunately the Elgin Marbles are taken," he replied.

"They will be the centerpiece of the collection," Mr. Kimberly promised. "A world-class collection that will attract international acclaim."

"Oh, I see!" The girl smiled conspiratorially, pushing the door closed. "We're playing patron of the arts again—our name on yet another brass plaque. Do we get a prize when we reach a hundred?"

"I wouldn't be so flippant if I were you," the woman countered. "It's your name that going to be on it!"

Her face fell. "Mine? What's all this got to do with me?"

"You're the benefactor." Mr. Van der Laar's tone was matter-of-fact. "It's time you pulled your weight in the family too."

"This is an important public legacy." Mr. Kimberly tried to make the proposition sound more attractive. "You'll be contributing a significant cultural endowment to the city of Boston."

"Oh, I'm certain that's just what people need!" the girl scoffed. "Another bloody vase! So lazy of them to spend their days waiting in breadlines when they could be going to the museum!"

"It's more than that. It's about setting an example; giving people something to aspire to," Mr. Kimberly told her. "We who can have a duty to educate and enrich the lives of others."

"And who are 'we' exactly, to educate anyone?"

"Don't be stupid!" The older woman sighed. "You're a very lucky girl. I don't know why you insist on making everything so difficult!"

But the girl wasn't listening.

She'd spotted me.

I picked up my handbag. "I really should be going, sir."

The older woman swiveled round, looking me up and down as if I'd only just manifested out of the blue. "And you are?"

"This is Miss Fanning, from Winshaw and Kessler," Mr. Kimberly said, to introduce me. "Miss Fanning has been good enough to deliver these at this late hour. Miss Fanning, may I introduce you to Mrs. Van der Laar and her daughter, Diana."

"Oh, yes! I *have* seen you before!" Suddenly Diana grabbed my arm. "Yes . . . I remember now! I *knew* I recognized you!"

"You know each other?" Mr. Van der Laar looked faintly appalled.

"I sometimes go to the lectures at the Athenaeum," I said quickly, trying to ease my arm away from Diana's grip. "Perhaps we've met there?"

Something changed in Diana's face. "You know," she said slowly, "I think that must be it. They're so informative, don't you find?"

"You've never been to a lecture in your life!" Her mother dismissed the idea. "I doubt you've even read a book!"

"Lovely to see you again." I inched toward the door.

"Oh, no! Wait!" Diana was surprisingly tenacious. "It wasn't the Athenaeum. I know where it was! It was Marblehead, wasn't it? Weren't you on Nicky Howerd's yacht last July?"

I blinked at her. "I . . . ah . . . Nicky?"

Mrs. Van der Laar turned. "You know Nicky?"

"Oh yes!" Diana gave my arm an affectionate squeeze. "Pinky Cabot Lowell was there as well, and weren't you completely monopolized by Johnny Coolidge? I remember how we all struggled with those lobsters! It was a lobster bake," she explained. "We had to crack them open ourselves and dig out the meat with our fingers!"

"How revolting!" Her mother shuddered.

"I think you were the only one who managed it!" Diana laughed.

"The Howerds always have dreadful food. It's a point of pride with them." Mrs. Van der Laar looked me up and down. "Who are your people?"

"My people?" Suddenly I was in quicksand, sinking fast.

"Let me guess." Mr. Van der Laar held up his hand. "With your fair hair you must be Nordic or German. Am I right?"

"I'm . . . well, the truth is . . ."

"Yes?" Diana seemed to be enjoying herself, a gleam of mischief in her eye.

"Well, actually"—I straightened—"I'm from Albany. I'm in town visiting family."

"And you're *working*?" Mrs. Van der Laar made it sound as if I were standing on a street corner in a bad part of town.

"Actually, the shop is owned by a friend of the family. Mr. Winshaw is a highly respected archaeologist. He's away right now, on an important expedition, and they needed someone to lend a hand."

"Young women today!" Mrs. Van der Laar rolled her eyes. "I can't imagine what you're all thinking of!"

"Some say working builds character," Diana told her.

"Character isn't built, it's bred." Mr. Van der Laar leaned against the mantel, elbow dangerously close to the Greek vase. "Where were you schooled, Miss Fanning? Abroad? One of the Swiss boarding schools?"

"Ah, no. Not really." It was dreadful to be the focus of their combined attention. "Mother always wanted to, but we never got round to going. . . . I'm afraid I'm simply something of a reader."

"Well"—he smiled again—"you appear to have read all the right books. Perhaps we should get Diana a library card, Mother."

"Too much reading is a bad habit. No one likes a girl who squints." Mrs. Van der Laar turned to her son. "Light me a cigarette, will you? We must go in. You know how unbearable Charlie Thorndike gets when he's been drinking."

He took a silver cigarette case out of his breast pocket. "He's easier to deal with when he's drunk. I've got a business proposal that will benefit if he's worse for wear."

"Oh, but you must come to supper sometime!" Diana looked to her mother. "Don't you think?"

"Of course. Our food is much better than the Howerds'. And we rarely ask guests to butcher their own meat." Mrs. Van der Laar took the cigarette offered her. "We don't often get to meet any of Diana's friends. Where do you live, Miss Fanning?" Before

I could answer, she rang the bell by the door. "I'll arrange for Morris to drive you home."

Mr. Kimberly hurried to her side and held out his arm. Diana's mother looked back at her son. "Don't be long. I don't want to be left alone with Thorndike."

"I won't leave your side," Mr. Kimberly assured her, escorting her out.

"You don't count," she informed him.

Mr. Van der Laar held out his hand to me. "Don't let my sister corrupt you, Miss Fanning. She's a terrible influence." He stopped, noticing the black agate ring on my finger. "What's this?"

I hadn't realized I'd slipped it on. "Oh, just something that came in the shop recently. Nothing much."

I tried to remove my hand, but he held it firmly in his own. "It's yours?"

"Not exactly. But I often wear the pieces we sell, so people can see them on." I removed it. "Have a look if you like."

He turned it over. "So it's for sale?"

"Well, I'm afraid it hasn't been valued yet."

"What is that?" He peered at the figure. "Some sort of angel?"

"I believe it's one of the three Fates. Clotho, perhaps."

He looked impressed. "Well, go on—name your price. What do you want for it?"

I wasn't prepared for this at all. "I couldn't possibly—"

"My God, Jimmy! You'd pluck the ring off a girl's hand!" Diana cut in. "Leave her alone!"

"When I see something I like, I buy it." He shrugged. "Is that so wrong?"

"Yes." Diana draped herself across the arm of a chair. "Because you only want what you can't have."

He laughed, looking at me with those unnerving, clear eyes. I smiled, feeling awkward and foolish and very much trapped.

Then he gave up, handed the ring back, and sauntered over to the door. "You forget, little sister—there's nothing I can't have."

After he'd gone, Diana sighed. "Aren't they appalling? I hate them all." She got up and took my arm, as if we were old friends. "You will come, won't you? To supper?"

I pulled away. Now that everyone was gone, my hands were trembling from nerves, my heart pounding. "What are you doing?" I struggled to keep my voice low. "Are you trying to get me fired?"

She seemed genuinely confused. "What are you talking about?"

"Do you think it's funny? Pretending I'm some debutante or one of your society friends? Because I don't!"

Her face went blank.

"No one knows I was in the hospital!" I hissed.

"Well, I won't tell!"

"And I'm not from Albany! I don't know any of the people you're talking about!"

"I never thought you were, darling. Though," she added with a smile, "you did well. Albany threw the old goat. She knows everyone in Boston, but upstate New York? Nicely played!" She chuckled. "She won't know what to make of you now!"

I could've slapped her.

"You think this is a joke, don't you? But if they knew I was lying, I'd lose my job! This is nothing more than a bloody parlor game to you!"

I marched out into the entrance hall, and she trailed after me like a wounded child. The sound of distant laughter echoed down one of the adjoining hallways.

"Go back to your party," I said.

"Don't be that way!"

Mr. Abbott emerged. "Morris is ready to drive you, Miss Fanning." He opened the front door and handed me an envelope. "From Mrs. Van der Laar, miss."

I was so shaken, I'd almost completely forgotten about the payment.

"Thank you, Mr. Abbott." I jammed the envelope into my handbag and headed down the front steps.

It was dark now, colder. Morris was waiting by the car.

"Look, I wasn't trying to make fun of you!" Diana called, trying to keep up with me. "Honest. I think you're magnificent!"

"Go back inside!"

But she kept following. "You see, she's such a snob, my mother, I can't help myself! And it was so unexpected, actually, to see you again."

"Fine."

"No, I mean it!" She grabbed her arm. "Really." She was shivering in her flimsy gown. "You have no idea. It's so lonely here. I'm sorry I put you on the spot. It's just, I hate the way they try to bully me into things."

An icy gust of wind slammed up against us. Morris hurried up the steps with a car blanket and draped it over her shoulders.

"It's all right," I said, calmer now. "But don't you see? I can't afford to make mistakes. I just want to put everything that happened behind me."

Her face fell. "Yes, I see. I only wish I could."

I climbed into the back seat, and Morris closed the door. As he reversed, I saw her standing alone on the front steps, wrapped in the car blanket, her face a ghostly white in the glare of the headlamps. Behind her figures moved in silhouette against the golden glow of the drawing-room windows: men in tuxedos, women in gowns, holding champagne glasses and cigarettes.

Morris sped on down the long drive.

Even though it was late, I asked him to drop me back at the shop. I let myself in and left the envelope on Mr. Kessler's desk.

Then I took off the black agate ring.

Had it brought me luck or just trouble?

Certainly Mr. Van der Laar had found it interesting—too interesting to remain a secret, I decided. I left the ring on Mr. Kessler's desk too and turned out the light.

Then I sat awhile in Mr. Winshaw's battered chair, petting Persia and staring at the map on the wall. For some reason I felt strangely euphoric, the way one feels after a narrow escape. For a while, I couldn't work it out, and then suddenly I knew why I felt giddy and my head was buzzing.

They'd believed me.

As angry as I was at Diana for forcing me to play along, it had been surprisingly easy to be someone else. Even that snobbish old woman Mrs. Van der Laar had bought the story.

It reminded me of a bracelet someone had tried to sell Mr. Kessler a few days before—a Victorian diamond-and-sapphire cuff. The woman was distraught to let it go; it was an heirloom given to her by her late husband. But Mr. Kessler had taken me in the back and shown me that while the sapphires were real, the diamonds were only paste, though quite cleverly done. But the real stones lent authenticity to the fake.

Tonight, Diana had turned me into a diamond.

Running my fingers through Persia's thick fur, I thought about the woman with the paste diamond bracelet.

And about all the shiny things that were only as real as you thought they were.

On Saturday evening Angela and I went to a matinee show of *Grand Hotel* at the new Paramount movie house on Washington Street. It was the first time we'd been out together since I'd come home, and it felt just like old times—putting on our best hats to meet and sharing popcorn in the front row of the balcony. Afterward we strolled arm in arm to the trolley stop, pretending we were Greta Garbo.

"I just want to be alone," Angela purred, mimicking Garbo's husky contralto.

I pressed my hand to my forehead dramatically. "I have never been so tired in all my life!"

Then I walked Angela back to her mother-in-law's house. Carlo's mother, the widow Menzi, had only two surviving children, Carlo and his younger sister Catherina, who was still in high school. She lost three children to illness and had two more stillborn before her husband died. Antonio Menzi had owned his own barbershop at the top of Hanover Street for years; the Menzis had done well for themselves and their remaining children. She was pleased when Carlo chose Angela for his bride; she considered the Russos to be one of the few families in the neighborhood on par socially with her own. They were both firmly established, and even though she'd sold her husband's shop long before, she liked to think of them both as business owners, real middle-class Americans.

I'd never been to the Menzi house before. Located on a quiet back street, it sat well away from the tenements and was one of the nicest in the neighborhood, with a narrow front porch and a heavy oak door with leaded-glass windows on either side.

"Come in and have a cup of tea," Angela offered. "Carlo's study-ing all night for an exam, and otherwise I'll have no one to talk to—except for my mother-in-law," she added, wrinkling her nose.

"I don't want to disturb everyone."

"No one's here but Catherina and the old owl, watching me!"

I knew she wanted to show the house off, even though she tried to pretend otherwise. Neither of us had ever lived in a house before. Even though the Russos were successful, they still lived above the bakery.

"Come on!" Angela unlocked the door.

"Okay. Just for a minute."

It was far more spacious than it looked outside. There was a front hall and a stairwell going up to the second and third floors with a carved wooden banister and a pretty stained-glass window on the landing, showing two brightly colored peacocks in a garden. On one side of the hall was a living room; on the other, a formal dining room with a dark mahogany dining set and a real crystal chandelier. From the dining room window there was a view of a small back garden, surrounded by a wooden fence, with a stone bird feeder and two plum trees. It was a long way from the damp, crowded apartments we'd grown up in—that I still lived in. Angela wasn't just married, she was advancing.

I nodded at the stained-glass window. "That's nice."

"Yes, I suppose it is." She barely glanced at it, trying to make out as if she'd never really noticed it before.

Catherina was lounging on the sofa in the living room, listen-ing to a radio play on a large freestanding Zenith radio. It was the latest model; the voices sounded so crisp and clear, it was as if the actors were in the same room. When she saw us, though, she turned it off and followed us into the kitchen. It was one of those newer-design kitchens with a linoleum floor and all the latest appliances.

"Catty, this is my friend Mae." Angela introduced us, putting fresh water in the kettle and lighting the stove.

Catherina was a small, delicate girl with large black eyes. She smiled at me, twisting a few strands of hair round her fingers nervously. "Hello."

"Very nice to meet you. What's this?" I pointed to a bright green machine with the word *Maytag* on the front. It had a squat, round tank. "Is that some sort of icebox?"

"Oh no! That's the washing machine," Catty said.

"Really?" I opened up the lid and looked inside. "Where's the mangle?"

"It doesn't have a mangle. It spins the clothes instead," Angela explained.

"Spins them! How's that?"

Catty giggled. "It makes an awful noise!"

"But you don't have to worry about getting your fingers caught," Angela said. "You just put the clothing in with the soap and leave it. When you come back, it's all done."

"You're having me on!" I sat down at the table while Angela took out a tin of biscotti. "Does it come with a magic wand too?"

"May I ask you a question?" Catherina blushed.

"Of course." I helped myself to a biscuit.

"Is your hair real?"

"Catty!" Angela fixed her with a stern look.

"It's okay." I smiled. "No, it's red really. But I dyed it for a job."

Catherina's eyes widened. "What kind of job?"

"A salesgirl. In a shop on Charles Street."

Catty slid into a free chair. "Did you do it by yourself, or did you go to a shop? It looks real." She touched the top of it lightly.

"Actually, my mother helped me. She works in Stearns, and one of the hairdressers in the beauty shop gave us a bottle of bleach and told us what to do. It was easier than I thought."

Angela took a teapot down from the cupboard and three cups. "It's not polite to ask personal questions," she reprimanded her young sister-in-law. "You know better than that."

"I don't mean anything by it. I think it looks grand! Like a film star."

Opening a jar of tea, Angela spooned a few teaspoons into the pot. "That's not the point."

Catherina blushed again. "You're quite famous, aren't you?"

"*Me?*" I laughed. "Hardly! Who says that?"

"Carlo. He says you have quite a reputation. That you'd been engaged once and then ran off to New York instead."

I stopped laughing. "Carlo told you that?"

"What were you doing in New York? Were you in a show?" she persisted.

"Honestly, that's enough! Where are your manners tonight?" Angela snapped, her face suddenly red and flushed.

"He says you went to speakeasies and jazz clubs, drank bootleg gin! What are they like really?" She leaned in eagerly. "Are people very depraved and glamorous? Did you see any mobsters?"

"Angela—" Mrs. Menzi was standing in the doorway. "I didn't realize you were home." She was wearing a fashionable if conservatively cut dress of heavy blue crepe, and her graying hair was arranged in the kind of neat marcel waves that came from a real salon. "Hello." She nodded to me with the kind of practiced graciousness that comes from a public position. "Catherina, dear, come with me, will you?"

"But why?" Catherina whined, deflating.

"Because I asked you to," her mother said evenly.

As soon as they'd gone, Angela tried to explain. "Carlo's an idiot, Mae! You can't pay attention to anything he says. He's just getting his own back because he knew that I wanted you at the wedding and you didn't come." She poured the hot water into the teapot and sat down again. "He has a few beers, comes home, and starts running off at the mouth. And you know what girls are like at that age. The world is one big stage show to them."

"But how did he know about the . . . about the drinking?"

"Well, I, ah . . . I suppose . . ." She frowned, suddenly flustered. "Look, Carlo's my husband, Mae! Of course I *tell* him things! What do you expect me to do?"

Not only had she broken my confidence, now she was pretending like it didn't even matter. "But that was private! I expected you to keep it that way."

She didn't answer me but poured out the tea, even though it hadn't brewed long enough and was still too weak.

We sat staring, silent, at our watery tea.

"I'm sorry," she mumbled after a while. "Really I am. I never thought Carlo would tell anyone. Actually, I'm sure it's just"—she stopped, backtracking to correct herself—"I mean, I'm sure he hasn't told anyone *outside* the family . . ."

My stomach sank. She was making matters worse.

"But I have to talk to someone, and you were away for so long!" Somehow she had managed to twist the whole thing round. "He's my *husband*, Mae! I can't keep secrets from my husband!" Angela was never very good at apologizing. She had to be right, which naturally meant everyone else ended up in the wrong. But this was the first time she'd ever chosen someone else over me. Now she was married, her allegiance had shifted. "Why did you have to go away? Why?" She veered from regret to anger, like a car out of control. "You think I'm too stupid to understand, don't you? You won't tell me the truth because you think I'm an idiot! Just because you're smarter, more clever. I may not have gone to secretarial school—"

"I never said that! I never said you weren't smart!"

"Then why, Mae?" Suddenly her eyes glistened with tears. "Why did you have to leave me here by myself with no one to talk to?"

She was crying now. Angela almost never cried; she was too stubborn. Even as a child, she'd preferred to lash out rather than let anyone see her give in to tears.

I took her hand, though it was an effort.

"Actually"—she wiped away a stray tear—"there is something I've been wanting to tell you . . . something I haven't told anyone else yet, not even Carlo." This was a peace offering, an olive branch. "I think I might be, you know . . ." She laughed awkwardly, cheeks flushing again, bright pink. "Well, *you know*!"

"What?"

"Pregnant," she whispered.

My hand went limp. *"Really?"* Of course it had only ever been a matter of time, but for some reason I never thought it would happen so soon. "Oh, Angie!" I tried to swallow, but my mouth had gone dry. "That's wonderful news!"

"Shhhh!" She pressed her finger to her lips. "Like I said, I've not told anyone. I'm not really sure yet."

"How far gone are you?"

"Maybe a month . . . maybe six weeks. I can just feel it. I wake up queasy."

"Oh. Oh my goodness!" I said stupidly, remembering my own dreadful bouts of morning sickness.

Angela tilted her head forward so that her forehead rested on mine. "I always thought we'd have our children at the same time," she reminded me softly. "That we'd do it together."

"I'm not going anywhere. I'm here now," I managed.

"Promise?"

"Promise."

She grinned uncertainly. "It's good news, isn't it?"

Her happiness shone a blinding light on the one thing I didn't want to see.

"Yes. Very good news."

Later Angela saw me to the door, gave me a long hug good-bye. I was halfway down the street when I realized I'd left a glove behind. Walking back up on the porch, I heard voices in the front room.

"She's not a good example. Especially to a young woman."

"But she's my best friend. I've known her all my life!"

"You need to think not just about yourself but about Carlo, about his standing in this community. And about *this* family. You're a Menzi now. This is a respectable household."

There was a pause.

"She's my best friend," Angela said again. But she sounded uncertain, tired.

"Really? Where was she on your wedding day?"

No response.

"Some friendships you are meant to grow out of." Mrs. Menzi's voice softened. "You've done so well for yourself. You've come so far. Think of how far your children can go with the right opportunities."

Angela didn't say anything. Her silence was enough.

I couldn't bring myself to knock on the door again. Instead I walked without direction, my mind blank, like the fuzzy, distorted static sound on a radio between stations. After a while I stopped in front of the old North Church and sat on the steps outside. It was late now, the air thick with fog and cold damp. I lit a cigarette.

Across the street a couple of vagrants were rifling through the garbage cans in the alley, collecting anything that might be edible or warm. They were setting up camp for the night; a few wooden vegetable crates marked the edge of their territory.

I took a deep drag, exhaled.

When we were girls, Angela and I dreamed of growing up together, marrying, having families of our own, sharing baby clothes and recipes. We promised each other we'd live on the same street, next to one another.

Angela was doing exactly what we'd planned.

But I wasn't that person anymore. I didn't want to be different; I hadn't planned it but I was. I was never going to live in the house next door to Angela Menzi or be part of her world, no matter how hard I tried.

I flicked a bit of ash; it fizzled on the wet pavement.

Like the men sleeping in the shadows on newspaper across the street, I wasn't welcome.

I'd have to find somewhere else where I belonged.

Mr. Kessler was laughing.

I was in the back, washing up cups, when I heard him. At first I thought it was a mistake. Then it happened again.

I poked my head round the corner to see what was going on.

He was with a woman. They had their backs to me and were looking at the little German writing desk. I knew he was telling the Mozart story by the way he was moving his hands. Then she turned, and I recognized her profile under the black netting of her hat.

It was Diana Van der Laar.

There's nothing quite as unsettling as being surprised by someone who knows your worst secrets.

"That's a delightful story!" She touched Mr. Kessler's shoulder affectionately, as if he were her own grandfather. "I only wish I were furnishing a house!"

And he laughed again, all boyish charm.

Certain women have a knack with men, using the simple fact that they're female endlessly to their advantage. Diana was one of them. She wore her beauty and wit with the same easy confidence with which she wore her black veiled hat—at a jaunty, slightly dangerous angle.

Mr. Kessler saw me in the doorway. "Well, there she is!" He beamed as if I were suddenly a beloved child. "Miss Van der Laar has stopped by to thank you, May. She told me you handled the situation expertly the other night."

My heart stopped in my chest. "What situation?"

"Oh! Just how you dealt with Mother." Her laugh was as light as a fluttering trill, played on the top notes of a piano. "She can be very difficult, but you knew just how to handle her. In fact, Mother was so delighted, she's asked you to supper!"

I gave her a stiff smile. "You didn't need to come all this way. A telephone call would do."

"But of course! We're old friends, you see," she explained to Mr. Kessler, smiling sweetly.

"Really?" Mr. Kessler looked at me over the top of his glasses. "You never told me that!"

"I was wondering," she continued, "if I might walk you out, May. I mean, as it's nearly five."

"We don't close until five thirty."

"Oh, but I don't mind. I'll wait," she offered. "You have so many lovely things here."

"Oh, *please*! Don't keep your friend waiting!" Mr. Kessler insisted. "Get your coat! I'll see you tomorrow."

I knew he did mind. He normally greeted me at the door in the morning with his pocket watch in his hand. But now he waved me away like a proud father, pushing me out the door on a first date with a very eligible young man.

I got my coat and hat, seething beneath my smile. The other night was bad enough. I didn't want Diana pitching up whenever the mood struck her and ambushing me.

Once out on the street, my smile vanished. "What are you doing?"

"I just wanted to talk. And look." She gave me a naughty grin. "I got you out early! Isn't that a gas?"

"This is my *job*! Are you trying to get me fired?"

"Of course not!" She had the nerve to seem indignant. "How many times do I have to tell you? In fact, I'll buy something, I promise! Anything you like."

"I don't care if you buy anything! Didn't you listen to me? Didn't you hear anything I said the other night?"

"I like your hair."

I stopped and stared at her. "What?"

"Your hair. Do you know how long I was looking at you before I could place you?" She reached out and touched a gold curl. "How clever are you? You've really managed it."

"Managed what?"

"You've disappeared, haven't you? Managed to give them all the slip. You're a whole new person."

She said it with both admiration and envy, but implicit in her observation was the accusation of deceit.

I folded my arms tight across my chest. "I'm not trying to fool anyone."

We both knew I was lying. But she had the good grace not to show it.

"Of course not. You're just trying to survive."

I knew then she wasn't just humoring me; she really understood.

"Just have a drink with me," she persisted. "That's all I ask. I've come all this way."

"What? In your limousine?"

"Actually, I took the train. Come on, I know a place nearby." She slipped her arm through mine. She had a way of behaving as if we'd known each other for years that was both disconcerting and strangely flattering. "Only it would be so embarrassing for both of us if I had to beg. And I will, you know."

We walked for a block or so and then turned down a steep flight of stairs leading into a small place called Blake's. Located on the lower floor of one of the large brownstones, it had a hazy, smoky atmosphere, like a private gentlemen's club. The interior was surprisingly luxurious, with dark red leather booths, gleaming brass light fittings, and rich wood-paneled walls. A group of businessmen were seated at a large round table in the center of the room, dining on oysters, lobsters, and steak, talking loudly and drinking from teacups a liquid that certainly wasn't tea. It was the kind of place I'd never dream of going into because I couldn't afford a squeeze of lemon, let alone a meal. But for Diana, it was like popping into a coffee shop. As I followed her to the table, I tried to look vaguely bored, as if I'd had far too many oysters in my life and couldn't bear to see another.

The maître d' sat us in a booth, and a waiter came up.

Diana pulled off her gloves. "You can have anything you want. I mean, if you're hungry."

I was hungry. The rich savory smell of grilled meat made my mouth water. But I didn't plan on staying long. "Coffee, please."

The waiter brought us both coffees, and when he'd gone, Diana leaned in. "Look, I'm not trying to hound you, really I'm not. But what I said the other night was true. You're the only person who understands what it's like."

"So what are we going to do? Hook rugs and swap stories? We're out now. We're meant to forget about it and be normal."

"What if I can't forget? What if I don't want to be normal?"

I shrugged, dropped a fat sugar cube into my coffee.

"Actually"—she dug around in her handbag—"I have something for you."

She put it on the table between us, and my skin went cold.

It was Dr. Joseph's silver pen.

Seeing it again made me feel slightly queasy, as if I were standing on a high precipice, staring down into a long, dark abyss. I could almost hear the nib scratching against the paper. I picked it up. It was heavier than I thought it would be. His initials, "FAJ," were engraved on the side. "How did you get this?"

Diana took a dainty sip of coffee. "I took it upon myself to relieve Dr. Joseph of it."

"How?"

"He was stupid enough to turn his back on me. Let that be a lesson to you," she added.

I turned it over, feeling the weight of it in my hand. Every time Dr. Joseph had written something down, our fate hung in the balance.

"Why did you take it?"

"Why not?"

"Well, what if you'd been caught?"

"What if I had?" She didn't seem bothered. "What were they going to do? Lock me away?"

I thought of Mute Mary working away furiously at a never-ending supply of rugs; the view of the gardens from behind the barred windows; the line of empty wooden chairs, bolted to the floor in the hallway outside the treatment room. "They do worse things than lock people up, you know."

Her face clouded. "Yes, I know."

I was fascinated and frightened at the same time.

"So what am I supposed to do with it?"

"My God! It's like having coffee with Eliot Ness! Nothing. Do nothing with the damn thing!"

"Well"—I put more sugar into my coffee, just because I could—"I don't want it. You can keep it."

Sitting back, she eyed me steadily. "I see right through you, you know. You're a fraud, May. A complete and total fraud!"

"That's rich, coming from you!"

But she just shook her head. "Takes one to know one."

"I don't know what you're talking about."

"Sure you do. There's no need to lie to me. Remember, I was locked up too."

I wanted to laugh. "In your own private room!"

"Face it"—she nodded to the rest of the diners—"outside, we're just impostors—cardboard cutouts of the women we're meant to be. Putting on the right clothes, making all the right noises. But all the while, my head is like a ticking time bomb, ready to explode." She looked down at her neatly manicured hands, began picking at the smooth red nail varnish on her thumbnail. "But that's not the worst thing. The worst thing is, I can't tell anyone."

"Well, what am I meant to do about it?" I snapped.

She banged her fist on the table, so loud that even the businessmen shut up. "Stop pretending it didn't happen! Stop hiding!"

"I'm not!" I hissed, suddenly embarrassed.

"Let me ask you something: How many people even know where you were?"

I glowered into my coffee cup. "That's not the point. It's private."

"It's private because you *can't* say it out loud! There's a difference. No one wants to hear about your time in the cracker factory. Trust me. I know."

She was right. The trouble was, I didn't want to hear about it either. It was hard enough just managing the cardboard version of myself without trying to be real at the same time. If anything was likely to send me round the bend again, that was it.

I focused on Dr. Joseph's stolen silver pen. "I don't know what you want," I muttered.

"Neither do I," she admitted dully. Then catching the waiter's eye, she waved him over and held up her coffee cup. "Honestly, isn't there anything more interesting you could put in here?"

He came back with two new cups, filled with whiskey.

It had been a long time since I'd had a drink. I'd almost forgotten the power it had to smooth over the rough edges, iron out the wrinkles in my head. From the first sip, I could tell it was top-drawer stuff, spreading through my veins like rain on scorched desert earth. I eased back, took out a pack of cigarettes. "Do you want one?"

"Sure."

I lit them, passed one over.

She raised her cup, took a deep drag. "So, been to any good ceilidhs lately?"

"You never told me why you were locked up in the first place."

"I tried to hang myself." She exhaled. "It wasn't the first time. Apparently practice does not make perfect."

"Why did you do it?"

"Why indeed?" She picked a bit more varnish from her thumb-nail. "I told you: I'm not like the other girls."

"So what happened? Rope not long enough?"

"Wrong sort of knot, would you believe? I'll never make the sailing team now. Next time I'm going to turn on the engine of one of the cars in the garage, light a cigarette, and listen to the radio until I fade away."

"Next time?"

"A girl has to keep her options open."

I wasn't buying her bored sophisticate act. "At least you have a car, sister!"

"My goodness! You really *do* have a chip on your shoulder! Or I could try the old head-in-the-oven."

I rolled my eyes. "Don't you have staff? How are you going to get anywhere *near* an oven?"

"You're right!" She started to giggle. "I'd have to ask Cook to step around me!"

"They'd probably bring you a goddamn pillow for your head!" I laughed, choking on my own cigarette smoke.

She laughed too, so hard that she had tears in her eyes and her hat fell off onto the floor. The waiter rushed to pick it up, and she told him, "Keep the coffee coming."

"Look at us!" She sighed, wiping the tears from her cheeks. "We can't even kill ourselves!"

"There must be a correspondence course we can take."

She raised her teacup. "Welcome to the first official meeting of the No Way Out Club. Very exclusive membership—failed corpses only."

I felt better now, like I could breathe for the first time in weeks. "A girl just needs to let off steam every once in a while, that's all.

A little of what you fancy does you good." It was something my mother would say when she bought extra butter or real cream. Her vices were so innocent.

I gave the pen a sharp flick so that it spun round wildly on the table. "What are we going to do with this damn thing?"

"I know what to do." She picked up her cocktail napkin and gave it a big kiss in one corner, leaving a bright red lipstick mark. Then she wrote across it, "Thanks for the good time! By the way, you left this in the hotel room, sweetie! Xxxx, Poopsie."

"I'm going to mail that pen back to Mrs. Verdent with this." She grinned.

I was starting to like this girl.

"You know, I think I am hungry," I confessed.

"So am I." She signaled to the waiter. "What do you want? Steak? Lobster? Both?"

"Steak." I took another drag and gave her a look. "I swore off lobster after Nicky Howerd's yacht party."

Afterward, stuffed with steak and a little worse for wear, Diana hailed a cab. "Come on," she insisted, climbing in. "I'll drop you. It's too cold to take a trolley."

"It's out of your way. On the other side of town."

"Get in before I have him run you over," she threatened.

The cab driver wasn't thrilled about going into the North End. As we wound our way farther from Beacon Hill, the neighborhoods changed dramatically. Old houses were hacked up into tenements, spidery black fire escapes winding up the sides. The buildings were closer together, sagging and worn down from the weight of many lives piled on top of one another. The streets became crowded with people and noise, and the taxi had to swerve round several horse-drawn carts. Uncollected garbage gathered in abandoned lots. Soon makeshift fruit and vegetable stalls blocked every corner, and laundry blew in the wind between buildings like flags on a massive black ship, sailing nowhere. Children huddled together on the front stoops, playing marbles, or ran across the busy roads in packs, many without coats or hats, dragging their brothers and sisters, barely old enough to walk, behind them. Every once in a while a window would open on one of the upper floors, and a woman's dark head would pop out. She'd shout something in Italian, throw down a few coins tied in a cloth square, and one of the children would grab it before anyone else could and scurry off to perform an errand. It was all so familiar to me, I hardly noticed. But Diana stared out of the window like a tourist in a foreign land, transfixed.

"Where are we?" she asked.

"Still in Boston, would you believe?" I tried to play it off. But watching the expression on her face, I saw the place differently too. It seemed filthy and crowded, the way I imagined the streets of Tangiers or Morocco—not like an American city at all. "You're in the North End."

We passed the cigar maker, rolling thin cigars by the window of his tiny shop. Next door was the pawnshop, overflowing with secondhand radios, men's suits, musical instruments, lamps. On the corner was Contadino's grocery with its magnificently displayed fruit and vegetables, stacked in pyramids. As always men were crowded round the chestnut oven, smoking penny cigars and debating politics, while the children, inching between their legs, tried to squeeze closer to the warmth.

"What are all these people doing?" she wondered.

"What do you mean?"

"Well, why are they all outside?"

"The only place they can go is out. There's not enough room inside."

A sagging old Model T braked in front of us, blocking the road while a heavily pregnant woman and three small children climbed out of the back seat. Several bystanders came up to talk in Italian to the driver, who, deep in conversation, gave no sign of moving.

The taxi driver leaned on his horn and rolled down his window, shouting. Nobody paid any attention.

"I like it here," Diana said, settling back in her seat, pulling her fox stole tighter round her shoulders. "Everything's happening. Do you like it?"

"I'm used to it. But it's like living in a fishbowl—everyone knows everybody's business. What I wouldn't give someday to have a place of my own!" I tapped the driver on the shoulder. "I'll get out here," I told him.

As she opened the door, Diana grabbed my hand. "Same time tomorrow?"

I hesitated only a moment before nodding. "Sure."

We began to meet nearly every day after work. Going to the same restaurant, sitting in the same booth. Sometimes we only stayed for a coffee; other nights Diana treated us to a meal.

Soon Ma became suspicious. "Do you have an admirer, Maeve? You're not seeing Mickey Finn again, are you?"

"No, Ma. Anyway, Mickey's a decent man."

"I don't care if he's the pope, he's not good enough for you. You used to come back at all hours, smelling of liquor and beer!"

"I'm not seeing Mickey!"

"Then where do you go every night?"

"I have a friend, that's all. A girl I met in the shop."

Ma liked to be kept informed. "What type of person is she? Where is she from?"

"What difference does it make?"

"Who you spend time with makes a difference. You don't want to fall into a bad crowd."

She didn't realize *I* was the bad crowd.

Two days later Diana had a taxi waiting. "I've got something to show you," she said.

We drove through the downtown and across to Beacon Street, almost to Kenmore Square. We got out in front of a large new apartment building, Waverly Mansions.

"What are we doing here?" I asked.

"You'll see." She grinned.

A doorman in a smart red uniform held open the door. "Good afternoon, Miss Hanover."

"Good afternoon, Charles." She sashayed past him into a foyer with marble floors and shining brass elevators.

"Why is he calling you Hanover?" I whispered.

But she just winked. "Patience, my dear."

We went up to the fourth floor, where she took a key from her handbag and unlocked an apartment. The nameplate on the door read "Hanover" too.

Inside was a neat little one-bedroom flat with a small kitchen, a bay window, and a separate bathroom. Tastefully furnished with new furniture in bottle-green fabric, it was warm and snug, and both the kitchen and bathroom had modern plumbing, with pink tile walls and floors.

"Well? What do you think? Isn't it heaven?" Diana sighed.

I looked round. "You mean this is *yours?*"

"All mine! I got the idea from you, when you talked about a place of your own. I decided that I wanted one too. A hideaway that no one knows about. That is"—she smiled—"nobody but you!"

"You mean you just bought it? Out of the blue?"

"No, I'm renting. But isn't it wonderful? And the best part is—no one knows it exists, just you and me. We're completely free to do as we please!"

I felt the sharp, unpleasant sting of envy. Everything was so easy for her; no sooner did she have an idea than it effortlessly materialized. I tried to ignore it. "So, who's Hanover?"

"Oh!" She shrugged off her fur coat, tossing it onto the sofa. "That's me, of course! Miss Julie Hanover, secretary! That's what I told them. What do you think of my new identity?"

Was she making fun of me?

"You mean, a secretary like me?"

"That's where I got the idea! Isn't it a hoot? Can you imagine me typing letters and taking dictation? Hanover was the name of my first nanny. May I get you something to drink?" She was enjoying playing hostess.

"What do you have?"

"Well . . ." She opened the kitchen cupboard. It was empty. "Nothing!" She laughed. "Water?"

"Then I'll have water."

We sat down, and Diana opened her handbag again, taking out another key. "Here. All the members of the No Way Out Club get one." She pointed to a private telephone extension on a side table. "I'll give you the number. Just ring before you come, that's all I ask."

I stared at her. "Are you serious? My own key?"

I wasn't so jealous now.

"Why not?" She kicked her shoes off, propping her feet up on the coffee table. "I think it's an excellent idea. We'll have no one to answer to, no unwanted guests, and no house rules. We'll do anything we please!"

I dangled the key from my fingertips; like everything else in Waverly Mansions, it was freshly cut, shiny and new. Apparently there were no limits to what Diana could do or have. And now she was offering me the same immunity; the chance to do whatever I pleased, without limits or explanations.

"You know this is insane," I told her, slipping my shoes off too and curling my feet underneath me. "Your house is so enormous, you could have your own wing!"

"So? I need a place where I can breathe." She looked across, hurt. "You're not the only one who lives in a fishbowl. I thought you'd understand."

"I do. It's just, well, it's so beautiful. Filled with so many lovely things."

"Is it? Well, they're only things. Anyway, I like secrets. What people don't know can't be interfered with." She stretched out, closed her eyes. "The secret life is the only real life. Everything else is just a disguise."

A week later there was an article in the *Globe* announcing that socialite and budding philanthropist Diana Van der Laar was donating two extraordinarily rare Greek artifacts to the Art of the Ancient World wing of the Museum of Fine Arts. She was described as a "world-class beauty with a Continental upbringing" and a family with "extensive foreign interests" that meant her personal wealth was "beyond considerable." There was also a photograph of her, looking very pale, quite exquisite, and exceptionally bored.

Mr. Kessler was beside himself with excitement, waving the paper at me when I came into work.

"Look! It's your lovely friend!" He flapped it around like a flag. "There's a public reception on Thursday! We must go. I only wish we'd been mentioned by name." He looked at me eagerly. "Perhaps you could suggest she do that next time."

"Actually, we never discuss that sort of thing." I made it sound as if it were somehow beneath me. But in fact she'd never even mentioned the museum reception or her society-page feature. It was odd reading about her in the papers as if she was a stranger.

"Well, there's no harm in asking, is there?" He bustled past me. "Still, this is a real feather in our cap! It confirms our reputation as a respected international source. This reception could be a platform for even more high-profile sales!" Then, as an afterthought, he added, "You must be sure to wear something nice, Miss Fanning."

I shot him a dark look. "Don't I always?"

"We might get our picture in the evening edition." Then his face changed. "Oh dear! Cards!" He hurried into his office and began digging through his desk drawers. "We must order new business cards immediately! How could I have been so stupid as not to request them sooner?"

I trailed in behind him. "Don't worry. I'll do it now."

"I'm not worried, but it must be taken care of!" He was rushing around in such a state that he became short of breath.

"Are you all right, Mr. Kessler?"

"Asthma." He paused, gasping a little. "This fog doesn't help. I'll be fine."

I pulled out his chair. "You'd better sit down."

"No, I want to get to the printer. It is imperative that we have cards by Thursday."

"You don't look well. You should rest awhile."

He opened his bottom right-hand desk drawer and pulled out a little vial. "I have something here. Benzedrine. It's new." He broke off the end. "The doctor says it works immediately. Clears everything. Now don't fuss."

When he'd gone, I telephoned Diana at the apartment, but there was no answer. I even went so far as to ring her Cohasset home, only to be told that "Miss Van der Laar has a great many obligations this week and is presently indisposed. However, I will inform her that you called. Would you like to leave a name?"

"No, no, that's all right," I mumbled, feeling as if now I was the one chasing her.

Hanging up the phone, I gnawed at my thumbnail.

The Diana I knew was a hard-drinking, rebellious prankster who had practically blackmailed me into being her friend. But to the outside world she was an elegant, accomplished society beauty with admirable philanthropic ambitions.

The real Diana existed somewhere between these two extremes, in the private world of secrets she was so protective of, but I wasn't sure where.

I thought of my own past, layered with different versions of myself. The tricky part wasn't the roles you played, but which ones you ended up believing yourself.

That evening I met Ma downtown after work, and we went to the sale basement of Filene's to buy a dress for the reception. Normally, we would have chosen a pattern from the Butterwick pattern book and Ma would have made it herself. But time was tight. Filene's was a department store, but not nearly in the same class as Stearns. The basement was famous for its sales and plummeting prices. Here great crowds pillaged the sprawling underground rooms, roaming from bin to bin, rail to rail, trawling for bargains.

In the end, we couldn't find a suitable dress; Ma chose a very fine black wool crepe skirt instead, cut on the bias. It was a size too big and had been reduced even further because one of the seams was coming loose.

"It's the simplest thing in the world to repair," she said, folding it over her arm. "And the fabric has a lovely drape."

But for the first time in my life, I resented Filene's basement. Before, it had always been an exciting treat; who knew what you might find on the 75-percent-off table or hiding at the back of the store in the Last Chance section? But tonight everything looked common and shabby. I was tired of people pushing and shoving and digging around like animals. I wanted a new dress— something fashionable, delicate, and pretty. Not a funereal skirt, cheap and practical.

"It's too big. It makes me look like a giraffe in mourning," I told her.

"It's too big *now*," Ma corrected me. "But by the time I get through altering it, it will fit like a glove." She paused to riffle through a bin of last season's blouses. "This is an excellent piece. You can wear it three seasons out of four, at work or in the evening, and it flatters you, which is the most important thing."

I picked sullenly through a rack of women's dresses, all last season and the wrong size. I couldn't help thinking of what Diana would be wearing; of how Mr. Kessler referred to her as my "lovely friend," while I was an Amazon. "Mr. Kessler said he wanted me to wear something nice," I persisted. "They'll all be wearing day dresses and suits."

"This is *nice*! Besides, men don't know what they want until you give it them." She held up a red-and-white knit top with a small tear in the collar and then rejected it. "You'll look elegant. But I'll tell you what will look ridiculous"—she took my arm, pulling me toward the cash register—"is all five foot nine of you covered in some dreadful floral tablecloth. Only short women can even attempt florals, and in my opinion, even they should give them a wide berth. By the way, what do you think of turbans?"

I looked across at her. "I'm sorry? Did you say turbans?"

"That's right."

"Are you going to be a fortune-teller in a fair?"

She ignored my sarcasm. "I'm thinking of knitting a few for the Widow's Society stall. I thought I'd do something different this year."

Every year the Widow's Society of Boston hosted several charity events to raise money. This year they'd booked a stall outside of the North Church during the Declaration Day Parade. Obviously they'd decided to push themselves artistically.

"Yes, but *turbans?*" For a woman who'd just lectured on the dangers of floral fabrics, this was really quite an aesthetic leap.

"Well, we can't keep making socks and doilies every year. Apparently people want something new. And Frieda's started making aprons." (Here was the crux of the matter.) "Out of nowhere, she just announced it at the planning committee meeting, as if we'd known all along. And now Rosemarie says she's learned how to make little coin purses out of leather. You know she works at the shoe factory? Well, she's allowed all the scraps she wants."

Ma was nothing if not competitive. She wasn't going to allow Frieda or Rosemarie to get the better of her.

"I'm not going to be the only one making socks, I'll tell you that much! See, the idea is, you can pop it on when your hair is setting and you need to go to the shops, or when you're cleaning, or even as a hat in the evening. Movie stars wear them."

I doubted this very much. "Where did you get that idea?"

"I saw an article in *McCall's*. Apparently Gloria Swanson *lives* in them."

Ma had received aid from the Widow's Society when she first came to Boston to pay her first month's rent, and later on to tide her over just after I was born. Although she hated to receive any form of charity, she was proud now to be a contributor. Every year she made dozens of thick socks, woolly hats, delicate lace collars, handkerchiefs, and elaborate, painstaking doilies to raise money for other women in similar circumstances. She even served on the refreshments committee, baking dense, dry scones, which, I noticed, were inevitably the last to go on the sweets table.

"I mean, socks are socks! The Marine Society has socks coming out of their ears, and their stall is only across the street this year!" Ma was working herself up now. "I want to make something that will sell. Frieda's aprons are nothing special. The cotton's rough. But people seem to like the colors. And, of course she can make them so much faster, so it looks like she's been slaving away, night and day—"

"It's a grand idea." I cut her off. "I'm sure they'll sell like hotcakes."

"Do you think?" She suddenly seemed unsure of herself, a rare occurrence. "I know they're a risk, but sometimes you have to go out on a limb, don't you think?"

"Ma, isn't it time you graduated from the Widow's?"

She scowled at me. "What are you talking about? They would fall apart without me!"

"I mean, isn't it time you found another man?"

"Oh, honestly!" She wrinkled her nose like I was a bad smell. "I'm far too old for any of that nonsense!"

"No, you're not! That's what you always say. And it's not like men don't notice you. You know they do."

She pretended to be deeply interested in a table covered with long underwear. "I have too much to do. I'm busy."

We filed into the payment line behind a woman and her two small boys. The woman had a man's winter coat in one hand and her brawling boys by their coat collars with the other. I watched as she gave each of them a smack on the head. "I just don't want you to be lonely," I said.

"I have you. And when you're gone, I'll get a little dog. One of those ones with curly hair."

"A poodle?" I giggled.

"That's right. A poodle! I'd rather have a poodle over a man any day!" She opened her pocketbook, took out her purse.

"I can pay, Ma."

"No, I want to," she insisted. "You've done well to get this job. I'm proud of you. When you came back I was afraid you'd go back to Mickey and well, who knows what. But I'm glad to see you've grown up, Maeve, and are becoming quite the respectable young woman. Regardless of your hair," she added.

Ma never gave compliments if she could give advice. Now the warmth of the smile softening her features unnerved me. Even in tender moments, she raised her chin upward, as if she were being pulled forward into some tremendous future like the masthead of a ship.

I was unused to praise, wary of it, especially from her. It often proved only the harbinger of some future disappointment gathering on the horizon.

"Thank you," I mumbled, staring at the sales assistant's quick hands folding the skirt, putting it into a bag. "Thank you very much."

I couldn't bear to look upon the satisfaction in my mother's face any more than I could stand to stare too long at the sun.

The public reception at the Museum of Fine Arts, Boston, took place the next afternoon. Mr. Kessler closed the shop early, and we took a trolley to Forsyth Park, walking across Huntington Avenue to the imposing "new" building. The vast marble gallery in the Art of the Ancient World wing, with its high ceilings and polished wooden floors, was crowded with guests, journalists, and newspaper photographers, snapping pictures of well-known faces from Boston society.

I hadn't been to the museum since I was little. Ma had taken me once on a rare afternoon off. We'd strolled through the galleries crowded with visitors, unsure of what we were looking at or what it all meant. We got in the habit of pausing where others paused, eavesdropping on strangers' opinions, trying to see what others saw. But in the end we spent more time staring at the fashionable ladies than at the paintings or artifacts.

Now here I was again, still daunted by the opulence, history, and grandeur. This was the domain of better educated, more sophisticated people; those who, instead of going to see the latest Marx brothers comedy, chose to admire a Rembrandt or a Turner.

As we came up the stairs, I hesitated on the landing. In front of me congressmen were flirting with Broadway entertainers, sports celebrities and socialites charmed captains of industry, art critics argued with scholars, and venerable old dowagers lit the cigarettes of charming young playboys.

Mr. Kessler was never more comfortable than in an academic institution. Museums and galleries were his natural habitat. "What are you waiting for, Miss Fanning?" He shimmied sideways, working his way through the crowd. "Come along! We have business to conduct!"

I caught a glimpse of a long tea and coffee buffet through the crowds, laden with cakes and confections, set up in a smaller, adjoining mezzanine. In the center of the main gallery a stage area had been constructed next to a new display case, cloaked in heavy black cloth and guarded by two museum security men.

I searched for Diana. This was her moment, but she was nowhere to be seen. I spotted Mrs. Van der Laar standing next to the stage, however, holding an untouched cup of tea the way a bad actor clings to a prop. She was in a heated conversation with a woman whose sour expression advertised her irritation even from across the room. Both were scanning the faces in the crowd with nervous intensity. Exquisitely turned out, the other woman wore a very simple deep royal blue tea dress and an exceptional silver-fox-fur stole that perfectly offset her pale complexion and sterling hair. It was strange to see a woman whose face was so young with such a head of thick, snow-white hair; the effect was both surprising and chic. I must have been staring; at one point she turned and caught my eye. But her disdain was so obvious that I blushed and immediately looked away.

I found Mr. Kessler talking to a couple of rather eccentric-looking gentlemen who, I deduced, were other dealers. He had availed himself of coffee and a generous pile of free macaroons.

"It came through Istanbul," he was saying as I approached. "Of course we don't auction anything. We're not Bonhams or Christie's! But I knew who to call, and that was that. He bought them immediately!"

"Quite right," one of them agreed, jamming a chocolate éclair into his mouth.

"But this"—Mr. Kessler smiled, rolling his eyes heavenward—"this is beyond my wildest dreams! To see some of our pieces join a *national collection*!"

This clearly struck a raw nerve; terse smiles followed.

"In fact, I'd like to have a word with Mr. Kimberly." He cast round anxiously. "Have you seen him? I have some suggestions for the Anglo-Saxon exhibit."

One of the other dealers jerked his head. "He's over there. Behind the senator."

"Here." Mr. Kessler thrust his empty coffee cup and plate into my hands. "I must speak to him before the ceremony." And he was gone, plowing his way across the room.

"You must be Kessler's blonde," one of the men guessed.

"My name is May. With a *y*," I informed him, in what I hoped was a withering tone. I looked round for somewhere to leave the dishes but couldn't find one.

"Don't be cross!" The man laughed. "He's been bragging about you."

"I find that hard to believe." I tried to catch sight of Mr. Kessler. "Why does he want to talk to Mr. Kimberly so badly?"

"Why?" The man looked at me strangely. "Because he's the head curator, of course!"

I hadn't realized the man I'd met at the Van der Laars' was buying pieces for the collection he oversaw.

"Another bequest, another exhibit," the man went on. "Kimberly's done well for himself."

"He certainly has," the other man agreed, taking out his cigarette case. "He's got to be relieved about that."

"Why relieved?" I asked.

He offered me a cigarette, oblivious to the fact that I didn't have a free hand. "He was on sticky ground before. There was talk of a replacement. Perhaps temporarily redirecting funds. But now the Van der Laars have stepped in and saved the day—again."

"It's getting to be a habit." The first man helped himself to one of Mr. Kessler's uneaten macaroons. "Two years ago they donated an excellent Ancient Roman war helmet and spear." He nodded to a case at the far end of the gallery. "They're starting to make quite a name for themselves."

His companion exhaled. "Good on Kimberly, that's what I say. He's no fool. He's got a talent for digging out new money. And he isn't afraid to ask anyone to the table."

I was surprised by this last remark. "What do you mean?"

The two men exchanged a look.

"Well, the Van der Laars are rich, no one's disputing that. But no one's quite sure where the money comes from. Or where they come from, for that matter. Some say Denmark, others Germany. It's not old money, that's for sure. They're not really the kind of people one usually solicits for such public contributions."

"And that matters?" I couldn't help but feel slighted on Diana's behalf.

"They have no history. No cachet."

"Let's just say they benefit from the social connections," concluded the first man, popping the last bite of macaroon into his mouth. "But the quality of the pieces, the focus on classical Greece and Rome—you have to hand it to them, it's a very shrewd calculation on their part."

"No doubt guided by Kimberly," his friend pointed out.

"No doubt."

"Why calculated?" I wanted to know.

"The pieces that you donate are your calling card; they have your name on them, simple as that. Do you want to be associated with primitive aboriginal wood carvings or the Venus de Milo?"

"Classical collections guarantee good press. And impress all the right people."

"Unlike your African fertility statues." The man smiled. "Speaking of which, any news from Winshaw?"

I'd assumed Mr. Kessler had told them the pieces came through Mr. Winshaw, but now it appeared he hadn't mentioned it. I wondered if there was a reason for his subterfuge. "Ah, no. Not that I'm aware of."

"I'm not surprised," said the other man, glancing round for an ashtray.

"Did you know him?"

"Oh, yes! Everyone knows Winshaw!"

"Except me," I told them. "I was hired after he'd already gone abroad."

"That's probably a good thing!" They both laughed.

"Why?"

"Oh, he's a terrible womanizer!"

"Absolutely!" his friend agreed, flicking his ash into the remains of Mr. Kessler's coffee. "You couldn't leave him alone with your mother!"

"Oh." I'd expected him to be older, like Mr. Kessler. I pretended to be only casually interested. "So he is a handsome man?"

"He's attractive," the man with the cigarette said, "but it's more his personality than his looks. Who knows?" He shrugged. "He's been off the radar a long time now—probably pushed his luck too far. He could be dead, for all we know."

"No, he's not dead," the other one asserted. "Winshaw's too

wily for that. If he's gone missing, it's because he's not ready to be found yet."

Just then Mr. Kimberly stepped onto the stage, and the room went quiet.

"Ladies and gentlemen, I want to welcome you to what is surely one of the most remarkable acquisitions in the recent history of the Museum of Fine Arts, and certainly a milestone for the Art of the Ancient World collection. We are now well on our way to rivaling the classical collections of both the Metropolitan Museum of Art in New York and the Philadelphia Museum of Art with these exceptional examples of classical Greek vase painting, dating from 456 BC." The security guards removed the black cloth with a flourish, and there was an audible gasp, followed by applause. Mr. Kimberly raised his hands to silence the crowd. "And we owe our tremendous good fortune to the incredible foresight and devoted civic generosity of one charming young woman . . ." He turned, his eyes scanning the room, and everyone turned too, looking for the girl of the hour. But she wasn't there. Finally, in desperation, he gestured to Mrs. Van der Laar. "My friend and a great friend to our dear city, Mrs. Jacob Van der Laar."

Mrs. Van der Laar stepped onto the stage and gave him a stiff nod of the head. Mr. Kimberly took her hand, and a flurry of flashbulbs went off. She blinked, clearly irritated, as Kimberly pulled her in closer, posing for the cameras.

I took the opportunity to slip into the unattended tea room and finally dispose of the dishes. I was about to go back into the main gallery when I heard voices, whispering quietly. I followed them. Tucked into one of the marble alcoves, hidden from view, Diana was seated on a wooden bench next to a small boy, chatting pleasantly, perfectly oblivious that she was missing her own party.

She looked up as I approached. "Oh! May!" She seemed not just surprised but shocked to see me. "What are you doing here?"

"I'm here with Mr. Kessler. For work," I reminded her.

"Oh, yes." I could see her making the connection in her head, and she relaxed a little. But it struck me that she was so instinctively guarded.

"The question is: What are *you* doing?" I pointed out. "Aren't you meant to be, well, onstage?"

"When am I not onstage?" Then her face brightened as she indicated the little boy next to her. "Let me introduce you—this is Andrew. My most favorite cousin. We've just been amusing ourselves away from all the hubbub." She gave him a smile. "We like the museum but not really all these people, isn't that right?"

The boy shook his head solemnly. He couldn't have been more than eight or nine, dressed in a gray flannel private school uniform. He had dark hair, and round wire-rimmed glasses framed his large blue eyes. He looked past me rather than at me and was holding a cloth school bag tightly on his lap.

I held out my hand. "It's a pleasure to meet you."

Andrew nodded but kept his eyes down. I let my hand fall to my side.

"Say hello, darling," Diana prompted.

"Hello," he murmured.

"Is that your school bag?" I asked.

"Oh, he takes that everywhere, don't you?" she said brightly. "It's his explorer bag."

"Really?" I knelt down. "What have you got in there?"

He shrugged, edged away. "I don't know."

"He likes certain books, don't you? He takes them everywhere with him, just in case."

"What a brilliant idea!" I smiled. "I wish I'd thought of that. I have some favorite books too. What are yours?"

Andrew tilted his head, looking at me directly for the first time, out of the corner of his eye. Then slowly he opened the satchel and pulled out a large field guide, *Brentworth's Encyclopedia of Insects and Beetles*. Its cover was tattered, its pages clearly well thumbed. He opened it up to a life-size drawing of a gigantic horned black beetle. "This is one of my books. It's got many magnificent color illustrations," he said.

"Yes, it has!" I agreed. "What a beautiful big beetle!"

"It's a Hercules beetle. The Hercules beetle is the most famous and largest of the rhinoceros beetles. It is native to the rain forests of Central America, South America, and the Lesser Antilles. The beetle has also been observed as far north as southern Veracruz in Mexico."

It was as if he were reciting from the book word for word. "So it is. How clever you are!"

"Yes, he's a very clever boy." Diana smoothed his hair down affectionately. "You can ask him absolutely anything about insects, and he can tell you exactly what you need to know."

"That's handy. Will you show me your favorite?"

Andrew's brow wrinkled in concern. "I don't have a favorite. I like them all equally. It would be wrong to choose one over the other." There was a thin edge of panic in his voice.

"Of course," I said quickly. "That's an excellent attitude to take. But you might find one or two especially interesting."

Pausing, he considered carefully. Then, flipping through the pages, he landed on another color illustration. "This is a giraffe weevil from Madagascar. It's called that because of its . . ."

"Oh, for God's sake, will you put that stupid book away!" The woman with the silver-white hair was standing over us, arms crossed. She spoke in the same clipped accent as Mrs. Van der Laar. "I told you, I don't want you dragging that thing all over town with you anymore!"

Startled, Andrew let the book slide off his lap and fall to the floor. Diana quickly picked it up and put it back into his bag.

"It's my fault, I'm afraid." I stood up. "I asked him to show me a few pictures."

But she ignored me, addressing Diana instead. "Where have you been? Your mother had to make the presentation herself!" Her eyes narrowed. "Have you been here, hiding, this whole time?"

Diana seemed to recede, shrinking back from her. I'd never seen her defer to anyone before, not even in the hospital. "I'm sorry. I didn't realize the time. We just wanted to find somewhere quiet, that's all. The echo hurts his ears."

"*Echo?* What echo?"

"The echo of all the voices, off the marble walls," she explained weakly.

"Don't be ridiculous! You're always coddling him. How you can throw away every single opportunity that's given you is beyond me! You've ruined it—the entire thing!" She thrust her hand out, speaking to Andrew. "Come on now. Cousin Didi has been very foolish and selfish. I think it's time you went back to boarding school, don't you?"

"No, Elsa!" Diana sprang to her feet. "I'm sorry! I didn't mean it!"

"Then you should've thought of that earlier." She snapped her fingers impatiently at the boy. "Come on!"

Clutching his bag, Andrew reluctantly took her hand, and they walked back into the main gallery.

Crestfallen, Diana stared after them.

"Who's that?" I asked.

"Elsa. My aunt."

"Your aunt?" She seemed too young to be the sister of Mrs. Van der Laar.

"She's my mother's stepsister," she explained.

"Her hair is so—"

"I know. It's mad, isn't it? She had a very high fever when she was younger, and it changed overnight." Diana leaned her head against the portico. "I'm in it now. Though if they had it their way, I'd be cutting ribbons and giving speeches all over Boston."

"Well, why does it have to be you? As long as it remains in the family, what difference does it make?"

"Oh, May! How else are they going to marry me off? I wasn't a debutante and I'm not a socialite and I don't have my picture in the right sorts of magazines and in fact, if anyone did know anything about me, they'd discover that I'm mad as a box of frogs! The only thing left for me is to become a patron of the arts!"

I wasn't sure what to say. Here was a problem I would never have to face.

"Did you see the speech?" She looked quite worried now. "Did my mother really bungle it?"

"No. It only lasted a few minutes. I think it was universally agreed that everyone was exceptional and wildly generous and that was it. Why?"

"Elsa can be a cow. And when she's in a bad mood, she takes it out on Andrew." She peered into the crowded room. "Poor little mite!"

Mrs. Van der Laar and Elsa were talking to Mr. Kimberly with Andrew wedged between them, staring down at his shoes. Elsa had her hand anchored on Andrew's shoulder; I could practically feel her manicured nails digging into his flesh.

Now that the ceremony was over, the tea room began to fill again. I tried to cheer her up.

"Have you seen the display yet?" I asked. "Aren't you even a little curious to see your name on a brass plaque?"

"After all, it's a lovely name, Diana," said a man behind us.

We both turned.

Very thin and gangly, with a narrow pale face and round soulful eyes, he smiled shyly, his chin sloping straight into his long neck at such an angle that he looked a bit like a turkey. He peered at Diana with a look of impish irreverence. "The girl who didn't show," he crowned her. "Only you could throw a party and not come!"

Instantly her charm ignited.

"Hello, Charlie." She held out her hand. "Did you miss me?"

"We all did! You're the only reason I came. Your first brass plaque—shouldn't we celebrate?"

"Maybe another time." She lowered her voice to a naughty whisper. "Now you wouldn't spank me, would you, Charlie, if I didn't want to do what I was told?"

He flushed bright pink and swallowed hard. "I don't expect I'd ever presume to tell you what to do, Diana." He pressed her fingers to his thin lips before walking away.

I stared at her in astonishment. "Who was that?"

"Mr. Charles Henry Peabody, the third. Of the Massachusetts Peabodys."

My face must have given me away.

"Ever heard of the Peabody Museum of Natural History?" she prompted. "Or the Peabody Institute? Or perhaps the Peabody Academy of Science? And then of course, there's always the family banking business, the Peabody Hotel, and the city of Peabody, Massachusetts, if that doesn't ring a bell!"

"Oh!" I turned again to see where he'd gone. "You mean Ichabod Crane there owns half of Massachusetts?"

"Precisely."

"Diana!" Someone else called from across the room. "I say, Diana!"

A rather squat man was pushing his way through the crowd toward us. He was wearing a double-breasted navy jacket with a private yachting club emblem on the breast pocket and a rather garish foulard of red-and-gold silk instead of a tie.

"Oh, dear!" She sighed. "Brace yourself." Her face crinkled into an involuntary smile. "It's Nicky Howerd."

"Diana!" Nicky arrived panting from the effort of negotiating the short stretch from the pastry table to us. Another triumph of inbreeding, he was short with a strange egg-shaped torso that made his trousers balloon out below his waist. He looked younger than his years, with ruddy round cheeks and colorless slicked-back hair. He beamed at Diana, jamming his hands into his pockets and rocking back on his heels, which struck me as a Humpty-Dumpty scenario in the making. "Well, fancy seeing you here!"

Diana smiled weakly. "Where else would I be, Nicky?"

"Oh, oh yes, of course!" He jerked a shoulder toward me. "And who's your pretty friend here? Aren't you going to introduce us?"

She caught my eye. "But Nicky"—she frowned innocently—"you already know May."

His face went blank.

"She was on your boat last summer." She smiled sweetly. "The lobster bake? We all had such a good time, didn't we?"

"I can't recall when I've laughed harder," I chimed in.

Nicky's eyes grew round with panic. He forced a smile.

Diana gave him a friendly poke in the chest. "Don't tell me you can't remember! *Really?* You honestly don't remember May Fanning?"

I poked him too. "From Albany?"

The last thing Nicky had was a poker face. "Why, yes!" He nodded. "Yes, I seem to recall . . ."

"To be honest," I whispered, leaning in, "my hair was a different color then."

"Oh!" Relief washed across his face. "Oh, yes! *Now* I remember! Of course!" He held out his hand. "It's good to see you again!"

I shook it. "Always a pleasure."

He turned back to Diana. "I hear your brother's back in town. Visiting from the Dark Continent, is that right?"

"Yes. I'm afraid it's true."

"We must put something in the diary." He nodded to me too. "For all of us! What do you think, Diana? It's been months since we've gone out, and I'm pretty sure you still owe me a dance!"

She smiled, linked her arm through mine. "It's getting late, Nicky. And I'd better go and at least look at this damn display before I leave."

"So I'll give you a ring, then, shall I?"

"Yes, you give me a ring, Nicky."

"And you'll answer this time?"

"I think you've lost weight, haven't you?" She pushed me into the other room. "So good to see you. Don't have too many petits fours!"

Dear Miss Fanning,

I've been to many of the places on the map in my office; they're all extraordinary, filled with mystery and beauty but also plenty of ordinary people too, living life with all the cares and concerns that we have back home. Next to the Pyramids at Giza are tribes of people living in shacks and tents, women baking bread and scolding children, men haggling over livestock. So it's very different and exactly the same. And I believe they all worry about being good, even though they pray to different gods in different languages, some of whom I hope listen.

I search this world for rare artifacts so that I, and others, might wonder at their age, craftsmanship, and most of all authenticity— the truth of the thing. I may be sentimental, but I believe there's value in what's real, even if it's been very much battered by time and fate, even if, when it's discovered, it's only a fragment of what it once was. No matter how common the object, be it a clay spoon or a jeweled ceremonial necklace, it has purpose and integrity. Can't the same be true of our lives, no matter how mundane?

Look after Kessler (did he tell you I was missing? Perhaps I'm simply not in the habit of asking for permission to go where I want to go) and try not to think too much or too hard. Philosophy is like smoke—it fills the air, blinds us yet vanishes quickly, leaving nothing behind. Action is key; in motion, we are all of us magnificent.

So there you have it. If the world were good, Miss Fanning, it wouldn't be interesting. But in my experience, when it's real, it's very interesting indeed.

Sincerely,

B. Winshaw

The letter arrived on a wet gray morning in late March. I read it standing in Mr. Winshaw's office. Then, closing the door, I reread it again, several times.

I'd sent the wrong letter.

But he'd responded.

He didn't write like a Lothario; he sounded intelligent, curiously romantic.

No matter how common the object, it has value and integrity.

For someone who discounted philosophy, he had quite a poetic point of view. And he'd taken me seriously; my foolish little rant about being good had found a thoughtful and attentive audience in a stranger who was thousands of miles away.

When Mr. Kessler asked what I was doing, I folded the letter quickly and hid it in my pocket. Just being able to take it out and read it anytime I wanted gave me an excited, euphoric feeling, quite out of proportion. And since Mr. Winshaw hadn't asked directly for me to convey anything to Mr. Kessler, I figured I had every right to keep it to myself.

In fact, I was already composing my response in my head.

Dear Mr. Winshaw,

Well, it's nice to know you're alive. And you'll be pleased to hear that we've received your latest shipment (are those your old vanity cases?). Now the Greek vase and plate are part of the permanent collection of the Boston Museum of Fine Arts so not a bad day's work, I suppose.

Mr. Kessler is fine by the way (thank you for asking). He practically levitated with pride at the public reception and had to be physically restrained from making a speech. Luckily he's easily distracted by macaroons. I don't know where you pick up these baubles, but you certainly do know how to make an old man very happy.

As for the business of being real and the inherent integrity of clay spoons, I would ask you this: If the mundane in Boston is as worthy as the fragments of ancient Babylon, why is it that you travel so far and so often? Why dig in the dirt of a foreign land to discover what you already have at home?

You cannot fool me, Mr. Winshaw. Either you are a criminal on the run from the police or Boston is not to be confused with the cradle of civilization, no matter what the Daughters of the American Revolution would have us believe. No one ties themselves to the mast of a ship heading for Boston Harbor, because the mermaids do not sing here.

And yet I think we all go mad with longing for their wayward song.

Sincerely,
May Fanning

After the museum event was over, Diana and I began to spend more and more time together. Whether her social obligations had diminished or she was simply happy to ignore them was less clear. But she shifted into an almost frantic devil-may-care pursuit of excitement and pleasure. We took to meeting regularly in the apartment after work. She kept a store of proper liquor sequestered from her family's seemingly endless supply and very occasionally even remembered to stock something to eat, but best of all there was privacy. We'd drink, smoke, listen to the radio, and venture out on what Diana called "hazards." These involved dares, designed by Diana to keep us from getting too bored.

After a long day, I was happy to stay put, but Diana needed constant stimulation. "I'm starting to go numb," she'd say. "Let's liven things up a bit. I feel as if I'm disappearing into the sofa!" Pulling me up again moments after I'd kicked off my shoes, she'd drag me to the door. "Come on, let's get out of here!"

Her favorite dare was "I Can't Believe It's You," a game that involved going to a crowded place like the train station or a hotel lobby where we would choose a complete stranger that the other would have to pretend to know. I was always terrible at it, hesitant and awkward. More than once I ended up chasing people down the train platform. But Diana never failed to give a star performance, running up and throwing her arms around them, covering them with kisses and tears of joy. Baffled, delighted, occasionally even pretending to know her too, they invariably yielded to her unique combination of plausibility, charm, and conviction. She always won. Extra points were awarded if you managed to begin each round with the phrase, "I can't believe it's *you*!"

Other times she liked to sit at a drugstore counter and spin stories to anyone who would listen, a pastime she dubbed "The Big Good-bye." She'd pretend that she and I were on our way to a nunnery and desperate to be kissed one last time, or that we were female aviators about to embark on a dangerous transatlantic flight, or sometimes fledgling actresses headed to Hollywood for a screen test. While I struggled to be convincing, she was both inventive and often touchingly believable. By the time we left, people were lining up to shake our hands and wish us luck, sometimes even asking for our autographs. She called it "practice."

"Think of all the lies you have to tell in life," she used to say.

Diana could fall into almost any character with such ease, I sometimes wondered if she'd forgotten it was all fiction. But then, when we were outside, she'd hang on to my arm and laugh until tears rolled down her face. "They're so gullible! My God, May! They'll be looking for our names in the papers for *weeks*!"

Being with her was like regressing into a very privileged, expensive childhood where the games were more dangerous but no less frivolous. I had the dizzying if slightly unnerving sense with Diana that anything was possible; we might be nuns or actresses, socialites or scoundrels; any folly might be carried by sheer audacity. Her only rule was that we never invite anyone from her own set to the apartment. "Our little secret," she'd say. "We don't want anyone getting wind of it and ruining things."

"What does it matter?" I was a little irritated that we weren't going anywhere more glamorous when she obviously had cachet at any number of fashionable venues.

But Diana was adamant. "You don't understand. They can't be trusted."

"With what?"

She didn't answer, but in her typical eccentric fashion ferreted out Dr. Joseph's silver pen from my handbag and put it over the transom of the front door. "There! That will protect us. The No Way Out Club is for members only!"

That didn't mean we were always alone.

Sometimes I'd arrive to find the flat filled with assorted strays she'd picked up that afternoon—deliverymen, waitresses, or taxi drivers—guzzling all the liquor, eating sandwiches, and dancing. "Come in! We're having a party!" she'd shout over the music. "Ernie here has just bought his own cab! Isn't that marvelous?"

Or there were evenings when I'd find her alone, lying on top of the bed, still in her coat, listless and mute.

"Are you all right?"

No response.

"Talk to me, Di."

But she'd be far away, behind a veil of slow blinking silence.

"Come on now. Sit up." I'd take off her shoes and coat, get her a drink. We'd sit side by side, under the covers, listening to the radio.

She'd lean her head on my shoulder. "You do love me, don't you?"

"Sure."

"No matter what?"

"No matter what."

"Even if I'm not the way you think I am?"

"Especially if you're not the way I think you are."

Occasionally she wanted to talk about the past. "Why did you take the razors into the bathroom, May?"

These were my least favorite conversations.

"I guess I forgot I'd already shaved that morning."

But she had a habit of digging until she got right underneath the skin. "Have you ever done anything you regret—something you can't fix no matter how hard you try?" She'd curl in closer. I could smell the warmth of her hair, the sweetness of her perfume. "Do you believe in providence? That God has already chosen our lives for us?"

I thought of the safety pin in my coat pocket, the one I never took out. As much as I teased Ma about her superstitions, I couldn't quite bring myself to live without them.

"I believe in luck," I told her. "And fate. And God. And free will. But nothing so intractable as providence. If I did, I'd stay in the bathroom with the razor blades. You have to have hope."

Then one day I came back from the post office to find Mr. Kessler talking to a customer. The man was leaning against the counter, chatting in a low voice, hands in the pockets of his immaculately tailored suit. His hat was cocked just so, obscuring his right eye. He had the same dangerous ease I'd seen so many times in the clandestine nightclubs and speakeasies of New York City and found so attractive; the way certain men had of sidling up to a bar and taking over a room. It was an absolute confidence that couldn't be mimicked or taught.

Then Mr. Kessler waved me over. "May, there's someone here to see you."

The man turned.

It was Mr. Van der Laar.

"Good afternoon." He took his hat off, and I was struck again by how similar he was to Diana, the unusual pale blue eyes and dark hair; only there was something about the way he looked at me, a directness in his gaze, that unsettled me. "I hope you don't mind me calling in. I seem to remember that you're a friend of Diana's, aren't you?"

"Is she all right?" I asked.

It came out rather chilly. I didn't trust him being here, although I wasn't quite sure why.

"Couldn't be better. Actually"—a single lopsided dimple appeared in the center of his left cheek—"I was in this part of town and thought I'd stop by, see if I could convince you to come for a drink with us tonight. We're meeting some friends, and I thought you might want to join us."

"Really? Diana never mentioned it."

"Well, she doesn't know yet. I want to surprise her."

This struck me as odd. "Why?"

He flashed a smile in Mr. Kessler's direction, caught his eye.

Taking the hint, Mr. Kessler slipped into the back office.

I didn't like being alone with him. Taking my coat off, I moved behind the counter, putting some distance between us.

"I suppose I'm a typical big brother, a little overprotective perhaps, but I like to know who her friends are. And after all, you've known her awhile, haven't you?"

"Not that long."

He tilted his head to one side. "I thought you knew her in New York, didn't you?" He said the words so lightly that the hairs on the back of my neck stood up. "From before?"

My chest tightened. Was he referring to the hospital?

I ignored his question. "So you're here to check me out, is that it? Go on, then." I twirled round so he could take a good look. "What do you think? Will I do?"

"You're making fun of me. And maybe I deserve it," he admitted. "But you see, Diana's a very sensitive girl. She pretends to be sophisticated, but actually she's surprisingly naive. I live abroad most of the time, and I'm afraid I've failed to look after her the way I should."

"Does she need looking after?"

"More than you know. There have been some unsuitable companions in the past, people who've tried to take advantage of her."

He seemed determined to offend me.

"And you think I might be one of them?"

He held up his hands, laughed. "You're too quick to judge me! Actually, when she mentioned you again, I was pleased."

"What did she say?" The question came out before I could stop it.

He paused a little before saying, "Only that you'd been a good friend. Someone she could talk to. And she needs a friend, Miss Fanning. Someone who can be trusted by all of us."

Our friendship was fast becoming public property, to be endorsed or discouraged as he saw fit.

"There's a little place I know called the Friday Club," he went on. "On Massachusetts Avenue. Members only. Have you been?"

I shook my head.

"Well, then, why don't you let me treat you? They have a heck of a band! And who knows? I might even ask you to dance."

It felt more like a summons than an invitation.

"I don't know. I might be busy leading small children astray."

"How does one get an appointment?" He grinned, and again the rogue dimple appeared. "Look, I'm sorry if we got off on the wrong foot. What do you say, Miss Fanning? Will you do us the honor?"

For all the time we spent together, Diana had never invited me to meet any of her other friends. And the offer to dine with her family had quickly fallen by the wayside. I wasn't sure if that was because she didn't want to put me in the position of lying or because she didn't think I'd fit in—something that had occurred to me before, but that I avoided thinking about.

It was as if he could read my thoughts.

"It's strange, isn't it? The way Diana keeps people all to herself."

"What do you mean?"

He gave me a quizzical look. "You're not the first, you know. She's never been very good at sharing. She always likes to keep one special friend all for herself. I wonder what she's hiding—you or us."

I didn't like the way he talked about her. Or me.

"I'm sure she doesn't care one way or the other," I said.

"You're probably right. So, shall I have a car collect you? What's your address?"

"I'll, uh . . . no . . ." My mind raced. I hadn't meant to agree, but part of me was curious. "I'll meet you there. What end of Massachusetts?"

"Near the Regent Theatre. We'll see you out front at nine."

He put his hat back on, heading for the door. Then suddenly he stopped and, as an afterthought, pointed to the glass display case. "Actually, I thought I might pick something up. You don't still happen to have that black stone ring you were wearing when we met?"

I was tempted to lie, to say it was already sold. But of course when I'd shown it to Mr. Kessler he'd insisted in displaying it right in the center of the case that Mr. Van der Laar had just been leaning on. In fact, he'd probably already seen it. "Yes, of course. It's Roman, made from agate and gold." I took it out, handed it to him. "Possibly third century AD."

"One of the three Fates—isn't that what you said?" He slid it onto his finger. The ring seemed made for him, dominating his hand. "What do you think?"

"It suits you," I had to admit.

"I suppose it's a good-luck charm."

"Well, fate can mean a lot of things—from tragedy to triumph."

"I don't believe in luck anyway. I prefer to make my own destiny. So, do you think I should buy it?"

I had yet to make a significant sale on my own. But it was also my favorite thing in the whole shop. I could feel him watching, waiting for my response.

"I leave that choice entirely in your self-determining hands," I said.

Pulling out his wallet, he counted out a stack of crisp twenty-dollar bills. It was as easy as that—he wanted it, he got it.

"You know, I'll think of you now every time I wear it." It was such an odd thing to say, especially as he'd been so insulting before. "Good afternoon, Miss Fanning. I look forward to our date." He tipped his hat. The gold of the ring caught the afternoon light as he pushed open the door.

I looked down at the space where the ring had been, at the

slight indentation left in the green velvet. Had he sensed it was my favorite?

What did he mean when he said I wasn't the first?

Mr. Kessler came out again from his office and removed the cash from the register, counting it out and nodding with approval. "I knew you'd be good at selling."

I gnawed at my thumbnail. "What about commission, Mr. Kessler?"

He folded the money, put it into his breast pocket. "Let's not get ahead of yourself, Miss Fanning."

I was in the kitchen in my stockings and robe, eating a plate of scrambled eggs while ironing my black crepe skirt, when Ma came home.

She stood in the doorway, unbuttoning her coat. "What's going on?"

"I'm going out," I said, swallowing another forkful of eggs.

"Where?" She unpinned her hat. "With whom?'

"You don't know them. I've only just met them myself. Ouch!" I managed to burn the tip of my finger. "Damn it!"

"Here, let me do that. You'll ruin that skirt. How many times do I have to tell you? You must protect the fabric!" She hung up her coat and took over ironing while I finished my eggs. She smoothed the seam flat before unfolding a handkerchief over the wool crepe. "Whoever it is, I certainly hope they're worth all this fuss! Better not be Mickey."

I couldn't resist showing off a bit. "Actually, it's Diana Van der Laar and her brother. They've asked me to go to a private club with them."

"Van der Laar?" She stopped ironing. "You mean, *the* Van der Laars?"

For once, I'd managed to impress her. "They're regular customers at the shop. Why?" I played it up to the full. "Have you heard of them?"

"Of course! *Everyone* knows them! They're one of the wealthiest families in the city!" She was obviously struggling to fit us all on the same page. "How did you meet them?"

"Mrs. Van der Laar bought a piece from the shop, and Mr. Kessler asked me to deliver it to their home."

"You mean the big house? By the sea?"

"That's the one." I put my plate in the sink. "The daughter, Diana, well, she just took a liking to me. I saw her again at the Museum of Fine Arts, and now they want me to go to a club with them on Massachusetts Avenue."

Her eyes were as wide as a nun's in a brothel. "But why didn't you tell me you knew the Van der Laars?"

"I *am*, Ma!"

"But we have so much to do!" she fussed. "What time is it?"

"*We?*"

She held up the skirt, which of course hung flawlessly. "The Van der Laars are extremely well connected. This is an opportunity, Maeve! A once-in-a-lifetime chance! If you're friendly and charming, who knows where you might end up? But you must be careful," she warned. "If you act carelessly or drink too much or speak out of turn . . ." She stopped; the threat of failure hung in the air, potent enough to leave unsaid.

I'd never seen her quite so worked up.

"I know how to behave, Ma. I'll be fine."

But she just nodded mechanically, her mind already racing

ahead. "Keep the conversation light and gay, understand? Avoid anything to do with politics or money or religion. . . . Laugh at everything, but not too much, mind you, just enough to show you're good company. Act interested, no matter what the topic is." She stopped, her brow furrowing. "I only wish it wasn't a nightclub," she fretted. "A nightclub is so . . . *informal*!"

She always had a talent for transforming good news into some unforeseen obstacle.

"If it were any more formal, I wouldn't have anything to wear," I pointed out.

This backfired terribly. She turned on me with a face like the Lady of Shalott. "Actually, what *are* you going to wear?"

"Well, the red knit top . . ."

"Oh, no!" She shook her head emphatically. "No, that won't do at all! They'll be in gowns, Maeve! If only I'd known sooner!"

Her worry was contagious. Now I was starting to panic too.

"What should I do?"

She thought a moment. "Come with me."

I followed her into the bedroom. She opened the closet. Inside hung an untouched white blouse, bought two years ago to go with the gray suit and never worn. It was made from a soft semi-sheer rayon fabric that fluttered slightly when it moved. "Hand me my shears."

I took the shears from the sewing basket by her bed. "What are you doing?"

She laid the blouse flat on the floor and began to cut. Off came the sleeves and then the collar.

"Ma! You can't! You're ruining it!"

She paid no attention. "Thread the needle, Maeve."

Folding the sleeves carefully, she placed them on the dresser, to be salvaged at a later date. "I'll turn them under and make cap sleeves. Pass me the pins. And we can give it a mandarin collar, which is very fashionable now. In the dark the fabric will look like silk, and no one will know the difference." She flashed me a smile. "Maybe a nightclub isn't so bad after all!"

She was in her element, solving problems, working at speed. She'd never been my ally before, for getting ready for a date. With Mickey, there was only opposition and dismay.

Now I watched as she deftly transformed the blouse, her fingers quick and skilled with the delicate material. She added a thin trim of black cord around the neckline from a supply of fabric scraps she'd collected from work and kept in her sewing basket. The result was simple but effective.

I put it on, along with the black skirt, and stood in front of the mirror. Ma took a navy blue satin sash from another dress that had long been remodeled and fixed it to my waist. The result was dramatic; it almost looked like a real store-bought gown.

"It's beautiful." I was touched, grateful and guilty at the same time. She'd never even worn the blouse. "Very stylish."

"Maeve! Your shoes!" She pointed to my feet. There was always some fresh hurdle. The black pumps that were perfectly fine during the day now looked worn and faded from too much wear in the snow and rain. "You'll have to borrow mine."

Her shoes were almost a whole size too big for me, but she was religious about wearing overshoes in the winter and carrying her "good shoes" to work with her in a separate net bag. So we stuffed the toes with newspaper and I made do.

Rummaging through her sewing basket again, she pulled out the discarded black net from my damaged hat. Then she carefully snipped the wide grosgrain ribbon from her own winter cloche and tacked the net to it. We fixed the ribbon in my hair so that the net fell just over my eyes.

"It gives you an air of mystery." She stood back, satisfied. "It's not just what you wear, but how you wear it. Think of simplicity as a choice. A statement."

Then to top it all off, she took out her pocketbook and handed me a five-dollar bill—almost half the weekly food budget. "Here."

"No." I put my hand over hers. "I don't need it."

But she insisted. "I don't want you to be beholden, Maeve. These people won't take you seriously otherwise. Rich people are far meaner with their money. I don't know why, but it's true. And you'll need to take a cab back at the end of the evening. On your own." She fixed me with a serious look. "Do you understand?"

I did. She didn't want anyone seeing where we lived. Tonight was a magic act; it depended on misdirection and sleight of hand if the illusion were to be pulled off.

"Be on your best behavior." She adjusted the sash a little, smoothing it flat. "Polite, charming, and a little aloof. Better to be vague than obvious. If you don't know something, just change the subject."

"I'll be fine," I said for the hundredth time.

All her ambitions massed together in her eyes like a great army of hopes, chafing for opportunity and success.

"And above all, act like a lady. As you do, so you will become."

I was late and out of breath from running by the time I got to the Regent Theatre. Twice my mother's shoe had fallen off, and I'd had to go back and get it, hopping on one foot so as not to run my stocking. Now a packed house was letting out from the seven-thirty show, people pouring out onto the pavement. Standing alone by the balcony exit, jostled by the crowd, I suddenly felt ridiculous, over- and underdressed at the same time. James and Diana were nowhere to be seen. The wind was icy, and I shivered in my plain wool day coat, struggling to keep the makeshift hat Ma had made from blowing away. This was a mistake. I'd rather be one of the people coming out from the film. There was still time to leave, to catch the trolley back home and spend the evening listening to the radio instead.

Then a hand grabbed my elbow. "Surprise!"

It was Diana, wrapped head to toe in a downy white fox fur cape. But she looked odd—her eyes wild, dilated and glassy. "We're going to have such fun tonight, aren't we?" She threw her arms round my neck, and I was enveloped in an embrace of thick, soft fur. It smelled of her perfume, a rich, heady mix of jasmine, orange blossom, and musk. "James cannot let me be," she whispered in my ear. "Not for a minute! Apparently he thinks I'm so much more interesting than I really am!" And she giggled hysterically.

By the time she let go, a loud crowd of six or eight people were clustered around us. James had his arm around a girl in a clingy silver gown and black mink coat. She was laughing and calling him "Jimmy" in the trademark flat-voweled accent of the Boston Brahmins. With her shingled hair, dark-red bee-stung pout, and gravity-defying figure, it was difficult not to stare at her. "This is Smitty," James said, introducing her to me.

"*He* calls me Smitty," she corrected, offering her hand as if she expected it to be kissed. "But my name's Charlotte. You can call me Lotte." Then she looked up at him. "Where are we going, Jimmy?"

"The Friday Club."

"Oh, goody! I lost my shoes there last week!" And she and Diana started giggling again, so hard that Diana lost her balance and I had to hold her up.

"What's going on?" I whispered. Clearly the party had already begun elsewhere and they were all well under way—everyone except me. "Have you been drinking?"

"Oh, better than that!" She stumbled, stepped on my foot, righted herself again. "Fairy dust, from Harlem! I'd give you some, but it's all gone now." She stuck out her lower lip sadly. "Smits made me share!"

"I see."

This wasn't at all what I was expecting. I thought there'd be chauffeured cars to drive us, sober, polite conversation, entry into an exclusive club—not extra girls and Harlem snow. James put his arm round Smitty's waist, and she clung to him like ivy. Still, I played along, smiling and laughing too, just as Ma had instructed. "So, shall we go?"

There were only three girls to five men. I couldn't quite tell if Diana was with anyone. If she was, neither she nor her date seemed very bothered. Instead, she slipped her arm through mine and pulled me close. "Promise you won't leave me!" An unexpected twinge of tenderness tugged at my heart. I needed a friend tonight.

The rest of the men were content to lag behind, smoking cigarettes and arguing about whether Al Capone should be released from jail to help find the Lindberg baby. No one bothered to introduce them. Snow flurries danced round us as we made our way down the street.

Near the far end of the block we turned into an alleyway and stopped at a dirty wooden door. It opened a crack, just enough for a hushed conversation to take place. Once in, we followed James down a dark flight of steps, through the back kitchen of a Chinese restaurant, and along to another guarded doorway. It looked like nothing more than an old coal cellar. But once inside, the Friday Club opened out into a vast maze of underground rooms lit by candles on the tables and paper lanterns dangling above. It was decked out with a mishmash of discarded theatrical props. Paper palm trees wilted on the walls, and an enormous Chinese dragon was suspended from the ceiling. Onstage the backdrop was from a Christmas pageant, a pink-and-green candy city receding into a golden sunset. It reminded me of every second-rate club I'd seen in New York, as haphazard and unsophisticated as a high school dance. However, the clientele was distinctly upmarket. Despite the shambolic surroundings, diamonds glittered, and beaded gowns and satin shoes shimmied up against tailor-made dinner jackets and black ties; so many furs were tossed onto the backs of cheap wooden chairs that it looked like an Alaskan trading post, and velvet evening coats formed black pools of fabric where they'd slithered to the floor. And there were faces I recognized from the papers, not just Boston papers but New York ones too—politicians, society hostesses, actors and actresses. And just as James had promised, the band was top-drawer—a sextet from Chicago called the Moonbeams. With the help of an extra-large tip, he wangled us a table near the dance floor.

"Here, Miss Fanning." He pulled out a chair with mock formality. "I want you to have a good view of the stage."

"Thank you."

Smitty watched as I took off my coat. "Oh my!" She giggled, catching James's eye. "That's quite an ensemble!"

"Yes, I suppose it is a bit modern," I admitted, smiling even though I wanted to smack her across the face.

Diana turned on Smitty. "Haven't you seen *Shanghai Express?*

Those mandarin collars are all the rage. Everyone's *mad* for Chinese this year!" She managed to make it sound as if Smitty were some backward hillbilly. "I adore it!" she cooed, sitting down next to me. "*So* Fu Manchu!"

A waiter came up and unceremoniously delivered two bottles of nameless liquor and only half a dozen glasses. One of the men began pouring. Whatever was in the bottle was amber.

"We haven't got enough glasses!" he called out over the music.

"I'll share with you." Diana took a drink and then passed it to me. I could smell whiskey, but I thought of my mother's warning, of the way Smitty was already treating me like I'd crawled in through the back door. "Not right now, thanks."

"What?" James leaned in. "I hope you're not part of the temperance league."

Smitty wrinkled her nose. "I hate a wet blanket!"

"I'm just a little under the weather, that's all," I fibbed, taking out a cigarette. This was a fast crowd; I didn't want my abstinence to make me look prudish. "I suppose I overdid it—I was out till dawn last night."

"With whom?" James offered his lighter.

"Oh, you don't know them. Old friends."

"I know *everyone*." Smitty pushed her chair closer. "Tell me who had the nerve to throw a party without me! Was it the Lyalls? No, it couldn't have been. Or Joss Davenport?"

I really hated her.

"It was a private house outside town," I said, "with a glass conservatory and an indoor pool. I can't remember exactly where it was . . ."

"Didn't Nicky Howerd take you?" Diana cut in. "I never pay attention when someone else is driving."

I gave her a grateful smile. "That's right. Though I'd have

turned him down if I'd realized I was going to have to stare at him all night in swimming trunks."

They all laughed, except Smitty.

"Oh, lord!" She rolled her eyes. "I'm so tried of pool parties! Especially in the winter. I'm glad I wasn't there, actually."

I couldn't help myself. "Too bad you weren't invited."

She stood up and shook off her mink, which slid unnoticed to the floor. "Come on, Jimmy!" She held out her hand. "Let's dance!"

They made their way onto the crowded dance floor, and soon Diana had joined them on the arm of one of the nameless men. I was left sitting on the far side of the table across from the three others, pretending to recover from a night of debauchery I'd never known. Instead, I smoked my cigarette and tried to look as if I were enjoying sitting one out for a change. The music bounced, flapped, and soared, filling the room with a thick current of sexual electricity. I would have liked to dance. Only a few feet away from me, Smitty draped herself over James. He pulled her close. Her slim hips melded into his so completely that they seemed like a single swaying organism. It was the kind of blatant physical ease whose origins couldn't be disguised. I looked for Diana, who was laughing and reeling awkwardly with her out-of-step companion. A big lad with large feet and broad shoulders, he seemed more willing than able. But Diana wasn't in need of a partner so much as ballast, to keep her from spinning into other couples.

I shot a surreptitious glance across the table. One of the spare men looked up, caught my eye. I smiled, but he quickly looked away.

What a bunch of bores. Or snobs.

Could they tell my dress was homemade?

My fingers wrapped automatically round the whiskey, the cool glass pressed against my palm.

Here was the fastest and surest way to get into the party mood.

"Pardon me, dollface, but you remind me of someone!"

I let go of the glass, looked up. "Rusty? My god!" I laughed with relief at the sight of a friendly face. "What are you doing here?"

"I could ask you the same thing. Heard you were out of town." He sat down. "Looks like you came back." He grinned.

Orestes "Rusty" Manetti was Pina's brother-in-law. Angela used to tease her sister because all the Manetti brothers had heroic, classical names like Romulus, Remus, Orestes, and Agamemnon. "You're going to have your work cut out for you when you start a family!" Angela would say. "How about Caesar?" I'd never spent much time with Rusty and only knew him through Pina, but it was nice to see anyone I knew.

"What are you doing here? Is your wife with you?" I asked.

"Shame you missed the wedding. Hell of a party!"

"I know. I feel bad about that. And you're not answering my question."

"Neither are you." He nodded to my hair. "I seem to recall you being a redhead. Took me about ten minutes to figure out who you were. Where's your date?"

"I haven't got one. I'm here with a group."

He jerked his head toward the Bores. "Where'd you pick up that lot?"

"Just lucky, I guess."

"Looks like they all got the same mother." He squinted. "What are they doing over there? Knitting?"

"Probably drawing straws to see who has to dance with me."

"What are they? Blind?" He stood up, buttoned his suit jacket with a flourish. "Well, if they're not going to dance with you, I will."

I could've kissed him.

I was at home on the dance floor and began to relax. We made a good couple. Rusty was attractive, as dark as I was fair with strong features and black eyes rimmed with thick long eyelashes. When we were younger, people called him Pretty Boy—hardly the worst name on offer in our neighborhood, but he still had to fight with almost every boy in a ten-block radius before they stopped. Rusty had what my mother called "an eye for the chance." If there was something going on anywhere in the North End, he was usually in on it. He imported cigars, procured books and newspapers from the old country, and could broker a good deal for you if you wanted a secondhand car, a new house, or a loan to tide you over. He had interests in half a dozen local businesses and ran twelve different shoeshine corners all over the city. He also had a wife, three children, and any number of casual girlfriends.

And I could see why.

He made a girl feel like she was a diamond and he the gold setting, designed to show her off. Navigating the dance floor with daring and a certain Latin flamboyancy, he dipped and spun me round like he was a matador, playing to a packed stadium. They were the kind of moves that could throw a lesser dancer off, but for me, they were fun. We even got a round of applause from the tables near the dance floor.

"Hey, you're not half bad!" He whistled. "Did you pick up some new steps in New York?"

"Maybe just a few."

"Look, your friends seem like idiots. Why not come and sit with us?" He nodded to a crowded table in an alcove. "We've got some real Canadian Club, fresh off the boat from Jersey."

"I'd like to, but I'm meant to be on my best behavior tonight."

He twirled me again. "Sure you don't want a night off?"

"Sorry to cut in, old man." James put his hand on Rusty's shoulder. "But I think this dance is mine."

I looked at him in surprise.

"Really?" Rusty took a step back, nodded to Smitty. "What about the kid wearing the silver handkerchief with no spine?"

"Oh, Smitty? I believe her dance card is free." He wrapped his arm firmly around my waist. "I'll introduce you if you like. She's very friendly."

Rusty held up his hands. "No, thanks! I've already got more friends than I know what to do with!" He gave me a wink. "You all right, Red? Don't forget my offer."

"I won't. Good to see you."

James watched as Rusty picked his way through the crowd. "Where'd you pick up that guy?"

"I found him under the table." I was irritated that he'd ruined my fun. "He must've fallen out of someone's pocket."

"Why'd he call you Red?"

"I'm a Communist."

He searched my face. "You're lying, right?"

"We were plotting the downfall of Western civilization when you cut in. The revolution is the week after next. You may want to mark your calendar."

He pulled me in close. It's a strange thing to find yourself in the arms of a man you don't like. I'd dealt with it every night at the dance hall. But something about James Van der Laar made the experience even more galling; perhaps it was that I was meant to be grateful to him, as my host.

"Well, he looks a bit suspect. I thought he might be bothering you. They let anyone in nowadays."

I could feel his warm breath on my cheek, his hip against

mine; a firm hand pressed into my back, guiding me. He moved with confidence, never second-guessing himself, and more than any other man I'd ever danced with, he wasn't shy about taking command. It was different from Rusty, who kept you on your toes. I felt like a thing, an object to be placed anywhere at his will. At the same time, this certainty was a relief. Without meaning to, I relaxed against him, and our movements were effortless and assured.

Where I came from, men smelled good if they'd had a bath. But James Van der Laar was far more refined than that. A musky, leathery cologne blended with the heat of his skin, creating a subtle masculine scent; his dark hair was slicked back, sleek and shiny; pearl studs shimmered against his starched white shirt-front. He reminded me of a certain type who occasionally graced the Orpheum—the kind of man who didn't need the company of a professional dancer, who were most sought after by the girls and very often got extra dances for free. We called them Princes. But if he thought he was doing me a favor right now, he was wrong.

"On the contrary," I said coolly. "I was quite enjoying myself."

"Are you not enjoying yourself now, Miss Fanning?"

He was so sure of my answer. There was no response that wouldn't sound petulant. So I ignored the question. "If anything, it looks like you're the one who needs protection."

"From Smitty?" He smiled. "I don't think so! We've known each other for years—and she's engaged."

"Maybe someone should tell her that."

He looked at me sideways. "You're not jealous, are you?"

"It's difficult, but I've just about got myself under control."

"And what makes you think this is all chivalry on my part? Perhaps I have an ulterior motive."

"Oh, I see!" I laughed. "Am I to be vetted again?"

I'd hit the mark; he colored a little. "Why is it that I have to work so hard with you?"

"Because you're lazy." It came out before I could stop myself.

"Maybe I am," he admitted, frowning. For the first time, his smooth exterior was rumpled.

"Men who get what they want usually are."

"You don't know what I want, Miss Fanning."

"Then why don't you tell me?"

I was used to flirting; I'd spent months in New York flirting for a living. And no doubt James Van der Laar was an old hand too. But this wasn't flirting; it was more like fighting. Ma's voice rang in my head—charm him, don't offend him. But his arrogance was more than I could bear.

For a moment he just stared at me. Like Diana, he had blue eyes that seemed two shades lighter than humanly possible—like pools of clear, cold water. Then he put his cheek to mine and spoke very quietly in my ear. "I wanted to hold you and feel your body against mine, Miss Fanning. That's why I cut in. Not to save you or to ask you questions or to be polite. But so that I might smell the sweat on your skin up close."

It was such a shocking thing to say; I knew my face was flushing. "I should slap you!"

But he held my wrist hard. "You won't. Not tonight, at any rate."

My heart quickened, my body warmed beneath his touch. But I willed my muscles to relax, to appear indifferent even though my mind was in confusion.

He held up his hand. "This ring must be lucky."

"I thought you didn't need luck."

"I don't. But I like it just the same."

The music stopped.

I stepped back. "And now your luck's run out. If you'll excuse me, I really must find my political comrades."

I could tell by the look on his face that he wasn't used to people walking away from him. And for the first time that evening, I felt like I had the upper hand. As I wove my way between the crowded tables, I knew he was watching, so I slowed down a little, moving lazily, almost as if I were bored. And I noticed that James wasn't the only man whose eyes followed me.

It was just like at the shop. The more unattainable something was, the more valuable it became. And while I couldn't compete with the breeding or bank balances of any of the other girls in the room, I had one advantage: I wasn't afraid to leave.

James Van der Laar was dominating, profane, and yet compelling. I didn't like him, but I also wanted him to be watching when I left and waiting for my return.

When I came out of the stall in the ladies' room, Diana was there, back pressed against the wall. "I've been looking for you. I haven't been able to be alone with you for five minutes. I'm glad you're here."

"Well, actually, I didn't have much choice." I checked my lipstick in the mirror.

"What do you mean?"

"Your brother came to the shop and enlisted me. Said he wanted to meet your friends."

She frowned. "Did he say anything else? Anything about me?"

"No. Who's this Smitty girl? She seems familiar. Is she famous?"

"Someone I went to school with. You've probably seen her picture in the papers. She's been engaged four or five times."

"And she's a friend of yours?"

"She was. Now she's found more interesting company."

"Why does she keep getting engaged?"

She shrugged. "Fickle, I suppose. Breaks it off at the last minute. It's getting to be something of a joke. So James just turned up at the shop?"

I nodded, taking out my compact. "I wanted to ring you first, but he wouldn't take no for an answer. He was quite persistent."

"Yes, that's the thing about my brother. He is very persistent, especially where girls are concerned. The thing is," she went on, "he's something of a louse, May. I know it's mean of me to say, but I think you should know."

I stopped powdering my nose, looked at her through our reflections in the mirror. "Why are you telling me?"

"I'm just saying, because he's really a dreadful cad." She went on quickly. "I mean, I *adore* him! After all, he's my brother. But he's so *unbearable*! So careless, in fact." Her face was suddenly drawn and tense. "And most of all, I don't want to see you upset or hurt."

"*Me!*" I laughed. "I can assure you, he doesn't interest me in the least!"

The tension in her body eased, as if she'd been holding her breath. "I'm sorry. I'm being stupid. But you see, he's an imperialist at heart—very interested in anything that doesn't belong to him."

I shot her a look. "And to whom exactly do I belong?"

"Me, of course!" She wrapped her arms round my waist. "You're mine, May Fanning. I paid one very expensive silver pen for you, remember?"

"I thought that was a gift."

"All gifts are bribes." She kissed my cheek. "You know that!"

She seemed happy now, at ease. But it reminded me of what James had said to me in the shop. *You're not the first, you know.*

As we walked out, I saw James circulating, making his way from table to table. Smitty had joined him, leaving her own unique impression. She'd stolen someone's cigar and was smoking it provocatively, draping herself around various men, ignoring the women completely. In contrast, James greeted each person with all the high-wattage sincerity of a political candidate at a rally—firm handshakes, slaps on the back, and wide smiles. He seemed to know everyone, and they in turn beamed up at him, enthralled, as if he was some hero returning from the war. Here was the social opportunity my mother had been talking about, a chance to meet new, important people. But of course it was Smitty on James's arm, not me.

He looked up briefly and caught my eye, but I looked away, pretending to be sharing a private joke with Diana. I wouldn't so much as glance in his direction again. He would have to come to me.

Back at the table, the Bores had become rowdy. Having failed to enlarge their circle of acquaintance and left too long to their own devices, they reverted to more insular pursuits. Ties loosened, hair disheveled, here they were in one of the most exclusive clubs in Boston, playing cards.

I couldn't believe it. "Who brings cards to a nightclub?" I asked Diana.

"It's Toepen, a Dutch drinking game." She tried to pour another drink, but the bottle was already empty. "Just ignore them, they're South African—completely feral. Mother can't stand them. Of course they don't fit in anywhere civilized."

"South African?"

"We have some land there, an estate," she explained. "It belonged to my father before he died. James still spends a lot of time there. He never comes into town, but he's got a few of these apes in tow. He likes to drag them everywhere."

"Why?"

"Don't ask!" She groaned. "He's involved in the local politics. Believes in building an independent government, blah, blah, blah. Honestly, if you ask, he'll bore you stiff about it. You see"— she nodded to them—"they all come from old Afrikaner families. Most of them are as rich as Croesus, they just don't know how to chew with their mouths closed or how to hold a conversation that doesn't involve cattle." She leaned in closer. "James pretends he's entertaining them, but I know they've been told to keep an eye on me. They're nothing but great big babysitters!"

Out of the corner of my eye, I saw James working his way back toward our table, glowing like a triumphant prizefighter fresh from the ring. I didn't want to be sitting here waiting for him when he got back. "Well, then, why don't we give them the slip?" I suggested. "You can introduce me to some of your friends instead."

"All right, then," she agreed. "Let's mingle!"

But before I knew what she was doing, Diana had made a bee-line for the stage and ducked behind the curtain.

There was nothing for me to do but follow.

I was hoping to meet some of her social circle. But instead we ended up backstage with the band, who were taking a break, sitting around on a sagging old sofa, smoking and drinking.

"What are we doing here? I thought we might crash another table!" I told her.

"But I want to make new friends. I know all those people, and they're hideous!"

"Yes . . . but . . ." I jerked my head toward the musicians and whispered, "they're *Negroes!*"

"Oh dear," she said flatly. "Try to be civilized. It's not contagious."

Strolling over, she wrapped an arm around the singer's shoulders.

"Gentlemen"—she smiled sweetly—"my friend and I simply *adore* the way you play! Do you mind if we join you?"

It didn't take long before Diana knew all their names and where they came from and was perched on "Savoy" Johnson's lap, giggling while he pretended to play the piano on her long, slender arm. I sat next to them, wondering exactly how she always managed to evade expectation, making the most bizarre situations seem utterly reasonable.

Savoy was smoking something he called a "Mighty Mezz," a loosely rolled, sweet-smelling cigarette that he offered to Diana. She inhaled gingerly before passing it on to me.

"What is it?" I asked warily.

"Don't worry, Iceberg, this will melt you!" He chuckled.

I didn't like his tone. "Why are you calling me that?"

"Because you're cold as ice, and that sour face of yours could sink a ship! What are you afraid of?" he teased. "That you might melt?"

They all laughed, including Diana.

I took it from him and inhaled hard, too hard. The next thing I knew, I was choking and coughing.

The horn player, Cairo Joe, slapped me on the back. "Take it gentle, sister!" He had a thin Duke Ellington mustache and limpid deep brown eyes. "Like blowing bubbles in reverse," he instructed. "Slow and easy!"

A flask of bourbon made its rounds, powerful and thick, and the knot in my chest began to loosen. In fact, I felt better than I had all night. I pushed off Ma's shoes. If any of them noticed the newspaper in the toes, they didn't say anything or care. Cairo Joe patted his knee. "Here, girl! Put those paws up here!"

And I did.

"You must be a dancer—look at those blisters!" he whistled.

The Mezz made another round. This time I inhaled gently. My face began to feel unusual—numb, as if it was made of rubber. And my scalp was suddenly so itchy. Off came the veiled "fascinator" hat, and the carefully coiffed curls tumbled free.

"Oh, she's melting!" Teacher, the drummer, pointed at me. "She's melting *good* now!" He laughed, only this time I laughed too.

The break was over. The band went back to play another set.

Diana and I sat alone on a broken-down sofa. Diana slumped forward and took my hand.

"Are you upset, darling? Have I been dreadful?"

I didn't care now about meeting society people. I felt much better. Capital, in fact. "Why would I be upset?" The words slid into one another, all vowels.

She shrugged. "I haven't disappointed you? Only, I can't breathe out there with all those snobs!"

I finally asked her the question that had been bothering me all night. "Don't you want me to meet your friends?"

"They're not my friends. They're my audience. Besides, I like it better back here. No one knows me." She smiled softly. "I like to lose myself, May." She paused, closed her eyes. "I like to drift away and never come back."

"Like a bubble. In reverse."

This struck us as funny. We laughed until our sides hurt, gasping for breath; Diana let out little snorting sounds that only made us laugh harder, and I nearly fell off the sofa onto the floor.

When we finally stopped, she grew thoughtful. "I hate my life," she confided. "I hate every inch of it. You have no idea what's it's like."

"Forget about it."

"I like to be where the action is."

"This is where the action is," I said, poking the sagging sofa. "There's plenty of action here."

"That's why I like you." She leaned her head on my shoulder. "I can be free."

We sat awhile, listening to the music.

Each note reverberated along my spine. I closed my eyes and felt it pulse through my body. Cairo Joe's cornet soared and dove, clear and sweet, while Savoy's fingers raced up and down the piano keys, like children chasing each other, playing tag.

Diana pulled me up. "Dance with me!"

"Are you mad?"

"We both are." She laughed. "Remember?"

We made our way out onto the dance floor. Wrapping an arm round my waist, Diana pressed her hips against mine and began to sway. There were shouts and whistles, clapping. Arms entwined, we shimmied and shook, throwing our heads back, arching our backs. On the drums, Teacher slowed the beat a fraction, in time to our rhythm; sleeves rolled up, sweat on his brow, he tilted his chin down, watching closely.

Diana, with her long, pale limbs and wild dark hair, held me close, her perfume mixing with the thick smoky heat and sweat. I closed my eyes; I could feel her hands in the small of my back, then over my hips. A sultry malaise weighed down on me, a dangerous aching. I was free. Free to do anything I liked. To hell with everyone and everything! I opened my eyes. Diana was smiling, tilting her chin closer, her breath warm against my face. She was looking at me so intently, so open and serious.

Then suddenly we were being pulled apart amid a chorus of boos. The Bores were dragging us back to the table.

"Time to go," one of them grunted.

"So soon?" Diana tossed herself into a chair. "Where's Jimmy?"

"He had to leave. That girl, the other one, she didn't feel so good."

"But I'm thirsty!" she sulked.

185 / Rare Objects

"So am I!" I pointed at the cards. "How about letting us play?"

"You'll lose," the blond one warned, sucking hard on the tail end of a cigar. He had the pink, puffy face of a schoolboy attached to the body of a wrestler. "And if you lose, you drink."

"That's all right, then." I gave Diana a wink. "We know how to do that!"

"We're playing for money," another cut in. He seemed to have been born without a chin; his face simply melted into his fat neck.

"If I didn't know any better"—Diana's eyes narrowed—"I would think you were being rude."

"I . . . I'm only saying," he mumbled, looking to his friends.

"We're thirsty," I reminded them. *"Really* thirsty!"

"And bored," Diana added. "I don't want to tell Jimmy you gave us a bad night out. He wouldn't like that, you know. And I'm not going home until I've had some fun!"

They muttered between themselves for a minute and then ordered another bottle of whiskey.

"Come on, then!" Opening my handbag, I brandished the five-dollar bill. "Let's see what you boys are made of!"

The game turned out to be more difficult than I thought. Diana lent me ten dollars, and then at some point the rules were changed so that we girls didn't need to bet money, but would have to sit on the winner's knee. After that, the details of the night became hazy, a blur of red faces, large laps, and sweaty hands. There was a car ride, loud singing, some of it in another language, and someone got slapped across the face.

The next thing I remembered was the sound of a motor running and something heavy and hot pressing against my stomach. With considerable effort, I opened my eyes. I was lying on the floor on my back, staring at a dimly lit ceiling. The motor was still going, like a large hand holding me down. Then suddenly it shifted. Two amber eyes blinked slowly. It was Persia, curled into a ball on top of me. I turned my head, wincing as a dull, thudding pain filled my temple. There was the map of the ancient world, on the wall over the desk. I must've made them drop me off at the shop and fallen asleep on the floor of Mr. Winshaw's office.

Pushing Persia off, I struggled to my feet. My skirt was on the wrong way round, my blouse was missing a button, and my stockings were split at the toe. Overcome with queasiness, I made it to the bathroom just in time. Bent over the toilet bowl, I stayed there awhile, Persia purring, weaving affectionately around my feet.

Afterward, hands shaking, I splashed my face with cold water. I looked like hell. My lipstick was smeared, my hair smashed flat on one side, the indent of the cushion button from Mr. Winshaw's chair pressed into my cheek.

Ma's words came back to haunt me. *If you act like a lady, then you'll be treated as one.*

Ladies didn't wake up on the floor, covered in cat.

The symphony of clocks at the front of the shop struck eight. Mr. Kessler would be here in half an hour.

I sank to the floor, head on my knees. If only I could lie back down and be still. Or die. Instead, with trembling hands I opened up my evening bag. It was empty except for a tube of lipstick, a folded hankie, and my powder compact. No trolley fare, let alone enough money for something to eat.

But right now I had to clean myself up, fast, or lose my job.

Stumbling into Mr. Winshaw's office, I searched through his desk drawers and found a tin of aspirin and thirteen cents in loose change.

Then I went into Mr. Kessler's office. The top right-hand drawer of his desk was locked. But below it, there was a large tin of Luden's Ole South Hard Candy Dainties and an envelope with a five-dollar bill inside. Rolling around in the bottom was the slim metal inhaler labeled "Benzedrine"—his asthma medicine. It cleared everything, he'd said. Cracking the lid, I breathed in deeply. The drug was sharp, both oily and acidic, scented with lavender. Then I took as many hard candies as I could hold.

Swallowing some aspirin, I headed back to the bathroom and washed my face, more carefully this time. A wave of nausea had me gripping the sink again, but I somehow managed to keep the aspirin down. Then I sucked on a couple of Mr. Kessler's hard candies. Gradually the wave of sickness eased. Smoothing my hair down, I patted my nose with powder, and by balancing my elbow on the sink and holding my right hand steady with my left, I finally managed to put on some lipstick. I didn't look good, but at least I looked better.

I still needed to hide the missing button. A shawl was draped over one of the tables on the shop floor, an Indian stole of very fine cream wool embroidered with gold silk thread. Shaking the dust out of it, I wrapped it around my shoulders. It hid an entire night's history.

But I was running out of time. Shoving another hard candy in my mouth, I headed to the back room to put the coffee on. My hands were still unsteady, but at least my head was starting to clear. It was as if somewhere in the back of my brain, a vista had emerged. It was only a thin line right now, but I could feel it expanding, widening.

It must be Mr. Kessler's medicine. I ducked back into his office, stole one more shot.

It was eight twenty-seven when I heard Mr. Kessler's key turning in the latch.

I stationed myself behind the glass counter, where I could rest my hands to steady myself.

Normally he was the first one to arrive.

"Good morning, Miss Fanning." He looked me up and down, not entirely without suspicion. "What are you doing here so early?"

"A mistake. I caught an earlier trolley. Would you like some coffee?"

(Best to keep moving. Not look him too long in the eye.)

"That would be fine." He hung up his coat.

I went to the back room and slumped against a wooden packing crate. Even that short exchange had taken it out of me. I needed to be still for as long as possible, but if I closed my eyes, the room would start spinning and I'd throw up again. So I just stared instead at the dirty broken tiles of the floor for as long as I dared before going back through.

Mr. Kessler was opening the cash register. He stopped, peered at me over the tops of his glasses. "I never thought to sell that as a stole." He pointed to the shawl.

I knew this wasn't a compliment. "Well"—I smiled, doing my best to seem charming—"that's why you have me, isn't it?"

He nodded, a little bemused. "You look pale. Are you sure you're quite all right?"

"We need sugar, Mr. Kessler. Shall I go out and get some? You can't have your coffee without sugar, now, can you?"

"No, I suppose I can't," he agreed.

"What good's an Amazon if you can't send her out hunting once in a while?" I got my coat.

Mr. Kessler gave me some petty cash. I went to a little grocery around the corner, bought a small bag of sugar, then went across the street to the drugstore. There I bought a doughnut, which I forced down standing at the counter.

By the time I got back and poured the coffee, my hands were reasonably steady and my stomach calmer.

"Something came for you." Mr. Kessler nodded to a letter.

"For me?"

"By hand," he added, looking at me out of the corner of his eye. I opened it. It read:

Dear Miss Fanning,

I believe I owe you an apology for abandoning you last night; however, Smitty turned green and had to be taken home. I trust by now you've discovered that young men are not to be trusted in drinking games with pretty girls. Another time, I hope to make it up to you.

James

Inside was a fifty-dollar bill.

"Where have you been?" Ma was waiting for me when I came in that evening.

Somehow I'd limped through the day, and I was exhausted. All I wanted was to sleep. "We were out too late," I told her, pulling off my coat. "So I stayed at the shop."

"At the *shop?*" She gaped in horror. "Are you mad?"

"Maybe."

I headed into the kitchen. It was cold. I opened up the icebox. There were a few eggs, a cheap cut of ham. All the bread was gone.

"It was late, and I didn't want to miss work. I didn't have time to come home. You don't want me to lose my job, do you?"

"You should have rung!"

"Right!" I jerked my head toward the outside landing, where the only phone in the building was located. "You mean the party line at three in the morning? Is that what you want? The neighbors knowing all our business?"

"You could have rung," she said again, firmly.

My head was pounding now. I didn't have the energy to argue. "You wanted me to go out with them! To see it as an opportunity! Well, I went!"

"Don't take that tone with me!"

"I'm too old for this, Ma! I went out, I went to work, and I'm home now. What else do you want to know?"

"I want to know that you're alive!"

"I'm not an idiot! Of course I'm alive!"

"Well, how would I know that? Do you know how close I was to calling the police?"

I glared at her, turned away.

"What happened?" she pressed. "Where did you go? Who was with you?"

Even greater than her anger was her curiosity. She sat down at the kitchen table.

"I danced with James Van der Laar," I told her.

"Which one is he?"

"Diana's brother. He's the one who invited me."

"Who was there? Just the three of you?"

"No, there was a whole crowd. We went to a private club, very exclusive. The Friday Club."

She shook her head. "I've never heard of it."

"That's the point."

A furrow deepened in her brow. I could see her mind working, calculating. "James Van der Laar. How many times did he dance with you? More than once?"

"He was very attentive."

"And who paid?"

"He did."

"Good." She nodded. "Very good. And did you drink?"

She knew damn well I'd been drinking; I probably still smelled of it.

"They all drink. What was I meant to do?" I asked her. "Make a spectacle out of myself?"

But her voice was steely, full of condemnation. "Nice girls don't, Mae."

"I only had one. One little drink! And I was fine." My hands were beginning to tremble again, and my knees felt weak. Whatever was in Mr. Kessler's vial had stopped working, and I was coming down hard. I had to get to bed.

"You don't look fine. You look as bad as you did when you were hanging around with Mickey!"

I sat down too, cradled my head in my hands. "You know, Ma, I just can't please you, can I? You wanted me to go. *Told* me to go. Then I did my best to fit in, and now you're attacking me for doing the very thing *you* wanted me to do!"

"I'm not attacking you, Maeve!"

I looked up. "Do you honestly think anyone wants to spend the night at a club with a girl who's teetotal? Think about it. Sitting across from some shabby little upstart who's looking down her nose at everyone?"

"You're not shabby!" She straightened, chin in the air. "Not by any means!"

I had to laugh. "Oh, yes I am! By *their* standards? Oh, Ma!

They were wearing furs and diamonds, and I had newspaper stuffed in my shoes!"

She suddenly seemed uncertain, pushing her fingers into her forehead as if she meant to press the wrinkles away. "That's not true. You looked fine. . . . You looked elegant."

"Oh, *please*! I looked like what I am! A dumb Mick out with a bunch of Rockefellers, making a fool out of myself! And are you going to begrudge me a little whiskey to take the edge off my shame?"

Her eyes widened with indignation, and something else, something I'd always known was there—fear. "You have nothing to be ashamed of! You're worth twice any of them!"

It was over now. She was defending me.

I took a deep breath, held my hands up. "Well, make up your mind, Ma. If you want me to make new friends, then I'll wear my skirt on my head if you tell me to. But I'm not going to be ripped to shreds every time an evening runs late." Then I opened my purse, took out a five-dollar bill, and put it on the table in front of her. "Here. You can have this back. Like I said, the Van der Laars paid."

She stared down at the money. Worn out after waiting up all night, she no longer had the energy or mental dexterity to combat my arguments. But she was stubborn and would hold a little longer, just for the sake of her pride.

I watched the men in the street below, gathering around Contadino's chestnut stove, and waited.

I'd considered sending the money back; had some pleasant daydreams imagining James Van der Laar's face when he opened the envelope and read my reply:

"Thank you, but no thank you. I'll make my own destiny."

How stunned would he be then?

But it was fifty dollars, after all. And I was broke again.

Fifty dollars meant bread for breakfast, cream in coffee, real cuts of meat without bone and gristle, plenty of coins for the gas meter. Most of all, it was a new dress—a real store-bought one, right off the rail, and a pair of evening shoes that fit.

Pride was a luxury I couldn't afford. Not yet.

Tomorrow I would go downtown and find the most fashionable outfit Boston had to offer—and not at Filene's, either. I just had to find a way of keeping Ma from being suspicious. Tell her I got commission, after all.

"I just don't want you ruining your chances," she said at last. "They don't come along very often. When you're young, you think you'll always have another opportunity, but it's not true." She was bewildered, second-guessing herself, which didn't come easy. "I only want what's best for you, Maeve."

I continued to stare out of the window, to think about where I was going to buy shoes. "Well, maybe it's about time you left that up to me."

Dear Miss Fanning,

The precise location of the cradle of civilization is a fiercely debated question, running the gamut of locations from Egypt and Mesopotamia to deepest South America, the South Pacific Islands, China, and even the Siberian Arctic. Apparently there's a thriving hotbed of preternatural progress nearly everywhere you turn, so who knows? Boston might turn out to be said cradle after all. For my part, I'm less concerned with the birthplace than those rare clues as to what it means to be civilized in the first place, and I have always suspected it has more to do with clay spoons than ancient monuments.

As for the mermaids of Boston Harbor, it's been a while since

I've heard their song, but if I'm not mistaken there's a sinister, slightly aquatic tone to your letters that's deeply suspect. Are you trying to drown honest men, Miss Fanning, with your imperious prose?

And yes, I have a vast collection of secondhand women's vanity cases, and am not ashamed to admit it.

Put that in your pipe and smoke it.

Yours, with Utmost Sincerity,

B. Winshaw

Then one day I realized the obvious: Mr. Kessler and Mr. Winshaw were collectors too; the entire shop was their collection. Everything in it revealed their personal preferences and interests, as well as hidden obsessions. Sometimes during quiet hours I tried to work out precisely who had chosen what. I discovered that Mr. Kessler had a soft spot for rather sentimental Victorian morality paintings with titles like *All Is Lost*, depicting the demise of a fallen woman on a moonless night, or *An Anxious Hour*, with a young physician watching with concern over a pale, sick child. At the same time he had an almost libertine appreciation for comfort, pomposity, and ostentatious ornamentation. All the French Empire, English Regency, and German Baroque furniture had been selected by him.

Mr. Winshaw remained more enigmatic; his contributions were haphazard, often challenging, and considerably less aesthetically pleasing. In fact, very little of his inventory ever seemed destined to sell—the squat African figures were his, along with the stiff-backed English chairs and a rather alarming bronze *Rape of the Sabine Women* that no one could possibly display in their home. He also had a fascination for scientific miscellanea—Georgian compasses, the brass dull and worn from centuries of use; a pair of deceptively elegant retractable seventeenth-century telescopes, gleaned from a violent shipwreck off the Irish coast; calculagraphs and ancient slide rules, as well as two very fine, remarkably complex Etruscan abacuses. He appreciated exploration and the practical objects of enterprise. But he also had a detailed eye for storytelling that occasionally surprised me. For example, two silver spoons sat next to each other in the glass display case. One day I made the mistake of separating them. Mr. Kessler was quick to set me straight. "You see," he said, "they go together. Both are English, and Mr. Winshaw likes them to remain side by side."

"Why?"

"Well, the older one is a rare York memento mori spoon from 1670. See?" He held it up. "It's engraved with a skull, and on the reverse a coat of arms. And along the stele are the words 'Live to Die / Die to Live.'"

"That's a bit grim for cutlery, isn't it?"

"Well, it reflects a very understandable preoccupation the Jacobeans had with death. After all, 1670 was only five years after the Black Death struck London. Now, in contrast, this one"—he indicated the spoon next to it—"has a fairly common motif for the time, featuring a bird sitting on top of its cage with the slogan 'I Love Liberty' beneath. That's a reference to John Wilkes, the English statesman, radical, and famous supporter of the American Revolution." Mr. Kessler's dark eyes had that particular gleam they got when he was teaching me something new. "There are only a hundred years between these two spoons, but note the change these years brought; from a dour puritanical obsession with death and loss to an optimistic Enlightened expectation of freedom. That's why Mr. Winshaw likes them side by side, to remind us."

"Of what, precisely?"

"That things change, Miss Fanning, and often in the most unexpected ways."

I took the opportunity to find out more about Mr. Kessler's own obsessions.

"Of all the things here, Mr. Kessler, what would you be most sad to part with?"

"Most sad? None of it!" he insisted. "I hope to part with all of it someday!"

"But which do you like best?" I pressed. "Which is your favorite?"

He stroked his beard, considering. Finally he pointed to a cherry Biedermeier pedestal table. "This is an exceptional piece."

His choice surprised me. It was relatively simple and restrained compared to his other selections.

"It reminds me of Vienna," he said. "The place where I was happiest, and the most refined city on earth."

"Then why did you leave?" I asked.

He shook his head. "It's a long story."

"We have nothing but time, Mr. Kessler. Go on," I coaxed.

"Where to begin?" Taking off his glasses, he rubbed them thoughtfully with his handkerchief before putting them back on.

"From the beginning, of course." I settled into the corner of a chaise longue.

He shrugged, resigned to the task ahead. "I will remind you that you asked to hear this when you are paralyzed with boredom," he said, sitting down. "You see, I came from a small Jewish village, in Yiddish a shtetl, in Galicia. My father was a cobbler and, for want of a better word, a handyman. Anything that needed to be repaired, he attended to it. Or at least he tried. I'm not saying he was talented in his field. In fact, he was rather clumsy. But that's what he did because that's what his father did, and his father before him. He was also a very religious, highly passionate believer. I think he would've liked to have studied Torah, but of course that wasn't possible. We were Hasidic." He looked across at me. "Do you know what that is?"

"I think so."

There was a single Jewish deli left at the end of Salem Street called Moe's, a remnant from another era when the whole neighborhood was Jewish. Now it was famous for being the only shop open on a Sunday. Most of the Jews had moved to Roxbury, where Jewish shops and businesses lined both sides of Blue Hill Avenue. I'd only been there a few times with Ma, who claimed they sold the best-quality fabric, provided you didn't mind dark colors. She said they were remarkable tailors. But in truth the place unsettled me. Mysterious, sullen men in shiny black coats and long beards conducted business in a strange guttural language. Their wives dressed in long sleeves even in summer, and little boys with skullcaps and curls longer than their sisters' played on the sidewalk, prayer shawls flapping behind them as they ran. They didn't mix. That was the most important thing I knew about them. No one knew what they were saying but they didn't want to be understood. And when you spoke to one of them, especially one of the men, they glared at you as if you were a troublemaker.

"Well," Mr. Kessler continued, "it was a small village. All the families were related through marriage. And the rabbi, everyone believed him to be a zaddik, a truly righteous man. Certainly my father did. The rabbi was like a Messiah to my father—he believed every word the rabbi spoke came directly from God.

There was always a trail of men following in his wake, day and night, hanging upon each syllable, hoping that being close to him would give them answers. But we were all very poor. The Poles hated us. They rode through every few months, bringing death and mayhem. With no one to stop them, they used to treat us like a drunk treats a stray dog, to be kicked and beaten at will without reason or regret. When I was young, I felt like I was suffocating in that village. I hated the heat in the summer, the terrible cold in the winter, the endless prayers and gossip and watchful eyes. I couldn't wait to leave. And I didn't believe the way my father believed; it didn't make sense to me, especially when things were so bad. So when I was fourteen, I left."

"Where did you go?"

"To Lemberg. I got a position in a printing house as a type-setter. There I was able to read anything I wanted, spend nights in cafés with socialists and Zionists and Bolsheviks. And there was a university there that took Jews. I slept on the printing press floor on reams of paper, worked all day, and went to school at night. When I graduated, I was lucky enough to get a posi-tion at the Austrian Museum of Natural History. In Vienna," he added with a smile. "I had never seen a place so beautiful, so refined. Everything about it was civilized and pleasing to the eye, from the golden-domed cupolas to the wide boulevards and grand public parks filled with scented flowers and exquisite young women."

It was difficult to imagine Mr. Kessler as a young man, eyeing up pretty girls.

"So it was the women," I teased, "that made Vienna enchanting."

"And the music and art and culture," he added quickly. "In my village, everything was gray, black, and brown. Even Lemberg was a dirty, crowded, ugly city by comparison. But in Vienna, even rain was romantic. It was the only place I'd ever been where I wasn't just a Jew. Here I was allowed to be an intellectual. A scholar, if I wanted. Such an age!" He paused, inhaling the memory of it, closing his eyes for a moment to savor the flavor of those forgotten days. "I advanced in my field, became a member of the Austrian Academy of Sciences. I wrote papers and had a black mustache the likes of which no one will ever see again!" He smiled. "And a young wife named Anya." His voice softened. "A Catholic girl."

"Catholic? What did your family say?"

"They disowned me. But in truth, I had disowned them first. I couldn't bear the oppression of my father's faith. I thought of myself as modern, cultivated, and educated. Too smart to be chanting prayers, rocking back and forth in a trance. I sent money back home, but I didn't bother, after a while, to include letters." His face darkened. "I thought I was right, you see. I was right, and he was wrong. That my father was foolish to believe as he did, weak."

He took a deep breath. "Anya died in childbirth. And then the pogroms began, spread throughout the region like a foul, unchecked disease, from Odessa to Minsk."

"I'm sorry?"

"Pogrom. A Russian word for massacre. Attacks on Jewish households. Raids lasting several days, murders, beheadings, children torn limb from limb."

I was horrified. "But why?"

"Because." He shrugged. "We're Jews."

"What about your family?"

He was quiet a moment, looking out of the window at the

empty street outside. "The whole village hid in the temple. The marauders sealed the doors and windows and burnt the place to the ground. I'm told it took days."

We both fell silent

Outside, the awnings across the street flapped forlornly in the wind.

"Did you ever marry again?" I asked after a while.

He shook his head. "I was offered a chance to teach, in Philadelphia. So I left. It's amazing how lonely a place where you were once happy can become. They say America is the place to begin again—*die goldene medina*, 'the golden country.' But I think there is only one golden age in every man's life. Vienna was mine. A brief moment when I thought I was the master of my own destiny."

Mr. Kessler got up, ran his hand over the elegantly matched surface of the cherry table, the beautiful grain of the highly polished wood spread outward from the center like an ornate inkblot, perfectly mirrored on both halves. "This was made in Vienna in 1840. The style was a great favorite with the rising middle class—the perfect marriage of form and function. And it was a very good way to tell the rest of the world who you think you are," he added.

He held his hand down, pressing it against the wood as if feeling for a heartbeat.

"There is a word in Hebrew—*nitzotzot*. It means 'divine sparks.' It refers to the infinitesimal fragments of godliness that inhabit everything—all of creation, both animate and inanimate. When something is used as it was divinely intended, these sparks are said to be 'liberated'; they shine, become a reflection of the face of God himself in this transient world." He looked up. "Do you see how this shines, Miss Fanning?"

I nodded.

"My father would have appreciated this. He never went any-where, never was much of a craftsman, lived his whole life in the *shtetl*. But I believe he would have seen God in this."

"I'd almost given up on you."

I turned round, surprised.

It was early evening, just after six. I'd stayed behind to finish Mr. Kessler's monthly accounts and was just locking up the shop. I had an arrangement to meet Diana at our regular haunt. But here was James Van der Laar, leaning against a parked car, hat cocked over one eye, smoking a cigarette. He was the last person I expected to see loitering outside.

"What are you doing here?"

"I want to show you something." Tossing his cigarette into the gutter, he held out his arm. "It's just around the corner. I want your opinion."

I looked down the street. "Is Diana with you?"

"No. Why?" A slow smile spread across his face. "Do you re-quire a chaperone, Miss Fanning?"

He had the same disquieting effect that he'd had the last time, irritation and excitement playing tug-of-war in my head. I didn't like being taken by surprise, but at the same time, I was intrigued.

I dropped the shop keys into my handbag. "What makes you think I have time to be abducted by you, Mr. Van der Laar? Don't you ever ring ahead? Or do you make ambushing people a regular habit?"

"So I'm ambushing you, is that it? Then I apologize. But this really is a business-related matter." He held out his arm again. "And it won't take long."

I thought of Diana, waiting for me at our regular table. "A business-related matter."

His smile widened. "You're not afraid of me, are you?"

"Should I be?" I took his arm. We began to walk, threading through the side streets, heading in the direction of the Common.

It was odd to be so close to him again; our last encounter had ended awkwardly, but now he strolled beside me as easily as if nothing unusual had happened. "Have you been well?"

"Cracking. And you?"

As we crossed the street, he changed sides so that I was farthest from the traffic. It was a common courtesy, but one that suddenly felt calculated and self-conscious.

"I understand I missed quite an evening the other night," he said.

I felt embarrassment rising; he was referring to his gift—a gift I'd never thanked him for. The money that had been so easy to take was now quite difficult to acknowledge, especially with my arm in his. "It was very kind of you, Mr. Van der Laar—"

"James," he insisted. "Call me James."

"Yes, James," I corrected myself, "very kind and unnecessary of you to pay my debts. However, I appreciate it just the same."

"I feel responsible. I shouldn't have left without seeing you home."

A uniformed nanny pushing a large baby carriage trundled toward us, and he pulled me in closer to make room. I recognized the dusky sweetness of his cologne, felt the certainty of his guiding hand on my elbow. It was the same sense I'd experienced when dancing with him, of being steered. I couldn't decide if I liked it or not.

"It was very kind of you." My words sounded stiff and disingenuous.

"I'm the kindest man you'll ever meet, May." He laughed. It was obvious I was struggling with pride. "May I call you May?"

"Yes. Of course."

"You see, I'm a bit old-fashioned. I believe a girl like you shouldn't have to pay for anything."

"A girl like me?" I looked at him sideways. "Am I a princess now?"

"You shouldn't have to be in order to be treated well. For example, you shouldn't have to work for a living."

"I couldn't agree more. But what if I like working?"

"What is there to like about it? Answering to someone else's beck and call? Waking early, coming home late? And for what?"

"Money. And there's the challenge, the chance to learn something, to be independent."

"Independent from what?" His gaze was unflinching. "A man who loves you and would look after you? Is that independence or mere stubbornness?"

Why was he having this argument with me?

"I'm afraid there aren't enough of those men to go around. Besides, not everyone wants to be kept."

"You sound like Diana. The two of you are quite close, aren't you?"

"Why?"

"I just wondered how much you knew about her."

"What do you mean?"

He shrugged. "She's not always what she appears to be, that's all. It's a good idea to be careful."

"What happened to the protective older brother?"

"I'm still protective. But I'm not naive. Not everything she says is true, May. Especially about our family."

"Like what?"

He didn't elaborate but instead asked, "How many people has she introduced you to? How many of her other friends? You're from out of town and don't know anyone here, right? But I'm willing to guess she hasn't helped you to meet anyone . . . Am I right?"

His words hit close to the mark.

He translated my silence. "See? That's Diana for you! She collects people, takes over their lives. But she lives in a world of her own creation. Sometimes it's harmless. But other times it has terrible consequences. Do you remember what they used to say about Lord Byron?"

I did, but I didn't like this conversation. "Why are you telling me this?"

"Oh." He gave me a strange look. "You're *loyal*!"

He said it as if he'd just discovered I was another species, one perhaps that he'd read about but never actually seen.

"She's my friend," I reminded him.

"That's to your credit," he admitted. "Just don't follow her down a rabbit hole. That's all I'm asking. I for one would hate to see you disappear."

We'd arrived at a large brownstone house on Marlborough Street. He took a key from his jacket pocket and, walking up the steps, unlocked the door.

"What's this?" I followed uncertainly. "What are we doing here?"

"This is a little house I was thinking of buying." He swung open the door, held out his hand. "Come inside and let me know what you think."

The "little house" was in fact a four-story mansion with eight bedrooms, a library, and its own ballroom overlooking a private walled garden in the back. The entrance hall and marble staircase were the finest examples of Italian stonework on the East Coast, he said. It was being remodeled, with updated kitchens and plumbing. Empty save for some ladders, tarps, and paint supplies left behind by the renovation crew, its gracious rooms echoed with grand possibilities; they seemed to be waiting for guests and parties and public occasions.

As we toured the ground floor, I felt a mounting sense of exhilaration, a giddy uncertainty that put me on edge. It was all I could do not to stare with my mouth open at the vast excess of beauty and space. Why was he showing it to me?

"It's all lovely," I said, a monumental understatement of my true feelings. "But why do you want my opinion?"

He turned to face me across the wide expanse of the drawing room. He was undeniably attractive, more attractive than I'd given him credit for. "Men like to have a woman's opinion, especially in domestic matters."

"I'm sure they do. But why me?"

"Well, this whole thing would need to be furnished in style befitting its age," he pointed out. "Do you or do you not work at an antiques shop?"

"Oh, I see." I was glad I'd restrained myself from gushing with enthusiasm. Almost everything he did or said was some sort of convoluted trap. But if I could sell him even a few pieces of furniture, it would be a coup.

"Well"—I scanned the room, as if calculating its dimensions—"If you're asking if we have enough furniture to fill it, the answer is no. Not yet, at any rate. But we could find it, I'm sure."

"So"—he took a step closer—"what do you think? Will it do?"

"That depends on what you want it for."

"Only time will tell." He shoved his hands deep into his pockets. "A home? A place to raise a family someday . . ."

"It would be best if you consulted the woman in question, then."

He was staring into my eyes, as bold as Napoleon, Alexander,

Charlemagne, or any man who'd ever invaded and conquered the world. "What makes you think I haven't?"

The question hung in the air between us.

"This house suits you." He came closer. "You look good in it."

"You make it sound like a dress." I turned, wandering through to the hallway, putting some distance between us. The light was dim now, the late-afternoon sun fading. Outside, an evening chorus of birds had begun, a sound one didn't often hear in the North End. But in this neighborhood there were trees, gardens— space. The song echoed hauntingly off the marble stonework, as delicate and hopeful as the pale light draining from the sky.

"I'm not here very often." He followed, stood in the doorway. "I'm leaving for New York again tomorrow. I'll be gone awhile."

Again, I wondered why he was telling me. But I only said, "You must let me know what you decide about the house. I will be glad to assist in any way."

"Will you think of me while I'm gone?"

He was so perplexing, so forward. This was another trap, I was sure. I tossed his words back at him. "Only time will tell."

"Give me something to remember you by."

"What? A lock of hair?" I laughed. "A poem?"

He came closer, drew me to him, kissed me.

I pulled away.

"Tell me you'll think of me," he said again.

My heart was pounding with fear or anticipation, I wasn't sure which. "Why?"

"Because. Because I want you to think of me as much as I think of you."

He reached for me again. And this time, I didn't move.

———

By the time I arrived to meet Diana, I was late and out of breath from running. The place was full, bustling with the first dinner service.

She was in our usual booth, chin in one palm, building a pyramid out of sugar cubes. Judging from its height, she'd been there some time. She didn't bother to look up when I sat down across from her.

"I'm so sorry!" I panted, trying to catch my breath. "A customer came in as I was closing, and wouldn't leave."

She balanced another sugar cube carefully on the final tier. "I've been waiting almost an hour."

"I'm really sorry."

"A customer, right?"

"Yes." I pulled off my gloves. "God, it's crowded! What's wrong?"

"Nothing. Only I went by the shop, and it was locked. I didn't see anyone."

I hadn't anticipated that. "They wanted me to look at something. To value it. In their home."

"How extremely unusual." She finished her masterpiece off with a little flag made from a book of matches. "What was it?"

I hesitated. "A table. Look, I'm sorry. I've never had to do that before, but Mr. Kessler was out, and I didn't want to turn away a sale. Why are you so angry?"

"I hate waiting." She looked up. "I especially hate waiting for people who don't show!"

"Well, I'm here now." I was beginning to lose patience. There was only so much penance I was willing to offer. "Why did you bother to stop by the shop in the first place?"

Her expression was hard, flat. "Because you work there." She signaled to the waiter. "I want something to drink."

The waiter brought us both teacups full of gin. Diana took a long greedy gulp, wincing as she swallowed. She didn't like gin, but it was all they had that day. "I'm sorry," she said after a moment. "I'm not myself."

"It's all right." I stared into my cup; I couldn't stop thinking about what had happened. It was as sudden and unexpected as being hit by a car and the whole encounter kept repeating, going round and round in my head, over and over again.

"You're somewhere else." Diana ran her fingers along her pearl necklace. "What are you thinking about?"

"Nothing. The table," I lied. "I'm sure I got the value wrong."

"We should run away," she said, frowning at the full dining room. "I hate this town!"

"Where?"

"Anywhere. Let's just go. Where do you want to go?"

I opened my handbag to look for cigarettes, but couldn't find any. I must've left them at work. "I don't know. I don't care."

"Of course they'd find us." She forced down another swallow. "They always do."

"Who? What are you talking about?"

"Though they would never think to look someplace like Kansas or Little Rock. If we were poor, well, they'd never guess that one. There's an idea!" She grabbed my hand, suddenly keyed up. "Would you do that for me? Run off to Arkansas?"

This was what James was talking about. She was in a world of her own creation.

"I'm not going to Arkansas for anyone," I said.

"If you loved me, you'd go."

"No one loves *anyone* that much."

She let go of my hand, sank back into her seat. "I suppose not.

Only"—she sighed—"I don't know what to do. I can't stay here. I'm suffocating."

I wasn't in the mood for her to be morbid or cryptic. There were far too many questions buzzing around in my head. I picked up a menu instead. "Do you want something? Shall we eat?"

"I'm not hungry. I don't want to stay here. I don't know why we always come here anyway," she added sullenly.

I didn't answer. I wasn't hungry either. All I wanted to do was go home, lie on my bed, and remember exactly what had happened, every single detail.

"I know. There's a place in Roxbury called the Black Rose. They have the best jazz in Boston." Diana downed the rest of her drink and stood up. "Come on, you'll love it! The place is full of criminals!"

"I'm tired. I don't want to go all the way to Roxbury. Not tonight."

"You'll be fine once you get there." She threw a few bills down on the table. "I know the landlady. She's a complete cow but she'll look after us. She owes me. I once paid off half the police department just so the band could finish their set."

"I'm not in the mood."

She put her hands on her hips. "And I don't want to stay. I can't go home. Not tonight. I can't stand it there!"

I ran my hand over my eyes. "Then go to the apartment. Stay there!"

"Alone?" She made it sound as if it were a punishment.

I wanted to laugh. "Why not? God, I'd give my eyeteeth to be alone for a night!"

Her face changed. "What are you saying? That you're tired of me?"

"No, just that I'm *tired*!"

"Where did you really go tonight?"

She was like a terrier with a bone.

"Why don't you believe me?" I snapped, all the angrier because she'd caught me out.

"Because you're lying. Who were you with?"

"Not everything is your business! I don't belong to you, you know!"

"How thoughtful of you to inform me." Tossing her mink over her shoulders, she flounced to the door, making a grand exit.

She was trying to take over my life, just as James had said. I wondered why I hadn't seen it before.

Still, I picked up my gloves and followed her out. The temperature had dropped. It was raining. "Look, maybe another time," I called, pulling my coat tighter. "I just can't manage it tonight."

But she was already flagging down a taxi. "Off you go, then. Do what you like."

"Aw, don't be that way! Diana!" I caught her by the arm. But she winced in pain and pulled away. "What's wrong?" I pushed up the sleeve of her dress. The dim light of the streetlamp illuminated a raised pink lattice of small, carefully executed cuts just above her elbow. "Jesus! What's this?"

"It's nothing." She twisted her arm free.

"What do you mean, it's nothing?" I was appalled by how deliberate the cuts were. "Who cut you?"

"No one. I did it."

"*You?* But why?"

"You wouldn't understand."

"Why not?"

She stared at me hard. "Because you have nothing to cut out, May!"

Her words frightened me. "What does that mean?"

She waved as another cab approached, and it slowed down. "Are you coming or not?"

"Why are you cutting yourself?" I demanded.

"Because"—she spat the words out—"it's hopeless! The whole thing is hopeless! You have no idea what I've lost, how I struggle . . ." She stopped herself, seemed for a moment to teeter on the brink of tears, and then shouted, "You don't even care! You care nothing for me!"

"What? Because I don't want to go to Roxbury tonight?" I shouted back. "That's *insane!*"

Water dripped from her chic little hat onto her face. Her lips were drawn tight and her eyes round with fury. "Do you think that's insane?" She gave a hard little laugh. "You have no fucking idea!" And she gave me a shove that sent me stumbling backward into the rails of a wrought-iron fence. "Why don't you just leave me alone?"

She climbed in and slammed the door, and the cab drove off.

I stood on the sidewalk, wet and shaken, full of guilt, regret, and something else . . . relief.

Being with Diana was a liberating, unholy adventure. It was also dark and strange and, tonight, even a little terrifying. James was right.

Just like Lord Byron, she was mad, bad, and dangerous to know.

Then, without any warning, Mr. Winshaw returned.

Mr. Kessler sent me to collect some prints from the framer, and when I came back, he was no longer alone; someone was in his office with him.

As soon as I saw him, even before he turned round, I realized it must be him. A briny, sunbaked scent of faraway shores and foreign spices clung to his hair and clothes. And there was the way he stood, leaning against the doorframe as if he'd spent his entire life in doorways, coming and going, with never any intention of staying. Tall and lean, he was clearly no follower of fashion. His trousers were a size too large, cinched in by a worn belt, as if he'd bought them for another man; his shirtsleeves were rolled up to expose tanned forearms and large, rough hands—workman's hands, callused and red. He could've been a vagrant, but he had the confidence and ease of a man in complete possession of himself. He and Mr. Kessler were laughing about something; Mr. Kessler was actually giggling uncontrollably, slapping his hands on his knees. Suddenly I caught a glimpse of what he must have been like as a child. He had a pixieish delight and readiness for laughter I'd never seen before; his whole face was illuminated with happiness.

I stood outside the door, prints in hand, listening. Mr. Winshaw was describing the passage from Istanbul to Athens on a local fishing boat manned by Bulgarian smugglers. But it was the rhythm and full rounded tone of his English accent that captured my imagination. It was the voice of a natural storyteller. He reminded me of the archetypal guests of ancient fables, wayward travelers who appeared unexpectedly just before nightfall to sit by the fireside and recount incredible tales before disappearing again in the morning.

Mr. Kessler saw me standing in the hallway. "Miss Fanning!"

Mr. Winshaw turned. He was somewhere in his late thirties or early forties, with light, sandy hair streaked with gray, an aquiline nose, and a wide, intelligent forehead. His lucid gray-green eyes catching the light, he fixed me with a direct, inquisitive gaze. "So, this is Miss Fanning? Well"—he gave a slightly awkward laugh—"I must say you're not quite what I was expecting!"

"And what were you expecting?" I asked.

"Someone older. Someone not quite so . . . so *blond*," he admitted, glancing at Mr. Kessler.

"Miss Fanning is a very capable girl," Mr. Kessler assured him.

"I have no doubt." Still, he frowned, changing the subject. "Has Kessler been treating you well?"

"Yes, I'm very grateful to Mr. Kessler."

"We're all grateful to Kessler."

"I'm sorry I wasn't here when you arrived. Only you didn't give us fair warning."

"Oh, Winshaw never writes!" Mr. Kessler said. "You're lucky if you get so much as a postcard in six months!"

I looked down at my shoes, suddenly self-conscious.

Apparently it was contagious.

Coloring a little, Mr. Winshaw tossed his jacket onto his desk. "Writing is overrated, don't you think? One should only ever bother if there's something to say. Now"—he rubbed his hands together—"shall we unpack these things?" And he headed toward the back room, calling over his shoulder, "You didn't think I'd come back empty-handed, did you?"

We followed him. There were three large wooden crates, covered in customs stamps. They too smelled of the sea and rain, of exotic harbors and distant lands. Mr. Winshaw used a crowbar to open them, while Mr. Kessler and I unpacked various treasures like excited children opening gifts on Christmas Day. And they turned out to be packed in Mr. Winshaw's distinctive fashion, using old suitcases and rolls of cheap muslin.

I held up a battered brown leather valise. "You're slipping, Mr. Winshaw. This isn't nearly as fashionable as some of the others in your collection."

"Yes, well, it seems there are fewer women traveling these days.

I can't imagine why. The lost-and-found department at the shipping port had only these sad leftovers."

"So you scour through lost luggage, is that your secret? And what, may I ask, do you do with all the clothes?"

He grinned. "I can't tell you all my secrets, Fanning. We'd have nothing left to talk about."

He opened another trunk and passed us a baby-pink hatbox. The thrill was even greater than when Mr. Kessler and I had unpacked the vases. Inside was a collection of rare items from the ancient Middle East.

"Most of these are plaster casts, done on site at the expedition in Ur," Mr. Winshaw explained, "but there are a few exceptional original pieces. What do you think?" he asked Mr. Kessler. "If they don't want them here, Pittsburgh or Cleveland will take them, don't you agree?"

"That's likely." Mr. Kessler nodded. "Maybe even New York."

"I heard they weren't buying right now."

"That's what they say officially, but no one else has anything like this." Mr. Kessler held up a bronze sculpture of a female deity with clawed feet. "Look at this! Isn't she extraordinary?"

I came closer.

Extraordinary was right. Her face was lovely, even peaceful, her figure full and voluptuous, yet her head was crowned in horns and her legs transformed below the knees into the sharply taloned feet of a bird of prey.

"Who is she?" I asked.

"Well, that's a matter of debate," Mr. Winshaw answered. "She could be Ereshkigal, ruler of the underworld of ancient Mesopotamia, or Ishtar, the goddess of sexual congress, love, and war, or even the demoness Lilith."

"She's magnificent! Look"—Mr. Kessler turned her round—
"her wings are facing down; that's the symbol of the underworld.
I doubt she's Ishtar."

"But she could be an *aspect* of Ishtar," Mr. Winshaw pointed out.

"Is that what Woolley thought?"

"I don't know what Woolley thought." Mr. Winshaw frowned
impatiently. "Not all of us defer to Woolley!"

Mr. Kessler wasn't listening. He turned to me instead, overcome by a sudden swell of emotion. "You see how lucky we are?
This isn't just a job. It's a privilege—a vocation! So few people
have a real *feel* for the life of objects. Or the significance of time."
He held the figure up. "To hold a fragment of the ancient world
in the palm of your hand and admire its artistry, to wonder at
its purpose, to pause and consider the vast empires that rose and
fell around it while this frail scrap survived, against all odds,
is to touch the very mind and soul that made it—across centuries, across continents! Across everything that divides cultures
and human beings. This is an honor, Miss Fanning. And a responsibility." He placed it carefully on the table. "We're custo-
dians, stewards. When we cultivate relationships with serious
collectors, encourage them in their investments, watch a collection grow, plan its next acquisition, what we're really doing is
shaping a legacy that, with any luck, will survive intact for
generations. Our scholarship, our aesthetic judgment, ensures
that."

"There's no need to lecture her." Mr. Winshaw laughed. "She's
a secretary, not a curator!"

Mr. Kessler was about to reply when the bell on the door of the
shop jangled as a customer came in. "Excuse me, please."

He went to the front, and I was left alone with Mr. Winshaw.

I watched as he used a crowbar to open another crate. "I *am* interested, actually."

"Are you? Well, good. That will help you to make sales." He tossed the lid aside. "I understand you've already made a good start."

"Really?"

"Kessler told me it was you who sold the ring of Nemesis." He dug out another case.

I couldn't work out what he was talking about. "You mean the black agate ring?"

He looked across. "You *did* know it was Nemesis, didn't you?" He made it sound as if it were the most obvious thing in the world.

I suppose my face gave me away. "I thought it might be Clotho, one of the three Fates."

Up shot his eyebrows. "Is that what Kessler said? Really?" He gave a low whistle. "The old man's slipping!"

"No, I looked it up. On my own."

"*You?*" He put the crowbar down. "And why did you presume to do that?"

I could feel myself flushing, suddenly on the defensive. "I just thought—"

"Well, you shouldn't." He cut me off. "It's not your place. You should have consulted with Kessler; he would have set you straight. We must be careful," he warned, "to identify things accurately. Can you imagine if someone bought something, believing it to be an ancient Greek artifact, if it was in fact Etruscan?"

I didn't know the difference between Greek and Etruscan either. Clearly he thought I was an idiot, completely out of my depth.

Strained silence followed.

I thought of James and the way he'd bought the ring, saying it made him think of me. If it wasn't a good-luck charm, what was it?

Persia padded in, weaving around Mr. Winshaw's legs, purring loudly. He gave him an affectionate scratch under the chin. "You haven't got any tea, have you, Fanning?"

"*'Fanning'*?" It was bad enough to be reprimanded like a child. "I do have a first name, you know!"

"Sorry." He gave me a slightly apologetic look. "It's an English public school thing—you get used to people calling you by your surname. Actually, it's a sign of affection."

"Only in England is it a sign of affection when someone forgets your name."

"They don't forget it. Chances are they never learned it in the first place." He smiled.

"So"—I decided to swallow my pride—"tell me, then: Who exactly is Nemesis?"

He looked at me as if I'd asked him to teach me the alphabet. "Nemesis is a Greek goddess. The name Nemesis is derived from the Greek words *nemêsis* and *nemô*, meaning 'dispenser of dues.'"

"Dues?"

"Punishment," he elaborated. "What's coming to you. She balances good fortune, Thyke, against hubris. Actually, retribution is a more accurate way of thinking of it."

"You mean revenge?"

He winced slightly, as if the word were philosophically clumsy. "That's one way of putting it. A little simplistic, though."

"Forgive me. My Greek's a little rusty."

I took the kettle into the bathroom and filled it.

The first time I'd seen the ring, wrapped in that dirty hand-kerchief it struck me as unusual. Perhaps it was just my imagination, but I recalled the strange, compelling aura that seemed to surround it. Was it more than just symbolic?

Going back in, I turned on the hot plate. "Where did you get it?"

He was stacking up the empty cases. "I'm sorry?"

"The ring of Nemesis. I was wondering where you got it."

"It came from a Swiss collector. Part of a considerable private collection—the same family that sold the vases."

"Why did they sell?"

He shrugged. "I'm not sure, really. Some personal inclination."

"It was wrapped in a dirty hankie. You know, we almost completely overlooked it."

He pulled out another case, in a particularly anemic shade of eau de Nil. "And so did the customs officials. That's the point. They tend to confiscate jewelry when they can. It sells quite easily on the black market."

I took the tea down from the shelf. "Is it bad luck?"

"The ring? Well, it would be bad luck if you lost it—it's worth a lot of money." He unwrapped a small stone plaque covered in rows of cuneiform writing. "Why?" He looked across at me. "You're not superstitious, on top of everything else?"

I stopped what I was doing. "On top of what, precisely?"

"On top of being blond, doe-eyed, and all of sixteen years old!" he laughed.

"Doe-eyed?"

"It's a compliment! Don't be so touchy!"

I was ready to pitch a cup at his head.

"Like not remembering my name?" I asked. "And I'm twenty-five, actually."

"Fine." He held up his hands. "Look, we've never had an assistant before. And certainly not a girl."

"Does that mean you don't want one?"

"I didn't say that. I just meant, well . . . you're not what I was expecting, that's all."

I spooned the tea leaves furiously into the pot. "And what were you expecting?"

He shrugged. "I thought you were older."

"What difference does that make?"

"It just . . . well, it just does! Anyway," he said, changing the subject, "you were asking about the ring."

"I wanted to know if by wearing it, one is invoking Nemesis. Like a curse?"

"You *are* superstitious!" He chuckled, leaning back on an empty crate. "Wait a minute, May Fanning—is that May, short for Maeve, by any chance? You're Irish, aren't you? I'll bet you grew up with little people and banshees and leprechauns and all sorts!"

His cockiness rankled. "Can you please just answer the question?"

He scooped Persia up, and the cat went limp with pleasure in his arms. "Nemesis is a goddess, but she's also more than that; she represents a force, a fundamental aspect of the equilibrium of the universe. It's not really a matter of her being good or evil, cursed or lucky. She's simply part of the way of things."

I folded my arms across my chest. "So you're incapable of giving a straight answer, is that it?"

He tried again. "Look . . . each action has its reaction. We tend to see things in terms of good luck or bad luck, but in the end, what really matters is not the twists and turns of fate but what you do with them. After all, your character isn't measured in your circumstances, but by your attitude and actions."

"Oh I see! Like a classic hero—'Made weak by time and fate, but strong in will / To strive, to seek, to find, and not to yield.'"

The closing lines of the poem came out before I could stop myself. I'd read them so many times, they were like a prayer repeated over and over in my head.

Mr. Winshaw stopped petting Persia and stared at me. "Did you just quote 'Ulysses'?"

Now I had his attention.

I pretended to concentrate on stirring the tea. "I suppose I did."

"*You* know 'Ulysses'?"

The disbelief in his voice was maddening.

"Well, let's see. That's the one about the great warrior of the Trojan War, stuck on an island and given the promise of an immortal life with a beautiful goddess, but who'd rather be pummeled at sea by Poseidon than live out his days quietly in paradise. Am I right?"

He put Persia down. "Actually, it's about craving your own mortality. Being hungry for life, for obstacles, no matter the cost."

He always had to have the upper hand.

"Ulysses wants to test himself," he continued, "to feel alive. After all, what's immortality but death, really—a vast, golden emptiness, devoid of the only true experiences that make life worthwhile?"

"Do you honestly believe that the suffering of life is preferable to heaven?"

"Heaven isn't a place, Fanning!" He rolled his eyes as if he'd been pushed beyond the limits of human endurance. "Why does everyone assume it's a destination—some celestial version of Grand Central Station? It's a state of being! The unshakable certainty of *who* you are and *where* you fit in the world! The slings and arrows of outrageous fortune aside, we suffer most when we try to be someone or something we're not."

He spoke in grand, abstract concepts the way other people

chatted about the weather or politics. I'd never met anyone so willing or able to dissect metaphysical ideas. Not that this impressed me much.

"Oh, how terribly *English* of you! So we should all stay firmly in our place, is that it?"

"Of course not! We have to test the limits—we're human!"

"And so we *have* to suffer," I concluded.

Talking with him was like being tossed into a dangerous, fast-moving current; one had to swim hard against the unrelenting tide of his arguments.

"Yes! Absolutely! Don't you see? Our souls are forged in adversity. Without it, we're shapeless, indistinct! Suffering isn't punishment, it's a catalyst!" He began to pace the floor, as if he were pulling ideas from the air around him. "Why, a man might think himself capable of anything when life is calm, might imagine himself equal to great sacrifice, dignity, or courage. But only in our desperate moments do we truly know what we're made of or who we are. The hour of our calamity is the only true test of our character—without it we're unformed and incomplete!"

"And what if the hour of our calamity is our last?" I countered. (Apparently I had just as many philosophical opinions as he did, which surprised me.)

Quite suddenly he stopped pacing. "Now there's a question," he admitted. Some inner shadow darkened his fervor. "Then we die," he said quietly. "But we die having truly lived. And nothing can diminish that."

Whatever that shadow was, it had diffused his enthusiasm for the argument. He turned back to unpacking again. "It's always been one of my favorites, that poem. How do you know it?"

"You'd be surprised, Mr. Winshaw. They give library cards to anyone these days. Even secretaries."

Mr. Kessler coughed in the doorway. "Is he lecturing you?"

"He's trying to." I poured out the tea and handed them each a cup.

"Don't let him batter you with his atheism and intellect," Mr. Kessler warned, picking up the cuneiform tablet.

"I'm not an atheist! I believe in gods," Mr. Winshaw protested. "I just haven't decided which ones."

"How can you say that?" I passed him the sugar bowl. "There is only one god!"

"Really?" He was quite easy to provoke. "And would that be yours, mine, or Kessler's? Or"—he held up a finger—"are we all right? Is the god you choose the god you deserve?"

"Oh, dear, Mr. Winshaw!" I sighed. "How can you ask such questions?"

"How can you not?"

"Why, you believe not only that you can choose your god depending on your mood, but that you can *design* him as well!" I shook my head in wonder. "Could you possibly be more arrogant?"

Mr. Kessler snorted in delight.

"Isn't that what men have been doing since the history of time?" he replied, clearly enjoying himself again. "Besides, it isn't arrogance."

"What is it then?"

"Necessity."

Mr. Kessler looked at me. "I told you. You will be here all night, arguing with him. And by morning, you will be no closer to a conclusion."

I took a sip of the hot tea. Mr. Winshaw was intellectually vain. But he spoke about things no one else discussed, ideas I didn't even know I believed in; he was like a whetstone, sharpening my thoughts and mind. Perhaps he was sent to refine my character through suffering, I thought wryly.

That evening, on the way home, I stopped into the library and, sitting at one of the long wooden tables, I looked up Nemesis.

The goddess of retribution avenging both evil actions and redressing unjustified good fortune, Nemesis was the eternal embodiment of avenging justice for those who committed crimes with apparent impunity, or who had inordinate good luck. Bringing an often sudden and terrible balance to bear in human affairs, she portioned out both happiness and unhappiness, taking care that neither was too frequent or excessive in any man's life. Often depicted as a comely winged goddess, her symbols were the apple branch, rein, lash, sword, or balance. And at her feet turned the great wheel of life itself, for she was the inescapable force that conquered all, rolling the proud from on high into the dirt and bridling the arrogant and unfaithful with her unshakable bit. For all were her subjects, from beggar to king, and none escaped her whip of misery.

So the wheel on the ring wasn't a spinning wheel, but the ever-turning wheel of fortune. And she was holding a whip, not a thread. Were Cupid and Psyche present because of the goddess's inclination to right the wrongs in matters of love?

I closed the book, resolved to do my research properly from now on.

Still, I couldn't help thinking of the ring, and the man who wore it. The man who'd taken over my thoughts and imagination. James Van der Laar was like a disease, spreading through my mind and body, even in his absence.

At night I lay in bed, imagining his hands on my skin, his body on mine.

I might have been infected, dying even. But I didn't want to be cured.

Mr. Winshaw turned out to be an invigorating if somewhat anarchic force in the daily fortunes of Winshaw and Kessler. He didn't work regular hours, he wasn't much interested in the actual business of selling things, and his presence often resulted in chaos—like the morning Mr. Kessler and I arrived to find all of the furniture out on the sidewalk. Apparently Mr. Winshaw had risen early with a vision, hired a couple of drifters from the Common to help with the lifting, and cleared out everything in the shop. Then, somewhere in the middle of putting things back, they got hungry and decided to go for breakfast, leaving it all on the pavement. I was instructed to sit outside and keep an eye on things while Mr. Kessler frantically tracked them down. Luckily people took it to be a clearance sale, and I sold a mahogany campaign desk and the Limoges tea set before they returned.

Already Mr. Winshaw was planning his next journey; there was talk of Egypt and also South America. And before that, he was scheduled to teach in Philadelphia for a semester. He had a voracious appetite for information, attending lectures, concerts, and plays almost every night. His office became even more overrun with stacks of newspapers, books, and journals, as well as piles of unopened mail, which he steadfastly ignored. He had an opinion about absolutely everything, which he never hesitated to share and might easily adapt or abandon, depending on his mood. And he became irritable and even sulky if no one bothered to argue against him. But what was truly exceptional was the lightning speed of his mind, the ease with which he leapt from one idea to the next, linking seemingly unrelated subjects until they formed a vast tapestry of contrasting perspectives and views. It was the challenge he enjoyed, more than the theories. His loyalty was not to the conclusions he reached so much as to the capacity of his mind to reach them.

It was easy to tell he was a bachelor; his shirts were poorly ironed, his trousers too big, and he seemed to survive largely on cigarettes and Hershey bars. Persia followed him everywhere with the silent devotion of a familiar, but he wasn't the only one. Mr. Winshaw was rarely alone in the evening; there was always an attractive woman trailing behind him, ready to make him a home-cooked meal or take him in hand. Mostly he resisted their attempts at domestication, though occasionally there was a small victory, and he would arrive dressed in a newly pressed shirt or a jacket that fit him before reverting to his old ways.

One of his more regular paramours was a girl named Selena, who worked at Freeman's Auctioneers downtown. An appraiser in the fine jewelry department, Selena was only a few years older than me. With her soft black curls, deep brown eyes, and enviable figure, she had a knack for hypnotizing clients, especially men, and Mr. Winshaw was no different. She had a slow, calculated way of moving and speaking that I suspected gave the impression that she was more intelligent than she was; making her comments seem considered and elusive rather than merely banal. And I quickly learned that if Selena was in the room, chances were she was acting out a private scene in which other people merely figured as bit players. There was little point in trying to steal the limelight from her.

Once or twice she'd come in before closing time to meet Mr. Winshaw, always eyeing me up as if I were a particularly pathetic stray dog. She pretended to take a maternal interest, defending me against his imaginary attacks. When he called me Fanning, Selena always jumped to my defense. "She has a *name*, Ben!" And then she'd roll her eyes at me as if to say, *Men!* To be honest, I was a little disappointed that such an ordinary girl could capture his imagination.

But the man I'd written to, the mysterious clever stranger who'd been so charming on paper, rarely seemed to match with the man who now wandered round the shop, debating politics and religion with anyone who would listen and planning his eventual escape.

The letters themselves were never referred to again. I sensed he was a little embarrassed that he'd written to me at all. I couldn't forget the look of surprise when he'd met me for the first time, the sudden realization that I was, after all, only a secretary. Still, I kept them. I liked that man. I missed his thoughtful consideration and clarity. I only wondered where he'd gone.

"He sounds like a snob," Angela said as we were walking back from church early one Saturday evening.

Normally I went to church with my mother at the Cathedral of the Holy Cross. But since New York, I'd avoided going at all, something Ma sighed and fretted over every Sunday. I knew there'd be no forgiveness for me there. But when Angela asked me to join her for mass at the local Italian church, St. Leonard's, I didn't even hesitate. St. Leonard's didn't feel like church to me. Where the Holy Cross was grand and dark and Gothic, St. Leonard's was unashamedly bright, ostentatiously Baroque. And my Irish sins weren't the jurisdiction of the smooth-faced saints that lined the walls in brightly painted robes, their large brown eyes mimicking the Mediterranean features of their congregation. No, my shame belonged across town, with the cold marble deities that stood as unblinking sentinels against moral decay.

But then I'd always found the theatricality of the Italian celebrations, especially the endless feast days of the summer months, irresistibly exotic and entertaining. In the North End, statues of the saints were paraded regularly through the streets, sometimes covered in crisp dollar bills and prayers and accompanied by loud marching bands. They headed long processions with the whole neighborhood following behind, singing and clapping, all wearing their best clothes. And on Easter Sunday, little girls and boys dressed like tiny brides and grooms were presented before the congregation for their first communion, the girls in white dresses and veils, their ears already pierced.

Ma had always been appalled by our neighbors' gaudy adoration. "God doesn't want us to throw a party. He wants us to remember our sins and repent! To regret what we've done."

The Italian saints were far too vivid for her liking—Saint Lucia holding her eyes on a little silver plate, or Saint Agatha offering her breasts like two splendid cakes on a gold tray. At the Holy Cross, there were no statues dressed in white silk finery and gold brocade gowns, no real jewels in the Madonna's crown, no noisy parades though the street. For the Irish, Catholicism was a sacrifice, an open wound that brought persecution and hardship. But for the Italians, it was celebration.

Angela preferred going to church on Saturday evenings so she could have an hour or two alone on Sunday morning with Carlo. And it gave me a chance to see her on my own, away from her new family. Although we never spoke of it, we both quietly accepted that I wasn't welcome to spend hours sitting on the Menzis' front porch with her, gossiping. Still, I craved Angela's normalcy and stability, even though I didn't necessarily want it all the time. She was the soothing antidote to Diana's unfettered excess, reminding me of simpler, more straightforward times. So I began joining her regularly after work on Saturday evening for mass, walking her back home afterward.

"Mr. Winshaw a *snob*?" This struck me as funny. "Oh, he'd be furious if he knew that! He fancies himself as quite a man of the people."

"An intellectual snob," Angela clarified. "People who imagine that they're cleverer than everyone else and therefore superior. They're the worst."

"I don't think he's that. It's not snobbery." I tried to put my finger on it. "It's more like impatience."

"With what?"

"I don't know. . . . Actually"—I realized it suddenly—"I think it's with me! As if he'd expected more of me and was disappointed."

Angela was indignant on my behalf. "Well, that's ridiculous! What more are you meant to be? I wouldn't bother to pay him any attention."

"Oh, I don't!" I assured her. "Anyway, Mr. Kessler seems happy with me."

"He's the one who hired you. You're a good secretary. Best in your class." She said it with pride, which warmed my heart.

Only being a good secretary didn't seem as much of an achievement anymore. I kicked a bottle cap into the gutter. "Actually, he did suggest a lecture series on ancient civilizations beginning in late August at the public library, if you want to go . . ."

"*Me?*" She snorted. "To a lecture?"

"Why not?"

"When would I have time for that? Have you forgotten?" She patted her stomach. "My spare time is running out!"

"Oh, yes. Of course."

"Anyway, you don't want to get involved with all that. You'll never meet anyone at the public library except bookworms."

"It's not about meeting anyone. It's about learning something."

"Yes, but you said Mr. Kessler was happy. So why bother?" She shrugged. "Why make more work for yourself?"

Angela was nothing if not practical. I wondered if Diana would be willing to go. It had been a while since we'd spoken—a couple of weeks of stubborn sullen silence on both ends. I was surprised by how long it had lasted. At least I had an excuse: I'd been busy, distracted by work and Mr. Winshaw's arrival. But I still didn't want to be the first one to call.

"Stop in with me to my parents'," Angela said. "They'd love to see you. And Mama's made *garganelli.*"

"*Garganelli?*" I looked across at her. "Why, what's wrong?"

Garganelli were little cylinders of pasta rolled out on a ribbed wooden dowel with a pencil and looked like quill pen points. They were also quite time-consuming to make. Delicately flavored with fresh nutmeg and lemon zest, they were served with cream, pancetta, and fresh peas. But in the Russo household, *garganelli* were the delicious outward manifestation of profound inward unease. Mrs. Russo only made them when she was troubled. Ridding the kitchen of everyone, she would crack eggs, fold the flour in, and sit down to roll out several hundred in much the same way that other women picked up their knitting. With her hands occupied, her mind was free to mull and brood, to turn over her difficulties in the hope of glimpsing an unexpected solution.

The result was rich, faintly perfumed, and comforting, but it was also an elegant response to the unexpected trials of fortune. Some problems could not be solved. But Maddalena Russo transformed worry into artistry, a defiant refusal to be undone by circumstances that sustained rather than diminished.

"It's Pina," Angela said. "They let go of another two hundred men at the canning factory yesterday. Her husband, Augie, was one of them."

Pina was due in less than a month.

"What are they going to do?"

"I don't know. His brother Rusty says he can find him

something, but Rusty's such a slippery character. Mama's convinced he's a criminal and has ties to the Black Hand, which of course is ridiculous. But that doesn't stop her from carrying on." She sighed. "They'd just put a deposit on a house, but now they won't be able to take it. I just hope they don't lose the money too."

"I'm so sorry." I thought of Augie (short for Agamemnon): not nearly as charismatic as Rusty, he was an earnest, soft-spoken man, but it was really Pina who ran the show.

"Come and eat." Angela gave my arm a tug. "The whole family will be there."

"Yeah, well, Pina hates me."

"No, she doesn't!"

I gave her a look. "Oh, yes, she does!"

"Well"—Angela grinned, not bothering to deny it anymore—"as long as she's busy hating you, she's not giving me any trouble, and that suits me just fine. She has to find fault with someone! Besides, you owe me one. Oh, look!" She bent down, pulled a gold-foil chocolate wrapper out from under the wheel of a parked car, and held it up triumphantly. "One for the box!"

"You don't still collect those, do you?" I laughed.

"Some habits die hard." She handed it to me. "Does it smell?"

I gave it a sniff. "A little. You know, you can buy as much chocolate as you like now."

"That's cheating!" She gave me a gentle dig in the ribs. "It's about the hunt, Mae. Not about the chocolate."

"Of course." I folded it neatly, handing it back to her. "Go on, then. One for the box."

One of the first things Mr. Kessler arranged after Mr. Winshaw's return was a visit to the Museum of Fine Arts to see the

"Winshaw and Kessler collection," as he put it, in its illustrious new home.

It was a wet, windy spring day, the kind that begins dismal and tempest-tossed and ends in Wedgwood-blue skies and sunshine. Mr. Kessler insisted we all go, first thing in the morning. Mr. Winshaw, who generally wasn't much use before noon and appeared to have slept in his clothes from the night before, lagged sullenly behind us as we got off the trolley, chain-smoking cigarettes, while I tried to be cheerful despite the rain that was slowly ruining my hat and dampening my curls.

Still, none of this mattered to Mr. Kessler, who radiated pride like a lighthouse over a black sea as he led the way into the Art of the Ancient World wing. He strutted past high scaffolding where half a dozen painters were diligently working on a new large-scale mural. There were the beginnings of a pastoral scene of ancient Greece, with billowing clouds, golden figures, and temples overlooking rolling green valleys.

Mr. Kessler stopped in front of the glass cabinet that housed both the plate and vase. "And there you have it!" he announced with a flourish. "Displayed just as it should be, right in the center of the room!"

Mr. Winshaw nodded, jamming his hands into his pockets. "There you have it," he agreed.

We all stared.

"Isn't it magnificent?" Mr. Kessler asked after a while.

"Very."

"This is a milestone. The first of many!"

"Absolutely."

Mr. Winshaw was resigned about seeing the final outcome, no matter how prestigious. I wondered if it had to do with the fact that once a piece was sold, the chase was well and truly over.

For Mr. Kessler, an artifact in a glass case was a triumph, but for Mr. Winshaw it was the end of a long, rigorously fought romance.

I decided to leave them to it. Instead I wandered around the gallery, which I'd never been in when it was empty. It was intelligently laid out, and obviously a lot of money had been spent on it recently. In addition to the mural, there were new cabinets and informative displays. I noticed the other Van der Laar bequest—a full set of polished bronze Corinthian armor and a spear, impressively preserved and heroically splendid—was also featured. The helmet, with its thick horsehair fringe, and the articulated shining breastplate were worthy of Achilles himself.

I moved along to an adjoining room. A pair of life-size Archaic Greek statues dominated: two identical figures carved in red marble, naked and flawlessly proportioned, standing with the same foot forward, hands clenched by their sides.

They were magnificent and yet bound with the static tension of their own perfection.

"They're *kouroi*, which means 'youth' in Greek," Mr. Winshaw said, coming up behind me. "Brothers, in fact; Kleobis and Biton. See how they're symmetrical? To the Greeks, they represented everything that was considered to be best in masculinity—strength, physical excellence, piety."

"Piety?" It seemed an odd word to use.

"A certain kind of piety," he allowed.

"They look so stiff."

"Well"—he took out yet another cigarette—"there's nothing natural about perfection. That's their downfall, you see. The myth says they were such admirable examples of manhood that their mother prayed to the goddess Hera to reward them with the best gift the gods could give a mortal."

"And did she?"

"Absolutely. Hera killed them in their sleep at a religious festival, so that they would be remembered always and worshipped as heroes."

I gave a low whistle. "If that's what she does to people she likes, you *really* don't want to end up on her bad side!"

"Living a long life meant nothing to the Greeks compared to the immortality of honor."

Reading the plaque, I was startled to see the name of the benefactor: "Made possible by a generous donation from Diana Van der Laar."

When had this happened? Here was another event in Diana's life she'd never even mentioned to me, that I'd discovered by accident. And to my irritation, I felt a stab of loneliness.

"What does it say?" Mr. Winshaw asked.

"Just that this was donated by the Van der Laars too."

"Well, aren't they civic-minded?"

"Why, Winshaw! Can that really be you, back from your travels?"

We turned. Philip Kimberly was strolling across the great hall, arms spread wide like a gracious host greeting a tardy houseguest. Wearing a wide pinstripe suit and a radiant gold silk tie bound in a large double Windsor knot, he crossed the marble floor looking every inch the fashionable man-about-town. He'd recently grown a small, thin mustache that made him look faintly like William Powell. As he approached, the air around him was scented with the delicate freshness of lemon vetiver water.

"Good to see you, old boy!" He shook Mr. Winshaw's hand. "So, what do you think?"

Mr. Winshaw brushed a bit of ash off his rumpled trench coat. "It looks like you've got some new pieces and some new patrons. The Van der Laars certainly have been generous."

Mr. Kimberly raised an eyebrow. "To both of us, wouldn't you say? So, how long are you in town?"

"Who says I'm going anywhere?" Mr. Winshaw shot a stream of smoke at the ceiling.

"Oh, it's not like you to ever stay anywhere for long." Mr. Kimberly laughed. "Besides, I'm curious. If I were smart, I'd have you followed and try to snatch those prizes before you do! Where'd you get that vase, for example?"

"Oh, well, that would be telling."

"You know, you should come for drinks at my club sometime, tell us all some stories of your adventures. It's very comfortable, and there are a number of people I could introduce you to. People who might be useful."

But Mr. Winshaw was impervious to Mr. Kimberly's charm. "That's more Kessler's area than mine. Why don't you invite him?"

Mr. Kimberly hesitated, gave a sharp little cough. "You know the rules. Be fair now. I'm only trying to help."

"You know me." Mr. Winshaw shrugged. "I prefer useless friends."

Mr. Kimberly's face flushed, his ears turning bright pink.

Mr. Kessler came up, bursting with excitement. "Mr. Kimberly! They look very well, don't you think?"

Mr. Kimberly smiled thinly. "I'm glad you approve. What do you think of our redecoration?" He gestured to the painters behind them.

Mr. Winshaw narrowed his eyes to better see the mural. "What is that exactly? A satyr? Playing *panpipes*? And are those nymphs frolicking across an open field?"

Mr. Kessler flashed him a warning look.

"It's a metaphor, actually," Mr. Kimberly explained indulgently, gesturing to the vast marble hall. "Here lies inspiration and hope. A glimpse of what we could be again. Another golden age."

Mr. Winshaw flicked a bit of ash onto the floor. "Only it's a myth."

"Well"—Mr. Kimberly straightened—"I'm sorry if you don't approve. Of course we're planning to increase the collection over time. We've got a few patrons now who are willing to invest considerably and are always eager to collaborate with dealers who understand our vision."

Mr. Kessler gave Winshaw a panicked look.

I couldn't bear the tension anymore. "I see Diana has made another bequest. Congratulations! It's a wonderful piece."

They all looked at me.

Mr. Kimberly frowned, only just recognizing who I was. "But of course, you know her, don't you?"

"I'm only sorry I missed the reception. We had such a good time at the last one, didn't we, Mr. Kessler? What a success!" I added, a little too brightly.

"Yes, well . . ." Mr. Kimberly tugged his cuffs down over his wrists with a quick, sharp movement. "I'm afraid on this occasion the family wanted something more discreet. Especially after the last incident."

He was no doubt referring to Diana's refusal to put on a satisfactory public show.

"Well, maybe next time we can come?" Mr. Kessler suggested, giving me a grateful smile. "We so enjoy working with their entire family."

As we were leaving, I hung back to speak to Mr. Winshaw.

"Why did you put Mr. Kimberly on the spot like that?" I whispered. "Can't you see how important this is to Mr. Kessler?"

"I understand better than you know, Fanning," he said, heading down the stairs.

"Then how could you embarrass him?" I asked, struggling to keep up with him.

He stopped abruptly, turned on me. "You have no idea what you're talking about!"

"Really? Well, then, enlighten me!"

"When we first started out, Kimberly was just an assistant, trying to get his foot in the door of the museum. He approached Kessler about some small pieces for the Egyptian gallery. They were modest but first-class—scarabs and the like, in excellent condition. Kimberly agreed on a price but after delivery only paid half. He promised Kessler they would go into the main collection, that he would repay him over time. But it turned out he'd sold them on to a private buyer for considerably more money."

"You mean he cheated him?" Mr. Kimberly, with his dapper suits, Hollywood mustache, and lectures on civic idealism, was a thief? "But why didn't Mr. Kessler go to the police?"

"Because he knew Kimberly could easily destroy his professional reputation if he chose. He's the kind of man who promises anything to get what he wants."

"Then why does Mr. Kessler continue to deal with him?"

"Because he can't afford not to. Nobody can. And Kessler's pragmatic. Kimberly's a loathsome creature. I'm only sorry that Kessler has to deal with him at all," Mr. Winshaw added, carrying on down to the foyer.

I straggled along after him, feeling stupid. "I'm sorry. I guess I jumped the gun."

"I guess you did."

"You must think I'm naive."

"It's normal to give people the benefit of the doubt. But remember, Fanning, for those ascending the social ladder, other people are only rungs. And this is a town of climbers."

"Well, in any case"—I sighed—"I don't think Mr. Kessler is speaking to you."

Mr. Winshaw looked across at Mr. Kessler, who was walking, head down, very quickly ahead of us. "Kessler's heard everything I have to say anyway."

After a few more days I gave in and wrote to Diana. I sent her a postcard of Bunker Hill and wrote "I surrender. Any chance of reconvening the No Way Out Club?" on the back. I sent it to the apartment in Waverly Mansions. But I got no reply.

Her silence bothered me more than I liked to admit. A couple of times I walked over to Waverly Mansions after work and was on the verge of letting myself in. Instead, I stood outside, staring up at the windows of the apartment, straining for a glimpse of her. I didn't want to go up to the apartment and find her there with other people, new friends. As difficult and unpredictable as Diana could be, she was also the only person who understood my need for freedom and who never judged me for it. There was sanity in our madness together that I couldn't find with anyone else. So I ended up walking away. I needed her, apparently more than she needed me. But it was her refusal to even acknowledge me, her complete and utter disregard, that wounded me the most.

Then one afternoon James Van der Laar turned up at the shop again.

I hadn't seen or heard from him in weeks. And yet he walked in as if he knew I'd been waiting for him. I had. I didn't like that either; it was dangerous to think so much about a man I didn't really know. And his confidence disturbed me, almost as much as my excitement at seeing him again.

"Have luncheon with me," he commanded, casting a restless eye around as if searching for something and vaguely irritated not to find it.

I resisted the urge to accept immediately. "Why?"

He picked up a Victorian silver letter opener, twirled it between his fingers. "Because. I've come all the way from New York to see you, May Fanning. Because you've taken residency in my thoughts and, quite frankly, I'm considering charging you rent for the time and space you occupy in my head."

He looked straight at me, and I felt my entire body warm with the sudden flush of power. Still, I held my ground.

"It's too late for lunch. And you forget, I'm at work. Mr. Kessler won't allow it."

"I'm an important client. Mr. Kessler will be only too happy to part with you. Now"—he held out his arm—"come and bathe me in the glaring light of your cynicism, Miss Fanning. I long to be scrutinized, judged, and found wanting."

We went to Locke-Ober, an old French restaurant on Winter Place. The maître d', Bernard, had been there almost as long as the restaurant itself and was as small and wrinkled as an old crab apple, with shockingly black hair that could only have come from a bottle. He fell upon James as soon as he saw him. "Ah, Mr. Van der Laar!" he gasped. "It's been far too long! *Far* too long! And who, may I ask, is this ravishing creature?"

"This is Miss Fanning." James introduced us.

"But she's exquisite!" Bernard took a step back. "A vision! Like something from a wonderful dream!"

I'd never had such a reception; I glanced at James to see if this was all some elaborate joke.

But he just smiled. "I'm sorry I didn't ring ahead, Bernard. Can you fit us in?"

"For you, anything! But we must find the perfect table to show off Miss Fanning!" He cast a beady black eye around the room. It was surprisingly crowded—crammed with fashionable couples, dining late, people with nowhere to go and nothing to do until it was time to dress for cocktails.

"Here!" Bernard ferried us to a table at the center of the room. "Now you will make all the other women jealous!"

Finally alone with James, I felt self-conscious and out of my depth. After weeks of imagining this moment, I was suddenly subdued and formal. The grandeur of the place, the other couples looking across at us, recognizing him, the absurd obsequiousness of Bernard, all put me on edge. Under the table my leg jogged up and down uncontrollably, and I had to cross my ankles to hide it.

But James was careful to put me at ease, and immediately ordered champagne, a bottle so old and venerable that its label was yellowed and it was covered with a fine layer of dust. "The family pays to keep a private stock here," he explained. "All acquired before the Volstead Act, so no one can touch them. We're doing a public service, you see—ensuring it doesn't fall into the wrong hands."

I'd never had champagne before. And it never occurred to me that anyone would be so extravagant as to drink it during luncheon. But when I looked around, there were ice buckets at almost all the tables. It was apparently the "done thing," and

James acted as if it were no less than what I expected. I tried to act that way too.

The waiter popped the cork and poured.

"Here's to you." James raised his glass.

"Here's to all of us." I raised my glass too.

The smell of crisp green apples and fine bubbles tickled my nose, behind it the seductive promise of a door unlocking in my head, of my nerves evaporating and an elegant, gay afternoon unfolding easily before us. From the very first sip, a glorious relief spread through me.

Ignoring the menu, James ordered for both of us in French, sending waiters racing back to the kitchen to meet his requests. Plates of delicately flavored fish in saffron sauce appeared, with *pommes dauphinois* and cold asparagus in vinaigrette, food so delicious I had difficulty concentrating on anything else.

"So, where have you been lately?" he wanted to know.

"Nowhere," I said in between greedy bites. "Why?"

"I wonder why we haven't seen you. I know Diana's quite fond of you. I suppose she'll be in touch when she gets back."

"Back?" I stopped mid-mouthful. "Back from where?"

"Saint-Tropez. Didn't she tell you?"

It never occurred to me that she might be traveling. "I'm afraid not."

"Well, she has a mind like a sieve. She goes every year. The sun does her good. Personally, I prefer Monte Carlo. Or Beaulieu. Have you been recently?"

"Recently? No. Not recently."

"Perhaps next year we will all go together, what do you say?"

It was all so beyond me, I couldn't help but laugh. "And how am I to manage that? Flap my wings and fly?"

He seemed surprised that I might find it difficult to nip over to France.

"Well, what if someone took you?"

"And why would anyone do that?"

"Because you're an extraordinary girl. Do you honestly think I would spend time with you if you weren't exceptional?"

"Perhaps you're doing a public service, like with the champagne. Ensuring I don't fall into the wrong hands."

He leaned in closer. "The average person is little more than cattle, waiting to be told what to do, what to think. But you have intelligence, beauty, and something else, something they haven't got and can never hope to have. You're made of superior stock. Anyone can see that. Look at your coloring, the symmetry of your face—at how tall you are!" I winced, and he laughed. "Forgive me, but you have the body of a championship racehorse. Not just anyone is fit to ride you."

I flushed bright red. "I'm changing the subject now, Mr. Van der Laar."

"Change it all you want, Miss Fanning. But I'm warning you: I won't allow you to underestimate yourself again."

It was a heady combination—the champagne, the flattery, the utter conviction of one's uniqueness in the world. I didn't mind being lauded as beautiful, bright, and a creature of uncommon destiny.

"Now"—he refilled my glass—"I want to know everything about you. Your favorite color, the name of your first pet, where you've traveled . . ."

"What was the name of your first pet?" I batted the question back at him.

"A gelding called Mercury. Mad as a box of frogs and fast as wind. Go on"—he nodded—"your turn."

"It was a parrot," I fibbed, "named Charlie. Had a mouth like a sailor and used to fly around the house chasing the dog. God, we all loved him!"

"Was it a big house?"

"A rather ramshackle Victorian affair. Nothing compared to yours."

"And what about your family? Tell me about them."

"My family . . ." I took out a cigarette, buying myself time. "My family are quite eccentric, I suppose. Lately my mother has become convinced that turbans are all the rage—isn't that hysterical? She's even threatening to knit me one!"

"What I wouldn't give to see you in a knitted turban!" He chuckled. "How ghastly! Do you miss her?"

"Pardon me?"

"It must be hard, being away from her."

"Oh, yes!" I'd forgotten about my Albany upbringing. "Yes, of course!" I exhaled, nodding a little too emphatically. "She's an odd bird—sweet, but odd."

"What about your father?" He really did want to know everything. "What was he like?"

"Ah, let me see." I paused. "Well, he was a writer . . ." (That wasn't quite grand enough.) "And a professor, actually. A very refined, intelligent man. The parrot was his. He died a long time ago, when he was still quite young."

"That must have been difficult."

"It was. It means, well, that I haven't got quite the financial security that some people have." I was taking a risk, hinting at our circumstances.

"There's no shame in that."

I looked at him sideways, trying to read his expression. "My mother and I, we live quite modestly. It's one of the reasons I work."

"You're resourceful. It speaks to your character. I admire that."

It was a gracious response, one that put me at ease. "So, you haven't told me anything of where you've been or what you've been doing."

"Too dull. I spend most of my time either in New York or abroad."

"In Africa?"

He looked up. "How do you know about that?"

"Diana said you had a family estate there."

"Yes, that's right. But I've been in Germany a great deal recently. I'm exploring some prospects of my own."

"Like what?"

"Research mostly. The Germans have been hit badly by this depression too. But they're not nearly so complacent." He leaned forward. "I loathe how America has become a nanny state, holding people's hands and spoon-feeding them subsidy." He waved his fork at the other diners as if they were personally responsible. "But the Germans, I'm telling you, they're far more progressive than we are."

"So you're a politician?"

"Not exactly." He took another bite. "But I'm thinking about the future. I'm part of a brain trust, a group of men looking to the future of Africa. The Broederbond."

I thought I'd misheard him. "I'm sorry?"

"The Broederbond. It means 'brotherhood' in Afrikaans. It's actually a private organization. We work on behalf of Afrikaner interests."

I was confused. "You mean for the natives?"

"Good God, no!" He laughed. "Best to leave that to the missionaries! No, *Afrikaner*. The true African people."

"Oh. I see." I had no conception of what he meant.

He wasn't fooled.

"The Afrikaners have been in South Africa for centuries. Our ancestors came from Holland, France, Norway. We settled this land, made it civilized. Left to their own devices, all the native tribes do is slaughter one another."

I'd always imagined Africa as safari tents, dramatic sunsets, and vast windswept plains teeming with wildlife. "Still, it must be quite exciting, with lots of lions and elephants . . ."

"Well, there's plenty of good hunting, but don't believe any of that nonsense you read about the noble savage. Mind you," he said darkly, "they're nothing compared to the English. They're completely without a conscience. You see, we understand Africa. It's our destiny and duty to guide and shape it. That's why the Broederbond was formed, to take this country back. We have a responsibility to our homeland—" He stopped himself, smiling apologetically. "I'm on my soapbox again, aren't I? I'm boring you."

He wasn't, actually. It was another world, one I knew nothing about. But that didn't stop me from teasing him. "On the contrary. Naturally I find you utterly fascinating."

He shook his head. "Why are you so cruel to me when I'm buying you lunch?"

"Why are you buying me lunch?"

"Naturally I find you fascinating. You know"—his eyes narrowed—"you're the only girl I know who treats me as though I were the bellboy at a cheap hotel."

"Perhaps you should look into it. I hear the tips are quite generous."

"I doubt the uniform would suit me." Refilling my glass, he tipped the champagne bottle upside down. "Well, darling, I think we're going to need another one." He shoved the empty back into the cooler of ice.

"Really?" It had gone so quickly. In fact, an hour and a half had vanished. My worries about how we would manage to while away the time were unfounded. However, I really needed to get back to work.

But James was already waving to the waiter for more champagne. And calling me "darling."

"By the way," he asked as the next bottle was opened, "do you know the Beauvoirs?"

"I'm sorry, the whos?"

"The Beauvoirs?"

I shook my head. "And why would I know them?"

"No reason. Only I'm told they're quite a prominent family in Albany."

"*Oh!*" I laughed as if I'd misunderstood him. "Yes, of course! But what I haven't confessed is that I'm a recluse—I never go out or do anything of interest. You're the well-traveled one."

"Well, that may all change. I'll tell you, you're going to love the nightclubs in Berlin."

"Really?" My pulse fluttered, though I knew he was only flirting. "But I thought we were going to Saint-Tropez! How are we going to fit it all in?"

"I can't be expected to conquer the world on my own, now can I? You don't speak German, do you? I'll need someone to charm all those Huns."

"Hun charming is my specialty. Though I don't come cheap."

We laughed, took another drink. I felt sophisticated and urbane, dining on French food, discussing politics, planning foreign holidays.

Suddenly he took my hand. "I'm sorry if I upset you when I spoke about Diana last time. You're a good friend to her." His face was serious. "I'm glad she has you to talk to."

I was taken aback by his sincerity. "I'm very fond of her," I said truthfully.

"You may not know this, but she's been very unhappy in the past." He paused, choosing his words carefully. "Actually, she's been unwell."

"Really?" I acted surprised. "In what way?"

"All that's important is that if you feel she's doing something unwise, please let me know. I want to help, but I'm so far away most of the time, and things can change so suddenly with her. And if I'm honest, I'm frightened for her."

His words disturbed me. "Why frightened?"

"She's unpredictable. We've had trouble before." James reached in his inside breast pocket, took out his card. "I shouldn't bother you, but if ever something concerns you, if she seems to be in difficulty, will you ring me?"

I thought of the times I'd gone to the apartment only to find her withdrawn and silent. Her jokes about ovens and exhaust pipes echoed uncomfortably. What if she really was in danger and did something desperate?

He took my hesitation as rejection.

"I'm sorry. It's . . . well, it's just been so difficult . . . I shouldn't have asked. I just don't know what to do."

As he picked the card up again, he seemed suddenly lost, out of his depth. For the first time, I could offer him something no one else could, something he really wanted that money couldn't buy.

"Here." I took it from him, wrote the address of the apartment on the back.

"What's this?"

"It's a place. A friend owns it. If you're ever looking for Diana and can't find her . . . well, there's a chance she might be there."

"What friend?"

I blinked at him, aware too late that I hadn't thought the whole thing through. "It doesn't matter. Just a girl I know." Then I remembered the name on the apartment door. "Miss Julie Hanover."

It was clear I was hiding something, but he didn't press the point. "I'm indebted to you, May." His expression relaxed to one of relief and gratitude. "Really, you are my guardian angel. And Diana's, too—even though she may never know it."

"I'm no angel!" I assured him. But inwardly I was glowing at the compliment. The invisible gap I'd been struggling to breach between us closed. I wasn't just his guest anymore; now I was his confidante and equal.

It was just past four when I made it back to the shop. Mr. Kessler had gone, and Mr. Winshaw's office door was closed. He'd been preparing for his lecture series and was due to leave at the weekend.

The champagne had taken its toll. I went into the bathroom and splashed my face with water, relishing the giddy elation of success. The luncheon had gone better than I could've imagined.

When I came out, Mr. Winshaw was waiting for me, leaning against the doorway, arms crossed. "You seem to have gotten lost on your way back from lunch," he said.

"I'm sorry. I'm afraid the time got away from us. And well," I smiled apologetically, "I didn't want to be rude. Mr. Van der Laar is a client, after all."

This failed to impress him.

"It seems to me, Fanning, that his interest may be personal. Kindly restrict your client relations to more professional interactions."

"It was all extremely professional!" I objected, taken aback.

"Fine. Then maybe you'd like to tuck that blouse in before you go home."

"Home?" He couldn't be serious! "You're sending me home? Why?"

"You've been drinking. And in my experience, drunk women and fine china don't mix."

"I'm hardly drunk!" I straightened, discreetly working my blouse back into my skirt.

He stared at me. "And yet you're a long way from sober. What you do outside this establishment is not my concern. But during office hours Kessler is depending on you, and, quite frankly, so am I. Especially while I'm away. If you can't separate your personal ambitions from your professional duties, then perhaps you should think about handing in your notice."

"Personal ambitions?" His accusations stung. "What is it exactly that you think I'm after?"

He shoved his hands into his pockets. "I have no idea what you want. And I suspect neither do you. Which is a shame, really. Because behind all your false front, Fanning, you're really quite a clever girl."

He went back into his office and shut the door.

I yanked my coat back off its hanger.

False front? He had the nerve to talk!

Of course he was perfectly within his rights to be angry: we both knew that. I should've never let James order that second bottle of champagne. But what Mr. Winshaw didn't know and could never really appreciate was that it had been worth it.

That's right, I thought, fumbling with my coat buttons and readjusting my hat.

I'd be a customer in this shop one day, picking out furniture of my own. Then he'd see that, actually, I'd known what I'd wanted all along.

———

It was a balmy, pleasant evening in the North End, one of the first really warm nights of spring. Russo's bakery doors were open, and musicians—an accordion player, a mandolin player, and a violinist—stood on the sidewalk just outside, playing a mix of Neapolitan songs, Verdi, Puccini, and the occasional tune from a Broadway show. Most of the neighborhood had crowded inside, all talking, shouting, and laughing, and Umberto Russo's famous homemade red wine was making the rounds in small paper cups, along with delicacies baked for the occasion. Pina sat at the center of all of it, holding a large, round baby boy with a red face and a cloud of soft black hair, the newest member of the family, Ulysses Manetti. Behind her, her husband, Augie, stood with one hand on her shoulder, greeting everyone with a firm handshake and the occasional outburst of grateful tears. Since Augie lost his job, they'd struggled. Early every morning he stood in line for day work down at the docks, and both he and Pina were thinner, tired. The haughty voluptuousness that had defined Pina's beauty had dulled to a pensive fortitude. And instead of leaving the bakery, she would now bring her new son with her to sit in the kitchens with her father and brother while she continued to work the counter.

But today was a celebration. Rusty arrived with two boxes of Cuban cigars that were quickly passed around, and a bouquet of yellow roses for Pina. The oldest brother, Romulus, came in with antipasto platters laden with hard salami, mortadella, capicola, and slices of fontinella and provolone cheese for sandwiches. Gifts overflowed on the table next to them—an elaborate fruit basket crowned with an enormous pineapple from Mr. and Mrs. Contadino, stacks of knitted baby blankets in an assortment of colors, a white wicker basket with a soft flannel cushion, a shiny tin piggy bank from Angela and Carlo, muslin baby gowns, bags of fresh almonds and walnuts, and a good-quality secondhand baby buggy from Pina's parents, with double-spring action and large white rubber wheels.

Ma had knitted a tiny little wool jacket with an Irish lace collar, and I'd bought a pair of white kid booties to be worn at the christening, which we added to the pile.

The local policemen stopped by for a drink and cigar; children danced barefoot on the sidewalk in front of the musicians; two elderly men, *anziani* of the neighborhood, took it upon themselves to propose a series of toasts in Italian that were echoed enthusiastically. Soon Mr. Russo was opening another jug of homemade wine.

The baby was passed around for everyone to hold, and when it was my turn he nestled into the warm nook between my chest and arm. Pink-skinned and content, he was softly scented with the intoxicating, milky perfume of all newborns. I smelled his head, both touched and disoriented by the wave of instinctive protectiveness I felt.

Mrs. Russo laughed, put a hand on my shoulder. "That will be you someday soon!"

"What do you think, Jean Harlow?" Pina gazed at her son, cradled in my arms. For all their current difficulties, her face was relaxed and serene when she was looking at him. "Why don't you stop chasing your tail and settle down?"

I didn't bother to answer back. It was her party, and she could rib me all she wanted. Besides, I couldn't take my eyes off the tiny fingers that curled around my own. At the same time, I couldn't dispel the memory of the dingy doctor's office in Brooklyn, how long it had taken me to find the place. And the way the nurse had asked me twice, "Are you sure? Are you really certain you want to do this?" I tried to push it from my mind.

Later I sat out on the sidewalk on a couple of wooden crates with Angela, herself now just beginning to show. We shared a salami sandwich and a cigarette, listening to the music and enjoying the tenderness of the early evening breeze. The sun was setting behind the buildings. A delicate bluish gray shadow saturated the evening sky.

We watched as a couple of skinny little girls bounced up and down in time to the music, laughing hysterically. They had straight Buster Brown haircuts, long, thin faces with large brown eyes. They reminded me of us when we were little—too skinny, too theatrical, wearing hand-me-down clothes and secondhand shoes.

"Did you hear about Mickey?" Angela asked.

"What about him?"

"Hildy's due in August. They got married last weekend. Her sister came in the other day, bragging."

Suddenly I felt winded, unable to properly catch my breath. "She's having a baby?"

The memory of our last meeting still haunted me.

"That's right."

I'd made my choice, and the rest of the world had moved on without me. I was invisible, erased, as if I'd never even existed.

Angela looked at me sideways. "I thought you were over him."

I nodded. "I am."

"Good. There are other fish in the sea." She took a final drag on the cigarette before grinding it out underneath her heel. "Hildy's a piece of work, though. My goodness, doesn't she have a mouth on her!"

She was waiting for me to join in the gossip, but I just sat there, silent. The subtle scent of baby still lingered in my nostrils, the weight of him in my arms.

"You know," she said, shifting, "Carlo has met some nice guys in his course. They study all the time right now, but when we have our own place, I'll invite you over to dinner."

I was on the verge of being a hopeless spinster. "I'm okay. Actually, I've got some prospects of my own."

"*Really?*" She leaned in closer, grinning. "Tell me everything!"

"I just meant I'm working a lot anyway, so I'm not really bothered," I said, backtracking.

"Oh, well. You don't want to put it off too long." And she rested her hand on the gentle curve of her belly. "I'm going to have another amoretti. Or two." She got up. "Do you want one?"

"No, thank you."

She went back inside, absorbed into the noisy crowd of her family. I pulled my legs up, rested my chin on my knees. Loneliness thudded inside me like a heartbeat.

Angela had left her cup of wine. I picked it up; it was almost full.

Ma came out, fanning herself with her hand. "It's so warm in there! I'm off," she announced, pulling on a pair of white crocheted gloves.

"So soon?"

She frowned, nodding to the cup. "Is that yours?"

"No." I put it down again.

"Well, don't be too late."

I watched as she headed down the street with quick, neat steps.

Dr. Joseph's words rang in my ears, "There is a line between normal and abnormal behavior. You've already crossed that line."

He was right. There was something fundamentally wrong with me. This world was real, solid. I could hold a baby and feel everything a real woman would. So why didn't I want this? Why didn't I want to marry Mickey or have his child or even meet one of Carlo's nice friends?

What did I hope to be instead?

Suddenly my heart was racing, panicked. I was fooling myself; no one would ever want me. James was little more than a chimera shimmering on the horizon—magnetic, alluring, but always out of reach.

One of the policemen stepped out onto the sidewalk, swinging his baton in time to the music. It was Jack Carney, a relative of my second cousins from the South End. A big, solid man, he cut a little caper, tipping his hat to me. (Clearly he'd had more than his fair share of the Russos' homemade wine.) I didn't like him. He made my skin crawl, with his large pink face and thick lips. "Well, if it isn't Maeve Fanning! Give us a dance!" He laughed. "You may be hiding that red hair nowadays, but I remember when you had a head like a four-alarm fire! You would dance all night long, Matchstick! Do you remember?" And he laughed again.

I tried to ignore him. The musicians played "Torna a Surriento." And the little girls began to dance again. They twirled, arms round each other's waists, slowly and dramatically, comical expressions of pathos on their faces.

"Don't tell me you're shy!" He leaned in, a gleam in his eye. "That mother of yours was never shy about anything, I can tell you that. We knew her back in the old country, before she turned into a saint and floated off to heaven. She was like you, Matchstick—a sight to behold!"

I hated it when he spoke about Ma. They'd come from the

same village, and he'd always had a soft spot for her—an affection she returned only with cold courtesy. But that didn't stop him from pressing his case each time he saw her.

"I don't know what you're talking about."

"Oh, yes, you do!" He jabbed at me with a thick finger. "She thinks she's too good for everyone now, doesn't she?"

I tried to get up. "I have to go."

But he stood in my way. "Come on, Matchstick! Give us a dance! Show us all how it's done!"

I wanted to punch his fat face.

Luckily his partner came out, hat in hand, smoking a cigar. "Come on, Jackie." He gave Carney a shove. "Let's get out of here."

They made their way down the street. Jack Carney twirled his stick, swaying a little as he went.

My hands were trembling. What self-possession I had left crumbled. I had to leave. Angela would be out again soon; everything she said, each question, felt like a searchlight, the bright beam exposing nothing but mistakes and cracks in my character.

I didn't go home. Instead I walked across town to the only place where I could be alone, Waverly Mansions. And when I unlocked the door, I found my postcard on the floor with the rest of the unopened mail. Apparently Diana hadn't been there in quite some time.

Once inside, relief washed over me. On the street, I'd felt as if my skin was transparent and everyone could see straight through me. Now I was safe. The apartment was perfectly quiet in a way that nothing in the North End ever was. But without Diana, it had the eerie emptiness and ambiguity of a hotel room.

Going into the kitchen, I opened up the cupboards and found a tin of saltine crackers and a bottle of real London dry gin she stocked just for me—the kind that couldn't be bought, even on the black market.

Settling into the sofa, I poured out a glass, lit a cigarette.

With the very first sip, the world began to soften, melt, and recede.

The smell of smoke woke me up. I came to with a jolt. It was dark outside. The dim lamplight cast shadows around the room. Across from me, Diana was sitting in one of the armchairs, and a stranger was standing near the window, his back to me, smoking.

"Relax." Diana's voice was calm and low. "Looks like you fell asleep."

The man by the window laughed—a hard, sharp sound. Even with his back turned, I could tell he didn't like me.

I blinked, looked around. The gin bottle was lying on the floor, half empty. The tin of saltines was unopened.

"I'm sorry." I tried to pull myself up. My tongue was thick and dry, as if it were made of felt. "I shoulda called. I'm sorry. I'll go."

"No. You need to sleep it off," Diana insisted.

"What time is it?" I was desperate for a glass of water.

"Three twenty." The man at the window exhaled, turned to face me. Only it wasn't a man. The soft curve of breasts filled out the man's suit jacket; the skin of her finely boned jawline was smooth. Gray eyes stared challengingly from beneath slicked-back hair. One hand in her trouser pocket, she walked over to Diana and placed the other on Diana's shoulder. Diana reached up to take it.

"This is Max," Diana said. "We're going to go to bed in a minute."

I stared at Max, trying to work out whether she was really a woman, or a man who looked like a woman, or perhaps not really there at all. If I concentrated hard enough, maybe both of them would disappear.

But they didn't.

"You're . . . you're going to bed?" I repeated.

"That's right," Max said.

I began to understand, though I wasn't sure that I wanted to.

"I'll go." I tried to stand, but my knees buckled, and I hit the edge of the table hard. Diana gasped in sympathy; pain shot through my legs. I tried to get up again, but the room was spinning. "I'm sorry, I know I should . . ." And then, out of nowhere, I began to cry.

With an exasperated sigh, Max jammed the cigarette into the side of her mouth and hauled me up by the shoulders. "Go to the toilet and wash your face," she commanded, steering me round the furniture. She wasn't the kind of person you wanted to argue with.

"I'm . . . I'm afraid I've had too much to drink," I said, sobbing.

"You don't say." Max pushed me into the bathroom.

I wept as I washed my face. Then somehow I managed to back into the bath, pull down the shower curtain, and throw up on the floor.

When I finally came out, someone, presumably Max, had made a bed on the sofa. There was a bucket next to it, and a glass of water on the coffee table. The gin bottle was nowhere to be seen.

"You're going to sleep now," Max told me. She pointed to the sofa. "We're going to bed too." Then she glanced at Diana, who stood up, as if on cue. "If you're sick again, aim for the bucket."

Max and Diana went into the bedroom and closed the door.

I sat down on the edge of the sofa, head in hands. My knees throbbed, and my nose was running. Only I wasn't drunk enough to pass out. One last shot was what I needed.

I was about to creep into the kitchen in search of the gin when Max called from the bedroom, "And don't even try to look for the bottle, blondie. I've got it here, with me in bed."

Sometime in the early hours of the morning, bleary-eyed and still half drunk, I came to. Diana was sitting across from me in a dressing gown, waiting. Gingerly, head throbbing, I eased myself up.

Before I could say anything, she pushed the glass of water across the coffee table toward me. "Drink. You'll feel better."

I did as I was told. But I couldn't sit upright for long; my head was spinning. I collapsed again.

"Are you angry?" I managed.

She shook her head, pulled her legs up underneath her. But her manner was serious, subdued. "Are you?"

I hadn't expected that. Seeing her now, everything—all the fear and hurt—faded. "Where have you been?"

"With Max." She looked toward the closed door of the bedroom. "I can't be myself around people who know me," she said after a moment. "Every once in a while I need to get away."

"I thought that's what this place was for."

She paused. "It's not far enough." There was a quiet sense of defeat in her voice. "There's madness, and then there's insanity. A little madness is one thing, but who wants to see your insanity, May?"

She didn't need to explain. I understood all too well. That's why I'd gone to New York. I needed not just time and distance but an entirely different city and life.

"But now . . . here you are." She shrugged awkwardly, her eyes glistening with tears. "Now you know. I told you I was different."

"I don't care."

She looked unconvinced. "You would if you knew everything."

"I don't care," I said again.

Wiping her tears away with her fingertips, she shook her head. It was an effort for her to have this conversation; I could feel the weight of her shame. "I never wanted you to know."

"Who am I to judge? If you knew where I'd been, what I'd done, you may not want to be talking to *me* right now!"

Her face changed, and she laughed, a hard bitter sound. "Because you drink?"

The way she said it, the fact that she said it at all, surprised me. I'd only meant to comfort her. "What do you mean?"

"Are you denying it? You drink *alone*, May! You drink more than anyone I know!"

Her words were razor-sharp arrows, expertly aimed.

"You drink too!" I shot back.

But she just laughed incredulously. "Not like you!"

"What are you saying?"

"What do you think I'm saying?"

We were like two gaping raw wounds, suddenly at odds with each other, at odds with ourselves.

"You think I'm a drunk?" I snapped.

"I think you already know what you are. But at least you can do something about it!" She got up and went back into the bedroom.

I wanted to leave, to storm out, but couldn't. I was too sick.

Instead I cried and fell asleep again.

When I woke up again, it was late in the afternoon.

This time it was Max sitting across from me, reading a copy of the *Saturday Evening Post*. She was wearing women's clothing, her hair combed into a very short bob. But I couldn't get the image of her as a man out my head.

"Where's Diana?" I rasped.

"She had to go. Asked me to look after you. You can't imagine how thrilled I was." She tossed the magazine down on the table. "Are you going to throw up again?"

"I don't think so."

"Peachy. Let's get you up."

I managed to wash and dress myself, and then Max dragged me out to a lunch counter and ordered plenty of strong coffee and pancakes, which she claimed to be the secret to surviving a hangover.

"How would *you* know?" I was feeling sick and pretty sorry for myself. Every noise reverberated through my skull, a constant symphony of clinking cutlery and clattering plates.

"I know more about hangovers than I'd like." Max added an extra teaspoon of sugar to my coffee, a liberty I only allowed because she frightened me.

"You've got to have a lot of sugar," she instructed. "To get over the shakes."

"I don't like pancakes."

"And I don't like cleaning up vomit." I watched in dismay as she drowned my pancakes in syrup. "You love sugar, blondie. You just like it in a glass." She set the syrup down with a flourish, enjoying being the boss, even if she resented looking after me at the same time.

I forced down a bite. I wanted to drink the coffee but was afraid that if I picked up the cup, I'd spill it. Max seemed to sense this. She waved down the waitress and asked for a straw, which she popped into my mug. "There."

I took a sip, grateful and humiliated at the same time.

"So . . ." She lit a cigarette, eyeing me suspiciously. "Who are you, anyway? And why does Diana care about you so much?"

"I don't think she *cares* for me," I corrected her. "Not in that way."

"Then why was she so particular about me staying, making sure you're all right?"

"We're friends. That's all." And then I added, just to be clear, "It's nothing, you know, nothing affectionate."

She inhaled hard, leaned back in her seat. "Is that right?"

I pushed the food around on my plate. "Why haven't I seen you before?"

"My family's here but I'm not in town that often. I live in New York now—I play horn in a private club in SoHo."

"Is that where you met?"

She nodded. "Diana visits, stays with me when she can. That's when her family aren't pushing her around, trying to turn her into a performing poodle. Anyway, you'd better not be taking her for anything." She exhaled, talking over a stream of smoke. "Just 'cause she's got money doesn't mean she's in the charity business."

I glared at her. "I've never asked for a thing! I'm not a charity case!"

She snorted. "You're doing a pretty good imitation, blondie!"

I hated that name. "Stop calling me that! I'm not actually even blond!" I jammed another forkful in my mouth. (She was right, the sugar did help.)

"*Really?*" She widened her eyes in pretend shock and laughed.

Our conversation had taken on the cadence and sophistication of a couple of bickering twelve-year-olds.

"You should mind your own business!"

"Diana is my business. She's my girl." Max smiled smugly. "Does that shock you?"

"Are you trying to shock me?"

"I don't care what you think. You or anybody."

"Then why do you let her cut herself?"

Her face changed. "How do you know about that?" She smashed her cigarette into the ashtray. "That's got nothing to do with me. I would never hurt her. Never."

"But you let her hurt herself?"

She glared at me. "Have you ever tried to stop her doing anything? Trust me, it doesn't work!"

I'd gone too far. After all, she was helping me. "I'm sorry. That was stupid—"

She cut me off. "Forget it. Diana's not an easy person to know. No wonder the two of you get along." She frowned, twirling her teaspoon between her thumb and forefinger. "You know, it's been difficult for her lately. She's not in a good way."

"What does that mean?"

"I'm only saying. Maybe you should steer clear for a while. Give her a chance to pull herself together."

After my scene last night and our argument, it wasn't surprising news. Still, I didn't like hearing it from a stranger. "Steer clear? Is that her idea or yours?" I asked bitterly.

For once she didn't rise to the bait. "I'm not trying to upset you. I'm just telling you straight."

We sat for a while before Max added quietly, "She can't look after you. She can't even look after herself."

"Well, I don't want looking after, so that's fine by me."

It was a childish response, but I couldn't quite manage to act any better than I felt. And I felt pretty damn bad.

Afterward Max walked me to the nearest trolley stop. Suddenly she became protective. "Are you okay to go home on your own? I mean, no one's going to give you any trouble, are they?"

"No. I'll be fine."

"Look, Diana wanted me to tell you about this man at the

Emmanuel Church on Newbury Street. Mr. Courtenay Baylor. He's some sort of doctor or therapist or something. Anyway, he helps people get on the wagon and stay there and, well, she thought you might want to know about it."

I stared at my shoes, miserable and alone. "I don't need any help."

"Don't be such an ass!"

"What's it to you, anyway?" I shot back.

Max jammed her hands into her coat pockets. Even in women's clothing she had a certain rough swagger that couldn't be disguised. "My old man died a drunk, and so did my oldest brother. My younger brother, Johnny, he's had a bit of luck with this guy." She shrugged, clearly as unhappy with the conversation as I was. "Like I said, Diana thought you would want to know."

I frowned. I didn't know what to say.

She took my silence as rejection.

"I told her it wouldn't make any difference if I told you!" She jerked her chin up defiantly, frustration overboiling. "I've seen how the whole thing plays out. It doesn't matter what you do, how you plead, what you threaten or promise. My brother, sure, he's okay right now, but it won't last. I know I'm just biding my time before I have to bury him too." Her eyes lost the fire of indignation, and instead bewilderment shadowed her face. "Just don't hang around Diana drinking yourself to death. Don't do that to her, understand?"

I turned away. I couldn't bring myself to answer.

Ma was sitting in the kitchen when I finally came in.

In front of her on the table was the blue-and-white willow-pattern teapot and cup—the cup empty, the ashtray full. She'd clearly been up all night and waiting most of the day. "Where have you been?" Her voice was flat and heavy, full of cold, hard anger.

I hadn't thought about Ma at all—that she would be worried. I was surprised by her drawn, pale face, eyes swollen and ringed with dark circles from lack of sleep.

"I . . . I'm sorry. I got sick and stayed at a friend's house."

Her face hardened. "A man or a woman?"

I absorbed the insult with a dull sense of shame. "Diana. Diana Van der Laar."

"Really." She didn't believe me. "And it never once occurred to you to let me know where you were? I don't suppose the Van der Laars have a telephone?"

My brain wasn't working fast enough to come up with an explanation. Besides, there was no excuse. I just shook my head.

Her upper lip curled in disgust. "So, this is how it is now? Coming and going at all hours, showing up reeking of liquor!"

I stood silent, cold, and sick. All I wanted to do was go to bed. "I won't do it again, I promise. I'm sorry, Ma."

"You're always sorry. You're always never going to do it again."

"But I mean it."

"You always mean it! Meaning it doesn't make any difference! All these years I struggled for you! Fought for you! Did everything I could think of to give you the best possible life, and this is how you repay me? You're throwing it away! Don't you see what you are?" She banged her fist hard on the table. "You're better than this, Maeve! You *have* to be!"

I'd never seen her so upset. She was the last person I wanted to let down, and yet the one I let down most often. "Ma, I'm . . . I'm trying . . ." I fumbled. "I really am!"

"I want you to talk to Father Grady."

"Father Grady?" Our parish priest, Father Grady was the very last resort—the final word on lost causes.

"You're drunk! *Again!* Just like last time! I thought when you went to New York, when you got away from Mickey, you'd put all that behind you!"

"I did! I have! I swear, Ma!"

Her eyes widened. "Don't you lie to me! Don't you *ever* lie to me!"

And with lightning speed, she picked up one of the Staffordshire teacups and smashed it against the floor. Then she grabbed the saucer and flung it down too.

"No, Ma! Stop!" I grabbed her arm.

"You ruin everything!" she screamed. "I'm glad your father isn't alive to see you now! You're nothing but a common little whore!"

Her words slammed into me, like a kick to the stomach.

She reached for the teapot.

"I'll go," I said quickly, frightened of her temper and what she was capable of. "I'll see him. I promise!"

She let the teapot go, and her features distorted into a grimace of painful sobs. She covered her face with her hands.

"I'm sorry, Ma." I tried to comfort her, but she recoiled from me as if I were some diseased creature, too foul to touch. Instead, she went into her bedroom and closed the door.

I stared at the floor covered in broken china, the shattered pieces.

I had to find a way to repair them. One way or another, I would fix things.

I hesitated by the door of the rectory office a moment before knocking.

"Come in."

Father Grady was standing by the window, looking out onto the schoolyard of the Holy Cross Grammar School below. It was recess, and the din of children running and shouting immediately took me back to my childhood. Those were pleasant memories, clearly defined in black and white. Children needed only a little sunshine and a square of empty space to be endlessly happy.

Father Grady turned. I hadn't seen him in over a year. He registered the difference in my hair color with a look of mild confusion, tilting his head to one side as if looking at my hair from a slightly different angle might suddenly make it red again. Then he gestured to a chair. "Sit down, Maeve."

Father Grady was from Kerry; he still had the gentle, lilting dialect of the southern Irish and the gaunt, distinguished features of an aging elder statesman. He'd known me all my life; he'd baptized and confirmed me, heard my first confession, and given me first communion. In the absence of a husband, Ma had turned to him for advice and guidance over the years. Secretarial school had been his idea.

Now, as I took a seat across from him, I could feel his concern and disappointment like a low-hanging dark cloud.

He nodded slowly, held his palms up. "Well, Maeve." He wasn't afraid to state the obvious. "Here we are."

I stared at his empty hands. "Thank you for seeing me, Father."

He said nothing. Instead, he waited.

Father Grady had years of practice in waiting behind him. He knew, perhaps better than any man in Boston, the art of silence. In a congregation full of first- and second-generation Irish immigrants, people uniquely skilled in the lavish use of language, he'd learned to navigate all manner of domestic, political, and spiritual crises by carefully rationing his words. He knew better than to argue, debate, cajole, or sympathize; any conversation was likely to muddy the waters of clear, calm reflection. Quiet unnerved his people, disarmed them. It forced them into that uncomfortable empty space where only God would go and where humor, charm, and intellect were of no use.

I looked down at the pattern on the rug, well worn and faded by sunlight.

"Things aren't going very well," I admitted after a while.

Still another minute passed before I added, "My mother, she thinks I've lost my way. That I drink too much, go out too often. I guess she's right."

Just saying it out loud seemed to open the floodgates. Taking a handkerchief from my handbag, I dabbed tears from my cheeks. "I've done things, things I regret, things I don't want to think about. . . . I've tried to change, Father. I've tried to be different. I've done everything I can think of—gone to different places, had different jobs, gotten new friends, but I'm still lost."

"One often meets one's fate on the road one takes to avoid it."

"I don't want to be this way."

He leaned back a little and pressed his palms together, fingertips against his lips as if on the verge of saying something.

Outside the children laughed and screamed.

"Well, aren't you going to tell me what God wants?" I prompted.

"I haven't a clue what God wants for you, Maeve. He doesn't talk to me about your life—he only talks to me about mine. If you are interested in what he has to say, you'll have to listen for yourself."

"But then why am I here?"

"You're here, I take it, because you've been told to be here. Am I right?" He smiled a little, as if we were playing a guessing game, and he'd won. "You're under the illusion that someone else is going to tell you what to do or how to do it. But I'm afraid you're a little too old for that now. Now is the time when you must take hold of your life, decide who and what you want to be. You've had a good education, a loving home." He gave an almost imperceptible shrug that reminded me of Mr. Kessler. "You know what to do." And with that, he stood up.

"Is that it?" Suddenly I panicked.

He looked at me carefully. "Is there something else I can do for you?"

"But you haven't given me any answers! I mean, I don't know . . . What if I don't even believe in God anymore?" I blurted, provoking him.

I expected a reaction, but apparently my doubts weren't as interesting as I thought they were.

"Well, luckily you don't need to believe in God in order for him to exist. His existence is not contingent on your being convinced. But as far as your life is concerned, well, that's another matter. I think you do need to be convinced, Maeve, of something. Even if it's only that you're not quite as uniquely flawed as you imagine you are." He held out a thin, gnarled hand. "May God go with you."

The interview was over. He turned again to look out at the schoolyard.

I walked into the dark stone corridor of the church.

The door closed, and the sounds of the playground, the universal echo of childhood, faded behind me.

Sitting alone on the back seat of the trolley, I stared out of the dirty window. I hadn't wanted to see Father Grady; I didn't think

I needed his counsel or advice. Now I was offended that he hadn't lectured me or given me an ultimatum. I felt utterly lost.

The trolley passed a Salvation Army soup kitchen. The line stretched down the street, round the corner; men of all ages, heads bowed, coats drawn tight against the cold, shuffling forward for watery soup and stale bread. Every day I watched them; it was normal now. Then I saw my own reflection staring back at me in the glass, the same round-eyed hollow look of hopelessness and quiet defeat.

To strive, to seek, to find, and not to yield.

I thought of what Mr. Winshaw had said to me when we argued: that I didn't know what I wanted.

I took out my wallet. There, folded into the bill section, was Alfred Lord Tennyson's poem "Ulysses," torn from Mr. Winshaw's book.

How dull it is to pause, to make an end,
To rust unburnished, not to shine in use!
As tho' to breathe were life! . . .
. . . that which we are, we are:
One equal temper of heroic hearts,
Made weak by time and fate, but strong in will
To strive, to seek, to find, and not to yield.

And there was the emphatic "Yes!" written in the margin.

I held my finger over it. I wanted this; I had a craving for "Yes!"—a physical longing that ached in my chest. But how could I find it? Where did it live, buried beneath the failure and disappointment of my life?

The trolley stopped at an unfamiliar corner, and suddenly I stood up, pushed my way to the exit, and got off. I stood there a moment, looking down one street and then the other, unsure of where I was or which way to go.

Then I began to walk, very quickly.

I walked to feel the strength of my body in motion, the building momentum of possibility. And most of all just to remind myself that I could.

Part Two

The cold spring softened, blossomed. Early summer arrived green, fresh, and fragrant. Cherry trees exploded into lush candyfloss blooms on Charles Street, and the thick damp fog of winter's chill dispersed, leaving behind a tender, delicate warmth.

Now I propped the shop door open and filled vases with bright red tulips. People strolled along the streets, taking their time, lingering longer in the evening. The shop stayed open later and customers drifted in, staying to browse.

Life was quiet and uneventful, temporarily suspended, like an intermission between acts. James Van der Laar still formed the central focus of my thoughts though he was abroad, traveling between continents. I consoled myself that I could use his absence to pull myself together, a hope that sustained me through the dull hours of peace and quiet that followed Mr. Winshaw's departure to lecture in Philadelphia. It was surprising how much I missed him too.

As for Diana, there was no word. What she'd said the last time I'd seen her still smarted, not least because she was right. My thoughts and feelings about her were as tangled as a ball of fishhooks; I was both sorry and humiliated, missing our former freedom and afraid of it, longing to be forgiven and yet dreaming of cutting things to say when we finally met again. I seesawed from shame to superiority and back again, with no resting place in between.

But I needn't have bothered: day after day it was just Mr. Kessler, Persia, and me. And after work I went to see Mr. Baylor, the man Max had told me about.

"You seem much better, Miss Fanning," Mr. Kessler commented one morning. "Much calmer," he elaborated.

"I suppose I am calmer," I admitted, pleased that someone had noticed a difference.

But I didn't expand, so he didn't pursue the point. Instead he accepted the change with the same grave attitude with which he accepted most good things in his life: as divine gifts that were diminished or even removed when questioned.

Initially, Ma was suspicious of my efforts. Why was I spending my evenings at an Episcopalian church, of all places, rather than at my own? And who was this Mr. Baylor? What could he offer that I couldn't find by going to either the library or confession?

But there was little point in discussing my private conversations with Mr. Baylor, the lay therapist Max had recommended at St. Emmanuel, with her. She wouldn't understand. Not because she didn't want to, but because she couldn't. That was one of the first things he explained to me—that people who weren't afflicted as I was wouldn't comprehend the lengths I had to go to.

Unlike with Dr. Joseph, I never confided to Mr. Baylor the details of my past, and he didn't ask. That alone made me trust him more than anyone else I'd ever met. Instead, his advice was entirely practical, his attitude strenuously positive. Once a hopeless alcoholic near death, Mr. Baylor had gone on to "cure" himself through his own techniques and was now devoted to helping others. He sat across from me week after week, in his comfortable study at St. Emmanuel, a trim, elegant man with lively dark eyes and an alert military bearing. It was impossible to imagine him drunk or debauched. But every once in a while he would share a story from his past, and I would realize that he'd known the kind of baffling misery I had too. This made it easier for me to follow his advice.

"First and foremost, you must accept that you have a nervous mind, Miss Fanning," he said, "full of fear and worry, prone to irritability and anxiousness. Like a fretting toddler, this mind needs to be calmed, reassured, and refocused."

"And how do I do that?"

"You must relax. Resist nothing and regret nothing! Now close your eyes, and I will guide you on how to still your thoughts."

It sounded simple enough, but it was surprisingly difficult in practice. In fact, I'd never felt as anxious and irritable as I did when I stopped drinking. Every sound grated, every thought raced out of control toward impending doom. Suddenly I was permanently on edge. It was as if I'd been numb before and could now feel every single shade and color of emotion—none of them particularly pleasant or manageable.

But Mr. Baylor had seen it all before. "If you want to know why you drank too much in the first place, try stopping."

So I kept to a strict daily schedule, just as he prescribed. I woke, ate, and went to bed at the same times, exercised by walking briskly, and practiced the daily relaxation methods he'd taught me. Underneath, however, my head churned, soaring between giddy anticipation and depression. "You must remain positive," Mr. Baylor advised. "Do something physical when the urge strikes—clean the oven, iron, scrub the floor." One of the benefits of my "Episcopalian regime" (as my mother put it) was that the apartment was always spotless.

The shop became a refuge. It was easier to keep my mind relaxed and focused when I was working. I began to arrive early and was regularly the last one to leave at night. "Refocus your mind!" Mr. Baylor had urged with his trademark emphatic energy. "Life isn't going to just fall into your lap, Miss Fanning. Go on! Try something new!"

So I tried my hand at creating window displays, which I was rather good at, and spent hours thumbing through antiques catalogues, trying to teach myself how to identify styles and eras. Pieces I'd dismissed before became interesting, silent ambassadors of vanished ages. The hard English mahogany chairs were as stoic and unyielding as the puritanical age in which they were crafted, while the gilded French Empire chaise in sea-green silk was as opulent and voluptuous as a courtesan of the Belle Epoque. I began to develop an eye and an appreciation for where I was and what I was doing. And right now, I had to believe that was enough.

Then suddenly, Diana reappeared.

It was on the day Mr. Kessler finally sold the Mozart tea table that I saw her again. Charlie was wrapping the table in old blankets, getting it ready to load onto a truck, when Diana strolled in through the open shop door as if nothing had ever happened, wearing a blue summer dress and bright red sandals. She looked tanned and lovely, and had a white Yorkshire terrier on a red leather leash with her.

"Oh, look!" She ran her fingers over the top of the table, gave a sigh. "I was going to buy that! For my little hideaway, Mr. Kessler!" She stuck out her lower lip. "I feel so *betrayed*!"

The dog growled and barked at the African figures while Charlie stared at her, open-mouthed, as if he'd never seen a female before.

"But I have another one here." Mr. Kessler hurried over to an eighteenth-century traveling bureau. "This one is a *much* finer piece."

"But it's not listened to Mozart play scales," she said sadly. "I cannot live with such a lack of musical appreciation in my furniture. Surely you understand that!"

Only after she'd charmed everyone else did she turn her attention to me. It was as if she needed to prove that she could still dominate all men in her path—that this power mitigated her relationship with Max and trumped any ambiguity. I could feel her determination to show me, to prove her influence.

"This is Henry." She scooped up the dog and handed him to me; he licked my nose. "Isn't he adorable? Come and have a turn round the block with us."

As soon as we were out the door, though, the air of charm and lightness disappeared, replaced by an awkward emptiness.

There'd been so many things I'd rehearsed in my head, curt little speeches and questions, but now their intensity faded to dull confusion.

"How are you?" she asked tentatively.

"Great."

"You're angry."

I didn't know what I was.

"Forgive me." Her strange blue eyes were dimmed, hollow. "Please, May."

"I know I made an ass of myself that night, that I behaved badly—"

"That wasn't it." She cut me off, eyes focused on the ground. "It wasn't your fault."

"Then whose was it?"

"I didn't think you'd want to be around me . . . once you knew."

"I don't care."

And I didn't. I minded that she'd not been there when I woke up, and that Max had been the one to tell me to stay away, and I minded that she'd refused to see me. But what she did with Max didn't matter.

We walked on.

"I wanted to come sooner," she said after a while, "really I did. But to be honest, I couldn't remember where you worked."

I gave her a sour look. "You've been here a thousand times!"

"I know." She kept her eyes on Henry, trotting along just in front of us. "But you see, this time the treatments were more frequent, stronger. They tried something new too. Aversion therapy. When I came home, I couldn't remember anything for quite a while. It took me a week, May, even to remember your name."

She said it so calmly that at first I thought I'd misheard her. Then, even though it was a bright, sunny afternoon, I felt my skin go cold. "Where?"

"A private hospital in Maine."

"What happened?"

"Nothing I want to talk about."

Her evasiveness frightened me; I imagined the worst—her sprawled across a floor.

"Did you want to go?" I pressed. "I mean, did you choose to, or were you made to go?"

"What difference does that make?" she answered blankly.

Henry stopped by a tree to relieve himself, and we waited.

"Are you all right now?" I wanted reassurance.

She frowned. "I seem all right, don't I?" It was a genuine question, as if she wasn't sure.

"Why won't you tell me what happened?"

A deep furrow cut across her brow. "I fell in love," she admitted. "I fell in love with someone I shouldn't have."

I thought about Max, how protective she was. "But Max cares for you too, Diana. I'm sure of it."

"It's gone now." She took a deep breath. "They took it away in the hospital. Did you ever go to that man I asked Max to tell you about? The one at the church?"

"Mr. Baylor? Yes, I did."

"Did he help?"

"Yes, I guess he does."

"That's good. Really good." She smiled at me, relieved. "I want you to be happy."

Her concern touched me. Although I didn't want to admit it, she'd helped me that night. Her harsh words had made it impossible for me to ignore my problems. "He's quite clever about all sorts of things. Do you want to speak to him?"

"Maybe. I'm not sure."

"Have you spoken to Max since you've been back?"

"Why?" She looked up sharply, frightened or offended, I couldn't tell which. Her eyes narrowed, and she seemed to be calculating something, something that proved too difficult to discern from my expression. "No. I haven't seen her. And I'm not going to," she said finally.

We'd come full circle round the block and were standing in front of the shop again. Diana was uneasy now, on edge. She stared fixedly at the dog. "I'm better now. Much better than I was. It's going to work this time, I know."

Her determination made her seem all the more fragile.

"Diana—"

"Actually, I'm going to go home," she interrupted, smiling apologetically. "I get tired so easily. I just wanted to see you, to apologize. Coming here was probably a mistake."

"I've missed you, you know."

"Really?" Her eyes softened and for a moment she seemed hopeful. "Most people grow tired of me after a while. I wear them out. They like me in the beginning, and then when they see who I really am . . ."

"But not me." I took her hand. "Mr. Baylor's been good to me. You can trust him."

"Yes, I'll think about it. I promise." She removed her hand carefully, as if the physical contact were dangerous, possibly even painful. "I'm glad you're doing well, May. Really I am."

"You are too. You look really wonderful—so healthy and tanned!" I said, even though I didn't believe it.

"It's in my blood. We Afrikaners go brown at the first sign of sun."

Flagging down a cab, she climbed in, and Henry jumped up on her lap. I noticed her nervously twisting the pearls she still wore round her neck. "I'll be in touch," she called, reaching to close the door, "and we'll have some adventures. Just like old times!"

"Yes, that's right. Of course."

As the taxi pulled out, she rolled down the window, and the little white dog stuck his head out, barking excitedly.

"Mr. Kessler," I asked, standing in the doorway of his office, "have you ever heard of an Afrikaner?"

He looked up from his desk. "You mean from South Africa?"

"Yes."

He leaned back. "Are you referring to the Van der Laars? The Van der Laars are Boers. South African natives."

"But I thought African natives would be Negro, wouldn't they?"

"Not exactly. Boer is the Dutch name for 'farmer,' given to the settlers who came to Africa in the mid-eighteenth century to form settlements for the Dutch East India Company," he explained.

"You see, the company needed to colonize the area for its own stability, and not many Europeans were interested in going to Africa
at that time. So the original settlers were either rural Dutch or
Low German, mostly poor farmers, orphans, and later Hugue-
nots, French refugees seeking religious freedom." He looked at
me thoughtfully. "I suppose you're too young to have heard of the
Boer Wars?"

I shook my head.

"There were two wars, fought against British colonial rule in
South Africa; the last was particularly brutal."

I leaned against the doorway, trying to follow. "Why is that
important?"

"Well, Great Britain had both colonies and growing economic
interests in South Africa. The Boer Wars were conflicts for sover-
eignty and control of the region. And of course, especially in the
Van der Laars' case, diamonds."

"Diamonds?"

"That's right." He pushed back his chair, and Persia jumped
into his lap. "South Africa has some of the richest diamond mines
in the world. But they were only discovered in the Kimberley
region by accident about sixty or so years ago. The result was
something akin to the great gold rush here—the area was suddenly flooded with fortune seekers from all over the world, including the English and, most importantly, Cecil Rhodes, who
was an ardent imperialist. The Boers had already been living in
the region for centuries. They had their own language, government, and beliefs. However, Rhodes had his own very English
vision of Africa. The Boer Wars are the upshot of his rise to political power and his ambition to consolidate all the diamond mines
into a single controlling cartel. The Van der Laars are part of that
cartel—but only at a tremendous price."

"What do you mean?"

He paused, scratching Persia under the chin. "They say that Jacob Van der Laar was originally born Jacob Isaacs in Germany, son of a Jewish cigar maker. He was one of the many young men who went to Kimberly to make his fortune at the same time as Rhodes. And like Rhodes, he had aspirations of dominating the diamond industry. He did well in his acquisitions, changed his name, and married an equally ambitious young woman whose family were prominent political figures and landowners in the Boer republic of Transvaal. He set about creating his own cartel under the name Van der Laar. But when the Second Boer War broke out, business became increasing impossible for him.

"The Second Boer War was incredibly bloody," Mr. Kessler continued. "The Boers had a ragtag guerilla army of native farmers, up against the British Empire. Still, they managed to hold their own for quite a while. The British retaliated with a scorched-earth policy, burning down Boer farms and homes, interning the rebels' wives and children in concentration camps in an attempt to force them to surrender. Many of them starved to death."

"So what happened to Jacob Van der Laar?"

Mr. Kessler shrugged. "Nobody knows the whole story. Clearly a choice was made. Some say Rhodes made him an offer that he couldn't refuse."

"You mean he betrayed his wife's family in order to join the cartel?"

"It's difficult to say who betrayed whom, isn't it? Van der Laar came from nowhere and became incredibly wealthy within a decade. How he did that, what it took, no one really knows. The one thing we know for certain, though, is that the Van der Laars continue to be one of very few families with Boer ties to have any substantial diamond mines in South Africa today."

I thought of Diana and her continental upbringing, the careful accent that both she and James shared, perfectly proper without revealing anything other than the excellence of their education, and how she'd joked in the hospital about diamonds being "common" where she came from. "We Afrikaners." The phrase reminded me of James's nationalist loyalty to his homeland. And yet the Van der Laars were Americans now, building a name and reputation alongside the oldest American families in one of the first colonial cities.

"You said Jacob Van der Laar was Jewish, isn't that right?"

"Yes." He smiled sadly. "But Mrs. Van der Laar refuses to have Jews in her home. She left South Africa when her husband was still alive and has never gone back. Not even for his funeral."

"I see."

Mrs. Van der Laar had never forgiven him. Instead, she'd taken her children and decamped to a new country, one where they would recast themselves as upper-class philanthropists and socialites. Only the past couldn't be entirely rewritten, even by her. Their vast fortune still depended on the diamond mines, now under James's stewardship. And he had ambitions to rebuild South Africa along with a determination to restore his mother's people to power.

Their seemingly golden life of privilege had taken on a more complex, uncomfortable hue. But the conflicts and contradictions of their history also made them seem less removed from myself, more accessible. And it cast James's political convictions in a new light when I thought of the betrayal and bloodshed that had divided his family.

Persia jumped down, and Mr. Kessler stood up, brushing the fur from his trousers. "I realize you're friends with the Van der Laars. And I'm very happy to see you make sales. But you mustn't feel obligated to them in any way. Do you understand?"

"Of course."

"I just wanted to be clear." He smiled, but behind his eyes there was a shadow of concern.

Ma had recruited me to help with the Declaration Day Widow's Society stall. It wasn't my idea of a good time, but Mr. Baylor had stressed the importance of doing things for others, and seeing as I had nothing else planned, I agreed.

We woke early and were setting up in front of North Church by eight. It had rained in the night and now the air was fresh and clear. Frieda brought a thermos of hot coffee and paper cups, and Ma unveiled a plate of her now-infamous rock-solid scones. Rosemarie and I nailed red, white, and blue bunting around the edge of the tables while Ma arranged the wares, hanging several of Frieda's aprons from the society banner in pride of place.

Already the parade was bustling; stalls were erected, food sellers began to cook, and children with penny flags waved them wildly, rampaging through the streets in giddy excitement. Religious societies gathered under elaborately embroidered banners; I spotted Mrs. Russo in her best hat, heading up the San Panteleone Women's Society, proudly bearing both the Italian and American flags. Boy Scouts with scrubbed faces and freshly combed hair arrived in uniform to take their place in the parade behind the long lines of decorated veterans, from the Great War, the Spanish-American War, and even the Civil War. Behind them the Marine Brass Band tuned their instruments, and the Highland Bagpipes looked grand, if hot, in full kilts. The smell of popcorn and caramel peanuts perfumed the air.

"Put this on, Mae." Ma handed me a special red, white, and

blue turban she'd knitted for the day. It was a perfect example of the hazards of mixing patriotism and yarn.

"Oh, but Ma, it's so . . . so warm out!" I tried to give it back to her.

"Come on!" Frieda prodded. "Be a sport! I want to see it on, and we'll sell more that way."

So I wore the ugly turban to please them all.

The committee arrived to review the arrangements and oversee the sales. Elsa Van der Laar, with her head of silver hair, was among them, holding a reluctant Andrew by the hand. He had a flag and an untouched cone of bright pink candyfloss. Before, Elsa had appeared aloof and imposing to me, but now I thought I could detect an anxious irritation beneath her commanding exterior.

I saw her bend down to talk to Andrew. "Now behave yourself," she told him, sternly. "I won't tolerate any nonsense. Do you understand?"

"I wish I had my book." He frowned at his feet. "I want my book."

"You don't need the book. It's a parade, not a library! Look"— she pointed across the street—"all the other children are having fun."

"I'm not sure I like parades. But if I had my book—"

"Enough about the book!" she snapped. "Can't you just act like a normal child for once in your life? Now go sit somewhere and be quiet!"

He retreated to a far corner of the church steps and stared glumly as his candyfloss began melting in the sun.

Crowds gathered thick and noisy now, and the parade began, all cheers, shouts, bright searing music, and confetti. Teams of mounted police trotted past on chestnut horses; I spotted Jack Carney sampling the roasted peanuts across the street, tipping his hat to any pretty girl he passed. The soaring bagpipes filled me with teary sentimental patriotism, a nostalgic ache for a land I'd never known. But soon the stall was busy and we all fell into a quick rhythm, serving customers and handing the money over to the committee members to be counted out. I played the clown as I modeled the turban, pretending to be Gloria Swanson doing the dusting.

"Hey, Nora!" Leaning against the stall, Jack Carney took off his hat and mopped his wide brow with his hankie. "I'd like to see you wearing one of those!"

"I made them, Officer Carney." My mother smiled politely.

"Well, they're just swell." He grinned, jamming the damp hankie into his pants pocket. "I should've known they were your handiwork."

Rosemarie caught Frieda's eye and smiled.

Jack leaned in closer. "Maybe you'd wear one when I take you out for a drink later. What do you say?"

Ma concentrated on refolding the aprons. "You know me, Jack, I don't drink. Thank you for your offer, just the same."

"Well, it doesn't have to be a drink. It could be a meal. I don't suppose you've given up eating too?" He laughed, looking to the other women for support.

Frieda snorted. I glared at her, and she stopped.

"You're very kind, Jack. But I'm too tired now. It's already been a long day, and it's not even over yet."

The playful gleam in his eye disappeared. "It's always the same with you, isn't it? Too good for the rest of us, is that it? One of these days you're going to regret putting yourself above the world." He spat on the ground as if to punctuate his sentiments.

Ma gave him a long, hard look. "I don't see that there's any reason to be uncivil, Officer," she said finally.

"No, no need to be uncivil," he agreed sourly, sidling away.

Frieda whistled. "Now there's a man who can't take no for an answer!"

"No." Her gaze followed him as he pushed his way through the crowds. "None of the Carneys ever could."

The hours raced by, and soon the stall was picked bare of merchandise, the cash boxes bulging. The day had grown hot, and everyone was tired but elated. Even the turbans had sold, thanks to my efforts. The crowds had thinned, but the streets were still busy and the mood festive.

We were cleaning up when Elsa Van der Laar looked around anxiously. "Has anyone seen my son Andrew?"

He'd been sitting on the church steps. Now he was gone.

"Please, can anyone help me?" Her voice was louder, frustrated. "I'm looking for my son Andrew. Eight years old, glasses?"

"I know what he looks like. I'll help," I volunteered.

"We'll all look," the head of the committee, Mrs. Cabot-Wilkes, announced, glancing at Elsa nervously. "Eight years old, with glasses and brown hair. I'm sure he's just hiding."

"I knew he'd be trouble," Elsa muttered, her eyes darting over the faces in the crowd.

Soon the word spread and others were enlisted in the search, crawling under stalls and behind cars.

But something Diana had said in the museum came back to me, about the noise of the reception hurting Andrew's ears. The parade had been earsplitting.

I went inside the church and, after searching awhile, found Andrew curled into a ball, hiding underneath one of the pews.

"What are you doing under there?" I asked, kneeling down. "We've all been looking for you. It's time to come out now."

But he inched farther away from my outstretched hand. "I don't want to go home. I want to stay hidden."

"Why? You have a lovely home. Come on." I tried again. "Take my hand. Everyone's worried sick."

But he moved beyond my reach. "It's not real, you know."

"What's not real?"

"It could be them, or it could be me." His manner was calm, detached, as if he were more interested in being accurate than understood.

I sat back on my heels. "What do you mean?"

"When you're real, you feel real," he clarified. "And when you're not, you feel see-through, like a piece of glass."

It was such an unusual thing for a child to say. "But everyone's very worried about you."

"They can only see me because I'm not there. If I go back, I'll be invisible again."

His logic was curiously sophisticated.

"It sounds like a difficult situation," I admitted.

"It's not difficult exactly." He pushed his glasses up higher on his nose. "It's just impossible."

"But I can see you," I told him. "I'm talking to you right now."

He thought about this a moment. "You're invisible too," he concluded.

I tried a different tack. "Why don't I buy you some popcorn?"

"No, thank you."

"What about peanuts?"

He shook his head.

I sat down and drew my knees up to my chest. I was out of strategies. If I yanked him out, he was sure to make a scene. Besides, I was tired and not in the child-yanking mood.

It was so quiet here, white and full of light. There were no vaulted stone ceilings, no stations of the cross, no banks of flickering candles. Instead there was simplicity, a bright feeling of airy purity. Andrew was no fool; he'd chosen the best place to hide. I turned my face toward the sun streaming in through the tall windows and closed my eyes.

"Are you going to stay?" he asked.

"I don't know what I'm going to do," I told him. "Everyone's looking for you. I can't lie."

"I'll get in trouble."

I nodded. "That's likely. Unless . . ." I opened my eyes. "Look, Andrew, I have an idea."

When we came out, Elsa Van der Laar was surrounded by policemen, gathering details and taking notes. When she spotted us walking down the steps, her face changed from fear and worry to anger. Pushing aside the officers, she strode over. "Where have you been? Do you know how many people are looking for you? How selfish you are?"

By now a crowd had congregated, eager to see that Andrew was all right.

"I'm sorry." He glanced up at me. "I lost track of the time. I was praying."

Elsa Van der Laar blinked like a shrew thrust into the light. "You were *what?*"

"I was praying. You see, they died, didn't they?" he explained. "All those soldiers. Do you think they can see us?"

A thoughtful hush fell on the crowd. Then one of the policemen said, "Kid's got a point. Can't smack him for praying." He tousled Andrew's hair. "Tell your mother where you are next time, will you?"

Andrew looked up at him. "But she told me to sit there."

Now Elsa was wide-eyed and flustered. "I said be quiet! I said sit still and keep out of the way . . ." She floundered before grabbing his hand. "We've had enough excitement for one day," she declared, dragging him away.

Once the stall was broken down and everything packed up again, I was free to wander through the confetti-strewn streets. I felt the pleasant, easy contentment that comes from honest effort. I'd been dreading the day, imagining the boredom of being stuck side by side in a small stall with Ma and her cronies. But in fact they were funnier and fiercer than I'd given them credit for; less like widows, more like sailors on shore leave.

The Fire Hall on Salem Street had its doors flung open, music and laughter drifting out. Easily half the neighborhood was there; went in too. Long tables; laden with food ran the length of the room, and a band was playing. Children chased one another between waltzing couples and men still in their uniforms gathered in boisterous groups, telling tales, smoking, and drinking homemade beer.

Then I saw Mickey through the crowd, standing with his arm around Hildy. He was laughing. For years, I'd assumed that he could only be happy with me.

I backed away toward the door before I was seen.

But Jack Carney blocked my way. "Hello, Matchstick!" He grabbed me round the waist and pulled me onto the dance floor. "Your mother may not have time to dance with me, but you do, don't you?"

I could smell the whiskey on him, sweet and stale at the same time. I pulled away, but he held on tight. "Oh, no, you don't! You're going to dance with me until I'm done saying what I've got to say, understand?"

"And what's that?" I tried again to free myself.

He pressed himself up against me, his bloodshot eyes narrowed into two watery blue slits. "That mother of yours is nothing but a stinking little whore, do you hear me?" His grip tightened, powerful hands digging into my wrists. "You can tell her from me that I know for a fact she doesn't belong in that fancy widow's society!"

"What are you talking about?"

"You can tell her I know there is no Michael Fanning! That she was turned out from her house. Her family didn't want her anymore. No one did! The only thing she could do was climb on a boat."

"That's a lie!"

"Is it, Matchstick? You ever meet any of Fanning's people? Every hear of any of them?" He shook his head, a wide gap-toothed grin spreading across his face. "No, I don't reckon you did. 'Cause there aren't any!"

People were staring now; we were making a scene.

But I couldn't control myself. "That's a lie, you bastard!"

He only laughed. "No, you're the bastard, Matchstick! You forget, my family knew her from the old country, way before she was the Queen of the North End!"

I blinked at him, standing in all his swollen vengeful glory. My head was pounding, throbbing like a heartbeat, and the noise around me deadened into a muffled echo. Someone was calling my name, maybe Mickey, but I didn't want to see who it was. I just wanted to get out. So I ran, as a child runs from a gang of kids from another neighborhood, terrified and desperate.

Reaching the front door of my building, I stopped and stared up at the windows of our top-floor apartment. I was afraid. Afraid to go in, afraid of what I might say if I did.

There is no Michael Fanning! Your mother's nothing but a stinking little whore!

Suddenly my stomach lurched, and up came all the coffee and popcorn and dry scones, into the gutter. Afterward I sat down on the front steps, resting my head on my knees.

When I'd arrived in New York, I'd searched the drugstore phone book for Fanning relatives, hoping to find my father's cousin Ned. I'd found seven households with the name Edward Fanning, but when I rang, no one knew who I was talking about. They'd never met a Michael Fanning, never known anyone who'd attended Trinity College. But I never told my mother.

It's not real, you know.

Andrew's words echoed in my mind.

It could be them or it could be me. But it's not real.

Across the street, Contadino's had closed early but their awning was decorated with yards of red, white, and blue streamers, twisted into braids that caught each gust of early-evening wind. It billowed like a sail, bound for brave new shores. Underneath, in the front window, a sign was sandwiched between sacks of unshelled almonds and walnuts. It was decorated with two flags, one Italian, one American, and below was written:

> MEN LOVE THEIR COUNTRY, NOT BECAUSE IT IS
> GREAT, BUT BECAUSE IT IS THEIR OWN.
> —*Seneca*

The party continued all over the neighborhood and would go on long into the night. Music poured out of windows and doors;

laughter and gay voices rose and fell in waves. Children patrolled the streets unattended, collecting discarded flags in little self-important tribes, faces dirty with ice cream and chocolate.

An old Model T Ford packed with workers from the shipyards rumbled to a stop in front of me. The driver leaned out of the window. "We're headed to a party, Goldielocks. Wanna join us?"

Someone in the back seat held up a bottle. "Come on, sister! It's going to be a hell of a night!"

"Yeah, and my lap's getting cold!" another one called.

"Hey, don't break my heart, dollface." The driver grinned, flashing a dimple. "I think I'm already in love!"

They were good-looking guys, not too rough. I ached to lose myself in the company of strangers.

"How much have you got left in that bottle?" I asked.

The guy in the back seat shook it. "Plenty!"

But plenty wasn't enough. It wouldn't silence the noise in my head or numb the ache in my heart.

I shook my head, and they drove away.

When I did finally go upstairs, Ma was asleep on the sofa, snoring softly. Her dark hair was flattened on one side, her shoes had fallen off, and there was a hole in her stocking where her big toe stuck out. The table had been laid for dinner: cold ham and potatoes.

I watched her rising and falling breath, her hand curled into a child's fist under her chin.

Michael Fanning stared at me from the mantelpiece.

I guess I'd always known, somewhere inside, that he was too good to be true.

After all, the apple doesn't fall far from the tree.

———

Sleeves rolled up and wearing an old apron, I heaved another pile of old scientific journals out of Mr. Winshaw's office and stacked them in an empty box. Since his return from Philadelphia a week ago, it had become obvious that not even he could function among this level of chaos, so the task of cleaning his office out was delegated to me. Mr. Kessler tactfully referred to the process as "archiving" so as not to alarm Mr. Winshaw, who hated to throw anything away. But when the garbagemen came on Thursday, I would give them an extra dollar, and the "archives" would mysteriously go missing.

Luckily, the whole pretense was lost on Mr. Winshaw. Kicked out of his office for the day, he'd taken Selena to lunch and was now indulging in his favorite pastime—educating her against her will.

"Now this one is truly remarkable!" He took Selena's arm and guided her toward the row of dark wooden African figures displayed near the window. "If you wanted to make a unique investment in an area of art that's going to increase dramatically in value over the next twenty years, this would be the direction to move in, I guarantee you."

"But they're so ugly!" She clasped her alligator handbag in front of her like a shield, laughing. "In fact, they're extremely vulgar! I wonder that you display them in public!"

"How can you say that? Why, look at this one—it's a Madonna and Child. Probably mid-nineteenth century, wood, stone, beads—there's some glass in there too, can you see? The glass mimics the element of water, which is very important to the tribes of the Congo. They believe that water is the median that separates the living world from the afterlife."

Selena rolled her eyes. "You cannot possibly compare *that* to a Madonna and Child! It's so crudely done!"

He took a deep breath. "Actually, my dear, we refer to it as 'primitive art,' but in fact there's very little that's primitive about it," he explained patiently. "These pieces are just as difficult to make as any Italian marble."

"Oh, now you're joking!" She turned to me. "He doesn't make it easy for you to earn commission, now does he?"

I wiped the dust and sweat from my brow. "What commission?"

He ignored both of us. "What you're really seeing here is an entirely different set of aesthetic ideals from our classical Western ones. You have to broaden your mind! Here"—he drew her in for a closer look—"see how perfectly compact and symmetrical the figure is? She's holding her child on her knees, staring into the distance between the two worlds of the living and the dead." He looked at her eagerly. "Only a woman who's had a child really understands that threshold, am I right? You see, this idol was probably placed on an ancestral shrine to honor not just one mother but all the mother figures of the family."

"Well, I think they're hideous." She sighed. "Now, stop trying to convert me to your heathen ways and tell me what time you're picking me up for dinner."

I caught Mr. Kessler's eye and smiled. Nothing was better than watching Mr. Winshaw fail to batter someone into submission.

Hauling another box into the back, I put it on top of the others. But it toppled, spilling onto the floor.

"Damn it!"

As I piled the magazines and journals back up, I came upon a photograph that must have been jammed between the stacks. It was faded, dog-eared. It featured a much younger, teenage version of Mr. Winshaw standing between two other young men who were practically identical—most certainly twins. They were all wearing smart British military uniforms and laughing, arms round one another's shoulders, blurry around the edges where they'd been unable to stand still. Their broad smiles, sandy blond curls, and regular features echoed one another, variations on a familial theme. I turned it over. A place and date, "Oxford, 1914," were written along the bottom.

That was the beginning of the Great War.

Sunlight flooded the photo, shone around their heads like soft halos, as if they were blessed, chosen for some great destiny. Certainly they looked as if they believed that to be true. I recognized the familiar carefree arrogance of youth, a complete inability to conceive of any impending consequences that might possibly apply to them.

Here was a fragile moment; doomed, disappearing even as it occurred, like a wisp of smoke that appears and fades in the same instance.

I put the photograph back on Mr. Winshaw's desk. When I went back into the front of the shop, Selena had gone.

Deprived of his office and his audience, Mr. Winshaw turned his attention to me. "So, Fanning"—he trailed after me as I searched for a duster under the shop counter—"do you think those pieces are vulgar?"

"Of course."

"And you don't think they'll sell?"

"Never."

Apparently this was both a revelation and an irritation. He scowled at me, shoving his hands into his pockets, "Well, why not?"

"Because no one understands them, and they're disturbing. But then you knew that already. That's why you like them—because they intimidate others."

He thought about this. "I want to challenge people."

"Then you're in the wrong place." I found the duster, headed back into his office. "Bostonians don't want to be challenged. They're proud of their loyalty to the past."

"They shouldn't be."

"And if they weren't, you'd be out of business. Who would you sell those Chippendale chairs to? You should send the primitive art to New York, where people are more easily cowed by the threat of being parochial."

"You know"—he leaned against the doorjamb—"you're too smart to be milling about here all day."

I shot him a dark look. "Does it look like I'm milling about?"

"Yes, but what are you doing, Fanning?" He held up his hands. "I mean, what are you *really* doing here?"

"Is this a philosophical question, or are you trying to get rid of me?" Climbing on top of his chair, I wiped down the light fitting. A cloud of several years' worth of dust filled the room.

"Stop meddling!" Mr. Kessler called from his office. "You're going to talk us out of a perfectly good salesgirl!"

"Yes, but what if she's not a salesgirl? What about your ambitions and interests? What are your aspirations?"

"My aspirations are to pay the rent. As for interests, I honestly wouldn't know." I climbed down, took a step back.

The room looked worse than when I started.

"What are you drawn to?"

"I don't know." I wasn't sure which was worse: when he didn't pay attention to me, or when he did. "I suppose I have to think about it. It's too hot for these questions. My brain is made of cement today."

"Then you need to feed it!" he insisted. "When was the last time you saw a play or went to a concert?"

"A *play*?" I laughed. "I've never been to a play, Mr. Winshaw!"

"Why not?"

"People like me, we go to the movies."

"That's ridiculous, Fanning! And elitist. I've never heard you say anything stupid before, and that *is* stupid!"

"You've heard me say a lot of stupid things, and let me know it too," I told him. "Besides, cinema is the Shakespeare of the masses."

I tried to look at the office from a fresh angle. Maybe if we moved the filing cabinet into the corner, the door might finally open all the way.

"Help me, will you?" I took one end.

"Shakespeare is the Shakespeare of the masses!" He pushed from the other side, and we dragged the cabinet into the hallway. "Errol Flynn or James Cagney can't inspire the way Macbeth or King Lear can—there's no comparison."

"Fine. If you'll stop harassing me, I'll go to a play."

"And the symphony. You must go to the symphony."

There was a damp patch on the wall that the cabinet had been hiding. Moving it had been a big mistake.

"I'll take you," he said suddenly.

I looked at him in alarm. "Pardon me?"

"I have tickets to the opera on Saturday. It's Puccini—everyone loves Puccini."

"The *opera*! Oh no!" I shook my head. "No, thank you!"

"Why not?"

"I'm not Selena!"

"What does that mean?"

"It means I don't want to be lectured all night!"

He was offended. "I don't lecture anybody!"

Mr. Kessler could be heard chuckling in the next room.

"And I'm not going anywhere with a man who can't remember my first name!" I added.

But he wasn't listening; he'd spotted the old photo on his desk, picked it up. "Where did you find this?"

"On the floor." I moved in closer, peering over his shoulder at the three faces. "It's you, isn't it?"

He nodded. "With my brothers, Harry and Ralph."

"Twins?"

"That's right. Not quite identical, but close."

"So they were the good-looking ones." I smiled.

His face softened. "They were three years older than me."

"I didn't know you'd fought in the war. You all joined up at the same time?"

"We wanted to serve in the same regiment. But we were separated anyway. I was sent off to Arabia, because I'd been there before on digs, and knew the language. They never made it out of France. That was the last time we ever saw one another."

Too late I remembered that Mr. Kessler had told me that Mr. Winshaw didn't have a family.

He put the photo back inside the top drawer of his desk and then looked up at the disarray of his office, as if he'd only just noticed what I was doing. "You know, we should get rid of this all," he said finally. "Give these books to a library, take that old map down . . ."

The map?

"Oh no!" I was adamant. "You can't do that!"

He looked at me in surprise. "Ever since I've known you, you've wanted me to clear this place out."

"Yes, but not *that*! That's different. I won't let you!"

"Hello! Excuse me!" someone called from the front of the shop. I peered around the corner. It was a deliveryman, carrying a large bouquet of white roses. "Excuse me, miss. I'm looking for May Fanning?"

"That's me!" No one had ever sent me flowers before. I hurried to take them from him. The arrangement was enormous, almost too unwieldy to hold, with blooms nearly as large as my hand. "My goodness!" I laughed, delighted. "Aren't they beautiful?"

"Sure." Mr. Winshaw jammed his hands into his pockets. "If you like that sort of thing."

I pulled out the card.

HOPE YOU HAVEN'T FORGOTTEN ME, FRA LINE.

SATURDAY NIGHT?

James

My delight transformed to a childish joy and relief. I thought I'd been the forgotten one. And after the incident with Jack Carney, I'd wondered if he was right, if I were nothing more than a mistake, the legacy of an unfit mother. But James didn't see me that way. And here, out of the blue, were two dozen old-fashioned white roses to prove it.

Mr. Kessler emerged from his office. "Well, look at that! That must be fifty dollars' worth of roses!" He shook his head in admiration. "You know, they fly them in all the way from California."

"So you have an admirer. Good for you." Mr. Winshaw jiggled the change in his pockets. "Though I've heard it said that men who make grand gestures are usually trying to hide something."

"And I've heard it said that men who make no gestures shouldn't judge those who do," I replied.

"Aw, come on! It's a cheap move. Any man can buy a girl flowers!"

"And yet they don't. Besides, why is it a cheap move? How are men meant to show they care?"

"With their conversation. Their attentiveness." He tapped his forehead. "The adroitness of their minds!"

"In that case, it's a good thing someone thought of sending flowers."

"Look, Fanning, I'm merely pointing out that to my taste, this is, well"—he shrugged—"it's a little *vulgar.*"

"That's rich, coming from a man who escorts a different woman around town every night of the week!" I buried my nose in the soft, waxy petals, inhaling deeply. A rush of hope and possibility filled me. Nothing Mr. Winshaw said was going to dampen my spirits now. Besides, he deserved to be put in his place for once. "What *heaven*! I really must put these in water. Don't you have some culturally stimulating event to go to? Some young female mind to expand?" I smiled sweetly. "Something to dig up in a foreign land?"

"Oh, I see!" He leaned back against the counter. "So a few weeds is all it takes to win a woman's heart! You're selling yourself cheap. Far too cheap."

"You're not fooling anyone," I informed him, going into the back of the shop to find a vase. "You haven't got the courage to send flowers! And as for the opera, I regret that I will have to decline. I have another engagement for Saturday night."

As I was filling the vase with water, Mr. Kessler came up behind me, standing in the doorway. "You know," he pointed out, "nobody speaks to Winshaw quite the way that you do."

"Well, now somebody does. Don't you think it's about time?"

"Yes." He nodded thoughtfully, tugging at his waistcoat. "Yes, I do."

They were just closing up for the day at Russo's when I knocked on the window. Angela was sweeping the floor and looked up to see me on the other side of the rain-streaked glass, holding up the gigantic bouquet. She squealed with delight and hurried to unlock the door.

"Oh my goodness, Mae! Where did you get those?"

"From a man—a real honest gentleman!" I swaggered inside. I'd never been able to sit across from Angela and brag about having a respectable beau.

"Who? I want to hear everything!"

Mrs. Russo came out from the back kitchen, wiping her hands on her apron. "Mae! We haven't seen you since Pina's party!"

"Mama! Just look at her flowers!"

"Yes." She nodded. "Either someone's been very naughty, or they're about to be. Come!" She pulled out some chairs. "Sit down. I'll get coffee."

We sat and drank coffee while I told them all about James Van der Laar, how he'd first introduced himself, invited me out with his friends, taken me to lunch . . . I took a few liberties, made a few careful edits to the tale, but most of it was true.

"Well, clearly he's sweet on you!" Angela said when I'd finished, easing back in her chair to accommodate her growing bump.

Mrs. Russo wasn't so easily convinced. She looked down into her empty espresso cup and frowned. "Is he Catholic?"

"I'm not sure." (In fact, I was certain he wasn't.)

She held up her hands in disbelief. "*Dio mio!* What are you thinking? Have you introduced him to your mother?"

"No. Not yet."

"Well, when?" Her finger went up. I knew that finger, we both did. Here came a lecture. "Here you have a suitor, right? A man needs to meet the family sooner rather than later. After all, the family is what matters! The family tells you everything you need to know about the person. The family is what is left after the roses fade."

"It isn't like that," I explained. "He's not a suitor, not like in the old country."

"Then what is he?"

I glanced across at Angela, who rolled her eyes sympathetically.

"Mama, you're too old-fashioned," she chided.

"I'm old! Of course I'm old-fashioned! But you can't make a life on a wish and a prayer. You need reality. He needs to know who you are, where you come from."

"What does that matter?" Angela argued. "Who cares about the past? People don't worry about that nowadays."

Mrs. Russo ignored her daughter, instead speaking to me. "Does he know anything about you? Where you live? Where you come from?"

"I suppose."

"You *suppose?*"

It never failed; Maddalena Russo had the power to disarm me in a heartbeat, to pull back the thin veil of wishful thinking and poke at the raw insecurities beneath.

"All your life, Mae, and I've known you all your life, you love to live in storybooks and movies. Like when your boyfriend is a boxer or when you run off to New York. But life is no fairy tale. When you meet a man, you have to *think*, not just *feel*. Where they come from, where they're going, what they believe in . . ."

She didn't understand. I came from nowhere and had a past

not even I wanted to know about. "I just haven't had much luck in love."

"Luck?" she snorted. "Luck is for gamblers and fools! You make a choice!"

"You're too serious, Mama!" Angela reprimanded. "He sounds like a nice man. Why can't she have a little fun?"

Maddalena Russo sighed heavily, pressing her warm, rough hand over mine in a rare show of tenderness. "Because happiness isn't made of fun. It's made of solid, real things. It's made of paychecks and clean clothing, and hot food and healthy children, and a man who can look you in the eye when he comes home because he has nothing to hide. It's not so rare. In fact, it's so common people don't notice it. They look for roses when they should be looking for indoor plumbing."

Ma, on the other hand, was thrilled about the bouquet. She couldn't have been more delighted if they'd been given to her.

We didn't have a vase big enough for all of them at once, so she divided them between several small ones, placing them throughout the house. Humming "I'll Take You Home Again, Kathleen" softly to herself, she carefully trimmed the stalks and fussed over each delicate arrangement.

Then, quite uncharacteristically, she insisted upon making an appointment with M. Antoine at the beauty salon. "Sometimes it's wiser to spend a little money than save it. And I've seen M. Antoine's waves—they are truly a thing to behold!" Her eyes shone with pride and excitement. "You are on your way, Maeve! You are on your way!"

———

Saturday night James took me to the Oak Room for supper, at the Copley Plaza Hotel. Grand in the old style, the Oak Room was decorated with carved wooden paneling, leather chairs, and stuffed deer heads staring down at diners with black button eyes. Now that it was summer, electric fans were tucked into corners behind palms, and a drowsy orchestra played sentimental favorites while regulars dined on vichyssoise, lobster Thermidor, and baked Alaska.

My hair gleamed in golden marcel waves, and I wore a dress of red-and-cream-striped lawn that grazed my ankles, made from a Butterwick pattern Ma insisted was identical to a Norman Norell ensemble that had sold out immediately at Stearns.

When we sat down, James waved away the menus. "Don't even bother looking. Just order anything that takes your fancy."

"Are you sure?" I laughed. *"Anything?"*

"They know me here."

"All right. Then I'll have what you're having."

"Don't you even want to know what that is?"

"No. I want to take my chances."

When the waiter came, James told him we would both "have the usual," so I was none the wiser.

I noticed that his ring was missing. "What happened?" I pointed to his hand. "Don't you like it anymore?"

"Oh!" He stared at where it had been. "I seemed to have left it somewhere. It will turn up sooner or later. These things always do."

Then he produced a small jewelry box from his pocket and put it on my plate.

My heart sped up. It wasn't a ring box, but still, I'd never been given a gift of jewelry before. I could feel the other diners watching, eager to see what was inside. I pretended to be calm. "What's this?"

"Nothing. A trifle." He smiled, leaning back a little, instinctively giving the rest of the room a clear view.

Inside was a slim brooch in the shape of an arrow, studded with diamonds. "Oh, James!" Taking it out, I held it up, and there was a universal murmur of approval.

"Do you like it?"

It all felt so unreal. These were diamonds, an entire row of them. "It's beautiful!" My voice trembled a little, more from shock than anything else. It was such an unexpected and lavish gift—too lavish.

"Here, allow me," he said, pinning it just below my shoulder.

"What's all this for?" I smiled as if I were in the habit of receiving jewels with supper.

"For you, May. It's for you," he said, shrugging it off. "Don't you want me to spoil you? Or do you insist on being a woman of independent means?"

"I think diamonds go with independence very nicely!" I said, relieved and yet confused by his casual attitude. Was I being provincial?

A bottle of champagne arrived, courtesy of the management. "It's always good to see you, Mr. Van der Laar," the maître d' told us, shaking James's hand enthusiastically. "And with such a lovely companion!"

I watched anxiously as the maître d' made a great show of opening the bottle and pouring out two glasses. Under the table, I twisted my napkin tight. Mr. Baylor had told me how to keep away from bars, speakeasies, and late-night parties, and how to guard against the miserable hours of loneliness and despair. But

I was completely unprepared for the more perilous moments of romance and celebration. Now I felt like an actress playing a scene in front of a full house—only I was about to ruin it all with the wrong lines.

James raised his glass. "To us."

"To us," I echoed, raising my glass too.

He took a sip. I sat frozen, glass midair.

What was worse? Drinking or not drinking?

Then suddenly something snapped, and I felt a sharp pain in my finger. The champagne spilled across the table; I had been gripping the glass so tightly, the stem had shattered in my hand.

"Oh, dear!" The maître d' rushed forward with extra napkins to mop it all up. "Are you all right, miss?"

"You're bleeding." James pointed to my hand.

I looked down. My finger was cut. "Gosh, what a mess!" I laughed awkwardly. "I suppose I should go to the ladies' and clean myself up."

Somehow I made it out of the dining room and to the ladies' lounge. There I ran my hand under cool water, staring at the diamond brooch in the mirror. I was on dangerous ground. This wasn't my world; I'd been admitted by mistake. Any minute now they would discover I was a fraud and show me to the door.

As I headed back, I was stopped by a familiar voice.

"Oh, I know you, don't I?"

I turned round to see Smitty on the arm of an attractive young man. They were both in evening dress; she was wearing a graceful strapless gown of gauzy black chiffon that flowed effortlessly. Her brow wrinkled as she searched for my name. "It's Mabel, isn't it?"

"May," I corrected her, certain she knew it anyway. "It's nice to see you again."

"What are you doing in *here*?" She cast her eyes round the lobby as if it were the most inconceivable destination on earth. "Are you with someone?"

I remembered the way she'd appropriated James the last time we'd met. "I'm just dining with a friend."

"Oh, I pity you!" She chuckled, giving her escort a knowing look. "That restaurant's an absolute *relic*! Full of old men with their mistresses!"

"I'm sorry?"

"Didn't you know? It's *notorious*! Alec and I are just having a quick drink before the show." She nodded to the bar across the corridor. "Of course, you and your friend are welcome to join us, if you like."

"No, but thank you. I really should get back."

Then she noticed the brooch. "Oh! Where did you get that?"

"Nowhere," I answered stupidly, caught off guard. "I've had it for years, actually. Why?"

"It's Cartier, isn't it?"

"It was a gift. I really couldn't say." I smiled apologetically. "I really must be getting back."

I could feel their eyes on me as I crossed the lobby to the main dining room, the marble floor echoing beneath my heels.

Once I was back, suddenly all I could see were the elderly couples that seemed to occupy the tables, the wilting palms, and James's slightly distracted look as he flicked the ash off the end of his cigarette. "Are you all right?" he asked as I slid into my seat.

"I'm sorry. I saw an old friend in the lobby and couldn't get away."

The dinner progressed from vichyssoise and oysters to an enormous chateaubriand. James told me about all the new Broadway shows and the best places to eat in Berlin, and promised to take me to both. He even asked my dress size, in case he had "time to kill" in Paris next month. But it felt dreamlike and insubstantial, as if I could no longer feel the ground beneath my feet. Perhaps I was just unused to happiness, I told myself. Maybe I needed to loosen up. And I couldn't stop thinking about the champagne that had spilled across the table. When we were finished, he stood up, held out his arm. "Shall we?"

But instead of leaving, he walked over to the elevator.

"Oh! You're staying here?" I asked, confused.

"I have a room."

"Oh! Shall I . . . shall I . . ."

The elevator doors opened, and he stepped inside. "Shall you what?"

I wanted to say, "Shall I wait here?" but I couldn't quite get the words out.

He looked at me expectantly.

I got in too.

Upstairs, he unlocked the door to a three-room suite. Even in the darkness, I sensed the expanse of space, the icy glint of chandeliers, the generous swags of silken curtains under the high ceilings. Not bothering to turn on the lights, he walked over to the open window. Far below us, the city blinked enticingly, illuminated by glowing billboards and neon lights; it lent the room a strange otherworldly luminescence and cast a bluish shadow across his face.

He stood there, back to me. "Do you like the brooch, May?"

The night pressed in upon me, heavy and black.

"Yes." My voice sounded hollow and far away.

"Good."

I waited for him to say something else, something tender or romantic, but he didn't.

Coming closer, he unzipped my dress. Moving without urgency, he took what was his now, lingering over the complicated fastenings of my lingerie and slipping his fingers beneath the fabric to feel the trembling warmth of my skin. When he'd stripped me bare, he stood back.

I watched as he poured out a large whiskey.

A warm breeze sent the sheer curtains billowing into the room like a ghostly sail.

I held out my hand, and he gave me the glass.

Then, smiling just a little, he took off his jacket and knelt down before me.

A week later Diana surprised me, ambushing me in the old style. I found her waiting outside the shop, sucking on a cherry lollipop.

"Hey, stranger," she said, offering me one too. "Busy?"

She seemed more her old self, impulsive and uncomplicated. I wanted nothing more than to slip back in time with her again and forget everything that had come between us.

"Not at all. What shall we do?" I asked, peeling off the wrapper and popping it into my mouth. "Shall we go to the apartment?"

She wrinkled her nose. "I haven't been there since I've been back. Have you?"

"No. We could go to the pictures," I suggested.

"It's such a nice evening. Let's get lost. We'll walk until we know what to do with ourselves."

She held out her arm, and I took it. And for a while everything difficult disappeared. I put James in a little drawer in my head and locked it tight. Tonight we belonged only to each other.

We walked down Charles Street and around the Common. It had been a hot day, and the park was full of people. We enjoyed making small talk for a while. She told me about how she was learning to play golf, even though she hated it, because her mother insisted that all the really "smart" girls did. They'd joined the country club at Chestnut Hill and hired a pro who, she was sure, was always drunk, no matter how early her lesson. She showed me the calluses on her hands and laughed about the dreadful shoes she had to wear. "I cheat, of course. I get my caddy to do it, though, so I can always pretend I'm outraged and fire him if I'm discovered."

"But that's dreadful!" I laughed.

"Oh, but I tip him so much he doesn't care," she assured me. "He's going to Princeton in the autumn, and I'm told they don't respect you at Princeton unless you cheat."

"Princeton?" I whistled. "I thought caddies lugged around clubs all day!"

"Yes, but they're all like that—going to college, zipping around in sports cars, and they have more expensive shirts and haircuts than anyone else. It's quite bizarre, actually. But I suppose they enjoy pretending to work."

She asked me what I'd been up to.

"Just work," I told her.

"I suppose your life is a desert now that I'm becoming a golf pro," she teased.

"I'm without hope of ever being happy again," I confirmed.

She looked out over the lush green lawns, at barefoot children playing tag in the cool grass and young couples lying in each other's arms. "I don't suppose you've heard from Max at all recently?"

"Me? No." Evidently she wasn't aware how badly we'd hit it off. "Why?"

"I just wondered." Then she added almost guiltily. "I don't really know why I asked. It's a stupid question." She began picking at the varnish on her thumbnail.

"Why don't you ring her?"

"No. It doesn't matter. It's a bad habit." She smiled quickly. "One I must learn to break."

"Do you think you'll ever see her again, just as friends?"

"No. I expect not. Though it's not as easy as I thought to control one's thoughts," she admitted sadly. "They go where they like, don't they?"

We carried on down the path that circled the pond. The evening had cooled down a little, and a gentle fragrant mistiness rose from the grass beneath the lilac-tinged sky. Eventually we came to the far edge of the water. Diana stopped. Sitting on a bench on the other side were a woman and a young boy. The boy had a notebook open on his lap.

"Isn't that Andrew?" I asked.

She nodded. "He likes to record the number of passengers on the swan boats. They often stop here on their walks, when the weather is fine."

Just as she said, Andrew was making notations, while the woman next to him, presumably his nanny, knitted in silence.

"He calculates which boats transport the most people throughout the year. He would do the same with trolley and railway cars, only he's not allowed. It used to be a rule that he wasn't permitted to stop, but Mrs. Hawkins is older than the other nannies, so she doesn't mind."

"The other nannies?"

"They never stay long. He goes through them like wildfire."

"Let's say hello." I started for the bridge.

"No." Diana put a hand on my arm. "Best not to bother them. I just like to check and see if they're there." Tenderness softened her features.

"I saw him, you know. Did he tell you? At the parade."

"No. I don't get to speak to him as often as I'd like." We stood a little longer before she asked, "Does he seem happy to you?"

"Yes. Why wouldn't he be?"

"I mean, he seems like a normal little boy?"

Andrew was undeniably unusual in some ways, with his remarkable memory and obsession with insects. "He's quite intelligent," I said after a while, "but he seems fine. Why?"

"Elsa says he has the most terrible temper tantrums, that the school doesn't want to keep him anymore. There's talk of sending him away."

"Away where?"

"Maybe abroad. To a French school."

"He seems a little young for that, don't you think?"

Diana nodded slowly. "I couldn't bear it."

"Is there anything you can do? Perhaps speak to your aunt?"

"I don't know. Maybe." She turned back to face me. "Do you still see Mr. Baylor?"

In truth, it had been a while since I'd been. I didn't want to tell him about James, about our time together, augmented by champagne and whiskey. "Sometimes," I lied.

"Does it help?"

"It's not easy," I warned. "In fact, it's much harder to maintain."

"But you can see improvement," she pressed. "You're getting better?"

There was an urgency in her voice that pricked my conscience. "Well, I'm not getting worse, am I?" It came out too sharp.

She lapsed into silence, absentmindedly running her fingers across her pearls.

"I want to be different," she said after a while.

"You mean, become a golf pro?" I joked.

"No, I'm trying, *really* trying, to change."

I didn't quite follow. "Change what?"

She gave me a look. "The way I am. I'm a moral defective. We both know that."

It shocked me to hear her sounding like Dr. Joseph—using words like *moral defective.* "You don't honestly believe that, do you?"

"I *know* that. If I don't face my failings, I can't change them. There's a minister, a spiritual leader of the Reformed Church, Dr. Alder. Elsa's arranged for me to see him. He's helped many people, including her."

Her change in attitude unnerved me. "But you don't need a spiritual leader, Diana. You're not evil!"

She turned on me. "What do you think evil is, May? Don't you think that having a perverted nature, wanting to do things that both the church and society find repulsive and abhorrent, to the detriment of yourself and your family . . . don't you think that's evil?"

A chill went up the back of my spine. "Do you think I'm evil?"

She hesitated. "You're weak. Unable to control yourself," she said after a moment. "It's not the same."

"But you're not a bad person!"

She stared at me hard, irritation flickering in her eyes. "And if it's it not natural, then what is it?"

"Different!"

"No, *defective!*" she insisted. "Cripples don't choose to be lame, but they are, nonetheless, and we help them, don't we? We don't allow them just to hobble along when we can operate and make their legs straight! Well, maybe some people are simply born abnormal. Their characters are defective the way some people's bodies are. But if I don't try to change—I mean *really* try—then I won't know what I'm capable of."

She'd obviously been thinking about this for a while, but her arguments had the hollow sound of someone else's labored logic. She was only fighting with me so she could convince herself.

"What about the No Way Out Club?" I asked. "What about the freedom to do as you like, regardless of what others want?"

Suddenly doubt shadowed her face; her borrowed resolve faltered. "Some things are more important than freedom." She turned, staring again at the little boy on the other side of the lake. "They say Dr. Alder works miracles. So who knows? Maybe he can even cure me."

It was a wet, dreary afternoon, full of summer thunderstorms. Charles Street was all but abandoned. The rain beat endlessly against the tin shingles on the roof, and Persia sat crouched like a sphinx by the open front door, staring at the gutters overflowing with water.

Still in his overcoat and hat, Mr. Winshaw had just arrived from the train station. He'd spent several days in Philadelphia, discussing a future expedition in Turkey with colleagues at the University of Pennsylvania. The meeting had gone well. Plans were being drawn up; a proposed alliance with the British Museum had been suggested. Now, despite the dreary weather, excitement crackled around him like electricity.

"So"—he tossed his hat on top of a filing cabinet in the corner, smiling at his own skill—"with any luck we'll be able to leave in another month or so. The Germans have dominated that site, but there's room for expansion on our part. It's an enormous undertaking. I've no idea how involved it will be. It could take years."

"Years?" I hadn't realized he was leaving again so soon, and for so long. "What site exactly? Where?"

"Oh? Didn't I say? Pergamon, the ancient Greek city that legend says was founded by Arcadians. One of the most remarkable and complete Greek remains in the world. In the book of Revelations, it's called one of the Seven Churches of Asia." He put his feet up on his desk and popped a square of chocolate into his mouth. "Do you know the library of Pergamon was second only to the library of Alexandria in the ancient world? They've already excavated a theater, Roman baths, several temples . . ." He sat up, pointed to its location on his map. "Here we are, right on the Aegean Sea. The landscape in that area is magnificent!"

Mr. Kessler and I watched glumly as he stuck a pin into it.

"Actually"—he took a deep breath—"I've got a lot to get in order and not much time." He rummaged around on his desk. "My passport papers are here somewhere. They need to be reviewed. I should contact the British consulate and get a visa extension. You type, don't you, Fanning? You can help with that." He moved an old shoebox out of the way. "What's this?"

"Oh! That's mine," I said quickly, taking it from him. "I left it there this morning. I'm sorry."

"Been out shopping?" He gave me the sort of indulgent smile that was akin to a pat on the head.

"No, it's just some . . . well, actually"—I opened the lid to show them—"I broke one of my mother's teacups. I thought there might be some glue here to repair it."

Mr. Kessler picked up a few of the pieces. "A Staffordshire willow-pattern design. Very nice. But you seem to be missing quite a bit. It's been seriously damaged."

"I know." Every time I looked at the broken remains, it reminded me of our argument, and our disappointment in each other.

"Actually, there's a legend behind this design," Mr. Kessler said. "Do you know it? A pair of young Chinese lovers, betrayed. They die in the end, and the gods are so touched by their love, they take pity on them and immortalize them as doves. Though"—he looked doubtful—"I'm not certain this poor example will ever have a second chance."

"Leave it with me," Mr. Winshaw said. Obviously his good fortune had put him into a magnanimous mood.

"What's the point, if it can never be used again?" I put the lid back on.

"Fanning, I'm an archaeologist! I spend half my life piecing broken things back together!" He took the box from me, tucked it underneath his arm. "I think I can repair a teacup."

Mr. Kessler drifted back into his office, but I lingered. Picking up a stack of outgoing letters, I pretended to be checking their return addresses. "What a thrilling opportunity. You must be excited."

"Can't wait." He pulled out some files and rummaged through them for his passport papers.

"It's not dangerous there, is it?"

"The whole world is dangerous, Fanning. What difference does it make?"

"No difference." His glibness was irritating. "It's just a shame, that's all. That you're leaving so soon."

"What else am I going to do?" He closed the file cabinet; his search had been unsuccessful.

"Stay." I pointed out the obvious. "Why do you own a shop if you never want to be here?"

"Poor planning, I suppose." He picked through his desk drawers. "The sad truth is I'm feral, and there doesn't seem to be a cure. People have tried to housebreak me, but it's never stuck."

"What people?"

He looked up, surprised. "It's not like you to be curious, Fanning."

"I'm not." I backtracked. "Not really. I'm just trying to understand you."

"Oh. Well, I wouldn't bother. Look, if you like I'll clear all my things out. Give you some room to work while I'm gone."

I couldn't imagine the office or even the shop without all Mr. Winshaw's books.

"But this is your office, your things!"

"Yes, but—"

"You're coming back, aren't you?" It came out panicked and sharp.

"Of course." His eyes searched my face, perplexed. "You could always write," he said softly.

My whole body flushed from embarrassment and, even worse, excitement. Was he teasing me? Or was he serious?

I turned away so he couldn't see my face. "Honestly, Mr. Winshaw. I don't know where I'd find the time."

"Ouch!" Ma winced. "Take it easy, Maeve! That's a comb, not a rake!"

"Then sit still," I reprimanded, forcing her to face front. "Honestly, you're like a child who has to look at everything!"

She was sitting on a chair in the center of the kitchen with a towel over her shoulders, the floor covered in newspaper. "I don't know why you want it so short anyway." I stood behind her, trimming her wet hair. "It would suit you better long."

"Not when you get older. As one ages, one must adopt a more conservative appearance." It sounded like something she'd read in the pages of *McCall's* again.

I concentrated, biting my lower lip hard. Her hair was as thick as mine, with natural waves that she tamed every night with pin curls. Every time I cut a bit off, her hair bounced back even more unruly and full, like a mythical hydra. "Maybe you should've gone to M. Antoine."

"I have complete faith in you. Oh, look!" She strained to see out of the window. "Is that Mrs. Marinzano, wearing a new hat? My goodness, she's let herself go! I hardly recognize her."

"Stop moving!" I pushed her back into her seat again. "I nearly took your ear off."

"Why are you in such a bad mood?"

"I'm not in a mood."

"Yes, you are," she insisted. "You've been in a mood for weeks."

I knew she was right. I'd been irritable and anxious, even though I was trying my best to contain it. In fact, the only time I wasn't on edge was when I was either about to meet James or with him. When we were together, I could lose myself and forget about anything else. But as soon as we parted, my thoughts spun out of control. I'd never been jealous before, but now I was fearful and suspicious. I couldn't concentrate on anything else for more than a few minutes at a time. The sound of his voice had the power to send my heart racing with excitement. But by the same token, silence devastated me, leaving me empty and alone.

"It's nothing," I told her. "I'm tired, that's all."

"That's what you always say!"

"And it's always true!"

I didn't want to fight with her, really I didn't.

"Well"—she folded her arms across her chest—"I don't know what I've done wrong to make you snap at me!"

I decided to change the subject. "So, I've been thinking, Ma. Would you want to see a play with me?"

"A *play*? You mean, in a theater?"

"Of course in a theater! Where else do they have plays?"

She turned to look at me, again nearly losing her other ear in the process. "Since when do you go to the theater?"

"It's just something I wanted to do. You know, to broaden my mind."

"What kind of play?" she asked cautiously, as if I were about to subject her to something distasteful.

"There's a production of *A Midsummer Night's Dream* opening soon. The balcony seats seem reasonable, especially if you wait and buy them on the day."

"A *Midsummer Night's Dream*." Her voice became reflective. "That's the one with the fairies, isn't it? And the donkey?"

I was impressed. "That's right. How do you know that?"

"There was a woman I knew who used to read Shakespeare to the children when I was growing up, at the public library. I guess that one stuck with me."

Ma almost never talked about her childhood. I'd asked many times, but she was staunchly evasive, claiming she couldn't remember anything or that the details were so unremarkable that they weren't worth repeating. But now, out of nowhere, a random gem spilled out. This was the first glimpse into my mother's past that I could recall in a very long time.

"She used to read to you?" I prompted.

"That's right. On a Saturday afternoon. I went with my brothers. The children sat in a circle on the floor in front of her, and she did all the voices of the characters. That was in the days before radio; it was like magic to us. Of course, after my mother died, all that stopped. Father never let us go anywhere." She took out a cigarette and lit it. "But sometimes I used to sneak off anyway. It was warm and dry between the library shelves, and if you were holding a book, they couldn't kick you out."

"Didn't you go to school?"

She shook her head. "Not until later. But one of the librarians took pity on me. She gave me a job cleaning the ashtrays, sweeping floors, stacking books, and in return she taught me how to read." She took a thoughtful drag. "Miss Caroline Frears."

"And what kind of books did you read?"

"Novels. Serials. Dickens and Collins." She laughed. "Miss Frears thought they were lowbrow! She called *Bleak House* 'unspeakably vulgar'!"

I was fascinated. "You never told me that."

"She had very particular ideas about what constituted good taste."

"What was she like? Was she pretty?"

"No." She smiled. "But she was elegant. She told me, 'Act like a lady, and you'll be treated as one.'"

"That's what you say to me now!"

She nodded. "Once a month, on a Sunday afternoon, she would invite me to tea. She showed me how to pour and serve and hold my cup." She imitated the stiff-elbowed posture. "Like this, just so. And not to gulp my cake!" She chuckled, remembering. "She had a tea service very much like ours. Only it had all the pieces, right down to a matching sugar bowl."

I was hungry for more.

"And your brothers? What were they like? What happened to them?"

She gave a little shrug. "I'm not sure."

"What was your mother like? Was she kind? Did she look like you?"

"I don't remember."

"What was your father like?"

Her face changed. "He was a beast."

It came out hard as stone, an iron door, slammed shut.

I'd asked too many questions. The conversation was over.

Suddenly irritated, she ran her fingers through the hair on the side of her head. "You've not cut that short enough, Maeve. I can't sit here all day—I've got things to do!"

I combed it out again and began trimming off the ends.

"You know"—Ma flicked the ashes of her cigarette into her palm—"those plays are awfully long. You should go with someone else. I think I'm too old for fairy tales."

I was alone in the shop one morning when a gentleman came in, dressed in a boldly fashionable blue seersucker suit and lavender tie. His straw boater was tilted at a rakish angle, and he moved with a certain barely contained energy, as if he might burst into dance at any moment. His eyes were lively and sharp, his mouth curved automatically into a smile, as if he were forever enjoying some private joke.

He sashayed up to the counter. "Good day. I believe Mr. Kessler is holding something for me," he said, giving me a sideways glance, as if we were involved in a secret alliance. "My name is Mr. Tresalion."

"Certainly, sir. I'll have a look."

Mr. Kessler hadn't mentioned anything, but after searching, I found a box under the counter with a card on top of it, Mr. Tresalion's name written on it in Mr. Kessler's spidery hand.

"Here we go. This must be it." I opened it up.

Mr. Tresalion reached inside and pulled out a tiny blue-and-white porcelain container with a silver stopper. The entire thing fitted neatly into the palm of his smooth, manicured hand. "Oh, yes!" He beamed enthusiastically. "What have we here?"

I turned the card over. On the back, Mr. Kessler had written some notes. "'A miniature Chinese Kangxi period vase,'" I read out loud, "'from 1662 to 1722, with broken neck.' It says the chased silver top was most likely added in Amsterdam in the early 1800s to create a scent bottle with stopper."

Mr. Tresalion lifted the tiny silver stopper out. It was attached with a fine silver chain. "How ingenious!" He laughed, delighted. "The cleverness of people never ceases to amaze me! Let's see if any of the perfume remains!" He lifted the bottle to his nose. "I think I can smell jasmine." He passed it to me. "What do you think?"

I sniffed. "I'm not sure. There's *something*, but I can't put my finger on it. Possibly rose?"

"Possibly." He sniffed again. "Yes, I think you're right!" Turning it over, he examined the bottom. "It's still got the hallmark! That is good." He sighed with contentment. "Once a vase, now something completely different! That takes real imagination."

"Oh, yes! *Of course!*" Suddenly it dawned on me. "You're the gentleman I've heard about—the one who collects damaged goods!"

"Not damaged, my dear!" He shuddered. "Reimagined! Restored! But not *damaged*! They deserve more respect than that!"

"I'm sorry—I just meant, well, that Mr. Kessler's told me about you. You're one of his favorite customers!"

He smiled with satisfaction. "Mr. Kessler has been the very best dealer in helping me with my little collection."

"It *is* unusual."

"I like the unusual." He took out his wallet. "Can you imagine the moment when these things first broke? Probably dropped by some poor servant girl who had to endure the wrath of her mistress! Just think of all the carrying on! These things would have been so precious, so rare! It would have been a *terrible* moment!" He winced. "And yet here they are now, having survived all the screaming and tears!" He chuckled to himself, counting out two hundred dollars.

I stared at the pile of bills.

He gave me a quizzical look. "Is there something wrong?"

"Ah, well, it's just, that's an awful lot of money for something that's . . . well, broken, sir. Are you sure that's right?"

"Quite sure," he assured me, putting the bottle back into the box. "You see, no one ever bothers to save something that isn't valuable. There are other blue-and-white porcelain vases from the Kangxi period, but there will never be another one like this, one that's weathered so much and been so lovingly repaired." Tucking the box under his arm, he tipped his hat with a flourish. "Sometimes, my dear, being broken is the most interesting thing that can happen."

Friday night was the opening performance of *A Midsummer Night's Dream*, and the Colonial Theater was overflowing with people.

Unable to lure anyone into joining me, I'd decided to go by myself. I'd come straight from work and now stood in line to purchase one of the cheap day tickets. I felt self-conscious but was lucky enough to find myself waiting next to a pair of enthusiastic elderly brothers named Harry and George, who took me under their wing.

"Are you here on your own, dear?" the older, George, asked kindly.

"Yes. You see, I've never been to a play before," I explained, feeling a bit of a fool as I said it.

"Oh!" Harry gasped in delight. "Your first performance! Well, this is a treat!"

"You'll love it!" George insisted confidently. "You'll absolutely love it! All the men wear tights!"

"I'm sure I will, only I'm not quite certain how to get to the balcony."

"Just follow us, dear! You see"—he showed me their tickets— "as we were next to one another in line, we'll all be sitting in the same row."

"We're theater folk," Harry said proudly. "And no, I don't mean actors, I mean people who love the theater."

"We see *everything*!" George agreed. "I have a signed program from Sarah Bernhardt's *Hamlet*! It's an illness." He sighed, looking at his brother sadly. "A terrible illness."

And they both laughed.

Harry had packed some sandwiches and insisted I share with them. We sat on a bench across from the entrance watching as long cars pulled up, disgorging women in evening gowns and men in white tie to the expensive orchestra seats, and played "spot the critic."

George pointed to a thin man with a pinched face. "My money's on him. He looks like it's been a while since he's had a hot meal."

"What's that got to do with anything?" I asked, enjoying myself.

"Oh, dear! Critics aren't human—they don't need food. They live on the moans and sighs of all the dreams they've crushed!"

Soon the bells began to ring, and we all climbed up to the balcony together.

The play itself was an entirely unexpected experience. I'd read it years ago, but seeing it was completely different. I was prepared for something lofty and difficult, but instead the characters were robust, vivid, and very funny. I found myself leaning forward, straining to catch each new turn of phrase and twist of the plot.

The balcony was hot. Even with the windows of the mezzanine open, it was airless and sticky, the seats narrow and close. During the interval, everyone went out again onto the pavement to make the most of the fresh evening air. There was a pleasant companionable feeling among the crowd, of people who've been laughing together, having a good time.

"Come on, I'll buy you both a lemonade," I offered, feeling generous. "It's my turn to treat you!"

Together the three of us made our way into the main foyer, down the elaborate vestibule with its mosaic tiled floor, and through to the lobby. In contrast to the balcony, the lower interior was a symphony of Italian marble, gilded mirrors, and sparkling chandeliers. Here bare shoulders and diamonds glittered in the golden light and smoke hung in translucent clouds, softening reflections in the long mirrors. This opening-night crowd was more polished but considerably less impressed; an attitude of wilting boredom colored the conversation around us.

"He's not a good Puck."

"He's *far* too old! My God, he needs a cane to get from one side of the stage to the other!"

"The costumes are so dreary! Why is everything so darkly lit? Tell me we haven't booked for the *whole* season!"

"My goodness!" whispered George. "I think we've stumbled into a critics' *convention*!"

Then, across the lobby, I saw Diana talking to a group of people. Wearing a gown of filmy silver fabric, shimmering and elegant, she was telling a story, and everyone was laughing. A thin, pale man was standing next to her, his hand pressed proprietorially against the small of her back. I recognized him as Charlie Peabody, of the Massachusetts Peabodys.

"Isn't she lovely?" George gasped, following my gaze. "Do you know her?"

She'd been so vague about her plans for this evening when I asked her to join me. "Yes, yes, I do."

Harry gave me a push. "Well, go on—say hello! We're perfectly capable of buying our own lemonades."

As I came closer, Charlie turned. He whispered to Diana, and she looked up. "Oh, look who it is!" she exclaimed gaily, suddenly animated and larger than life. "How lovely to see you!"

"Hello."

"It's been so long!" She embraced me, kissing the air somewhere around my cheek. "May Fanning, I hope you remember Charlie Peabody."

Charlie gave a polite nod. "My pleasure."

"This is my dear friend May," Diana explained to the assembled group. "Forgive us for a moment, but we haven't seen each other in ages! So"—she wrapped her arm around my waist, drawing me off to one side—"tell me how you're getting on! Are you enjoying the evening?" she asked, steering me away from the others.

"I'm fine. But what are you doing?" I glanced back at her companions. "What's wrong?"

She sighed, suddenly tense, her voice hushed and urgent. "I need to speak to you. Privately. But now isn't the time."

I had the awful feeling of being excluded, like a child seeking out her friends, only to discover she's been replaced. "Am I intruding?"

"No. But I need to explain some things."

"Like what? What's happened?"

She leaned in close. "I'm engaged."

"What?"

"Charlie Peabody and I are going to be married," she said quickly. "I didn't want to tell you like this, or in front of everyone. We need to speak," she said again. "Can you meet me?"

"But . . ." I couldn't quite make sense of it all. "When did that start? Why didn't you tell me that you'd been seeing him?"

"What do you mean?" She sounded defensive. "He's a perfectly lovely man."

"But, Diana!" I nodded to Charlie, with his turkey neck and disappearing chin. "Are you serious? Is this what you want?"

"That's not the point!" Irritation lined her forehead. "I can't go into it all now, May! Tomorrow. Meet me tomorrow, and I'll tell you everything. Please, darling!" She flashed a nervous smile. "This is Charlie's crowd, you see—I can't keep them waiting! You understand, don't you?"

Since when had Diana ever cared about convention?

"Of course," I said, even though I didn't understand at all. "But Diana . . ."

"May, I can't!" she snapped suddenly, fixing me with a fierce look. "Not now!" And crossing back to her new friends, she was instantly absorbed again into the conversation.

I stared after her, cut adrift in a sea of tulle and taffeta, alone and out of place. I could feel the eyes of the room on me, whispers behind me.

I fumbled for a cigarette, humiliation burning my cheeks. Had I done something wrong? How was it possible that she could be engaged so quickly?

"May I?" Mr. Winshaw stood in front of me, holding out his lighter. He was dressed in white tie, clean-shaven and in a suit that actually fit, looking unnaturally polished and refined.

I was at once mortified and relieved to see him. "What are you doing here?"

He ignored the question, apparently dismissing it as too obvious to answer. Instead he lit my cigarette. "Isn't that your friend?" he asked, giving Diana a look. "The Van der Laar girl?"

"Yes."

He glared at her, and I realized that he must have seen the whole thing. "She seems to have misplaced her manners," he said coolly.

Then he put his hand on my elbow and ferried me farther away from Diana and Charlie and into the ambiguity of a crowded corner. Immediately I felt less conspicuous.

"Shall I buy you a drink, Fanning?" he offered. "You look like you could use one."

I was grateful and touched that he'd come to my rescue. "No, no, thank you. I'm all right. Where's Selena?"

"Head cold. Though the truth is, she's not much good at Shakespeare. She always wants to know why they don't just say what they mean." He glanced around the lobby. "Who are you here with?"

"Actually, I'm on my own. Expanding my horizons," I added, which only made me feel more idiotic.

He gave me a quizzical look.

"You know," I said, "I think I could do with some air."

We went outside. Even though it was only marginally cooler, just leaving the scene of my embarrassment was a relief.

We strolled through the interval crowds.

"So apparently you're not the philistine you pretend to be." Mr. Winshaw lit himself a cigarette too.

"It's better than I thought it would be," I admitted. "There may be something to this theater lark after all."

"The Puck's a little old, but then again, I don't think Puck has an age, do you?" He was trying to distract me.

But I couldn't seem to put the episode behind me.

I shrugged. "When you're a fairy, does age matter?"

"How do you know that girl anyway?"

"Diana? Oh, we met a while ago . . ." I gave him an unconvincing smile. "I guess I caught her at an inopportune moment."

The bells began to ring, ushering the audience in for the second half.

"Where are you sitting?" he asked.

"The balcony. You must be in the orchestra, aren't you?"

He nodded, suddenly concerned. "Are you all right, Fanning?"

I took another drag, nodded. "You go on. I'm just going to finish my cigarette."

"Really?" He looked at me closely. "You don't seem all right."

The truth was, I felt alone and utterly foolish. Perhaps Diana was ashamed of me, didn't want me lowering the tone of the evening. I focused on the marquee behind Mr. Winshaw as if it were particularly fascinating. "Actually, I think I'll head off now."

"I'll see you home." He pressed his hand into the small of my back protectively, guiding me toward the curb. Before I could stop him, he'd flagged down a cab. "Where do you live?"

"No, really," I protested. "I can manage."

But he opened the door, ushered me inside. "Don't be daft."

We sat next to each other in silence with the windows open, feeling the cool breeze on our faces.

The cab wound through the streets. It was warm that night. As we approached the North End, people spilled out onto the streets, escaping the cramped, airless apartments: men in their under-shirts and suspenders, women reeling in laundry and gossiping with neighbors. People had dragged chairs onto the pavement and were clustered in groups, talking and playing cards. One family had a watermelon sliced up on a wooden crate, and the husband was playing the accordion; that was enough for an impromptu party. And a group of older men played bocce in an abandoned lot.

The cab pulled up outside my block, and we got out.

"Well, this is where I live." I glanced at the watermelon crowd, dancing in the street. Why did they have to be so noisy?

"It's a lot like the real thing," he observed. And then, seeing the perplexed look on my face, he explained, "A lot like being in Italy."

I'd never thought of it like that. To me, it had always been the wrong end of town, not a small slice of an exotic location.

Mr. Winshaw dug his hands into his pockets, seemed to be weighing something up. "You know, Fanning," he announced out of nowhere, "you're clever."

"I'm sorry?" I thought I'd misheard him.

"You write well, you're perceptive, your intellectual instincts are good." He stopped, frowning a little, as if he'd suddenly real-ized he'd flattered me more than he'd intended. "The point is, you have ability. You could do things with your life."

"Thank you." I wondered why he was telling me this.

"I mean something real. Something of substance," he elaborated.

He had the uncanny knack of turning any compliment into an insult. "And what makes you think I'm not doing that now?"

"Those people, back at the theater, they're not worth your time."

"*Those* people?" I folded my arms across my chest.

He sighed with frustration. "You know what I'm talking about! Don't be seduced by the tinsel and the lights. You're worth more than that. To quote our favorite bard, 'All that glitters is not gold.'"

"Maybe, but have you ever noticed how gold glitters too?" I was irritated that he thought me gullible and starstruck.

"Well, fine." He gave up. "If that's what you want."

He took out a cigarette, lit it.

I scowled at my feet, kicked a bottle cap into the gutter. "Why do you always think so little of me?" I asked after a moment.

"So *little*!" He stared at me in amazement. "Why are you so determined to misunderstand me?"

"I understand you perfectly well. You think I'm shallow."

"I just told you that you were clever!" he pointed out.

"And then warned me not to be taken in by shiny objects!"

"Jesus!" Staring up at the sky, he took a long, hard drag. "Well, I suppose perhaps we're not destined to understand each other."

We both glowered in silence.

"Well, thank you," I said finally, "for seeing me home."

"My pleasure." He gave a sharp nod. "Good night, Fanning."

Then he headed off down the street, past the accordion player and watermelon eaters. In his white tie, he looked tall and debonair and, oddly, not the least bit out of place.

———

The next day a note was delivered to the shop from Diana.

I'm so sorry, darling. I wanted to meet with you but I just can't. Please don't hate me. I've thought about this all very carefully, and the truth is, I don't want to discuss it. I know you won't like it, but I don't want you to try to change my mind. No one knows better than me how strange this all must seem, but I have my reasons. I hope you're not cross. I've enclosed an invitation to my engagement party. I do so hope you'll come—even if you violently disapprove. I still need you, perhaps now more than ever.

> *Your friend always,*
> *Diana*

An engraved invitation was enclosed.

Mrs J. R. Van der Laar requests the pleasure of your company to celebrate the engagement of her daughter Diana Elizabeth Van der Laar to Charles Henry Peabody at their home in Cohasset, Massachusetts, from 2:00 in the afternoon onward.

I thought of the No Way Out Club, of the silver pen above the door.

All that was over now.

Diana had found an exit.

I continued to meet James Van der Laar at the Copley Plaza Hotel when he was in town. It was always the same. Flowers would

arrive at work, with a date and a time, and although I didn't want
to go, told myself I wouldn't, there was always another part of me
that couldn't keep away. Very quickly all pretense was dropped.
We didn't bother with the Oak Room anymore but dined in the
room. There were gifts—a sable stole, a jade bracelet, a silk night-
gown too beautiful ever to wear to bed—and always plenty to
drink, champagne followed by whiskey followed by brandy.

I drank only with him. And with the curtains drawn, lying
in bed, he whispered to me about the places we would go, the
things we would do. He told me how he couldn't do without me,
that he'd never cared for anyone the way he cared for me, how he
would be lost without me.

I wanted to believe him, and so I did.

I was lost with him or without him. And in that dark room,
with a drink in my hand, I didn't want to be found.

The day of Diana's engagement party dawned bright and flawless,
a warm sun-kissed morning with a clear blue sky. The Van der
Laars had booked two trains to deliver guests to Cohasset, where
a fleet of cars were on duty to ferry them onward to the house. At
Diana's request I took an earlier train, arriving at the house before
luncheon, just as the caterers and decorators were at full hysterical
pitch with final arrangements.

My nerves were strained taut with anticipation and fear; was
this the moment when my clandestine relationship with James
would become real? When I would walk from the shadows of
his life into the full glare of his family's awareness? Or would we
continue to lie, to greet each other like cordial acquaintances? All
morning I'd weighed the two possibilities against one another;
both felt unreal. And my own ambivalence unnerved me.

Diana had a suite of rooms on the south side of the house that consisted of a bedroom, bathroom, dressing room, and private parlor, all done in the same bright pearly tones with modern mirrored furniture. I'd never seen such a big bedroom; it was at least twice the size of our whole apartment. It looked like something from a movie set, with high narrow French doors leading to a terrace overlooking the sea. These were propped open; a cool, briny breeze swept through, tossing the sheer curtains into the air like feathers of smoke. Diana was curled into an armchair in her dressing gown when I arrived.

"Oh, thank God, you're here!" To my surprise, she got up, rushing to embrace me with a genuine outpouring of emotion. The distance between us melted as she clung to me, leaning her head on my shoulder. "I don't know how I'm going to make it through the day! I really can't tell you how much this means to me. You're the only one who understands!"

After so much time consigned to the edge of her life, I'd forgotten the strange, luminous warmth of Diana's attention. It had the power to dissolve resentments and disarm all doubts.

"I thought this is what you wanted." I looked round. It was a dazzling room; light danced from one reflective surface to another, casting a myriad of rainbows over everything. I was disoriented both by the opulence and by her sudden rush of affection. Being with her was as blinding as trying to find my bearings among the radiant shifting reflections.

She stepped back, held me at arm's length. "You're weren't fooled, were you?"

I didn't understand. "What do you mean?"

"The charade is for them, not for us. I had to play along."

"It seemed pretty real to me." The memory of the night at the theater still smarted.

"I can't afford to fail, May. But I don't really want to succeed either." Her smile was tinged with sadness. "I'm lost either way."

"Why do you want me here?" I asked. "You don't want my advice, you don't need my help. So why am I here?"

"I need your friendship," she said. "I need to be with someone who knows me, who cares. I'm frightened, May."

One look at her face and I could tell it was true.

Like tightrope walkers balancing on a dangerous ledge, we were trying to convince everyone, including ourselves, that we weren't afraid of heights. But at least when we were alone we could drop the pretense of being fearless.

"I'm just . . . I'm just glad you're here, is all." She took my arm, leading me out onto the terrace. An informal luncheon had been set up on a low table overlooking the lawns that rolled, rich and green, to the abrupt cliff face and the sheer drop to the sea below. Gulls circled; distant waves crashed against the rocky shore. Below, armies of staff assembled tents and tables, swarming like carefully choreographed dancers in a large-scale musical production.

Diana looked down on them, doubt lining her face. "I can't wait until this is all over."

"It's not too late to change your mind—"

"Shhh!" She pressed a finger to her lips. "Don't tempt me, darling. *Please!*"

Our time alone together was short. Soon hairdressers and a manicurist arrived, and the great juggernaut of a society event lurched into action.

The festivities began in the early afternoon with a swimming party, a polo match, and several musical performances. Guests arrived in waves, wearing anything from bathing costumes to morning suits. Gradually, members of the Van der Laar family put in appearances. Mrs. Van der Laar presided over a piano recital on the side lawn with Elsa, while Charlie Peabody played polo with surprising skill for a man so awkward off the field. Afterward an elaborate tea buffet was served before the guests changed for cocktails and supper.

Diana spent most of her time wandering from one room to the next, introducing herself and shaking people's hands like a visiting dignitary. I trailed along in her wake; more than once I was mistaken for her personal secretary. I didn't bother to disabuse anyone. So many of these people had never even met her before. And though she might have been nervous, she was an accomplished hostess; I marveled at the ease with which she talked to complete strangers. Here was the role she'd been groomed to play all her life, and as in the "hazards" she was so fond of, she acted her part with complete conviction and charm.

For my part, I remained happy to recede into the background. Like Diana, I was conflicted, trapped between excitement and dread, in a purgatory of my own making. Around every corner I anticipated seeing James. But he remained elusive; it was as though we were playing a grown-up version of hide-and-seek, and he was winning.

The afternoon waned. Diana wafted from place to place like a wisp of perfumed smoke, never settling. The tea concert ended, and the polo match was cut short so that everyone could dress for dinner. Long tents had been constructed on the front lawn, housing extra changing rooms, with rows of dressing tables, private cubicles behind swags of silk, and an army of extra maids on hand.

I was given the use of Diana's private parlor to change for

supper, and when I came back in my red-striped gown, Diana applauded. "How charming! Where did you get that dress?"

"My mother made it."

"Isn't she clever! It's just like one I saw at Stearns."

Her eye fell on the arrow diamond brooch I wore on the bodice.

"Well," a quizzical look creased her brow, "isn't that lovely!"

"I borrowed it." I said quickly, feeling conspicuous. Perhaps I should have left it at home.

"You know, Cartiers get their diamonds from us. That arrow brooch is one of their biggest sellers. I could get you one of your own, if you like it."

She made it sound as easy as passing the salt.

"Really?"

"There was a time when Mother used to give them as hostess gifts when we stayed with people. It's charming, don't you think?"

"Very charming."

Suddenly I wanted nothing more than to take off the brooch and my reproduction designer dress and leave the party altogether. But Diana was heading downstairs; she turned back and held out her hand to me. "Come on!"

She opened the bedroom door; the strains of an orchestra swelled, the sound of hundreds of voices laughing and chattering filled the air like an empire of exotic birds. We descended the stairs. Charlie was waiting in the crowded entrance hall; he looked up and gave Diana an anxious nod as she approached, and together they proceeded to make their rounds.

Waiters flitted by, glasses filled with champagne balanced on silver trays. I wanted to reach out and grab one, to wash my self-consciousness away in a few easy swallows, growing more and more translucent until I vanished altogether inside myself. But tonight was important, and I was on my best behavior.

Diana was walking away from me now on Charlie's arm, disappearing into the crush of people. I looked around for a familiar face. In the next room I heard Smitty's bored, flat drawl cutting across the din. So I went the other way, into the library.

The room that had seemed so vast months earlier was now cheek by jowl. I slipped through, pretending to be searching for someone.

"Oh! Hello! Say, you're Diana's friend, the girl from the lobster bake, am I right?" Nicky Howerd was looking very dapper but no less rotund in his black-tie attire.

"Yes, that's me!" I was grateful for anyone to talk to, even Nicky.

"How about a drink?" He stopped a waiter, took two glasses. "I think you and I have some catching up to do."

He handed me a glass, raised his. "Cheers!"

"Cheers," I echoed, watching as he took a swallow. It looked good. Maybe I would drink when James arrived, when we were together. But until then I wanted to be at my best.

"I don't suppose you've seen James anywhere?" I asked, putting the glass to one side.

"James?" He turned, peering through the crowd as if he expected him to manifest at the mere mention of his name. "Why, no."

"I thought he'd be here."

"Oh, well, Jim's not often in town these days. Spends his time on the Dark Continent." He leaned in conspiratorially. "Were you meant to meet him? Always been a great favorite with the girls."

I laughed, a bleating, slightly desperate sound. "No! Just surprised that the whole family isn't here, that's all. I've been playing lady-in-waiting to Diana all day. I just wondered."

His face fell. "Yes, Diana." Clearly he'd not recovered from the blow of her engagement. "I don't know why she'd go for a broom-stick like that. As dry as a piece of toast, if you ask me."

"He's not that bad!"

"Compared to some of her other prospects . . ." He drained his glass.

I didn't want him to leave; I put my hand on his arm. "There are more lobsters in the sea, Nicky."

He face widened into a grin. "Too true, Mary!"

"May."

"Yes, well, I'm only saying, too true!"

"Well, if it isn't Tricky Nicky Howerd! Slippery as an eel!" A young man was pushing his way toward us, hand outstretched. "Haven't seen you in years!" He grasped Nicky's palm, pumping it vigorously. "Is this your girl? Aren't you going to introduce us?"

Nicky looked at me as if he'd only just realized I was female. Then, chest swelling, he took my arm. "Mavis, this is Richard Cranley Saunders, or Soft Spot, as he was known back in Princeton. Could always touch him up for cash, isn't that right?"

"Perfectly true! Perfectly true," Richard assured me, delighted.

"I'm May Fanning."

"Well, May!" Richard jerked his head toward Nicky. "You've got a strange catch in this one!"

"Aw, come off it, Richard! You're going to scare her away!"

Richard screwed his eyes closed and made a strangulated gasp-ing noise that must've been a laugh. "Wouldn't want to do that, now would we?"

From then on I found myself being escorted by Nicky Howerd, who was only too pleased to pretend that I was his date for the evening. And while he wasn't thrilling company, at least every-one seemed to know him. We went out on the veranda, where Diana's mother raised a curious eyebrow in greeting, and I enjoyed the dubious pleasure of having Diana's earlier lie seemingly confirmed. Nicky introduced me to a long line of people who accepted me without question or, indeed, curiosity, people who spoke in flat languid tones about polo matches, trips to Europe, and yachting races.

"I'm having a devil of a time finding a good groom to replace Dawes. No one knows how to handle Dancing Joe the way he did."

"That's because he's an Arabian. You need a Spaniard. Or a Moor. I have a Moor. Speaks to Shalimar in some ridiculous babble, but his coat has never looked better."

"Has anyone else noticed how expensive the rooms at the Waldorf Astoria have become?"

"The service is abysmal!"

"It's too hot in the City. We're leaving for Bar Harbor on Tuesday."

Occasionally a vague political opinion was tossed into the arena; it fell like a cigarette butt onto the ground, smoldering only a little before being crushed out. It was clear that some of the men had political futures ahead of them, but it was a legacy, passed from generation to generation by the same discreet forces and unquestioned private alliances that had been formed centuries earlier. They had been born into a tide of cleaner, clearer water, sweeping them in a single, inevitable direction. None of them would ever know what it was like to swim upstream.

No one asked me who I was or where I'd come from; on Nicky's arm I blended into the fabric of their world seamlessly. Instead they simply picked up where'd they'd last left off on a continual twenty-year conversation on the exhausting prospect of being wealthy: on the many responsibilities, changes of clothing, and superhuman reserves of patience it required.

The cocktail hour progressed. I held off drinking by throwing myself headlong into a conversation with a great hulk of a girl named Becky Flint, a creature as wide as she was tall, who'd heroically crammed herself into a layered gown of sea-green tulle for the occasion. She sat miserably on a divan, legs slightly splayed, eyeing the trays of canapés as they went by—caviar toast, smoked salmon and crème fraiche, fois gras tarts, truffled quail's eggs, lobster mayonnaise, fresh crab puffs . . .

"I'm not to eat any," she said. "Mother says once I start, I can't stop, so it's best not to start in the first place. But honestly, what's the point in going out if I can't eat anything?"

"I know what you mean. It's maddening."

"It's torture," Becky confirmed sourly. "The girls who can eat them don't want them, and I want them and can't eat them. Something's wrong in this world, don't you think?"

"Terribly wrong. Come on. Let's wander round and count how many men look as if they're wearing toupees."

Becky hauled herself up. "We can start with my father, if we can find him."

In the drawing room, somewhere around the ninth undisputed toupee spotting, we ran into Diana and Charlie. Diana caught my eye over the sea of heads with a quizzical, slightly panicked look. We went over.

"Congratulations, Diana," Becky offered. "Gosh, your dress is nice!"

"Thank you." Diana took my arm; she seemed drawn tight as a tripwire. "Do you think you could help me with something? I need to fix my hair."

Ferrying me into an empty corridor, she leaned back against the wall and pressed her eyes closed. "I feel like my head is going to explode! Why can't it just all be over?"

I put a hand on her shoulder. "It will be over soon enough. You're doing so well," I assured her. "So very well."

"I *loathe* people, loathe chitchat!" She twisted her pearls between her fingers. "I especially loathe these people. Not a single one of them cares about me in the slightest! Or has the slightest idea of who I really am!"

"This isn't your real life, Diana. Remember that. Think of Max. None of this really matters."

"But it does matter!" she insisted. "It matters too much."

"Pardon me, ma'am."

A steward in a uniform stood behind us, a concerned look on his face. "Something's happened, ma'am. We were just getting ready to call for dinner when . . . oh, dear . . . How to put this?"

Diana sighed. "Now what?"

"I think it best perhaps if you come this way."

We followed him through closed doors into the dining hall, where long tables were laid out for supper. Crisp white linens sparkled in the golden rays of the setting sun. It was odd how they shone. Suddenly I realized why—the carefully set places were covered in shattered glass, glistening shards everywhere. "What's happened?"

"Someone has broken each and every glass!" the steward explained, his voice rising in panic. "We don't know what to do—it will take hours to clean!"

Diana's eyes widened in disbelief. "But who . . ."

Suddenly, in the far corner, there was a movement; two small, swinging legs. Hands folded on his lap, sitting very calmly on a dining chair, was Andrew.

"I don't know what to do! What to say to the kitchen!" the steward continued, wringing his hands.

"What's wrong?" Elsa walked in. "What's holding up dinner?"

Diana stared at her but seemed frozen, unable to speak.

"There's been an accident." I explained finally.

Elsa saw Andrew sitting in the corner. "You're meant to be with Mrs. Riggs upstairs. What are you doing here?"

Then slowly she caught sight of the shattered glass, and her face changed.

Flying across the room, she yanked Andrew up by the arm, her face white with rage. "Did you do this? Have you broken all these glasses?"

He winced in pain. "You're hurting me!"

"Please, Elsa!" Diana pleaded. "Don't!"

But she ignored her. "Answer me!" She shook him, hard. "Why would you do such a malicious thing? *Why?*"

"Elsa, please don't hurt him!" Diana begged.

Elsa turned on her. "He's mine, remember? I'm the one who looks after him day after day—I'll handle this!" Her hand landed hard across his cheek. Diana gasped. A red welt appeared on the soft pink skin. "Don't you understand what will happen?" Her voice continued to rise. "What is *bound* to happen if you continue to behave like this? Are you *trying* to get in trouble?"

Andrew blinked up at her through tears. "But Mrs. Riggs says that drinking is illegal. That you should all be arrested! And I don't want you to be arrested. I don't!"

Elsa let go of his arm. She teetered backward, stunned, like a person thrown off balance.

"What's going on in here? Why isn't dinner being served?" Mrs. Van der Laar and Charlie Peabody were hovering in the doorway. Then Mrs. Van der Laar noticed the glass. "Good God! What's happened?"

"There's been an accident," Elsa said matter-of-factly, taking charge. "Couldn't be helped, I'm afraid. We'll have to make other arrangements."

"I don't know what to tell the kitchen," the steward kept repeating to no one in particular. "I don't know what to say. We're meant to begin service any moment!"

Elsa glared at him. "Tell them to put the food on trays and serve it on the lawn. We will have a picnic."

"Are you *mad*?" Mrs. Van der Laar hissed, horrified. She looked to Charlie, who in turn stared at Diana in alarm.

"Oh, what fun!" Diana's voice was thinly edged with desperation. "Besides, it's a beautiful evening! Aren't we lucky? Open more champagne! We can throw rugs across the lawn! And light candelabras!"

"And for God's sake," Elsa commanded, "send the band outside onto the terrace! If anyone asks, there's been a leak in the dining room. But"—she shot her older sister a stern look—"no one *will* ask. Now hurry!" She clapped her hands, and the steward lurched into action.

Diana made a move toward Andrew, but Elsa intervened. "He's my responsibility, have you forgotten? You have more important things to attend to right now." She pointed her toward the door. "This is your party—deal with your guests."

"Be gentle," Diana pleaded.

Elsa's eyes narrowed. "I will do whatever I think is necessary. And now"—she nodded to Charlie—"so must you."

Charlie took Diana's arm, and they went back to the party, putting on a brave face about the sudden shift in arrangements. And the room was suddenly filled with a dozen waiters, all executing Elsa's orders.

The impromptu picnic turned out to be an inspired solution. The party that before had labored under all the ponderous formality of a state dinner was suddenly transformed into a gay carnival atmosphere. With the addition of extra champagne and dozens of flickering candelabras, the lawn took on a romantic bohemian air. Oriental carpets were brought out, strewn with piles of velvet and damask pillows where young and old alike lounged like sultans in a harem. Overstuffed armchairs and settees, transplanted from the drawing room to sheltered groves and beneath trees, made the scene look surreal and magical. Balmy breezes tossed through the silken folds of women's gowns as they waltzed on the grass in bare feet to the music floating from across the terrace. As twilight faded into darkness, stars appeared; long hedgerows and carefully cultivated gardens became convenient alcoves for secret assignations.

Mrs. Van der Laar, positioned in a leather wingback chair near a bank of white rhododendrons, continued to hold court over a coterie of aging friends and admirers. They were discussing travel across Europe and the difference in the railways from Germany to Italy.

"It's often impossible to get on a train at all!" lamented one woman. "We had to wedge ourselves into *third* class across Hungary. There was a *goat* in the carriage!"

"I should have waited for another train," Mrs. Van der Laar asserted as I walked by. "I always tell my children, one only meets first-class people in first-class places. Traveling with goats will never get you anywhere in life!"

They all laughed.

I carried on walking, peering into clusters of sprawling bodies, searching through the crowded lawn for James but unable to make out faces clearly in the wavering candlelight. The band was playing "You Do Something to Me," and the air of romantic intrigue struck a melancholy chord. Already the day had been exhausting; life in Diana's world was like being tossed into a pit with a bunch of very well-dressed, starving tigers. Holding one's own was a matter of survival, each interaction another skirmish in a never-ending war.

I walked until I found a quiet spot on a bench near a high stone wall covered in roses. This far from the rest of the party, I could finally hear the sound of the surf breaking on the rocks. In one direction lay the sprawl of bodies, laughter, and music; in the other, the black void of the sea, drawing me into the darkness like an outstretched hand.

It reminded me of Ulysses stranded on his paradise island, sitting on the shore, staring out at the ocean day after day. Behind me was everything I'd thought I'd ever wanted—wealth, privilege, beauty—but here I was, longing for the music to stop, the dancing to end, seeking out the silence at the party.

"Where were you?"

"Relax! I only just got in. There was an accident on the road from New York."

The voices behind the wall were urgent and hushed, a man and a woman. I wasn't alone after all. The wind and the sound of the surf made it difficult to make out everything they were saying but they struck me as familiar. I sat very still, straining to hear more.

"You promised you wouldn't bring her!"

"What am I meant to do? Leave her at home?"

"Did you tell her?"

"Not yet."

"What are you waiting for?" the woman hissed.

"I'll do it after the party. Tonight."

"You always say that!"

"I mean it." There was silence; the sound of a match being struck. "I promise, I'll tell her tonight."

"I'm not going to wait forever, you know. I've already waited too long!"

"You won't have to, darling."

"But why?" the woman whispered, her voice catching. "Why do you treat me this way?"

A while later, two figures emerged from behind the wall. The ends of their cigarettes glowed orange in the twilight as they walked back up toward the house.

Almost against my will, I followed them. Halfway up the lawn, they separated; the woman drifted off to the left, into a throng of people, and the man carried on. I hung back a little, keeping to the shadows as he climbed up the terrace steps.

Standing near the open French doors was a young blond woman in an exquisite pale silk creation and I recognized the distinctive bias cut of a real Vionnet gown. She seemed ill at ease, as if she were looking for someone, and as the man approached, she suddenly smiled, eagerly holding out her hand. He took it, lightly kissing her fingers.

It was James.

"Ha! Finally, I found you!" Nicky Howerd was walking toward me. "I've been looking for you everywhere! Thought you'd got lost or given me the slip!"

But I wasn't listening. "Who's that girl with James?" I asked.

Nicky turned, followed my gaze. "Oh, that's Heleen, of course. His wife."

In the end it was Richard Cranley Saunders, Soft Spot, who agreed to drive me back to Boston on short notice. Sitting numbly in the passenger seat of his roadster, I stared out the window into the uneven darkness. After a few brave stabs at conversation, he gave up and hummed quietly to himself for the rest of the drive.

When he pulled up in front of Contadino's grocery, he looked around in confusion. "Gosh, I don't think I've ever been here before."

"No, I don't expect you have," I said, climbing out.

"Oh. Well, good luck," he said, rather forlornly, as he pulled away.

In the east a rosy softness had begun to warm the very edge of the night sky, and the sweet smell of overripe fruit and the aroma of bread baking in Russo's ovens mingled in the dewy dampness of the early morning fog.

Lifting the skirt of my dress so that it wouldn't drag on the ground, I crossed over.

Yes, good luck.

I stood behind the counter, staring into empty space, at the dust particles dancing slowly in a beam of late-afternoon sunlight.

The summer that had been at first such a relief was now a sentence to be endured. The fan was on, rotating uselessly, and the door was open, but nothing moved. The air in the shop was heavy and still, smelling of centuries. Outside, people pushed through invisible membranes of humidity and lethargy. It was a morbid, narcotic heat, the kind that presses against the skin and weighs down thought, making children teary and adults bad-tempered.

I watched the tiny fragments, suspended, weightless. They were falling, very slowly; it might take them years to hit the ground, but they would end up there eventually.

"You're not yourself today, Fanning."

Mr. Winshaw lit another cigarette. He was immune to heat; years in boarding school and exotic climates had annihilated any expectations of physical comfort he'd once had. Sleeves rolled up, he sauntered out of his office, where he'd been confirming the details of his next expedition. He'd already booked his passage on a steamer to Athens, and was finalizing train connections. I'd noticed that as soon as he came back from the travel agent, he was a changed man; focused, considerate, even professional.

His excitement felt like a snub. Nothing could hold him here, not Mr. Kessler or the triumph with the museum or the business; not even the seductive Selena. And now he strolled from his office brimming with the kind of gracious concern that was only possible when one knew one was on the way out the door.

"What's troubling you?"

"It's hot."

"This is nothing compared to Crete in August. Or Baghdad."

I knew he would say that. Pushing my sweaty, damp hair away from my face, I shifted my weight from one dead foot to the other. Outside, a street sweeper worked his way down the pavement with his broom, drops of sweat dripping steadily from his brow.

Mr. Winshaw leaned against the counter. "Why, I've known nights in Caracas in South America—"

"I'm going to get a glass of water," I interrupted. It was abrupt, a verbal shove.

I came out of the back with a mug of water and gave it to the street sweeper, who drank it gratefully. When I returned, Mr. Winshaw was sitting in one of the uncomfortable English chairs.

"Not yourself today, Fanning," he said again, exhaling.

"What do you care?"

I sounded childish, and he grinned, which was galling.

"Why, you're all I think about! Day and night. What's wrong?"

"Nothing." I looked at the wall of clocks; I'd been staring at them all day. Now it was 5:17. "I don't suppose I could go early."

"Leave any time you like."

I'd expected more resistance.

He took another drag.

"You know . . ." I began, then stopped myself.

"What? What do I know?"

There was no need to say anything. No need to fight.

I did anyway.

"You know, it's really disconcerting." I eyed him darkly. "The way you come in and out of people's lives. I mean, for them."

"For *you?*"

"No! Not *me!*" His arrogance was appalling. "But Mr. Kessler, for example."

He waved my concern away. "Kessler doesn't mind. He's used to it. Besides, someone's got to go on these buying trips. He gets seasick. And sunstroke. And traveler's tummy," he added with a smile.

Everything about him was infuriating today. The way he slumped back in the chair, pretending it was comfortable when I knew damn well it wasn't; his self-satisfied smirk; his habit of inhaling his cigarette as if it were some rare, exotic delight; and especially the way he pretended that traveling around the world was as easy and commonplace as taking the bus across town.

"What about Selena? Doesn't she count? Don't you ever think about her feelings?"

Again, he laughed. "Oh, she's not waiting for me, of that you can be sure!"

"But what if she wants to? What if she *wants* to wait for you? What if you're breaking her heart?"

"I'm not breaking anyone's heart, Fanning!"

"Yes, you are! You break people's hearts all the time! You come in, trample all over everybody, and then leave! Just go!"

He stopped smiling; his eyes narrowed, and he gave me the same look animal trainers in the circus get when a tiger shows its teeth.

Cramming his cigarette into the corner of his mouth, he got up and took me by the arm. "I can't tell if you need a drink or a slap or both." He gave me a shove. "Go get your handbag."

"Why?"

"I said, get your handbag. We're going out."

I've been frog-marched many times in my life, more than most girls my age—normally out of bars and nightclubs, occasionally into a cab. But now Mr. Winshaw held me securely by the elbow and steered me around the corner to a dingy Chinese restaurant called the Green Dragon. Tucked into the basement of a laundry, it had bright red walls and low-glowing paper lanterns. A group of old Chinese men sat in a corner, smoking out of a strange container with a long mouthpiece, and a woman in a fitted silk dress with a high collar sat near the door, working the *Herald* crossword puzzle in ink.

She nodded to Mr. Winshaw as we came in. He led me to what must be his regular table, in the corner by the window.

"What are we doing here?" I demanded.

"Sit down."

The woman brought a pot of tea and two small china cups with no handles. The tea came out of the pot an almost colorless pale green, smelling faintly like dried grass.

"This is jasmine tea." He pushed a cup across to me and ordered something I didn't understand. I'd never had Chinese food before. The smell of unfamiliar spices wafted from the kitchen—fresh ginger, coriander, rice vinegar, sliced garlic—along with the rich, earthy aroma of fried noodles and roasting duck. Whatever the old men were smoking filled the air with a dense, sweet perfume. They moved like puppets with slow, careful motions, passing the long mouthpiece from one to the other, their faces unreadable, neither smiling nor frowning.

The woman bent in, voice low. "We also have plum wine. My husband makes it."

Mr. Winshaw looked across at me.

"I'm fine," I mumbled, and the woman left.

Alone now, he eased back in his chair, stretching out his long legs. Light caught the corner of his eyes, a flickering golden green. He folded his arms across his chest. "Well, Fanning, you now have my complete attention." And he waited.

I wanted to fight; to sulk and shout and toss words like grenades around the room. Mr. Winshaw could take it; he could handle anything anyone threw at him. Except now he'd disarmed me with strange tea and his full attention. It was a low move, a dirty trick.

I glared at him. "I don't know what you're talking about."

He just sat there.

"Honestly!" I fumed. "Are you so arrogant that you think that all you have to do is grace me with a few moments of your time, and magically everything will be fine?"

Again, nothing.

"You don't know anything about me! Not one single thing!"

"Then tell me."

A tidal wave of anger broke. "Don't you see? I *can't* tell you anything about me! There is nothing to tell that isn't . . . isn't . . ." My voice caught.

"Isn't what?"

"Bad!"

The navy window of his pupil widened, and the flickering light stilled.

I looked away. The very surface of my skin seemed to burn with embarrassment, and I couldn't bear to have him see me.

I stood up. "I have to go."

"Sit down."

"No."

He got up and took me by the shoulders, held me firm. "Sit down, Fanning."

The woman came out of the kitchen, carrying a tray of food.

"You need to eat," he said quietly. "Have you ever had Peking duck?"

I shook my head.

"You'll like it. I promise. The world is full of things, Mae Fanning, that you will like. Things you just don't know about yet."

We sat down. Mr. Winshaw showed me how to make duck pancakes with plum sauce, shaved cucumbers, and spring onions, and I began to talk, about James and Diana; about the apartment; even about the hospital and Mr. Baylor; about everything that had been pressing in, crushing me. It came out sloppily and unchecked, like a handbag tossed on the ground, private contents spilling out in all directions.

And he listened. Pouring out more tea, rolling more pancakes, asking the occasional question when he didn't understand. It was odd how easy it was to tell him almost anything; how nothing seemed to shock or disappoint him. He even smiled a little at times, as if he recognized my folly from his own.

The little restaurant filled and drained again. We had lychees and mandarin orange pieces on shaved ice for dessert. And when we finally left, it was dark out, the night air cooler. The shops were closed now, the streets empty. And the burden that had weighed on me eased like a breath held tight, suddenly released in a sigh.

Mr. Winshaw kicked a stone off the pavement.

"Why did you leave England?" I asked, suddenly curious.

"There was no reason to stay. My parents are dead. My brothers are gone." He took a final drag from his cigarette, tossed it in the gutter. "They died in France, while I was drinking mint tea and playing backgammon by the sea."

"What are you talking about?"

"I was aide to General Townshend at the Siege of Kut, outside Baghdad. A monumental military disaster from start to finish." He sighed, shaking his head. "When we surrendered to the Ottomans after a hundred and forty-seven days, the general was exiled to an island off Turkey for the rest of the war. He took me with him, along with a few of the other officers."

I remembered the map, a pin stuck in the tiny island of Halki off the Turkish coast.

"Over half our men died in captivity, starved to death or beaten by the Ottoman guards."

"I'm sorry."

He frowned. "I shouldn't have been there in the first place. My brothers and I, we were meant to fight together, that's why we joined. But Harry and Ralph died in the rain and the mud of the Somme . . . in horror . . . and I, I shouldn't . . ." His voice trailed off, but the furrow in his brow deepened.

He was drawing a conclusion, forming some unspoken belief about himself. I could feel his dedication to it. I also knew that, unchallenged, it had been allowed to grow inside his imagination and take root.

I stopped.

He looked back at me. "Are you all right?"

"And what?" I prompted.

"What are you talking about?"

He was playing dumb. But I knew him too well.

I rephrased the question. "And you shouldn't have what?"

"Nothing."

He tried to carry on walking, but I stayed put, folded my arms across my chest. "Do you imagine you're a mystery? Too difficult and complicated to comprehend?"

He glared at me. The idea that he was enigmatic was clearly precious to him. "You wouldn't understand," he assured me.

"No, I wouldn't. I've never been in a war. But what is it you think? That you should've done something differently?"

Apparently no one had ever challenged this perception, or probably any conviction he'd held before.

He glowered at me, but I stood my ground. After a minute he gave up. Instead he stared at his shadow in the glow of the streetlamp as it stretched far beyond the limits of his natural form, reaching out to touch the darkness around us. "My brothers shouldn't have died, Fanning."

"No, probably not."

"And I shouldn't have survived without them. They were better men than me," he said quietly. "They will *always* be better men than me."

"That's not possible," I said.

"I hate to disabuse you—"

"Don't talk rubbish. Besides, how would you know what kind of man you are?"

He considered this a moment before finally saying. "I was given special treatment. It wasn't fair. I don't deserve it."

"You were lucky."

"Luck?" He gave a hard laugh. "I would rather die from honest effort and endeavor!"

"Well, then maybe I'm the lucky one."

I could feel him looking at me, but I avoided his eyes, kept mine firmly on the ground in front of me.

We walked on, taking the long way back through the steep, narrow cobblestoned alleyways that wound through the night. Open windows brought sounds of radios, music, and laughter; of other lives, close and yet removed in their private world.

Finally we reached the shop.

I caught sight of myself in the window and remembered my first day with my new blond hair, imagining myself to be different. Tonight the weightless curls seemed contrived, faintly ridiculous.

Mr. Winshaw shoved his hands deep in his pockets. "You must navigate by means of your own natural compass." It was the only piece of advice he'd offered me all evening.

"And if my compass is broken?"

"Then you must learn to compensate. Sail a little crooked, make adjustments, but you must set your own course, or the journey is meaningless." He took out another cigarette, sat down on the front steps. "But for what it's worth, Maeve, I don't think your compass is broken."

"You called me by my first name." I sat down too.

"I must be tired."

I yawned, leaning my head against his shoulder. He still smelled of far-off shores and distant lands, but also of Peking duck, strong, earthy sweat, and the powdery sweetness of laundry soap. "Why do you have to keep leaving?"

"You and Kessler don't need me here. Besides, someone has to go out and land the big fish."

"Are you going to speak in maritime metaphors all night?"

"I have a few more good ones left. I'm working on one with a lighthouse and a ship in a storm."

I closed my eyes. "If I didn't know any better, I would think you were trying to impress me with the adroitness of your mind."

He said nothing, but put his arm around me. My body relaxed against his, and I fell asleep.

Just before dawn, a chorus of birds began. I woke up, neck stiff, Mr. Winshaw's arm still round me, only now it was limp and heavy, a dead weight. I wriggled out from underneath, and he shifted, automatically readjusting himself against the doorjamb.

Someone had left a nickel on the pavement in front of us, taking us for homeless. Rubbing my neck, I looked down at Mr. Winshaw, curled on the front steps, his face a picture of perfect contentment. He had the knack of wearing his circumstances with ease; even sleeping rough, he managed to appear in his element. Kneeling down, I tapped his shoulder. His eyes flicked open. "What is it now, Fanning?"

"It's time to go home."

Folding his arms into his chest, he closed his eyes again. "I'm fine."

"No, you're not." I shook him harder. "Someone will see you."

Eventually I got him into the shop, where he immediately stretched out on the floor as happily as if he were lying on a pile of down mattresses.

"Good night, Fanning," he said, shutting his eyes.

I opened the door. "Good morning, Mr. Winshaw."

I got home just as the early dawn light began to bleed into the night sky. The flat was still, Ma asleep. Outside, the street was peaceful too; it was Sunday, the one day of the week in the North End when business was not as usual.

I didn't bother to go to bed but instead ran a hot bath and scrubbed away the sweat and city filth, lathered my hair until the water rinsed clear. Then I lay soaking, staring up at the peeling paint on the ceiling, and thought about James Van der Laar, about how being with him had been like being drunk—unable to see straight and think clearly. And how seeing him with his wife had been like waking up someplace strange, coming to and discovering the horror of what I'd done.

And then I thought about Mr. Winshaw; of his arm around my shoulders and the way he would pause just a little, the light in his eyes sharpening, before he launched off on yet another tangent, like a man scanning the horizon for his next destination.

I sat in the bath until the water went cold and my fingers wrinkled, remembering his warm smell.

Afterward I made coffee and dressed. While the coffee was brewing, I dug around among the books underneath my bed until I found something I hadn't looked for in years—my old cigar box. Crammed right into a corner under a pile of old magazines, it was covered in a thick layer of dust. I opened it. There were the stacks of gold and silver chocolate wrappers, ticket stubs, long faded, stray buttons, and scraps of ribbon. Buried at the bottom was the bowtie. I took it out. It was older and cheaper than I remembered; in my childhood mind I'd believed it was made of black silk, shiny and smooth. But it was just cotton. I had made it into what I wanted it to be. There was nothing here of any value. But I couldn't bring myself to throw it away. So I put it all back and placed it under my bed again.

When Ma woke up, I was in the kitchen, beating eggs.

Pulling her dressing gown tighter, she stood in the doorway, confused. "What are you doing?"

"Making breakfast." I took down a skillet, put it on the stove. In the oven, slices of bread were toasting. "Sit down. It'll be ready in a minute."

She sat down. I scrambled eggs and poured her a cup of fresh coffee.

"You're never up this early on a Sunday," she said.

I divided the eggs and toast between two plates and set them on the table. "I thought I'd go to early mass with you."

She seemed more wary than relieved. "Really?"

"Uh-huh." I pushed a jar of plum jelly across to her. "I want to go to confession."

"I wasn't sure you believed in that anymore."

"I believe in believing in something, Ma."

I hadn't realized I thought that until that moment; until I'd been sitting across from her with no distractions, no noise, no James Van der Laar devouring all the space in my head. For weeks I'd avoided being alone with her; my anger and hurt were too raw. But out of nowhere, out of time and distance and loss, came this simple conclusion: it was better to believe in something than in nothing.

She'd given me that.

And not even Jack Carney could take it away.

I reached for the butter. "How's work?"

"Fine." Ma took a bite of toast. "Miss Craddox is getting married."

"Good for her. Are you going to apply for her job?"

"I don't know." She shrugged. "Maybe."

I felt a sudden wave of tenderness. "They don't deserve you, Ma."

She scowled, unused to sentiment. "You know, you're not looking after yourself. We need to dye your hair again." She waved her fork at me. "Your red roots are starting to show."

"I've been thinking. It's too difficult to keep up."

"No!" Horrified when I dyed my hair in the first place, now she was appalled that I might stop. "But you can't! What about your job?"

"Jeez!" I laughed. "I thought you hated it! Besides, isn't there something we can use—some rinse?"

"You mean henna? It's like mud!"

"So we cover me in mud, Ma."

"It's hardly dignified, changing your hair color like a vaudeville actress!" Shaking her head, she took another bite of toast. "Well, I always said, Maeve, you never should've done it. You should have listened to me in the first place."

"You're right. I should have."

The air changed; an autumn chill settled over the city in the mornings, and the leaves began to fall. It had been weeks since I'd heard from Diana; after her party she became caught up in the whirlwind of wedding arrangements and all but disappeared within the world to which she was raised. So I was surprised when out of the blue she rang me at the shop and asked me to meet her at the apartment one evening after work.

It was odd to be back at Waverly Mansions. I hadn't been to the apartment in months. It looked exactly the same, still pristine and new and oddly impersonal. Once it had been a haven, but now the space and freedom felt only empty and abandoned. I suppose we were the ones who were different.

When I arrived, Diana was already there, sitting on the sofa, smoking, wearing a light blue linen traveling suit. Her shoes were kicked off, feet curled underneath her. A suitcase was waiting by the door, keys and a train schedule on the table. Her hat and gloves were laid out neatly on the back of the armchair.

"Thank you for coming, May." Her tone was strangely formal.

Outside it began to rain, a sudden gust of wind rattling the window.

"What's all this?" I nodded to the suitcase as I sat down. "Are you going somewhere?"

"Just for a few days before the wedding." She attempted a smile, but there were dark circles under her eyes, and her skin was drained of color as if she hadn't slept in days.

"How nice!"

"Yes." She took another drag. "Lucky me."

I could feel the tension pull tight between us, though I wasn't sure why.

"Diana—" I began.

But she cut me off. "You know, I never use the place anymore, do you?"

"No."

"That's strange! You see, I came here the other night, for the first time in ages. I had to get away from my family. I wanted to be alone, to think." She paused. "But I wasn't alone for very long. Someone knew just where to find me."

I felt the bottom of my stomach disappear and my head grow light, as if all substance had suddenly drained away inside.

"He got the doorman to let him in." She gave me a wry smile. "James got to you, didn't he? I told you to stay away from him, but he always manages somehow."

I opened my mouth to deny it but couldn't.

The full weight of my accumulated lies and betrayals settled upon me. In the moment when I'd needed them, they'd appeared deceptively light, justifiable, even harmless. But now they threatened to overwhelm me.

She gave a hard laugh. "That brooch. That stupid, bloody brooch! I knew the instant I saw it, but I didn't want to believe. You're not the only one, you know. He used to get them in by the dozen!"

She meant to hurt and humiliate me, and she succeeded. I couldn't blame her for her bitterness.

"I'm sorry!" I tried to explain. "But he said that if you were in danger . . . that you'd done things in the past and you would again. . . . He was worried that he wouldn't know where to find you . . ." My thoughts knotted, tangled and confused.

"What else did he say? That I was a liar? Crazy?" Her voice was oddly calm. "I thought I could trust you."

"You can!"

"And then, of course, there's this." She placed the black agate ring on the table between us—the ring of Nemesis. "The cleaning lady found it under the bed. Am I mistaken, or doesn't this belong to you?"

I wanted to look away but couldn't. Instead I blinked stupidly at it.

He told me he'd lost it.

Leaning forward, she stubbed her cigarette out. "I could've sworn that you were wearing it the first time I met you at the house, May."

"It belongs to James. I wasn't here, Diana. I swear."

I could tell she didn't believe me. "Is this where you two meet? Here in the apartment I pay for?"

He'd used the apartment, but not for me.

"Go on." She pushed it closer. "You can have it back if you want. Something for your jewelry collection."

Her sarcasm was almost as painful as my sense of self-loathing.

"I don't want it."

"How noble!"

My anger flared. "That's not fair! It's not mine—it's his! And I wasn't here, Diana! Not without you!"

"You expect me to believe that?"

"No! I don't expect you to believe anything I say!" I got up, headed for the door. "But then, you never really trusted me, did you?"

"What are you talking about?"

I turned. "You always held me at arm's length, always kept me on the outside of your life! If he was able to come between us, it's because you let him!"

"Is that what you think?" She sounded incredulous. "That your duplicity is *my* fault?"

"You're just as manipulative as he is!" I shot back. "Coming and going as you please. Never telling anyone the whole truth. People like me are just toys to be picked up and tossed down whenever you tire of them. You have no loyalty, no true depth of feeling for anyone else but yourself!"

Her face changed, and her tone grew lethal. "You have no idea what you're talking about!"

"Of course I don't!" I paced the floor. "How could I? You never tell me anything!"

"You're not the only thing in my life, May. You're not the only person I have to consider!"

I laughed. "Now who are we talking about? Max? Charlie Peabody? Your posh new friends? Who is it this time?"

Her eyes widened in fury. Suddenly she grabbed the ashtray and threw it at me. I ducked and it smashed just behind me, against the front door, clattering to the ground. "It's Andrew, you fool!"

I stared at her in shock.

"It's Andrew!" she screamed again, her voice cracking. I realized she was crying. "I can't just do what I please—not without paying a price! Don't you understand? He's mine!"

She covered her face with her hands.

Stunned, I went to her side, knelt next to her. Her shoulders shook as she sobbed.

I felt around in my coat pocket and handed her a handkerchief.

She looked up, eyes swollen with tears, and took it.

"When I was fourteen, my father died. I hadn't known him very well—he had lived in Africa, and we, well, we, we'd lived in a lot of places. But it affected me quite badly. He'd left me the pearls. I wore them all the time. I wouldn't take them off.

"That same year, my aunt Elsa was very ill with a terrible fever. It turned her hair white at the age of twenty-three and left her barren. That's when my mother had an idea—that I would join my aunt and uncle on a trip around Europe. The journey was meant to restore us all. We were going to sail over on the *Queen Mary* and visit Italy,

France, Switzerland, Germany. Only Elsa still wasn't completely recovered. She spent most of the time in her cabin, and my uncle Peter and I spent a lot of time on our own. He was very attentive." She stopped, dabbed her cheeks dry. "Too attentive."

Like a camera lens coming into focus, suddenly everything sharpened, painfully clear. There was only the sound of rain drumming against the window; a million tiny little pinpricks against the glass.

"I was fifteen when I had Andrew. It was agreed that Elsa would take him. Agreed by everyone but me, that is. At first I didn't mind so much, I was still a child myself really. But as time went on, he was all I could think about."

I remembered how she had watched him in the park, from across the pond.

She looked down at her hands. "He's not like other kids. That's probably my fault too. Not everyone understands him. Elsa thinks he's mentally deficient. That he should be sent away."

"Can't you look after him instead? Maybe go away somewhere together?"

She shook her head. "The family has plans for me." She gave me a weary look. "I can't tell you what a disappointment I've been to them. Everything I do is wrong—who I love, what I am. They're repulsed by me. But at the end of the day, I have my uses."

"What uses?"

"I don't expect you to understand or approve of me, but I have my reasons for marrying Charlie. James wants a banking alliance, one that gives us a dominant position in the cartel. One that puts Afrikaner interests first. And if it will keep Andrew close to me, then it will be worth it. Of course, his behavior at the party made things difficult, very difficult."

"Are they threatening you?" I asked. "Are they trying to take him away?"

"They've taken him away from me before." She was done crying. She folded the handkerchief neatly in her lap. "My life is not my own, May. If I've not been honest about the details, it's because I can't be."

I looked at the suitcase. "Where are you going?"

"I don't know." She shrugged. "Nowhere. Sometimes I decide when I'm at the train station, buying the ticket. I pretend I have choices, that I can go anywhere, do anything. But it's just a game I play. I leave and come back. I always come back."

It reminded me of the elaborate hazards she used to love; small escapes from reality. No wonder she was good at them.

I had an idea. "But what if you really left? What if you traveled so far away no one could find you?"

"Then what would happen to Andrew? And what makes you think such a place exists? If I ever manage it," she said, "I'll send you a postcard. But you see, no matter what I do, what lengths I go to, James always knows where I am, what I'm doing." She looked across at me. "He has accomplices everywhere."

The hopelessness of her position was overwhelming. Worse was the role I had played in maintaining it. Tears of shame and re-morse worked their way down my cheeks. "I didn't mean to hurt you."

"It's funny. No one ever does."

I leaned my head against the side of her chair. "I'm sorry, Diana. Really I am."

"Oh, May!" She looked across the room, out of the window at the sheet of gray autumn rain. "I've had so few friends. So few people I can really call my own."

I was reminded of Max, of how protective she was, how loyal.

Her hand rested very lightly, almost tenderly, on top of my head. "I really thought you were one of them."

The day of Mr. Winshaw's departure arrived all too soon. Mr. Kessler was going to the train station to see him off, while I stayed behind to look after the shop. In the end, our parting was brief and awkward; he slapped me a bit too roughly on the shoulder and said, "Take care of yourself, Fanning," before picking up his bag and heading to the door. I didn't know what to say, so I just stood there, as wooden and ridiculous as one of his round-eyed African sculptures.

Then he stopped and dug a woman's silk scarf out of his coat pocket. For a second, I thought it was a gift. But instead he said, "Oh, listen, would you do me a favor? This belongs to Selena—do you mind dropping it off at the auction house for me?"

"Of course," I agreed, hoping my disappointment wasn't too obvious.

And then he left.

I folded the scarf, smelling thickly of Emeraude perfume, and put it in my handbag. Persia wound around my ankles. I tried to pick him up, but he pounced on top of Mr. Winshaw's desk and curled into a ball on top of his papers.

That night after work, I walked the several blocks over to Freeman's Auctioneers to return Selena's scarf. They were having an evening viewing prior to an auction, and I was directed to the second floor, where Selena was overseeing a collection of estate jewelry. As I approached from across the room, Selena recognized me, and her face lit up. "My goodness, I almost didn't know who you were! I absolutely *adore* your hair! How brave of you to go red!"

I didn't bother to explain.

"Mr. Winshaw asked me to return this to you." I handed her the scarf.

"Oh." Her face fell. "Thanks. Well, that's over then," she added grimly.

"What are you talking about?"

"I told him to keep it till next time." She gave me a rueful look. "That I'd pick it up when he got back."

"Well, I'm sure he just didn't want you to be without it. Perhaps he thought it was your favorite."

"I doubt it." She turned to face a mirror, knotting it expertly round her neck. "To be fair, it's not as if he didn't say as much early on. And he hasn't been very attentive lately."

"Oh. Well, men are idiots!" I was both relieved and yet oddly protective of Selena. "A girl like you, you could have any man you choose!"

"Yeah, well, I keep choosing the ones that don't want to be chosen."

"I've danced that step," I told her. "Not as much fun as it looks."

"Hey!" It suddenly dawned on her that I might be decent company. "Do you want to get a drink? I get off soon. There's a place around the corner that isn't half bad."

It would have been nice to go out, to shake off the low spirits that Mr. Winshaw's departure had brought on. But I'd gone back to working with Mr. Baylor and was determined to see it through this time. I pushed my hands into my pockets. "You know, tonight I have to get home. How about I buy you coffee someday instead?"

"Sure." She glanced around the empty department. "God! I hate late nights!"

I gazed at the glass cases filled with diamond necklaces and sparkling gemstones. "It can't be all bad."

"The worst thing is watching them being bought for other women. I came close once, on a pair of garnet earrings, but the man was too old and wanted too much for them, if you know what I mean."

Then there it was, among the other pieces in the case: the black agate ring of Nemesis, gleaming with the same dark luster it had the first time I'd held it.

I felt a sudden, sick flip-flop in my chest. "Where did that come from?"

"What?" Selena bent over to see. "Let's see. Yes, we got that in a couple of days ago, along with this string of pearls." She pointed to the necklace lying next to it. "Normally we don't take such small lots. But both are excellent pieces. Apparently it's Roman."

It was a shock to see it again. I had an eerie, uncomfortable feeling, as if it were tainted. It was more than just a ring; it was a harbinger.

"But *where* did you get it?" I asked again.

She slid behind the counter, pulled out a black leather ledger, and began thumbing through it. "Here it is," she said finally. "Lot number 133, a Roman gold and black agate ring with an image of a goddess on it, offered for sale by . . ." She squinted. "Oh, it's anonymous."

"What does that mean?"

"Well, it means the seller doesn't want to be identified. It happens all the time. Not everyone wants to advertise that they're forced to sell the family jewels." She referred to the ledger again.

"In this case, the proceeds go to a third party: a Miss Julie Hanover at a bank in New York." She closed the book. "Are you all right? You look a bit pale."

Miss Julie Hanover was Diana's alias. And those were her pearls too. But why was she selling her jewelry?

"It's not just any old goddess, you know," I told her. "It's Nemesis, the goddess of revenge."

Selena wasn't convinced. "There's a cupid on it. And it doesn't look very dangerous."

"Isn't that always the way?"

"So"—she leaned closer—"who did it belong to? Anyone famous?"

"I think I saw it in an antiques journal. The shop is full of them. It's just strange to see it in person, that's all. I must be tired," I apologized.

Stretching, Selena stifled a yawn. "Me too. Well, I guess pieces that old don't really have owners. They make their own way through time."

It was surprising to hear her being so philosophical. "That's one way of looking at it."

"Everything we sell will probably outlast us, isn't that an odd thought? It was here before we were born and will be here long after we're gone. God, how dreary I am tonight! That damn scarf has made me morbid. I need some good luck for once!" She sighed.

I felt in my coat pocket, took out the crooked pin my mother had given me months ago. "Here—" I handed it to her. "Maybe this will work."

"A crooked pin?" She laughed. "You don't believe that old wives' tale, do you?"

I shrugged.

She tilted her head provocatively, stuck out her lower lip. "Sure you don't fancy a drink?"

"That pout works on men, but not on me." I smiled. "Maybe another time."

As I headed to the trolley stop, I thought about the ring, how untouched it was by everything that had happened around it and would happen . . . Selena was right. It would journey from hand to hand, continent to continent, decade to decade—a time traveler made of agate and gold.

We were the fragile ones. The ones who, like Mr. Tresalion's salvaged objects, needed to be rescued, reimagined, restored.

The trolley came. I got on and sat next to the window, leaning my head against the glass. Beneath me the car swayed like a boat, heading through rough water. Emptiness swelled; tomorrow, it would just be me and Mr. Kessler again.

Where was Mr. Winshaw now?

The world is full of things you will like that you just don't know about, he had promised.

I closed my eyes and tried to imagine what I didn't know.

When I opened them again, a man was sitting across from me, reading the evening edition. Words seemed to float in front of my tired eyes.

"Diamond Heir in Fatal Shooting," read the headline. "Two Gunned Down at Plaza Hotel. Society Playboy Killed."

The body of James Van der Laar had been found lying on the bed in a suite in the Plaza Hotel with a bullet through his head. Next to him was the body of his lover, Charlotte Smith Reynolds, known as Smitty to her friends. A police investigation concluded she shot him first before killing herself.

It was, apparently, a well-known affair in society circles. James Van der Laar had a reputation as a serial seducer and barely bothered to conceal his adulterous relationships from his young wife. He'd known Smitty for years, and there were rumors that they were at one time engaged. However, his devotion to the Afrikaner cause made it impossible for him to marry an English-speaking wife. Instead he chose Heleen Van Bek, a fellow South African and daughter of the owner of the largest platinum mines in Rustenburg. Smitty continued to hang on, however, convinced that one day he would divorce. The papers speculated that when he attempted to end the affair, she became desperate.

I remembered the hushed conversation I'd overheard the night of the party; Smitty's pleas, James's promises. It had been effortless for him to lie—to me, to Smitty, to his wife. Like the air he breathed.

From then on, the press spent many editions combing through James Van der Laar's romantic past, sifting through a long list of suspected lovers—would-be actresses, socialites, chorus girls. Soon stories of the Van der Laars' Boer origins, South African diamonds as large as a man's fist, and shadowy dealings with foreign governments replaced the tales of sex and scandal. "All That Glitters" was the cover story in the *New Yorker* the next month. I didn't bother to buy it.

The scandal culminated in the announcement, discreetly posted by the Peabody family, that the engagement of Diana Van der Laar and Charles Peabody had been called off by mutual agreement. And that Diana, who had been traveling, would remain abroad for an extended stay.

There was no public funeral for James. Rumor had it that his body was sent back to South Africa and buried on his father's old estate.

His widow, it was said, did not attend.

The autumn progressed, a string of misty mornings and gradually cooler days and nights, melting into one another. The air became scented with the rich, earthy aroma of crushed fallen leaves and fresh rain. Streets that had been littered with bodies stretched out on lawns and lounging on doorsteps searching for relief from the heat emptied. Instead of drowsy lethargy, people moved again with purpose and industry; children went back to school, and life fell into a familiar routine.

Without Mr. Winshaw, the shop was quiet and ordered and dull. And now that Diana was gone, the world of the Van der Laars receded. The whole experience was like being caught in a sudden violent tempest that, now spent, left only a calm and placid sea. I saw Nicky Howerd walking down Beacon Street one morning, but he strolled right past me, lost in his own dim world. He didn't recognize me with my red hair, and I didn't bother to stop him. We had nothing in common anyway.

Instead, I turned my attention to a series of lectures at the Athenaeum in the evening and occasionally took Ma to the theater as a treat; we saw A Doll's House together, and she wept through the entire last act.

"It was like that, you know," she said on the way home. "You are so lucky nowadays. You young women have so many more choices."

Angela grew larger. Early one morning she awoke in a pool of blood and was taken to the hospital, where an emergency cesarean section was performed. The baby, a little girl, was so small that she was kept in the hospital for two months.

Angela named her Maddy for her mother.

I missed Mr. Winshaw. As the days went on, the feeling grew rather than diminished. And I realized that part of me—a really decent, admirable part—only resonated to the sound of his voice, to the impossible workings of his impossible mind. I didn't know what was worse, to be entirely without him or to have him return and to be close to a man who would never take me seriously.

One morning Mr. Kessler was going through the post when he handed me something.

"Do you have any idea what this means?" he asked.

It was a postcard, addressed just to the shop, with a detailed drawing of a Madagascar giraffe weevil on it. On the back was written:

Our collection is coming along brilliantly—only 27,000 more species to go!

   Original picture by Andrew Hanover

Signed,
The Secret Society of the Silver Pen
(Formerly the No Way Out Club)

Then at the bottom, in different handwriting was scrawled, "Stay away from pickle juice, blondie . . ."

Max, Diana, and Andrew . . .

"Yes." I smiled. "I have an idea."

Taking the postcard into Mr. Winshaw's office, I stuck a pin into the map on Madagascar.

The world was full of collectors, scouring the earth for pieces of themselves.

———

Then one evening I came home late from confession to find a man's hat sitting on the hallway table. "Is that you, Maeve?" Ma called.

I was on the verge of saying, "Who else would it be?" as I always did but checked myself instead. "Yes, Ma."

"Well, it's about time! You have a visitor."

I walked into the kitchen. Ma was sitting at the table with Mr. Kessler. They were drinking coffee, a plate of scones was halfway finished, and on the table between them was a large box.

"Mr. Kessler's been telling me what an asset you are to the shop!" Ma smiled. "He's says you've got the makings of a first-class antiques dealer."

I looked at him quizzically. "I do?"

Mr. Kessler gave a little nod. "Your daughter has a sharp mind and an eye for a sale," he confirmed.

"She gets that from me!" Ma squeezed my hand. "And look! He's brought you something."

I sat down. "What's this, then?"

"Mr. Winshaw asked me to collect it," he said. "Apparently it took longer than he thought." Mr. Kessler removed the lid.

Inside was a glass-domed case, like a miniature version of a Victorian diorama. Displayed on a black velvet cushion was the Staffordshire willow-pattern teacup. The pieces had been bound together with thin veins of gold. The cracks were now illumi-nated, gleaming under the light, a delicate map of misfortune and fate.

Ma stared at it. "Is that my broken cup?"

I nodded in astonishment. "I wanted to fix it. Mr. Winshaw offered to help."

"*Fix* it!" She laughed in disbelief. "This is more than fixed! Is that gold, Mr. Kessler?"

"It's gold leaf mixed with lacquer resin, Mrs. Fanning. The technique is called *kintsugi* and is Japanese in origin. It's not just a method of repair but also a philosophy," he explained. "It's the belief that the breaks, cracks, and repairs become a valuable and esteemed part of the history of an object, rather than something to be hidden. That, in fact, the piece is more beautiful for having been broken." He looked across at me. "There are only a few authentic Japanese craftsmen in the country. Mr. Winshaw took it to New York to have it done, and then had the case made here afterward."

"But why?" I wondered, amazed at the gesture. "Why would he go to so much trouble?"

Mr. Kessler and Ma exchanged knowing smiles.

"Well, if I didn't know any better, I'd say it's a kind of over-ture." Mr. Kessler chuckled softly.

I looked down, both embarrassed and thrilled.

"May I get you another cup of coffee, Mr. Kessler?" Ma offered, breaking the awkward moment. "You can have it in a gold-plated teacup if you like!"

"No, I'm afraid I've intruded upon your evening for far too long." He got up. "You have a lovely home, Mrs. Fanning. And those scones were most delicious."

"I can't tell you what a pleasure it's been." She rose too, took his hand. "It's so good to know that Mae is among the right sort of people. I can relax now, knowing that you've taken her under your wing."

I saw Mr. Kessler to the door.

"You have a nice home, May with a *y*. And a good family," he added with a nod.

"Well, there's only the two of us," I said, handing him his hat.

"To my mind, any more than one is enough. You're lucky." He gave a little formal bow. "Good night."

After he left, I went back into the kitchen. Ma was washing up. The teacup sat in the center of the table in its glass case, like a museum object. It struck me as funny that anything from our lives should be singled out as worthy of such distinction, let alone a broken cup. But it was like Mr. Winshaw to see ordinary objects in an extraordinary light. To him, even simple things held stories.

"Did you know, Ma, that the willow pattern has a legend behind it?" I asked.

She dried her hands on a tea towel. "A tale of two lovers, separated by death. The birds are their souls in flight."

"How did you know that?"

"Why do you think I chose it, Maeve?" She looked at me and sighed. "You're not the only one who's ever read a book, you know!"

After she left, I lifted the lid off and took the cup out again, turning it round, tracing the veins of gold with my finger. Ma was right—it was more than repaired, it was now an entirely different thing. No longer one of a set, its unfortunate fate had made it unique, a survivor. It was a Ulysses cup, I decided. Made weak by time and fate, but strong in will.

Then I noticed the wooden base. A carved motif ran along the edge—waves. I turned it over. There was an inscription on the bottom.

TO THE MERMAID OF BOSTON HARBOR

FROM A DROWNING MAN

Acknowledgments

I wish to thank the following people for their tremendous insight, copious notes, relentless re-reads, support, and above all patience during the completion of this book: my exceptional trio of editors at HarperCollins U.S., UK, and Canada—Maya Ziv, Lynne Drew, and Lorissa Sengara; my astute, unflappable agents—the stiletto-heeled Jennifer Joel and sensible-shoed Jonny Geller; and self-professed Classics geek Madeleine Osborne at the offices of ICM, whose extensive help and enthusiasm have been nothing short of heroic. I'm extremely lucky to work with such intelligent, dedicated individuals.

I also want to acknowledge my husband, Gregg Liberi, and my son, Eddie, just because I can and because you're the reason why all efforts are worthwhile.

About the Author

KATHLEEN TESSARO is the author of *Elegance, Innocence, The Flirt, The Debutante*, and *The Perfume Collector*. She lives in Pittsburgh, Pennsylvania, with her husband and son.

www.kathleentessaro.com